A game

Novels by Gary Alan Ruse
HOUNDSTOOTH • **A GAME OF TITANS**

OF TITANS

A Novel by Gary Alan Ruse

PRENTICE-HALL, INC., Englewood Cliffs, New Jersey

Fic
Rus

A Game of Titans by Gary Alan Ruse
Copyright © 1976 by Gary Alan Ruse

Printed in the United States of America

Prentice-Hall International, Inc., London
Prentice-Hall of Australia, Pty. Ltd., Sydney
Prentice-Hall of Canada, Ltd., Toronto
Prentice-Hall of India Private Ltd., New Delhi
Prentice-Hall of Japan, Inc., Tokyo
Prentice-Hall of Southeast Asia Pte. Ltd., Singapore
Whitehall Books Limited, Wellington, New Zealand

10 9 8 7 6 5 4 3 2 1

Library of Congress Cataloging in Publication Data

Ruse, Gary Alan.
    A game of titans.

    Bibliography: p.
    I. Title.
PZ4.R95Gam   [PS3568.U72]   813'.5'4   76-27370
ISBN 0-13-346080-0

Grand Eagle illustrations by Gary Alan Ruse,
based upon the nuclear airship design
developed by Francis Morse, Professor of Aerospace
and Mechanical Engineering, Boston University.

Kiev illustrations copyright 1974 by
Jane's Fighting Ships; reprinted with permission of
Jane's Yearbooks, London, England.

Book design by Hal Siegel

This book is dedicated
to all those who believe in the future
of lighter-than-air craft.

ACKNOWLEDGMENTS

As with my previous novel, *Houndstooth*, a considerable amount of background research in a wide variety of subjects was necessary in the preparation of this book. In that regard, I have been most fortunate to have the assistance of many people around the country and, in fact, the world. I wish to take this opportunity to thank them.

Francis Morse, Professor of Aerospace and Mechanical Engineering at Boston University, was kind enough to answer a great many questions about airships, both in correspondence and in a personal interview in Boston. More than a mere airship enthusiast, Professor Morse is active in developing plans for nuclear-powered airships. Some of the descriptions of the USAF *Grand Eagle* are based upon information furnished by Professor Morse concerning his Boston Airship design.

Carole Farrar of the Staff Secretary's Office, National Security Council, Washington, D.C., supplied some very helpful information concerning the operations of the NSC.

Marie Shroff and Neil Walter were courteous and extremely helpful with information regarding background and policy matters when I visited the office of the New Zealand

Consulate General in New York. Michael F. Chilton, Information Officer, New Zealand Embassy, Washington, D.C., also provided an abundant amount of information, as did J. G. Thomson and C. M. Kingston of the City of Wellington Public Relations Office, Wellington, New Zealand. I wish to thank them all for the time they took from their busy schedules.

At Homestead Air Force Base in Florida, Capt. Robert C. White, CBPO, 31st Combat Support Group, explained the command structure and personnel requirements likely to be encountered in an airship of the *Grand Eagle* class.

Anna C. Urband, Assistant Head, Media Services Branch, Office of Information, Department of the Navy, Washington, D.C., provided information and materials concerning the Soviet Navy and the aircraft carrier *Kiev*.

In London, Capt. John E. Moore, Editor, *Jane's Fighting Ships*, also assisted with information on the Soviet carrier *Kiev*, and Eugene M. Kolesnik, Editor, Jane's Yearbooks, granted permission to reprint the line drawings of the *Kiev* that appear in this book. I am grateful to these gentlemen for their help.

I must thank June Landsperg at Royal Tours in Coral Gables, Florida, and the staff of the Pacific Area Travel Association in San Francisco, California, for their assistance in obtaining information on Tongareva (also called Penrhyn by its British discoverers) and the other Cook Islands.

I owe a special thanks to Dr. Stephen Mallon of the University of Miami's School of Medicine Cardiology Department for invaluable help in the area of genetic heart disorders and their treatment, and also to Dr. Jacob Kline of the University's Biomedical Engineering Department for advice on the problems inherent in creating an artificial heart. Also, Lt. Frank Davis, in charge of Rescue Shift 3 at the Coral Gables Fire Department, helped with information on portable defibrillator units.

R. B. Morrisey, Manager, Public Relations and Communications at Teledyne Ryan Aeronautical in San Diego, California, furnished a good deal of helpful material on remotely piloted vehicles and their potential uses. Dick Tipton of the News Bureau at Bell Helicopter Company in Fort Worth, Texas, supplied helpful information on the Bell UH-1N twin-turbine helicopter. And John F. Pearson, Science Editor, *Popular Mechanics*, aided me in locating a number of useful articles on airships.

In San Francisco, a number of people helped with

much-needed information: Hollis Gray, University of California Medical Center; Dr. James Duncan, School of Natural Science, and Sheila McClear, Office of Public Affairs, San Francisco State University; and the staffs of the Chamber of Commerce of Greater San Francisco and the American Automobile Association Travel Desk.

In New York, Ann Whyte of Pan American World Airways Public Relations provided a considerable amount of material on Wake Island and its background that would have been otherwise unobtainable.

Bill Byers of Eastern Airlines' Flight Training Center in Miami provided information on emergency water-landing procedures. Jim McIntyre of Trans World Airlines and Mrs. Lee of Philippine Airlines assisted with information on Pacific passenger flights. And Bill Myers, Boeing Company Airplane Division, gave advice concerning passenger/cargo craft.

I am again indebted to the reference staffs of the following libraries: the Miami Public Library's Main Branch and Coral Gables Branch and the Otto G. Richter Library of the University of Miami.

And a special thanks to the members of my family who assisted with more than moral support this past year: my mother, who did final typing; my father, whose knowledge of World War II tactics has helped me more than once; my grandmother, a lover of books and main proofreader here at home.

Again, to those people who furnished information, I extend my sincere thanks and my apologies for any errors I may have committed while including that information in the framework of this book.

G.A.R., Miami, Florida

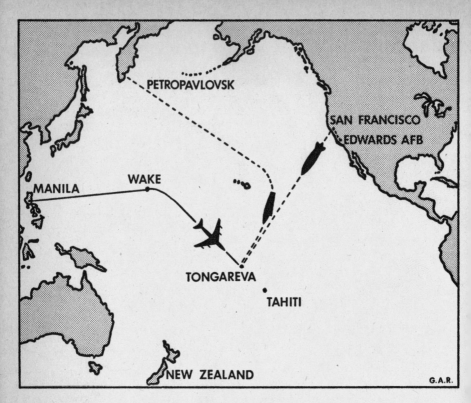

PETROPAVLOVSK

SAN FRANCISCO
EDWARDS AFB

MANILA   WAKE

TONGAREVA

TAHITI

NEW ZEALAND

G.A.R.

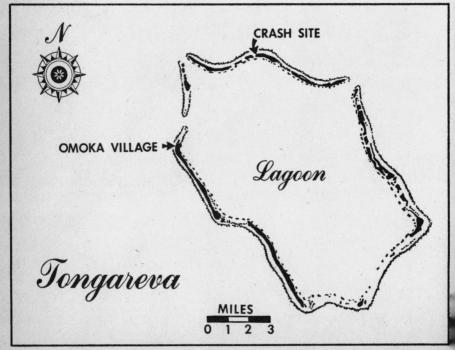

N

CRASH SITE

OMOKA VILLAGE →

Lagoon

Tongareva

MILES
0 1 2 3

CHAPTER ONE

At first it was only a speck on the horizon, scarcely noticeable in the Pacific Ocean's vast panorama of sea and sky. Then, as it drew nearer, the scream of its rapid descent became audible, building in intensity until it rose above the steady sounds of wind and wave.

The Trans-Pacific DC-8 jet aircraft should not have been in that remote and isolated part of the South Pacific. Its sudden presence there now was alien and unexpected.

Still losing altitude, it roared on toward Tongareva, a low coral atoll of the Cook Island group. Surrounded by seemingly endless miles of ocean, the island was the only visible point of land that broke the water's seething surface. Its vast central lagoon shone pale emerald within the narrow strip of sand and palms that framed it, sparkling like an enormous gem. There amid the Pacific's blue waters, Tongareva seemed to draw the approaching aircraft like a magnet.

First to see the jet were tuna fishermen a few miles from shore. In outrigger canoes little different from those of Captain Cook's day, with patched sails billowing in the breeze, the fishermen of Tongareva soon forgot about the importance of their morning's catch. Passing no more than thirty feet above their heads, the DC-8 hurtled along its shallow trajectory, rapidly closing the gap between itself and the shore.

Its flaps were down, exerting braking force to slow its onward rush, and little more than a mile from land the craft began to jettison the fuel from its wing cells. The highly flammable kerosene became a mist that mingled with the ocean's own salty spray.

Emptying the wing fuel cells would give the jet greater buoyancy in the water, but if the pilot's intention was to ditch offshore of Tongareva, then he had dangerously underestimated the plane's forward momentum.

Even as it skimmed the water, the jet was still moving at nearly 150 knots. The sleek fuselage skipped, like a stone thrown flat across a pond, then came down again to meet the water's surface. Its right wing digging into the crest of a wave, the plane began to skew a few degrees off center, plowing through the wave peaks at an angle. Then, close to shore, rock-hard coral formations less than a foot beneath the surf, caught the leading edge of the jet's nose. The plane shuddered under the sudden, violent impact, and the sharp edge of the coral head tore a raw gash along its gleaming underbelly. The wings wrenched away as the plane bounded off the reef's protruding coral for one last brief moment of flight.

Even now the jet was beginning to break up, fragmenting into sections that careened at varying speeds toward the beach. In another second they had impacted, with part of the plane's shattered fuselage plowing across the sand at a narrow strip of Tongareva's northern shore.

If people were screaming within the still sliding section of the plane, their sound could not be heard above the horrid, grinding squall of metal against sand and rock. . . .

The sound of the crash might easily have been heard a mile away. And it was heard, with awful clarity, in a stone and timber building located less than one-fourth that distance from the impact site. Had the jet been flying a fraction of a degree more to the east, the remote medical research center would have been obliterated in the disaster.

Within that building, Carla Jennings tensed suddenly as the awful sound grated on her nerves. The glass slide she had just removed from her microscope popped from her grasp, nicking her thumb in the process, and shattered into sharp fragments on the wooden floor below. She turned toward the sound, then froze in stunned silence as her mind sought to identify it. Behind her, Carla's assistant, Mary Akaru, uttered a string of words in the Maori language—a beseechment to the old gods for protection from the unknown. Almost as an afterthought, and with no sense of inconsistency, a short Christian prayer flowed from her lips.

In the next moment both were at the window, looking anxiously out at the wreckage. Carla Jennings was the first to recognize it.

"Good Lord—" Horror tinged her words. "It's a *plane.*"

Mary Akaru seemed reluctant to accept the fact. "No aeroplane's been here in years . . . nothing that big since the war. . . ."

Carla hesitated only a second longer, then bolted toward the door. "Come on! There may be survivors." She paused at the doorway long enough to grab up the fire extinguisher, kept there since the time the gasoline generator ruptured a fuel line and caught fire. Then she jumped down the three steps to the ground and started running.

Mary Akaru followed, somewhat more slowly. At forty years, with her heavyset build and stocky legs typical of some Polynesian women, she was not fast on her feet. She had barely reached the edge of the stand of palms surrounding the research building when the abrupt crack of an explosion came from the edge of the beach.

Carla Jennings had covered more than half the distance to the wreckage when the explosion came, and even though it was far to her right, she could feel some of its concussive energy.

Startled, she looked for the source of the sound. There, at the edge of the beach, one of the wings torn from the aircraft lay shredded and smoking. What had caused it to blow up, Carla could not guess. She felt a cold wave of fear. The plane itself might be on the verge of exploding into flames.

She paused, then ran on as the first faint cries and moans reached her from the ruptured jet. It was difficult to tell what kind of aircraft it had been. The entire cockpit section of the plane was standing in knee-deep water at the edge of the shore, tilted at an odd angle. Fragments of torn metal and mechanical systems littered the entire breadth of the island's narrow north shore, extending from the ocean side to the green waters of the central lagoon. The rear third of the plane was resting on dry land, more or less intact, at the end of a shallow trench dug by its own skid. The cries were coming from there.

As she ran, Carla glanced off to her left. In the lagoon, perhaps three hundred feet from water's edge, bubbles were breaking the surface in a tumultuous rush. Part of the wreckage had gone into the water, apparently. If it were part of the passenger section, there would be precious little time for survivors to free themselves and reach the surface. But for the moment there was nothing she could do to help them.

As Carla reached the main fuselage, she was nearly overwhelmed by the devastation around her. Besides the ragged wreckage of the once sleek aircraft, there was the human destruction as well. It was horribly apparent that many of the passengers had been killed upon impact. Perhaps a dozen or more seats had been wrenched free of their mountings, with people still strapped in them—some alive, some dead.

Carla fought back the growing urge to look away—to

run in the opposite direction and escape the horror. She had to do what she could to help. She was, after all, a doctor, and medical school had prepared her for the prospect of direct contact with death and injury. Or so she had thought. . . .

Forget how many were dead, she told herself. There were an equal number alive. *They* needed her. They needed her *now,* with all her wits about her, and with all the skill and quickness she could muster.

Amazingly, several people were already on their feet, stumbling about in a dazed condition among the fragments of wreckage. There was movement within the still intact section of fuselage as well, and Carla saw two women in stewardess uniforms working their way forward from the back. She started toward them, then halted as a cry for help came from her right.

One of the dislodged seats was on its side more than a dozen feet away. An elderly woman passenger was strapped into it, trying unsuccessfully to free herself. Only a few feet away from her a small puddle of jet fuel had dripped from an engine wrenched free of its wing. The fuel had started to flame.

"Please help me!" The woman waved feebly with one hand, still struggling to release the jammed seat belt that held her. "The fire! *Don't let me burn!*"

Carla raced to her side, then triggered the extinguisher, smothering the flames that threatened to spread. When she was satisfied that the danger of fire was momentarily past, she turned her attention to the woman. With some effort, she released the seat belt and helped the elderly passenger from her seat. Quickly examining her, she determined that the woman's injuries were relatively minor, but that she was almost in a state of shock.

She knew she was going to have to move the woman away from the area, and all the others as well. She looked for Mary Akaru, and saw that her Polynesian assistant had finally reached the crash site but was standing in stunned horror, both hands covering her mouth.

She shouted Mary's name, then looked around. One of the passengers was standing nearby. The man seemed dazed, almost uncomprehending of what was going on around him, but Carla managed to make him understand that he was to help her move the elderly woman out of the area of danger.

As they started to move away with the injured passenger, Mary Akaru took her place in transporting the woman, freeing Carla to return to help the others. As she did, a man dressed in the conservative clothing of a minister came limping toward her. His forehead was bleeding from a gash, and there was a trace of blood on his trousers, about knee-level on the leg he was favoring.

Carla extended a hand to help him balance. "Are you all right?"

"Yes, I think so," he said. "Nothing serious—just a few scrapes. Look—there are others that weren't hurt badly. We can help move those that are injured. We should do it soon. There's not much fuel on the ground, but there's a lot of flammable stuff here just the same."

Carla nodded, vaguely surprised by his familiarity with planes. "See if you can organize the others. Do what you can. I'll go check the injuries in the rear of the jet."

She hurried toward the gaping end of the rear fuselage. The nearly intact fragment of the jet was resting at a thirty-degree angle, which was going to make it more difficult for the survivors to get out, especially those with more serious injuries.

There was one benefit at least. In its slide across the narrow beach, the fragmented compartment had pushed up a considerable amount of sand at its leading edge, and the pile reached up past the lower luggage compartment, almost level with the passenger deck. Carla scrambled up the sandy incline and entered the craft.

Almost all the people she encountered in the first few rows were injured. All had abrasions and contusions. Some were in shock, and several had broken limbs. That much she could tell with hasty examinations. She could not even guess at the number and extent of internal injuries.

Carla saw the two stewardesses again, still working their way forward, helping free the passengers from their seats as they went. Carla wanted to reach them, but a seat broken free of the flooring blocked the aisle. She bent to examine the motionless, strapped-in passenger, striving to keep her balance on the sloping floor.

The man had no pulse. Judging from the marks and the odd angle of his head, he had been slammed against the metal framework of the seat across the aisle when his own seat had wrenched loose. His neck was broken.

Another passenger was coming forward. His carefully styled hair was partly disheveled, and the denim leisure suit he wore bore stains from his bloodied nose. But he seemed to have no serious injuries.

Carla looked up at him. "Help me get this seat upright. We have to get the aisle cleared."

The young man ignored her, trying to scramble over the fallen seat and its dead occupant. In his eyes was something bordering on panic.

Carla got to her feet, grabbed him by the arms, and shook him. "I said *help me get this seat up!*"

He turned and looked at her wildly, then broke free of her grip, shoving her backward against an injured passenger.

"Do it yourself!" he shouted as he lunged out of the plane and down the mound of sand.

Carla regained her balance and began to struggle with the unmanageable weight of the seat. She was getting nowhere until one of the stewardesses—the younger of the two, a blonde in her early twenties, only a few years younger than Carla— joined her. The two of them together were able to lift the seat and its occupant upright, finally clearing the aisle.

Carla's eyes met those of the young stewardess. "Thanks."

The blonde girl looked apprehensively at the man in the seat. "Is he dead?" she asked softly.

"Yes. And I'm afraid there are a lot more outside. The passengers sitting near the point where the compartment broke up didn't have much of a chance. Now let's get these people out of here and clear—"

Carla had looked away for a moment, and upon looking back she saw that the young stewardess was very close to collapse. Her face was milk-white, almost drained of blood.

"Can you manage?" Carla asked her.

"Yes ... yes, I'll be all right." She took a deep breath and brushed some of the tumbled golden hair away from her eyes. Some of her color seemed to return, but only a little.

"Let's start, then."

The process of removing the passengers from the wreckage began, carefully, but with an urgency that allowed no wasted moments. All survivors capable of walking on their own were directed out of the immediate area, and those who were fit enough to help carry out the injured were set to that task. There were only six, including the two stewardesses, but with Carla and Mary Akaru's aid they were able to remove at least four of the injured passengers on each trip.

6

It was a difficult and painful journey for many, but the ever-present danger of fire and explosion hurried them on, forcing the immediate evacuation of the crash site with time only to apply tourniquets to the most severe bleeding cases.

As they carried the last of the passengers out of immediate danger, Carla noticed that one of the men helping to carry an injured woman was struggling more with each step. He appeared to be in his late fifties, with graying hair and beard, and the few words he had spoken so far had been tinged with an accent Carla had not been able to pin down precisely. He had not sustained any serious injuries that she could detect, but it now seemed that the effort of the last three trips back to the plane were wearing him down enormously. Carla moved quickly to his side.

"Here—let me help. You've carried enough."

The bearded man started to protest, then suddenly changed his mind and allowed Carla to take over, nodding reluctantly. His features were damp with perspiration, more so than they should have been even in the warm and humid climate of Tongareva. Carla made a mental note to examine him more carefully as soon as there was a free moment.

That moment came sooner than expected. She scarcely had a chance to lower the woman she was helping carry to the ground when she saw the bearded man stumble. He dropped to his knees, then crumpled to one side, clutching his chest. His face contorted with pain and he let out a wheezing gasp.

Carla guessed what was wrong even as she rushed toward him. The outward signs were all those of a heart attack, and she silently cursed herself for letting the man help with the injured. Yet there was no way of knowing that he had a heart condition.

As she reached his side, the man fumbled in his pocket with one hand. She saw him withdraw a small bottle containing pills and quickly helped him remove the cap. The man brought one of the pills up to his mouth with a great deal of effort and put it beneath his tongue. Carla helped him into a more comfortable position, his back and shoulders raised, propped against a fragment of one of the dislodged seats. She loosened his tie and collar and noted that he seemed to relax somewhat, though his breathing was still irregular.

The capsules remaining in the bottle looked like nitroglycerine, but it was hard to be certain. The label was no help at all. The language was unknown to Carla, although it appeared to be Slavic.

She checked his pulse continuously, as well as his breathing and his color. After several long minutes his condition finally seemed to stabilize. Carla had to hope he would manage unattended for a little while at least. There were so many other things to be done.

At that moment, the throaty roar of an outboard motor caught Carla's attention. Looking to the south, she could see a small boat approaching from the lagoon side of the shore. It was running at full throttle and barely managed to slow down in time to avoid beaching itself on the shore.

Scrambling from the boat, James Akaru—the husband of Carla's assistant—rushed up the beach to the area where the survivors had gathered. His look of concern lessened somewhat when he saw his wife standing by Carla's side. James Akaru was slightly older than his wife's forty years, but his hair showed little gray, and his build was leanly muscular. His features had a tough and weathered look, but his face was clearly one that had smiled often and easily. He was not smiling now.

"I was diving for shell," he said simply. "I saw the crash. Bad . . . very bad. I feared it had hit your building."

"We were lucky it missed us," Carla told him. "Did you say you saw the actual crash?"

"Yes. I saw it coming in low, and then hit."

"Did part of the plane go into the lagoon? I saw bubbles coming up."

"I think so. There was a splash," James replied. "Hard to tell though, at the distance I was."

Reawakened concern showed on Carla's features. "Could you go down for a look? If there's anyone down there, they may have drowned by now, but still—"

James nodded and quickly turned back for his boat. Over his shoulder he said, "I'll look, ma'am. But drowning's the least of their worries."

The young blonde stewardess was approaching, and she was near enough to hear his parting words. She watched him push his boat out into the lagoon, climb in, and start it away toward the point where the wreckage had sunk.

"What did he mean by that?" she asked.

Carla glanced around at the stewardess, then returned her troubled gaze to the man in the boat. "The lagoon is not completely enclosed," she replied grimly. "There are three openings to the sea—they let in thousands of tropical fish. They also let in sharks. The lagoon is full of them."

The stewardess was aghast. "And he's going *down* there?"

Mary Akaru stood solemnly watching her husband's boat move out. "James dives in the lagoon four, maybe five times each week, miss, for the mother-of-pearl shell. He says the sharks they will not attack him, if his faith is strong and his prayers are said well."

Her face was firm and expressionless, and it was hard to tell if her own faith in his safety was as strong as it seemed. She fell silent after that—a silence the others did not break for a long moment.

It was then that the other stewardess pressed forward into the group. She was older than Carla, and her light brown hair was tied back in a severe bun.

"What about the rest of the flight crew?" she asked anxiously, in an accent that was decidedly Australian. "Are they . . . down there, too?"

Carla inhaled sharply in pained realization. "Oh, God—I didn't *think* to check the cockpit!"

She whirled around and started off on a dead run toward the opposite beach. The two stewardesses followed close behind her, as did the man in minister's garb.

Splashing through the shallow water past the edge of the beach, they reached the torn nose section of the shattered fuselage in less than a minute. Sitting at a slight angle in almost three feet of water, the cockpit was like the severed head of a gigantic snake. Around the gaping end, raw and twisted shreds of metal stuck out like bizarre knife points, razor-sharp and menacing. The waters of the Pacific lapped silently against the open end of the fuselage, dangerously concealing some of the lower sharp points.

It was difficult to climb up to the level of the deck, but Carla found a few safe handholds and pulled herself into the remains of the craft. The jet had fragmented only a few feet from the end of the cockpit section. The door that had separated the compartments was open, torn half off its hinges.

Carla entered, half hopeful, half fearful of what she would find. Early morning sunlight poured into the compartment through the shattered front glass. Tattered shreds of the crystallized safety glass hung like icy lace within the framework. Otherwise, the interior of the cockpit was oddly intact.

There were only two men within the compartment. One had apparently been thrown completely out of his seat and was sprawled face down on the flooring. Carla bent to check for signs of life. Judging from the position of the empty seat, the man was the copilot. He had several broken limbs, and more than a few areas of blood marred the trim uniform he wore.

But that mattered little now. The man was dead.

Carla checked the pilot next, finding similar injuries. And his fate had been no better than that of his second officer. She turned, eyes downcast, heading for the door and the open.

Expectant eyes searched hers eagerly as she appeared again and started the climb down to the shallow water. The older stewardess seemed to sense the answer even before she asked—

"The crew—?"

Carla shook her head. "Both dead."

"Both?" the young blonde asked oddly.

"Yes, both the pilot and copilot."

"But what about the navigator?"

Carla frowned, realizing that there should indeed have been a third man. "There were only the two—no one else."

The blonde gazed out toward the ocean beyond the reef. "He must have been thrown out, when the plane broke up. . . ." She shook her head slowly, and the full weight of the disaster finally seemed to come down upon her fragile shoulders. For the first time, tears began to run down her pale cheeks, and the first trickle quickly became a torrent that would not stop easily or soon.

Roughly eight hundred feet away, within the clear waters of the lagoon, James Akaru kicked stongly away from the surface of the water and the safety of a boat that was now only a floating shadow above him. His lungs held the only air he would have for the remainder of the dive. He wore only his swim trunks and a pair of goggles with lenses no larger than half-dollars. His hands were straight out before him, the right one holding a well-cared-for diver's knife.

There on the lagoon's bottom, a little ahead and beneath him, the last main fragment of the DC-8 rested, an open-ended cylinder of metal that shimmered in the changing patterns of light. Small tropical fish were already beginning to explore the dark cave that was suddenly a new part of the lagoon floor. And the fish were not alone.

Thirty or more black-tipped sharks swam in lazy, deceptively unconcerned patterns about the wreckage, probing a few feet nearer with each turning pass. James Akaru swam on, confident but wary.

At most, he had only a few minutes beneath the surface of the sparkling lagoon. His lungs had been expanded and strengthened by many dives, but there was still a limit to any man's endurance underwater.

Still conscious of the positions of the sharks, he swam to the open end of the fuselage and peered inside. It was hard to make out detail in the dark interior. Entering the flooded compartment, he paused briefly to allow his eyes to adjust to the dim light. There were a dozen or more large bubbles of air still clinging to the ceiling of the compartment, and his passage broke them into quivering globules.

In a moment he could see well enough to discern forms. It was clear that there were no passengers here, dead or otherwise. There were only a dozen or more boxy shapes, some extremely large, others quite small. All were held down by straps and mounting clamps barely visible in the sunken gloom. But no people.

Turning, James Akaru swam out of the fuselage and began his ascent to the surface thirty feet overhead. As he made his way up, he saw that the less dangerous black-tipped sharks had been joined by their brothers, the dreaded *papera*—the black sharks. The deadly inhabitants of the lagoon were actually more gray than black, but there was no quibbling about their ravenous appetites. Their danger was enough to test even a strong man's faith. James continued his ascent, more carefully now, and yet more quickly.

When he finally reached his boat and returned to shore, he found Carla bent over the bearded man, checking his pulse. As he approached them, the others crowded around.

"No people down there," he told them, his breathing slowing to normal. "Only crates—cargo of some kind. Lots of those. But no bodies. Not even any empty seats."

Carla's puzzled frown brought a quick reply from the older stewardess. "The aircraft is . . . *was* a Jet Trader model. We carried both cargo and passengers on the run to Hawaii. The cargo was in the forward compartment."

The bearded man still resting on the ground listened with an intense interest, then stared out across the lagoon with a look of deep concern.

"Wait a minute," Carla said quickly. "You say this was a flight to *Hawaii*?"

"Yes—Trans-Pacific Flight 47 out of Manila. Why?"

"You're about two thousand miles off course. This is Tongareva, of the Cook Islands. You're a lot closer to Tahiti than you are to Hawaii."

The blonde stewardess frowned. "But I don't see how that's possible!"

"Anyway, the how and why of it are the least of our problems," Carla said firmly. She gestured toward the rows of injured. "We're going to have to move them to the research facility. Some of the injuries we'll have to treat here first, but then we'll need something to transport them. There's some canvas and some lengths of wood back at the building we can use to make litters. I'll have to go get my medical kit, too."

The minister was dabbing at his forehead with a handkerchief already crusty with dried blood. But the bleeding from the gash had almost subsided. "I'll go along and help with the things you have to bring back."

"Good. I can use the help. In fact, I'll need someone else, too." Carla's eyes searched the others who had survived the crash with no serious injuries. The dazed man still seemed unaware of what was happening. The European man with the beard was out of the question—his own medication had temporarily stabilized his heart condition, but he could no longer be considered one of the fit. She quickly skipped over the denim-suited young louse who had knocked her over in the wreckage, and her eyes settled on a man standing a few feet away. He was holding an attaché case he had somehow brought with him from the wreckage, and was bending, fastidiously brushing away at the wet sand that clung to the lower pants legs of his brown suit. He seemed to be in his forties, and he looked more than fit enough to help.

"Sir—would you come along with me?"

The businessman looked up, realizing that Carla was speaking to him. "What? Oh—yes, of course."

Carla turned again to the two stewardesses. "You've had some medical training, haven't you?"

The older one answered. "Just the advanced first aid all airline flight personnel have to know."

"That'll be good enough for now. While we're bringing back the things we need, you two keep an eye on the injured. We shouldn't be gone more than a few minutes."

Both women nodded and headed in the direction of the other survivors. Carla motioned to her two recruits and started toward the stone and timber building a little over a thousand feet away from the crash site.

They reached the building fairly quickly, and while the men busily gathered up the materials necessary to make litters, Carla loaded her medical bag with all the antiseptics and dressings it would hold, then checked her stores for pain-killers and whatever else she might have use for in treating the injured. She set the bulging bag down by the door, where it would be ready the moment she left, and headed for the small room next to the lab area where the radio was kept.

She leaned forward over the desk that supported the heavy, multiband shortwave set and flipped the switch on. Nothing happened.

Carla struck the desk with her fist, both angry and impatient with herself. Running out of the room, she went around to the back of the building and started up the gasoline generator that supplied electrical power for radio, lights, and several pieces of medical equipment. As soon as the generator was running smoothly, she hurried back to the radio room and sat down before the desk.

Microphone in hand, Carla adjusted the radio's tuning dial for the emergency band monitored by all nations. With the power now on, she triggered the transmit button.

"Mayday, mayday—to anyone listening. This is Dr. Carla Jennings, at the World Health Organization research facility on Tongareva . . . repeat, *Tongareva*. A commercial airliner, Flight 47 of the Trans-Pacific line, crashed here on the island this morning at—" Carla paused to check her watch. It was 10:00 A.M. It was hard to believe that only forty minutes had elapsed since she had heard the sound of the crash. It seemed more like several hours. "It crashed at about nine-twenty. We have an unknown number of fatalities and injured, and we need assistance."

She hesitated a long moment, waiting for a reply—any reply. Then she triggered the transmit button again. "Is anyone listening? Please reply. We need help most urgently. *Mayday, mayday* . . ."

In Wellington, New Zealand, less than one hour after the repeated emergency radio transmissions had begun, it was 8:40 A.M. In New Zealand's capital, which was well into the Southern Hemisphere's summer season, the morning air was warm and still, an exception from the usual wind that characterized Wellington, a city rising like a natural amphitheater around the waters of Port Nicholson. Some residents would call it the calm before a storm, but the weather to come would not be the only disturbance felt in the capital.

In Lambton Harbour, the small leisure sailing craft normally abundant at this time of year were not out yet, but a number of the larger vessels, both cruise ships and cargo carriers, were already leaving wharves along the harbor's shore on journeys that would take them initially out around the Miramar Peninsula into Cook Strait, separating the country's North and South Islands, and from there to varied destinations throughout the world.

A half-mile from the wharves at the northern edge of the harbor, in the midst of the bustling city in which street names were an odd mixture of English and Polynesian, the heart of the nation's government was located. In assembly rooms and offices divided between the Takaka marble structures of the Parliament buildings and the older Government Building, possibly the largest wooden building in the world, the daily activities of political life in New Zealand occurred.

Those activities were at a standstill now, since it was Sunday morning in this part of the world, but one office was open, and it was the scene of an unplanned and hastily called meeting.

As George Derrence, Secretary of the Ministry of Foreign Affairs, reached the door of his office, he heard voices inside. Derrence, a distinguished diplomat in his fifties, was dressed in his Sunday best. He had been preparing for early morning worship services with his family when the call came on his private line, and he had been driven over immediately. The voices ceased as he opened the door.

His Deputy Secretary, Hughes Aberdeen, rose as Derrence entered. Aberdeen wore a coat, but beneath it was a sports shirt more suited for the beach. "Good morning, sir," he said, almost apologetically. "John's been helping out."

Derrence glanced briefly at John Peddington, division head of South Pacific and Antarctic Affairs, and managed a nod of greeting. He looked quickly back to Aberdeen, frowning. "What's this about, Hughes? What was it you couldn't speak about over the phone?"

The young man extended a wire service news release to Derrence. "There's been an air crash in the Cook Islands, sir. On Tongareva. Extensive fatalities and injuries—"

"Spare me," Derrence interrupted. "Shouldn't bother me, I suppose, but I have absolutely no tolerance for gore. Anyhow, what about this crash? I heard something of it on the radio on my way here, so it's hardly a secret."

"No, sir. But the media didn't carry the whole story. From what we were able to find out from the local representative of the airline here, the flight was bound for the Hawaiian Islands, and the passenger list included several foreign scientists scheduled to participate in the World Science Conference in Honolulu."

Derrence nodded, glancing over the news release. "Yes, I've heard of it. We've sent two of our own men there—an engineer and an environmentalist fellow, I think. But what's wrong—couldn't you have handled the rescue operation details yourselves?"

"We thought we could, sir," Peddington spoke up. "Hughes and I began checking on the procedure as soon as we got here. And then, about twenty minutes ago, the call came in from the American Embassy here."

Derrence looked up, his interest increasing. "The American Embassy? That quickly?"

"Yes, sir. They said something about the Hawaiian state officials relaying word about the crash, and offered whatever assistance they could to aid the survivors."

"Decent of them, but I think our own people can get there sooner."

Aberdeen picked up another slip of paper from the desk before him and handed it over. "That's not the problem, really. The strange part is the rest of the message. I wrote it down exactly as they relayed it, apparently from Washington. It says that the flight carried a radioactive materials shipment among the cargo. They feel that during the crash, the containers may have been broken open, and that there is a serious danger of exposure to these materials. They ask us to keep all rescue teams out of the area until a specially equipped American team can go in. They ask us to also alert the Cook Islands Government to the danger, and any other nation whose ships in the vicinity might feel compelled to render assistance."

Derrence frowned. "Can't say as I approve of that. The Cooks may be a goodly distance from us here, and self-governing in a limited way, but we still have jurisdiction over their international affairs."

Aberdeen nodded in agreement. "But the Americans were quite emphatic in their warning. The message was politely worded, but they left no doubt that they fully expected their advice to be followed."

"So I see." Derrence read through the official statement carefully, then a second time, then a third. Finally, he looked toward John Peddington, his tone serious. "What do *you* make of this?"

Peddington was silent a moment, then sighed inwardly. "I'm not really certain. It seems legitimate, I suppose, but still . . ."

"Yes—go ahead."

"Well, sir, it's just that the whole thing seems a bit odd, and I can't help but wonder if we should merely take them at their word."

"And you, Hughes—what's your opinion?"

"Basically the same," Aberdeen said. "I feel there's something phony about it, but what, I don't know. Even so, I don't think we can justifiably ignore their advice."

"Perhaps not," Derrence replied, clearly disturbed. He tossed the message from the embassy on the desk top and looked over the news release once again, as if some missing piece of the puzzle were lurking there in its innocent phrases. Suddenly, he looked up, tapping the news release with his finger. "If this plane was due to land in Honolulu, then *how in bloody blazes* did it end up on Tongareva? Not even a storm could blow it *that* far off course!"

Hughes Aberdeen shrugged helplessly. "There was no explanation offered, sir. Clearly there has to be more to it than has been said, but there's just no more information available."

Derrence began to pace the confines of the large outer office, keeping his thoughts to himself for several moments. Finally, Aberdeen interrupted the silence.

"Shall we notify the prime minister and the governor-general, sir?"

Derrence glanced briefly at Aberdeen, then resumed his

16

pacing. "No ... no, not just yet. Let us see how the matter progresses. And let us also see if we can expand our knowledge a bit, through *unofficial* channels. There must be something else we can learn, even if the Americans are keeping mum."

"And the rescue operations—?" Peddington responded. "Are we simply to go along with their wishes, and restrict all attempts for assistance?"

Derrence stopped his pacing. "Yes. Like it or not, that is exactly what we will do, for the time being. The Americans must have their reasons, whether as stated or otherwise, and we would do well to give them the benefit of the doubt. We will follow their 'advice,' gentlemen ... for the time being. ..."

Exactly one hour after Carla Jennings' urgent radio request for help, a squadron of Soviet naval vessels reached a point approximately seven hundred miles east-northeast of the Hawaiian Islands. Eight days earlier, they had left their home port of Petropavlovsk, on the coast of the Soviet Union's Kamchatka Peninsula. Administrative center of the region and a major seaport, Petropavlovsk served as base for most of the Soviet submarines operating in the Pacific, and was second only to Vladivostok as a port for surface vessels of the Russian Pacific Fleet.

And now a small unit of that fleet was crossing the great ocean. At the start of their voyage the progress had been slow. It was mid-December, and icebreakers had been used to clear a path through the frozen barrier that was forming in the North Pacific. The waters off Petropavlovsk were ice-locked most of the winter, as were many of the Soviet anchorages and sea routes. It was only natural that Russia had been the first nation to develop an oceangoing icebreaker, and the first to exploit nuclear power for the purposes of propelling the strong-hulled craft. For the Soviet naval and merchant fleets to have any mobility at all during the winter months, it was essential that the great ice barriers could be traversed.

But the frigid waters of the extreme North Pacific were far behind now. The heavily armed vessels that plowed the warm waters off Hawaii's northeastern shore were not scheduled to return to their own home base for several months.

And their journey did not go unnoticed.

High above those ships, a lone reconnaissance jet bearing

United States Navy markings circled, keeping pace with the steady forward progress of the vessels below. It maintained a respectful distance, even though there was little chance of open hostility from the Soviet ships. It was standard procedure to gain whatever information could be gathered concerning the movements and operations of Russian naval vessels anywhere in the world, and especially when near the coastal waters of other nations.

But this time there was a special reason for the recon pilot's continuing interest. Besides the two Kashin class destroyers, the Kresta class cruiser, two submarines, and support ships, there was one other vessel—a ship that dwarfed the rest and dominated the formation so totally that there was no doubt which was the unit's command ship. And there was also no doubt that the great ship below was the *Kiev*. There were only two ships of the Kuril class thus far, the *Kiev* and the *Minsk*, and the latter was reportedly still testing in the area of the Black Sea.

Rumors concerning the development of the Soviet aircraft carrier had been circulating for five years or more. At a length of 925 feet, the *Kiev* was somewhat smaller than the largest carriers of the United States Navy, but its design and armament were considered by some authorities to be more advanced. Its very existence was proof that the Soviet Navy was expanding steadily to a worldwide force, and a force to be reckoned with. The days of Russian sea power being used for mere coastal defense were past. The Russian Navy already possessed more ships of almost every class than its American counterpart. All that was lacking was an effective seaborne tactical air force—an essential element for the intervention capability desired by Soviet leaders.

Despite the constant threat of total nuclear warfare, and in some ways because of it, the ability to wage conventional warfare had gained importance as a factor in international power. Wide-ranging naval air capability was an essential tool needed to exercise that power, and in the game nations play for military and political influence, the mobility of troops and strike aircraft meant as much as, if not more than, the too-dangerous, overhanging threat of total destruction.

It was a game the Soviets played well, with deadly seriousness. And in that game, the *Kiev* and ships like it would be powerful playing pieces.

THE KIEV

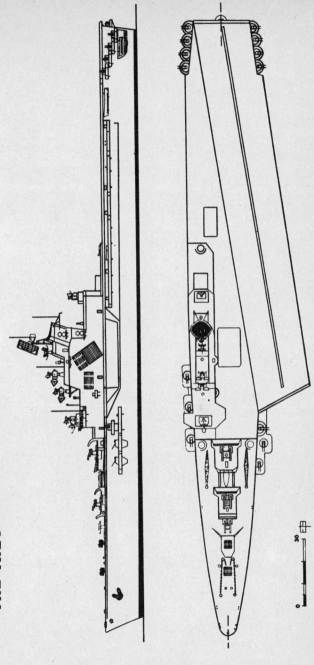

Rear Adm. Nikolay Bakhirev was a man well aware of the *Kiev*'s awesome power. He stood on the bridge of the aircraft carrier, feet planted firmly on the deck that rose and fell ever so slightly, cool gray eyes surveying the smooth and gleaming surfaces of the *Kiev*'s forward structure. With the ship's heavy gun armament, its multiple missile launchers, antisubmarine weapons, and tactical aircraft, it was easily the most powerful and versatile craft in the Soviet Navy. And Bakhirev relished the fact. To be commanding this squadron on its current mission was one thing—to be commanding it aboard the *Kiev* was quite another. For Bakhirev, it was the culmination of a long and distinguished career as a naval officer.

At his side stood Konstantin Dashkevich, captain first rank and the man technically in command of the *Kiev* itself. In the wide, many-windowed bridge, elevated a full thirty feet above the ship's flight deck, Dashkevich's view of the *Kiev* and the surrounding ocean could only be termed inspiring. His opinion of his superior officer was no less appreciative. Both men had had their officer's training at the Frunze School in Leningrad, and Dashkevich had served under Bakhirev during two previous commands. He considered the man to be the best naval officer he had ever encountered.

Five years younger than his superior, Dashkevich had hair nearly the color of rust, in contrast to the darker, graying locks of Bakhirev. He was also more slender, and his strong features were marred by a scar that ran along one side of his jaw—souvenir of a shipboard explosion six years earlier.

Turning to the young warrant officer who sat before one screen of the bank of radar equipment, Dashkevich asked, "Is our curious comrade still with us, Yakosev?"

Vasiliy Yakosev studied the glowing screen intently, not taking his eyes from it even to reply. "Yes, Captain. Maintaining the same reconnaissance pattern."

Admiral Bakhirev noticed Dashkevich's somber look. He raised an eyebrow amusedly, wrinkling his high forehead. "So we will let him have a good look, yes? Better that they see how strong we are rather than merely guess. The oceans are ours to sail at will, and the world will soon get used to seeing ships like this."

"Yes, Admiral," Dashkevich replied, but he did not lose his troubled look. He could not adequately explain why the presence of the American jet bothered him, and yet he could not entirely dismiss the feeling either. "At least he will have to leave us soon—I suspect he will be out of operating range before long."

Bakhirev nodded and returned his gaze to the sea before them. He was still surveying the technological marvel that was the *Kiev* when a lieutenant came forward from the communications niche and approached the two officers.

"Sir—" He extended a sheet of paper with a radio-teletype message to the captain. "This has just been relayed from Petropavlovsk—it is quite urgent."

Dashkevich took the encoded message quickly. "All right. Return to your post." He glanced over the first few lines, which identified the message's point of origin. Frowning, he turned to Bakhirev, his voice lower. "This is from Moscow!"

The admiral's own interest was already evident, and as he took the sheet from Dashkevich's hand, he was already starting for the plotting table. Using his key to unlock one of the drawers, Bakhirev extracted a code book and located the correct decoding section. He began to break the message down into its original form, and within a few minutes had converted almost half of it into readable copy. Bakhirev paused in his work long enough to scan back over the decoded section. His expression of curiosity changed subtly.

"What is it?" Dashkevich asked, facing the admiral from the opposite side of the plotting table.

"We are going to have to change course," Bakhirev said softly. "Prepare to contact the other ships in the squadron— they are to continue on their present course and mission. But the *Kiev* will be leaving them."

"Leaving them! But why?"

"Just do as I say," Bakhirev cautioned. "I will explain more fully later."

"Yes, Admiral."

It took less than ten minutes for the necessary radio communications to be carried out between the ships of the squadron, and for the *Kiev*'s navigation specialists to lock in a new course based on coordinates supplied by Admiral Bakhirev. As the great aircraft carrier began its slow turn to the south, another of the *Kiev*'s officers appeared on the bridge, emerging from the companionway at the rear. He headed unerringly for Admiral Bakhirev, pausing only once to take in the shifting angle of light within the bridge.

Dashkevich barely restrained a grimace as he caught sight of the ship's senior political officer. Although the man was only a captain third rank and had never in his career held a command position, he could and occasionally did make life miserable for the other officers. Not even a higher ranking officer could go against him without fear of repercussions from the highest levels of Soviet government. He was a representative of party doctrine first and foremost, and a naval officer second. That fact endeared him to none but the most idealistic of seamen, and his regular lectures on Marxist-Leninist principles never quite generated the revolutionary zeal he expected of the men.

Dashkevich nudged Bakhirev, whispering, "Grigorovich—"

Looking up at the approaching officer, the admiral's expression became chillingly firm. "Yes?"

Ivan Grigorovich managed to combine respect with arrogance as he stopped before the two men. "It was my understanding, Admiral, that we had orders to proceed directly to the coast of South America—"

"And so we did," Bakhirev said coldly. "But now we have *new* orders—direct from Moscow. I am following those orders."

"Yes, of course," Grigorovich replied, undaunted. "I shall be interested in knowing what our new mission is, since it may influence my training programs for the men."

"All in due course, Captain." Bakhirev turned away from the irritating young political officer, facing once more the rolling sea ahead. "For the moment, I can only say that it seems we are off on a mercy mission. And as for your training programs—I can foresee no problems that will affect either them, or the performance of this ship. . . ."

In southern California, over an hour later, it was 2:30 P.M. when Lt. Col. Stewart Gardner drove through the gate at Edwards Air Force Base, located on the western edge of the Mojave Desert. He had been driving almost a full hour, primarily along the state interchange up from the San Fernando Valley some eighty miles away, and at speeds that should have got him pulled over by the Highway Patrol in any number of places.

Gardner was both angry and curious about the alert

message he had received at 1:35. He had only just left the base at 10:00 A.M., after the perfunctory Saturday inspection at Company HQ. What with normal driving time, it was 11:30 by the time he had reached Martha's house for his weekly visit. Then after lunch with his wife's mother, he had gone on to the city's cemetery, stopping only to buy the flowers his melancholy ritual demanded.

The thirty-five-year-old air force officer had stood there before the headstones, hating the place and its dreary aspect, and yet never willing to forgo the weekly trips that had begun five years before. The pointless bitterness was gone now—there was that much at least. But he still felt incongruous and out of place there, even after all those visits. It was not right, he told himself—he was simply too young to have a wife and son dead and buried here. He had often feared that, in the course of his flying duties, he might leave his wife a widow dependent upon his limited government insurance. That was a burden carried by nearly every married military man. But the possibility that the situation would be reversed—that he would be the one left alone—had never even occurred to him.

He had only been at the cemetery a few minutes when the message had come. Martha herself had brought it, catching a cab from her house when the telephone call had come for Gardner. The tone of the call had unduly alarmed her, and in hurrying from the cab to the place where Gardner was kneeling, the poor woman had almost fallen, hindered by her cane and the heavy brace that enclosed her crippled leg—a permanent reminder of the tragic auto crash that had taken the lives of Gardner's wife and young son.

He had calmed Martha down, paid her cab fare, and made apologies for the trouble he had inadvertently caused. Then he had left for the base in his own car, as quickly as he could.

And now he had reached Edwards still wondering what could be so terribly important.

Gardner accelerated as he headed for the special access road, bypassing the main part of the base. His destination was an isolated section of the thirty-five-mile-wide government reservation, and a facility whose purpose was known to only a small percentage of the air force stationed personnel there. The road he was traveling now had been used by literally thousands of trucks over the past three years, transporting a great variety and quantity of materials in extreme secrecy. Rumors made the rounds among the base personnel regularly, but only the essential personnel and a few civilian contractors knew the true nature of the project. So far . . .

Gardner kept his windows closed as his car sped along, more against the wind-borne dust than the mid-fifty-degree temperature. He had driven this route often enough in the last three years. Not that he minded. He had originally volunteered for the project without even knowing what it was, simply because it afforded him an opportunity to stay in the area, close to his family.

His features hardened even more at the recollection of those first few years, when his air force duties were the only thread binding the fragments of his life. Perhaps because of that, the project was more than a mere assignment. It had become a reason for living.

Gardner suddenly looked ahead, squinting into the desert glare. He could see the "Farm" ahead, a brighter spot of light in the distance. Gardner was not sure just who had first tagged the facility with that nickname, but there was no denying that the place resembled a farm, or at least the enclosed greenhouse of one. The structure glistened in the sunlight, the silvery Mylar-coated Plexiglas panels that comprised its surface almost mirrorlike against the sky.

The rooflike structure was low—from a distance it seemed nearly level with the ground. It was only when you came within a mile of it that its truly awesome size could be perceived. Its height was not impressive, at a mere forty feet, but that dimension was small compared to the other two.

Over three hundred feet wide at the base it was, and fourteen hundred feet in length. In the space the structure occupied, eight football fields could have been laid down, side by side, with nearly enough room left over at one end for a ninth.

Closer now, the separation of the overlapping roof sections were visible, as were the train tracks running parallel with the structure. Tracks that supported dozens of wheeled platforms, which in turn supported the edges of the roof sections themselves.

On the other side of the greenhouselike building were the support facilities—the complex of buildings that included a large metal-forming plant and several materials storage warehouses. Activity there was halted now, temporarily, but if things went as planned, workers would be busy again within a year.

Gardner pulled up alongside the guard gate. Even here within the base, the special facility was fenced off and patrolled regularly. Gardner was recognized by the man at the gate, but still went through the motions of showing his clearance ID. Once inside, he drove to the parking area at the near side of the great structure. Emerging from his car, Gardner went straight for the small, one-story building that was so totally dwarfed by the greenhouselike building it was scarcely noticeable. A familiar face was there, waiting at the open door.

S/Sgt. Elizabeth Jordan stepped out of his way as he entered, her hesitant smile freezing as she sensed his grim mood and barely controlled anger. She was already dressed in the special unit's deep blue flight fatigues, a uniform that accented rather than underplayed the girl's attractive figure. Her brunette hair reached almost to her shoulders, and her blue eyes were riveted on his features in concern. But all this was lost on Gardner, who was staring at his immediate superior officer.

Col. John Curtis was in the center of the room, methodically going over a checklist. A towering Texan five years older than Gardner, Curtis did not look up. "You just *did* make it," Curtis said flatly. "I was about to use a replacement and have you flown out later by jet."

"Why?" Gardner said carefully. "What's up?"

"Something special. We just got our orders from Washington about thirteen hundred hours."

Elizabeth Jordan reacted to his remark instantly, taking advantage of the opportunity. "Which reminds me, sir—I came up to bring you these updates from the commo section. The final confirmation is here, plus some new information."

Curtis looked the sheets over carefully, then attached them to his clipboard, beneath his checklist. Glancing at Gardner suddenly, he said with irritation flaring, "You know, it's damn inconvenient having my senior flight officer eighty—odd miles away when an alert comes through!"

"I was on my own off-duty time," Gardner replied, still angry enough not to apologize. Still, he kept his temper under control. "The likelihood of an alert has been negligible up till now. Besides, you knew where to find me."

Curtis said nothing in reply, but kept his hard look.

Elizabeth Jordan looked away from Gardner, lest her own thoughts be too apparent. She knew as well as Col. Curtis where Gardner went every weekend, and although she sympathized with the man she also was concerned with his almost fanatical devotion to the dead. She had tried to express that concern on more than one occasion, only to be rebuked each time. Gardner had made it clear that the subject was taboo. So even though she wanted to say more about it, even now, she knew better than to press the issue. Perhaps with time—

"All right. Let's forget it," Curtis said sharply. "We've got a lot to do, and precious little time to do it."

He turned and headed for the back of the office and the elevator, which stood waiting with its door open. When both Gardner and Elizabeth Jordan had joined him in the veneer-faced metal cubicle, Curtis took the controls off hold and pressed the button that was second down from the top. The buttons were arranged as they normally were in elevators, with the difference being that their numbered sequence started with *one* at the top and increased with each succeeding button below. The car started down.

Curtis held the elevator on the second level long enough for Gardner to go to the flight crew quarters and change from his dress blues to the same special flight fatigues worn by the others. When he returned, Curtis pressed the last button and the elevator started down again, bypassing the intermediate levels containing offices, mess facility, medical facility, supplies, and all the other sections that were a part of the massive complex.

When at last the car whined to a halt, 275 feet below the surface of the desert floor, the door panels opened onto a plain concrete corridor thirty feet in length. Curtis and the others started for the far end, their heel-clicks echoing from the smooth surfaces of walls, floor, and ceiling. The temperature was several degrees cooler here, and indeed would have been cooler still if not for the balancing efforts of the complex's air-conditioning equipment. Both the depth of the installation at this level and the mirrorlike surface of the roof structure above kept the temperature low without much assistance. But the air-conditioning system was there to keep a balanced temperature, even in summer when the outside desert heat rose to well over a hundred degrees. In winter, it kept the subterranean chill to a manageable limit.

They emerged from the corridor into the hangar. Any

casual visitor, seeing the chamber for the first time, would have been awestruck by its immense scale. The roof, which let in a gray, diffused glow, stretched high overhead, more than three hundred feet at the highest point of its peaked structure. The width of the chamber was an equal distance, and the length of it was so great that detail at the far ends was difficult if not impossible to make out. Its volume was 115.5 million cubic feet, slightly less than NASA's massive Vehicle Assembly Building at the Kennedy Space Center in Florida, but totally open throughout, with no verticle supports save for the walls themselves.

But those walls were enough. Almost 1.5 million tons of concrete had been poured, in slow stages, over the steel reinforcing structures of the walls alone. Thirty feet thick at the base, tapering gradually to ten feet at the top, they rested on solid bedrock. The floor, consuming another 2,100 tons of concrete, had been poured within the boxy framework of the walls after they had set.

The floor space could have accommodated seven 747 jet airliners with ease, wingtip to wingtip, or harbored the Soviet aircraft carrier *Kiev* with room to spare. It could have, but in fact the hangar only held *one* craft within its spacious interior, and its dimensions nearly filled the great chamber.

As Curtis and the others walked, an electric tram whined past them, its flatcars stacked high with boxes. Some, wrapped in foil and sealed plastic, bore food labels, while others were clearly marked as emergency medical supplies. Everywhere, technicians in air force blue hurried about almost frantically, completing loading and final flight preparations.

"You don't mean to tell me we're going to lift off in midafternoon!" Gardner was saying.

"I mean exactly that," Curtis replied. "Today is a little sooner than our scheduled debut, but we have no choice."

Gardner nodded grimly. "I was thinking more in terms of the air currents up there at this time of the day."

"We'll manage. Just be glad it isn't summer."

At the moment, Gardner almost wished it *were* summer. With Christmas only a week and a half away, he would rather be through with the whole season and be well into next year. He began to hope that the mission would be an extended one. "What about the leak in the number four ballast tank?"

"Been taken care of," Curtis said smoothly, stopping before the bank of test and monitoring equipment concentrated along the center of the hangar's wall. "So far, all the systems check out at optimal level. And we can be thankful we've already conducted the hook-on tests—the Harriers are all stowed and ready."

"What about the heavy equipment—it hasn't arrived yet, has it?"

"Don't need it. Couldn't take it even if it was here. We need the extra payload and space for the return trip."

Curtis then checked the readings on the high-power air compressors that were warming up and presently venting their pressure through exhaust ports topside. Once it was time for lift-off and the hangar's top panels were open, air would be valved into the four large guide-columns located several hundred feet from each end of the chamber, one to a corner. In their present deflated state, they were only crumpled stacks of heavy nylon fabric, three layers thick and formed into cylinders thirty feet in diameter. Smaller air arteries within the cylinders would make them more rigid, and when the pressure valves were opened, the cylinders would inflate to their full height and extend roughly eighty feet above ground level. Their purpose was to prevent buffeting of the mammoth craft in the hangar during entry and egress, and so far, during night testing over the last month, the system had worked flawlessly.

Curtis turned suddenly as another tram whisked past, heading for the loading bays. Three medium-sized crates were tied down to its single flatcar.

"What are those?" Gardner asked.

"Some special medical gear," Curtis answered. "We had it transported over from the base hospital to augment what we have in sick bay. And two surgical nurses have been assigned for the mission."

"Even at that, we'll be traveling light."

"We can carry enough ballast to make the difference."

Gardner's mind began to work faster now as he was caught up more in the pressure of the moment. He moved quickly to the large relief map on the wall, his eyes scanning the terrain surrounding Edwards Air Force Base. So far, all flight operations and testing had taken place over the restricted zone well within the limits of the base. Gardner had known that eventually he would have to fly the ship out of the area. He just had not expected it to happen this soon.

His finger traced out a path along the surface of the

map. There was a narrow wedge of land, beginning at Edwards and stretching out to the coast, with the widest point of the triangle located between Ventura and the center of Los Angeles. Within that wedge there were virtually no mountainous areas to interfere with relatively low altitude flight. The other areas were less clear. Directly to the south and southeast lay the San Gabriel and San Bernardino mountains. Almost exactly to the north was the great chain of the Sierra Nevada. And to the west were scattered a number of lesser peaks.

Gardner glanced over at the colonel. "Are we going to be using the planned Pacific access route over Oxnard?"

Curtis shook his head. "Can't—we're not going in that direction immediately. We have to pick up some people first, northwest of here. And if you're thinking of looping around the coast, forget it—we haven't time."

"Then how?" Gardner looked back to the map. "We can't afford to go too high over some of those regions—we'll reach our pressure height and have to vent."

"No, we won't. I've had Roth plot out a flight path that will take us between Double Mountain and the Tehachapi Mountains. From there on, we'll follow lowland all the way, over the San Joaquin Valley."

Gardner was silent as he considered the terrain and the air currents likely encountered between the two mountain areas. Lieutenant Colonel Roth was no doubt a first-rate senior navigator, as navigators go, or he would not be in the program. Even so, Gardner had hardly any working experience with the man. Roth had only returned two weeks before after a three-month training program in Washington, in which a number of civilian and government agencies had provided information essential to understanding the nuances of his new assignment. But whatever the man's experience or skills, Gardner thought ironically, it was one thing to merely point out a path, and quite another to have to *follow* it.

At that moment there came a buzzing from the small radio transceiving unit clipped to Colonel Curtis' belt. He snapped it free, bringing it to his lips. "Yes, sir?"

There was a moment's pause, and then a voice issued from the unit's speaker, a voice that was mellow and unhurried, and tinged with a bit of Tennessee twang. "You about got it packed, John?"

Curtis hesitated as his keen eyes searched the hangar

area. The last of the loading bays had been secured and the electric trams were clear. Everyone—except for himself, Gardner, Jordan, and the ground crew—was aboard. Defense systems had been loaded and checked, and all was in readiness. The automatic release latches that held the ship secure were awaiting the electronic commands that would trigger them. The ship's cells were at normal volume already, and only the hangar's latch system kept it from the sky.

"Yes, sir," Curtis said smoothly. "We're operational."

The voice from the small radio unit answered back, "Then, gentlemen, anytime you're ready . . ."

Curtis clipped the unit to his belt and moved quickly to a different section of the complex equipment panel. Opening a covered switch box, he turned the key-shaped knob twice to the right, waited a moment, then pressed two buttons beneath it simultaneously. From somewhere overhead came the distant and somewhat muffled sound of huge diesel engines starting up. An instant later, a brilliant, almost blinding slash of light cut through the middle of the hangar, steadily expanding as the raw desert sun came into view.

High above, the telescoping sections of the hangar's roof were rolling away—parting in the middle as half of the sections moved toward one end of the fourteen-hundred-foot-long chamber and the rest moved toward the other. It would take a full fifteen minutes for the rolling panels to open completely, but by then Curtis and the others would be on the ship's command deck, ready and waiting.

Stewart Gardner turned to Elizabeth Jordan, acknowledging her presence for the first time. "Beth—has commo been processing current meteorological data for the flight path?"

"Yes, sir, it's on board. And of course we'll get updates as we go."

Gardner nodded, then turned as Curtis swiftly motioned them over to a small electric crew tram. They climbed aboard and the colonel switched its power on.

Pulling away from the main hanger control equipment, the tram sped off toward the far end of the chamber and the retractable boarding ramp leading up to the command deck hatch. Meanwhile, high above, the roof sections continued to open, pouring in more and more sunlight on the glistening craft that waited below, like a slumbering giant about to awaken. . . .

"You might say, blood bruises easily."

There was a small amount of laughter, more really than the joke deserved, but then all 150 assembled pre-med students were caught up in the Christmas holiday spirit. The young men and women who composed the group sat in one of the two lecture halls of San Francisco State University's old science building. The special weekend seminar had been going on since noon, with representatives of the University of California Medical School and a half-dozen specialists in the various fields of medicine explaining new developments and research projects with which they had firsthand contact. It was now a few minutes before 6:00 P.M. in San Francisco, but the students' attention, rather than waning, was still sharply focused on the man who stood before them and on the equipment he was demonstrating.

"That's facetious, of course," Dr. Paul Brandon continued, "but the fact remains that most mechanical systems presently used for pumping blood—whether in the traditional heart-lung machine, the kidney dialysis unit, or the several attempts at creating artificial hearts—most have a tendency to damage the red blood cells after prolonged pumping."

Paul Brandon was markedly unlike the professors they were used to hearing. He was thirty-seven, with sandy-blond hair, and his form was kept both trim and tanned by weekends usually spent on the tennis court. Instead of a dress shirt and tie, he wore a scarlet turtleneck sweater under a tweed jacket. His features were finely chiseled, almost Scandinavian in their contours, and if not quite perfect enough to be considered handsome, his face was at least pleasant enough to arouse the immediate interest of several young women in the first row. Brandon's dark eyes were steady and penetrating, and he seemed a man well in control of his destiny.

"An impeller can't be used because the rotating blades positively blenderize everything—plasma, corpuscles, the works." As he spoke, deep red fluid constantly flowed through the clear plastic tubes and filtering systems of the heart-lung machine behind him. Both it and the kidney dialysis equipment to his right pumped blood the same way—the fluid was progressively moved forward through a series of tubular coils by the action of rollers rotating within them, physically squeezing the fluid along in the spaces between. "Even in this system here, there is still more cell damage than we would like to have, and of course this can't be reduced in size sufficiently to be of any use in an artificial heart design."

Dr. Philip Norton of the San Francisco State University School of Natural Sciences was presiding over the seminar. Standing near Brandon, he fielded a question from a student in the middle of the room. "Yes, Feldman?"

"What about an electromagnetic system?" the young man asked. "Hemoglobin has a fair amount of iron in it—couldn't it be moved in that manner?"

Brandon smiled faintly. "I'm afraid not forcefully enough to do the job, although a magnetic field *is* being considered as a means of separating blood components. No, I'm sure what we have to do is find a way to *duplicate* the heart's own action. Which means we have to have a flexible, multichambered structure with valves, much as the heart has, and a means of causing that structure to constrict. And it has to be *reliable* enough to function continuously without trouble for at *least* a year, if not longer. Ideally, the system should be responsive to changes in the patient's activity, and composed of materials compatible with blood and the human system." He paused and picked up a device he had shown earlier, at the beginning of his speech. It filled his hand, and consisted of four discusshaped chambers formed of some rubberoid material, two above and two below a rigid nylon framework. In the center of that framework was a solid-state electronic timing circuit, encased in a clear material, and a set of solenoids with pressure arms resting above the upper chambers and below the lower ones.

"As I said before, this device, which we're developing at the Steinman-Keller Institute, is still highly experimental. The electrical power it requires is rather high, at present, but if the atomic-powered pacemakers currently in use prove reliable, then we may follow in that direction."

Five students immediately raised their hands with further questions in mind. But Dr. Norton, who had been checking his watch during the last few mintues, interrupted the proceedings.

"I'm afraid we've run overtime again," he said, then shrugged helplessly at a few groans of protest from the group. "I promised the dean we'd have the hall clear no later than six, and it's five after already. Besides," he added, smiling, "I'm sure you all can think of a better way to spend a Saturday night than sitting here on campus. Everyone's dismissed!"

As the students began to leave, amid the sounds of seats moved back, Norton turned to Brandon. "We'll have to have you back again, Paul. The students respond to you very well, and I think these little technological progress reports are a good balance to the more academic side of their studies."

"I'll try to come better prepared next time," Brandon replied, packing away his own equipment even as U.C. Medical School personnel prepared to load the heart-lung machine and other large display units into the van outside. "I'm afraid I've been neglecting my duties here since you gave me the advisory position last year."

Norton gave him a sympathetic pat on the back. "I know your time is at a premium. Especially these last few months." He was silent a moment as they left the lecture hall and started along the walkway leading to the parking area. Then as they walked, he said speculatively, "I've heard that the institute has quite a sizable investment tied up in your heart project. Are the stories true?"

"It depends on which ones you've heard," Brandon answered, almost evasively. Then, as if reconsidering, he added, "It's no secret, really. To date, they've put roughly two and a half million into the project."

Norton raised an eyebrow. "It seems the rumor-mongers have been underestimating!"

"Steinman-Keller expects to get it all back, and then some," Brandon explained matter-of-factly. "Presuming the project works out, which I think it will."

Norton shook his head disconsolately. "And I have trouble getting a mere thousand out of Funding for new classroom equipment. Ah, well—" He sighed, then as they reached the first row of cars he added, "As their key man, I wonder just how much *you're* worth to them?"

"Probably not as much as I like to think," he said wryly. "Well, I guess this is where we head our separate ways."

Norton realized that they were standing beside his own car. He nodded in agreement and started to unlock his door, then suddenly hesitated. "Oh, and there's something I'd better not forget, not if I want to go home tonight—I know it's short notice, Paul, but Margery *insisted* I ask if you could make it over to the house for a little dinner party later tonight, about eight-thirty. It seems the list is a little lopsided, and she was hoping you could balance it out."

Brandon gave him a knowing look. "What she means is, the group is short one eligible bachelor." He laughed faintly. "Phil, your wife is marvelous and a perfect hostess, but she's also an incorrigible matchmaker. Please—thank her for her kind invitation and tell her I can't make it tonight."

"All right." Philip Norton nodded understandingly. He thought he sensed behind Brandon's lighthearted reply a mood that was sadder and more reflective. He also thought he knew what caused it, but said only, "All right then—see you later, Paul."

"Good night."

Brandon watched him back the car out and waved him off, watching until Norton's vehicle disappeared around the bend in the road. Then he turned and walked on to the spot where his own car was parked.

He unlocked the door to his silver-gray Corvette Stingray and slid into the leather-upholstered seat. In a moment the engine started with a throaty purr and he backed out into the lane. He had just put it in forward and started up when the sound of screeching tires attracted his attention.

Brandon saw a dark car—perhaps black, but it was hard to be certain in the limited light—speeding along the lane that intersected the one in which he now drove. In the next second it turned the corner and pulled to an abrupt halt just in front of his car, blocking his path completely.

He tensed slightly, involuntarily, and watched as the car's driver threw open the door and stepped out. The odd shadows cast upon the man's features by the headlight's glare were enough in themselves to make him look menacing. Still, Brandon leaned out his window and called out to him.

"You're in the way!"

The stranger studied him a moment, then surprisingly called back, "Are you Dr. Paul Brandon. . . ?"

Brandon did not reply. He was not sure why he hesitated, but some inner feeling told him to be cautious. Maybe it was the knowledge that in the last two months alone, there had been at least three kidnaping or extortion attempts aimed at executives of large businesses within the San Francisco area. His position with Steinman-Keller would certainly qualify him as a target. Also, there was the question of why anyone would need to contact him here and now. Since his research work had begun, he was no longer on call at the hospital for emergency surgery, and as far as the police were concerned, with no next of kin, Brandon had no reason to be notified of traffic accidents or the like.

All these thoughts raced through his mind in a matter of seconds. Brandon already thought he could distinguish the outline of a gun at the edge of the man's open coat, and in the next instant, the issue was decided for him by the sudden emergence of a second man from the passenger side of the car.

Brandon waited no longer. Throwing the car into reverse, he stepped on the gas and sped back along the parking lane until he came to an intersection. Turning abruptly, he changed gears again and started off for the edge of the campus and the main road beyond. From behind him came the sound of car doors being slammed shut and of an engine racing. He knew he had no more than a few second's lead on them, but Brandon held on to the somewhat feeble hope that he could lose them in traffic.

He could see their headlights behind him now, and he tried to force himself to think clearly, seeking a way out of the situation. He could try heading for the nearest police station, but was not sure of its location or distance. There were a number of pay phones on campus where he could make a call to the police, but it would be foolish to stop long enough to do so—his pursuers would catch up with him before he could finish dialing.

He turned the corner and rounded another block, still heading for Nineteenth Avenue. The lights of the dark car behind swung around as well and shone brightly in his rear-view mirror. If nothing else they were determined, and their continuing pressure made Brandon increase his speed.

Skidding around yet another corner, Brandon aimed the car straight down a narrow lane that had guideposts on both sides. There was only a half block remaining before he would reach the edge of the campus and Nineteenth Avenue, and he was still maintaining a fair lead over the car behind. Once out in traffic, he would have at least a chance of losing them. And once out of sight, he could contact the police and get assistance.

But something happened that dashed those hopes and made his heart literally skip a beat. For ahead, turning the corner from Nineteenth, was a car identical to the first. It headed directly for him, then skidded to an angled stop that left it blocking his escape route.

In the mirror, Brandon saw the pursuing car closing the gap between them. He could go neither forward nor back, so he threw open his own car door and jumped out, preparing to flee on foot.

He had gone only a few yards when a voice cried out his name, loudly and sharply. Something in its tone and timber made him halt.

Looking around, his eyes fixed on the man who had emerged from the second car. Like the other two, this man was dressed in a plain business suit and topcoat and wore no hat against the evening's chill breeze. Brandon thought he had recognized the voice, and now, as he looked hard in the difficult light, he thought he recognized the man's features as well.

"Mr. Haddock?"

The man approached swiftly, yet without menace in his behavior. He reached Brandon's side, his expression grim and impatient. "We had a devil of a time finding you, Brandon. I take it you're not in the habit of letting people know where you're going."

"There aren't that many people I have to answer to," Brandon said bitterly, his tension now exploding into anger. "And what's the idea of having your people pop up, like Gestapo agents, chasing me across campus."

"Let's not overreact—"

"How do you *expect* me to react—I had no idea who they were, and I wasn't especially anxious to find out."

Haddock glanced over to the other car, appraising the situation. Finally, his tone cooled somewhat, his manner becoming more apologetic. "All right, I can see how it must have seemed to you. I'm sorry if there was a misunderstanding, but there's been no time for a lot of explanatory messages. We've been trying to find you for the past three hours. My men were already heading for the university just to check out a hunch when I received word that you were actually here. I'm sorry I didn't get here first so we could have avoided any worry on your part, but it didn't happen to work out that way. Now, are we going to stand here and argue about it, or get down to business?"

Brandon considered, and his anger was finally quelled by the logic of the matter. For Haddock and his men to seek him out this way, things must indeed be urgent. He would at least hear the man out.

"All right—what's happened?"

"The man I've spoken to you about before," Haddock began, his voice low. "He needs treatment—probably an operation—immediately, as soon as it can be arranged."

Brandon frowned. "I wasn't scheduled to see him for a week yet. From the information you provided, the man's condition seemed stable."

"It was, but it isn't now. It's imperative that he receive help. As we discussed it. I can explain on the way, Dr. Brandon, but I have to know immediately if you're going to help us."

Brandon hesitated. "Which hospital?"

"We can't do it in San Francisco," Haddock replied quickly. "You'll have to go with me to where the patient is at present."

Brandon's frown deepened, and he wavered a moment. But he *had* agreed to help. . . .

"All right, Mr. Haddock. I'll go, although I can't say I like your methods. We'll have to stop by the institute, though. I'll need some of my equipment."

"Yes, of course. It's on our way. But we have to get started at once." He directed Brandon to the dark-colored vehicle in which he had just arrived.

"What about my car?"

"One of my agents will drive it to your apartment house—you don't have to worry about that. We'll take care of everything, including a suitable excuse for your absence."

Brandon got into the car and settled back as the vehicle backed up, then pulled swiftly away onto Nineteenth Avenue, heading north. He looked at Haddock, but the government man was silent for the moment.

Brandon felt ill at ease with this man, even though he had promised to help him. He remembered the first time Haddock had approached him, a full month ago, with his strange request and desire for secrecy. Haddock had shown him his State Department credentials, and Brandon had confirmed, through a highly placed friend of his own in Washington, that the man was exactly what he represented himself to be.

That such a man would approach him was intriguing enough. The fact that the prospective patient discussed by Haddock was to be kept a mystery was downright bizarre. Haddock had supplied a complete medical history, including recent electrocardiograms, which had told Brandon a great deal about the physical condition of the man he was to treat. But it told him not one thing about who that man was. Brandon had protested the lack of a direct physical examination, conducted by himself, but there had been no swaying Haddock. All he would admit was that the patient was highly important and involved in sensitive international relations. Beyond that, nothing. At times during the last month, Brandon had wondered why he had gone along with Haddock's wishes. He was not sure, even now, if he had an answer.

The lights of the city glowed like a thousand fireflies as their car sped along. A little over four miles away, in downtown San Francisco, people would be involved in a vast variety of evening entertainments. Restaurants noted the world over for their fine food would be filled with patrons, as would the theaters, a short while later. Many residents would be out now, traversing the hilly blocks of the city, doing their Christmas shopping, perhaps in Ghirardelli Square, or in the numerous specialty shops of The Cannery or of Union Street which now had extended hours for the holiday season.

Their car turned right on Judah Street, and Brandon knew they were only fifteen blocks away from the University of California Medical Center. Traffic was fairly light, and they were making good time. When they finally reached the angled bend where Judah Street became Parnassus Avenue, Brandon began watching for the turnoff, in case the driver should miss it.

He found he had underestimated the man's knowledge. Going past the looping driveway before the Herbert C. Moffitt Hospital, the car turned right just before reaching the Neuropsychiatric Institute. A moment later, it turned right again and headed for the parking area alongside the East Tower of the Health Sciences Instruction and Research Building.

Brandon left the car, checked in with the guard, and entered the building. He took the elevator up to the floor on which the Steinman-Keller Institute maintained its research labs, and let himself into his office. Unlocking a metal cabinet at the rear of the room, Brandon hesitated for a moment, then removed a sealed box and slipped it into his medical kit. He paused long enough to remove another device from the cabinet, contained in a canvas case, which he tucked under one arm. Locking up everything again, he left the office and took the elevator down.

Outside, Haddock was waiting. As soon as Brandon

38

entered the car, it pulled out of the parking area and headed back to the main road. It stayed with Parnassus Avenue until it reached Willard Street, when it turned left, heading for Golden Gate Park, the thousand-acre recreation area that ran all the way from the Great Highway on the west to Stanyan Street on the east—three and a half miles long—almost halfway across the peninsular end of the county.

"Mr. Haddock," Brandon said at last, "don't you think it's about time you gave me at least a rough idea of who it is I am to treat?"

Haddock remained silent for a moment, then finally replied without looking at Brandon. "His name is Stefan Lorenz. His age and medical background you already know. He is Czechoslovakian, a Nobel prize-winning physicist whose genius is respected worldwide."

"The name is familiar," Brandon replied. "I seem to recall that he's been rather outspoken about political matters there."

"Yes, which is not the *safest* way to behave in a communist bloc nation. Lorenz is considered a dissident by the Czech government, and of course by the Soviets as well."

Haddock stopped speaking as the car pulled to a halt in front of Kezar Stadium. The gate had been left open, and Brandon could see a police car parked near the entrance to the structure. Brandon was puzzled, but said nothing.

As they got out of the car, Haddock motioned for Brandon to follow. They walked swiftly through the main corridor, and upon reaching the inside of the stadium, they could see that several of the lights had been switched on. The place was deserted, since the San Francisco Forty-niners were now using Candlestick Park for their home games and the high school competition had taken place the night before. Only one thing kept the old and empty stadium from looking normal.

Parked in the center of the grassy field, its silver fuselage glistening in the electric glow, a Bell UH-1N twin-turbine helicopter sat waiting, its engines idling as its rotor whirred steadily overhead, creating a *whupping* sound. The side of the ship bore U.S. Air Force markings, and one access door had been slid back.

Ducking lower than they had to beneath the whirling reach of the blades, both men climbed into the craft and seated themselves on the wide canvas and framework bench that ran from one side to the other. An aircrewman slid the door closed and latched it, then joined them in belting down securely.

The turbines began to increase their speed as the pilot fed the system more fuel, and the noise built up to a surprising level inside the craft. Then, with an abrupt feeling of detachment, the helicopter lifted up and forward, rising out of the stadium and steadily gaining altitude.

"This Lorenz," Brandon asked Haddock above the roar of the turbines. "How is he your responsibility?"

"Because he's leaving Czechoslovakia—for good," Haddock answered. "He had an opportunity to attend the World Science Conference in Hawaii and made contact with us about a month and a half ago. We made all the arrangements necessary for him to continue on to the continental United States once he arrived there."

"He's defecting?"

"Yes. And one of the stipulations of the agreement was that we would provide the best possible medical help available, which is where you come in, Doctor."

"And you say his condition has worsened?"

Haddock nodded gravely. "Definitely. The plane in which he was traveling crash-landed, on a remote island considerably farther south than Hawaii. We're going to have to reach the spot by air."

Glancing down as the helicopter continued its spiraling flight, Brandon wondered if they were heading for the nearby air force base, roughly twenty miles north of Oakland. "Where are we going to land now—at Travis?" he asked.

"No." Haddock said flatly. He had an odd expression on his face. "We're not going to land. We're going to rendezvous. And our immediate destination isn't down there below—*it's up above*...."

CHAPTER TWO

Paul Brandon gazed up in astonishment, leaning to his left to better see out the window in the closed port hatch. His eyes had been accustomed to the pale blue-white glow of instrument lights within the darkened helicopter cabin, and for an instant or two he had been unable to perceive anything in the greater darkness outside.

But now, looking in the direction Haddock indicated, Brandon could see the silhouetted form of something waiting above. What he had at first mistaken for the lights of a cluster of aircraft in fact belonged to just one object, unbelievably large, that loomed black against the indigo sky. Motionless against its backdrop of stars, the thing sent a chill along Brandon's spine that added to the cold he already felt, high in the air above a wintry San Francisco.

Brandon looked hard at the object, disbelieving what he saw, yet stunned by its reality. Looking almost like a great whale raised from the ocean's depths, the huge craft was cylindrical, with a gently tapering, almost blunt nose and a more sharply tapering aft end. Wedge-shaped fins were near the end, two on the vertical axis and two on the horizontal, giving the craft the aspect of a giant torpedo. Words from another age came to mind—dirigible, Zeppelin . . . *airship*. And yet the craft before him did not look like some relic from the past. The design was clearly more advanced than the pictures Brandon had seen of the earlier ships—for one thing, there was no underslung control car; for another, the small, outboard engines of the early designs had been replaced by a pair of gigantic propellers at the aft end.

Drawing nearer to the mammoth craft, the helicopter was dwarfed by it. The airship's propellers alone were at least seventy feet in diameter.

Brandon craned his neck to see ahead as the helicopter rose above the airship, heading for its center. There at the top of the hull, a rectangular pattern of lights glowed red in the darkness, marking an opening in the otherwise smooth surface. Bathed in the red glow of the landing lights, the space beneath that opening revealed itself to be a hangar.

The steady roar of the helicopter's turbines and rotors grew louder as the sound rebounded off the surfaces below it. Expertly, the pilot maneuvered the Bell UH-1N toward the very center of the opening, aiming for a small platform that was now level with the top surface of the hull. It too was outlined with lights, and by peering out and down to his left, the pilot could see the landing skid on the port side of the ship. His copilot was doing the same on the other side. Their aim was to lower the skids into special brackets at the sides of the landing platform, and with the breeze that was gusting over the top of the great airship, it took a full minute just to line the ship up properly.

THE USAF GRAND EAGLE

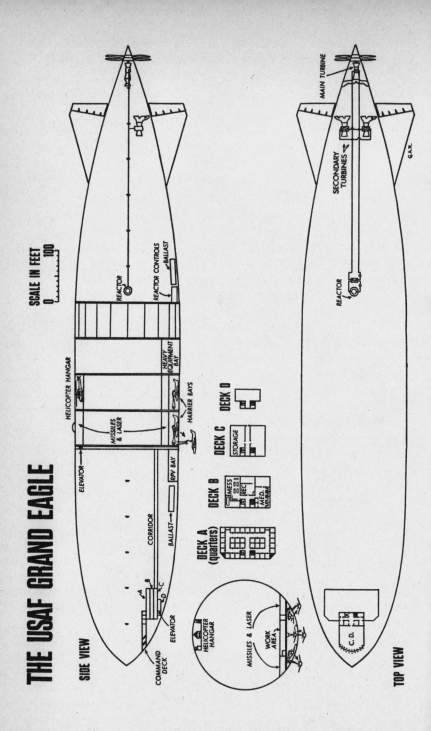

SCALE IN FEET
0   100

SIDE VIEW

HELICOPTER HANGAR

ELEVATOR

MISSILES & LASER

HARRIER BAYS

HEAVY EQUIPMENT BAY

REACTOR

REACTOR CONTROLS

BALLAST

CORRIDOR

BALLAST→

RPV BAY

ELEVATOR

COMMAND DECK

A
B
C
D

DECK A (quarters)

DECK B

MESS
REC
MED.

DECK C

STORAGE

DECK D

HELICOPTER HANGAR

MISSILES & LASER

WORK AREA

TOP VIEW

MAIN TURBINE

SECONDARY TURBINES

REACTOR

C. D.

G.A.R.

42

Instantly, clamps gripped the helicopter's landing skids and locked in place, securing the small aircraft. The pilot throttled off the engines and waited as the rotor spinned to a halt, then activated a servo unit that rotated the blades so that they lined up fore and aft, and locked them in place.

"On board, sir," the officer said into the small microphone attached to his flight helmet, and Brandon realized it was the first time he had been able to hear the man speak.

At once, the platform on which the helicopter rested began to lower to the floor of the hangar as air was bled out of the pneumatically operated system. In less than fifteen seconds it was down and locked. While the aircrewman opened the hatch, Brandon and Haddock unbuckled their safety belts.

As Brandon stepped out into the hangar with his medical kit and additional equipment in hand, a very tall man approached them. In the hangar's red glow, Brandon had the fleeting impression he had descended into a scene from Dante's *Inferno*.

"Gentlemen." The tall man greeted them with a hasty handshake. "Welcome aboard the USAF nuclear airship *Grand Eagle*. I'm Col. John Curtis." The voice had a Texas twang.

"Nuclear?" Brandon said. Then he noticed the oval unit emblem on Curtis' flight uniform: a silver embroidered design of the airship, viewed from the side, against a dark blue field, with red ellipses overlaid on the airship in the form of a symbolic atom.

"Our propulsion system," Curtis added. "Not our weaponry, in case you're wondering."

Haddock showed Curtis his State Department ID routinely, then put it back in his pocket. "How soon can we be under way, Colonel?"

"Just as soon as we get to the command deck." Curtis motioned them toward the front wall of the small helicopter hangar and the door that was located in its center, then turned back to the pilot, who was checking the locking brackets that held the small craft secure. After a brief exchange, Curtis switched off the landing lights, returning the hangar to its normal reduced lighting. At the touch of another control, the opening above began to close, mimicking the action of the airship's own giant hangar at Edwards Air Force Base.

Brandon paused a second to watch the panels close overhead, shivering in the chill of the unpressurized hangar, then turned and followed Curtis and Haddock. He clutched the medical gear like a lost and bewildered traveler might his luggage, his eyes taking in details as he walked.

Beyond the door was another chamber, equal in size to the hangar. Yet as large as it seemed, Brandon knew it could only occupy a tiny fraction of the airship's vast interior. The lighting was reduced here as well and was concentrated primarily along a narrow pathway running the length of the chamber. On both sides, stacks of cylindrical objects reposed in the near-darkness, and above were glints of light reflected from edges of some form of mechanical equipment. A permanent metal ladder led up out of sight into a higher level of the chamber.

Looking about, Brandon said, "These are missiles, aren't they?"

Curtis kept walking. "Yes, sir, they are. The air-to-air variety. They're primarily for self-defense—in anything this big, we'd be a sitting duck without them."

Brandon considered it a moment, then said. "You don't mean to say this thing's intended for combat?"

"Not directly."

"Then why the missiles?—unless you'd rather I didn't ask."

They had reached the far wall and a set of sliding double doors that were presently closed. Curtis pressed a button alongside them, and the doors whisked open with a slight hiss of air pressure, revealing a small elevator. Entering, he turned to face the others.

"Dr. Brandon," he began, "you're welcome aboard this craft. Our orders state that you're to be given VIP treatment, and that we're to help you do your job in every way possible. But I want you to keep in mind the fact that the *only* reason you're here is because Washington says it's necessary and because the State Department vouched for you as a good security risk. A lot of what you're going to see here is still considered classified and will be for some time. Do we understand each other?"

Brandon arched an eyebrow, then nodded. "I think so."

"Good." Colonel Curtis stood by the control buttons and waited as the helicopter crew caught up with them in the elevator. When the six men were all within the enclosure, he pressed the second button from the top.

The doors closed instantly and the cage started to drop, quickly but smoothly, and with little sound. Brandon studied the control panel with interest. There were only four buttons on it, and none bore any kind of markings or numbers. Presumably the crew of the immense airship did not need to be reminded where things were located, but the puzzling thing was that there were only four levels. Ten or fifteen seconds had already elapsed, and Curtis had only pressed the *second* button down from the helicopter hangar level. Brandon's curiosity got the best of him.

"Just how tall *is* this elevator shaft?"

"Roughly the equivalent of a twenty-two-story building," the colonel replied. "The *Grand Eagle* is two hundred and twelve feet in diameter at the hull's widest point, and twelve hundred ten feet from nose to tail rotors. And in case the length is a bit hard for you to grasp, think of it this way—if this airship were stood up on end alongside the Empire State Building, we'd only be forty feet short of matching its height."

Curtis had said it offhandedly, but the impact was no less extraordinary. Brandon tried to imagine himself, almost a mile over San Francisco at the peak of the Christmas season, standing in the midst of an aircraft the size of one of the largest skyscrapers in the world. While he was still struggling with the concept, Curtis and the other air force men abruptly turned to the opposite wall of the elevator. The sound of air pressure opening another door came from behind, and Brandon turned to see a second set of doors standing open at the rear of the elevator. Curtis led him and Haddock out, but the three helicopter crewmen remained behind, presumably heading for another level of the craft.

The elevator opened onto a corridor, roughly four feet wide by seven feet high. Brandon noticed that Colonel Curtis, who'd had to duck through the elevator door, now had only a few inches of headroom in the corridor.

"You can be glad you won't have to travel this route often, Doctor," Curtis said as they walked quickly along the corridor, which stretched away, perfectly straight, for what looked like a good city block. "There was no way to avoid the distance, really, with the forward compartments located so close to the nose of the craft. The one running aft to the turbine service areas is actually longer, but only the technicians have to use it. We thought of installing a moving sidewalk contraption, but the weight factor was prohibitive."

Brandon paused briefly to peer through one of the Plexiglas windows that dotted the corridor's walls, but he could see nothing. A heavy sheet of some type of synthetic material pressed against the other side of the Plexiglas, and beyond that was darkness. The gas cells, he reasoned, had to be on both sides of the corridor, surrounding it like balloons packed around a soda straw.

At the end of the long corridor were double doors that spanned its width. Curtis opened one of them and led the others through another, shorter corridor, with storage bays on each side, then stopped before an elevator opening out from the right wall. Opposite it were spiral stairs.

The control panel inside the car had buttons labeled for Decks A through D, and topped by one labeled *Command Deck*. Curtis pressed the top one. The light for Level C winked off as they started up.

"If you don't mind, Doctor, we'll get you settled in later. Right now it's more important that we get under way."

The trip this time was considerably quicker, and Brandon reasoned that the decks in this part of the ship were more closely stacked than the distant levels near the center. Emerging from the elevator, they started across the command deck. The short corridor crossed a longer lateral one that had several doors opening onto it, then terminated in a double set of doors with automatic closing devices.

Curtis pushed through one of them and held it aside for Haddock and Brandon to enter. Haddock went ahead, but Brandon stopped, awestruck. Stretching out before him, the command deck occupied an area fifty feet across and an almost equal distance from back to front. Arranged on both sides of a center aisle were a variety of electronic consoles, all with active glowing lights and visual displays. In the rear corners, two computer systems filled up a sizable amount of space. All in all, there had to be at least seventeen or eighteen air force personnel on duty in the airship's command center, and there were empty seats behind some consoles for at least a half-dozen more. The place was abuzz with equipment sounds and muted activity that seemed impressively efficient.

But the most remarkable aspect of the entire scene was the great curving window that ran the full width of the command deck, rising from floor to ceiling and sloping forward with the gentle curve of the airship's nose. The huge panels of Plexiglas that formed it were separated by narrow mounting frames, but the expanse was interrupted in only a few places by the longitudinal beams that formed the structure of the airship.

Beyond that great window was the nighttime sky, and below, the countless lights of San Francisco. It was a sight at once unreal and strangely beautiful.

But Brandon's attention was immediately distracted from that distant beauty. One of the airship's officers was approaching them, and Brandon assumed—from the marks of rank on the man's uniform and from Col. Curtis' alert posture—that it must be the commander of this remarkable craft.

Striding toward them with an easy gait, the air force officer appeared to Brandon to be in his early fifties. Roughly his own height, the man was slightly heavy, in an almost cherubic way. Receding gray-white hair formed an M on his high forehead, and a few loose curls hung casually at the point of the M, well above eyes that were childlike and bright. His mouth appeared to be permanently set in a wide, easy smile—a smile that crinkled the skin above his cheeks—but it rigidly held a small meerschaum pipe within its pleasant curve. Add a beard, Brandon found himself thinking, and the man would have made a good Santa. But when he spoke, the voice was mellow and easygoing, and more at home in the hills of Tennessee than the north polar regions.

"These our passengers, John?" he drawled.

Col. John Curtis nodded and introduced Brandon and Haddock. Then, turning more to Brandon, he said, "Doctor, this is the *Grand Eagle*'s commander, Maj. Gen. Bertram Smalley. This airship probably would not exist without General Smalley. It was primarily through his own efforts that the Air Force was persuaded to adopt the program."

Smalley grinned even more noticeably. "John here's going to be my press agent when I retire." Having squelched Curtis' praise, he added, "I can't really take credit for this ship, except for making a good sales pitch at the Pentagon. The real angels are the engineers who made it work. Right, John?"

"Yes, sir," Curtis said resignedly.

S/Sgt. Elizabeth Jordan made her way across the command deck from the communications center with a folded slip of paper in her hand. She remained silent as she reached the group of men, but positioned herself where the general could see her.

Smalley noted the urgent expression on the girl's pretty features. "Yes?"

"There are some further updates from Washington, sir. Captain Wylie is still running some through the scramblers and decoders, but he thought you should see this one." She extended the slip of paper and waited as he read it.

There was a subtle change of expression on Smalley's features as he studied the message. His eyes flicked up to Haddock, and he handed him the slip of paper.

Haddock's reaction was similar. He refolded the note and handed it back. "That's going to make things a bit tougher."

Brandon frowned. "What's wrong?"

Smalley hesitated a moment, then explained, "We've just been advised that the Soviet aircraft carrier *Kiev* has been diverted from its expected course and is heading for Tongareva. Navy plane spotted it. Looks like they've taken an interest in the fate of the crash survivors as well."

"Or at least one." Haddock said dryly.

"You mean Lorenz?" Brandon was skeptical. "But he's not even a Russian. Why would they want him badly enough to send a carrier?"

"You might say he's important to them," Haddock offered, then paused, apparently reluctant to explain further. He looked back to Smalley. "It shouldn't be too bad, should it? I mean, our airspeed should be a good deal faster than their maximum speed."

"Should be," Smalley admitted. "But from their coordinates it seems they already have a good head start on us. And our courses are close enough that we're going to have to pass pretty near them on the way. Could be—interesting."

Haddock considered the information. "I think I'd better send a message to my superiors at State. I may need clarification of something."

Smalley nodded, and Beth Jordan led Haddock off to the communications area. Then Smalley turned to Curtis. "I believe we're ready?"

"Yes, sir."

The colonel headed forward, and as Smalley started to follow, he motioned for Brandon to set his medical kit down and join them. "I think you might be interested in this, Doctor."

Lt. Col. Stewart Gardner was at the helm of the craft, at a low console near the great window. His two junior officers monitored display readouts and indicators on each side of him. Before all three men were television screens which showed views from a variety of positions on the airship's outer surface.

"Reactor readings all normal, sir," one of the men told him.

"Air lanes clear," the radar technician reported.

Gardner glanced up as Smalley and the others took places along the rail that stood close to the window. Looking out at the California coast, he suddenly realized that it would be the first time he had left the States since the accident that had claimed the lives of his wife and son. He pushed the thought away and returned his attention to his instruments. Switching off the automatic controlling systems, he brought the craft's flight functions to full operational status. His right hand went to the turbine control buttons even as his left tapped out the turning sequence on the board before him.

"Leaving stable hold," he said loudly.

In the darkness, the giant aircraft began to rouse from its rest. At the commands relayed back through numerous checking circuits, powerful servos adjusted the position of the massive fins' rudder planes. At the same time, the three big turbines located at the rear of the craft began to increase their power. The counterrotating rotors which had before been turning only slowly to help maintain the position of the craft now began to spin their lengthy blades faster and faster, until they became a blur.

At first ponderously, then with increasing speed and ease, the nuclear airship *Grand Eagle* turned away from the coast of California on its maiden voyage over the dark waters of the vast Pacific. . . .

On Tongareva, little more than an hour later, it was early evening. As always, the fading light brought a striking change to the island, achieving the seemingly impossible effect of making it appear even more alone and isolated within the ocean's expanse. Clouds ablaze with raw color sailed across the endless canopy of a sky grown dim, and those colors were echoed in the sparkling, tumultuous water. Toward the east, the line where sea met sky vanished in a blue-gray haze, making it hard to distinguish one element from the other. The ocean breeze, which had been warm throughout the day, was now cooling, and it stirred the coconut palms and set their fronds rustling softly. There was a sense of timelessness to it all, and of overwhelming power. And yet there was also a feeling of peace—of rest at day's end.

A sound of incredible sadness augmented that feeling. It came drifting across the lagoon from other, nearby islets of the great ringlike island that was Tongareva. A hundred or more voices rang out, many in separate, scattered groups. Singing had always been an important part of life in the isolated islands of Polynesia, even before Christian missionaries brought new songs and a new fervor. Tomorrow would be Sunday, the day of the traditional *uapo*, a hymn fest in which the islanders would engage in hours of singing, both devoutly religious and emotionally exhausting. But the songs tonight had a different tone and purpose. The islanders were singing hymns for the dead— the dead and dying of Trans-Pacific Flight 47. In some places, the Christian hymns mingled with the older *tangi*, the Maori dirge.

And in the stone and timber building that served as headquarters for the island's small medical research outpost, the business of tending to those who still lived continued.

"Is it very deep?" Jill Laudon, the young blonde stewardess who was one of the only two surviving crew members, sat near the end of a long wooden bench in the main room of the sparse facility, where six other survivors sought rest among the laboratory equipment. Her narrow shoulders were bent in exhaustion, for both the physical and the psychological strains of the day had been enormous, but her slender form was momentarily tense. Carla Jennings knelt before her, examining the girl's extended right leg and the long red line that marred its smooth surface.

Carla had cut away the stocking after removing the temporary bandage that had been applied immediately after the crash, and was now checking the extent of the wound. Glancing up, she sensed in the girl's worried gaze a concern that went beyond the immediate.

"It's not bad," Carla reassured her. "Only a nasty scratch, really. I don't think you have to worry about a scar." Carla paused a moment as she dunked a fresh swab into the bottle of antiseptic and gently applied it to the cut. She cringed inwardly as the girl stiffened, reacting to the stinging pain, but made sure the entire area had been treated.

Jill blinked away the moisture that started to form in her eyes. "Will you bandage it again?"

"No. It's stopped bleeding, and I think it will heal quicker if left to the air. Besides," she hesitated, smiling awkwardly, "and I hate to say this, but I'm afraid I'm going to need all the gauze I can spare for some of the others whose injuries are more serious."

Jill nodded, still wincing from the antiseptic sting.

Carla got to her feet and put a comforting hand on the stewardess' shoulder. She had liked Jill from the moment the girl had helped lift the fallen passenger seat within the shattered plane's rear fuselage. That first impression had been reinforced throughout the day, as Jill had uncomplainingly assisted in treating and transporting the injured passengers to the research facility, a tiring procedure which had taken hours. The girl had not once asked for treatment for herself, instead, helping Carla with the others who needed it more urgently. Carla felt an empathy for her as well. The girl might not be thought pretty by many men—her nose was a bit wrong, and her figure too slight—and that made her concern over the prospect of a scarred leg even more touching.

"We're all lucky you were here," Jill said, her voice beginning to show the weariness that had caught up with her. "If there hadn't been a doctor nearby—!"

"Luckier than you realize," Carla replied softly. "The resident doctor here died two months ago. I was already here, on a research grant, and I've been filling in until another doctor can be sent out from Rarotonga—that's the main island of this group, and it's a long ways away. There's a small hospital—really only a clinic—over at the main village of Omoka. I had some of the medical supplies brought here a little over a month ago, so I could handle routine medical problems and still keep up with my work." She sighed, stroking her forehead with the back of her hand. "But I sure never expected anything like this!"

"I should have realized *something* was going to happen."

Carla looked at her oddly. "Why do you say that?"

Jill hesitated. "I don't know if you believe in bad omens or not, but I do. Maggie and I weren't even supposed to be *on* this flight today. We had just come in to Manila on another flight at nine in the morning, and Trans-Pacific's supervisor

51

there had to put us on the next flight out at two in the afternoon. I didn't get even three hours' sleep!"

"He *had* to put you on the next flight out?"

"Yes. Oh, it wasn't his fault, really. Two of the regular girls scheduled for it got sick—food poisoning, I think—and couldn't make it. Someone had to go. We were the only ones available, so we went." She shrugged tiredly. "Is there anything else I can help with?"

Carla considered the offer. She knew Jill was almost dead on her feet, but still, she could use all the help she could get. "I don't know. I haven't had time to think about what needs doing next."

She looked around the now crowded main room of the research facility, glad for a moment's respite from the frantic activity of the morning and afternoon. The most urgent matters had been taken care of earlier. Those passengers most seriously injured were in a separate, larger room, the litters on which they had been carried in resting on crates and whatever else was handy to form crude cots. A few folding cots had already been in the facility, brought from the clinic at Omoka weeks before, but they were hopelessly outnumbered by crash casualties.

Carla had lost count of the number of broken limbs she had set and bound and the gashes and abrasions she had treated throughout the course of the day. Blood transfusions had been given to some, provided by islanders eager to help in whatever way they could. She doubted that she had enough emergency medical supplies and provisions to last more than a few days at most, but that was not her chief worry at the moment. Rescue and medical assistance had been promised, and she assumed it would arrive before the supplies ran out. What worried her was that several of the injured needed medical attention that she had no means of providing. Some would need operations for internal injuries, operations that would have to wait until help reached them—if indeed they could wait.

Here in the main room were those who bore the least injuries from the crash—those who had helped in evacuating the others, and who now were resting as comfortably as they could manage. Seeing them again brought to mind something Carla had overlooked in the pressure of tending to more important procedures.

"There's something I'd better do," she said suddenly, starting across the room toward the window where the other stewardess stood looking out. "You can help, if you want," she told Jill.

Maggie Newcombe, who had been senior stewardess on board Flight 47, gazed out at the stretch of sand where the battered remnants of a jet aircraft rested and at the lagoon beyond that. Her flight uniform was somewhat bedraggled now, but her light brown hair was still fixed in a prim and orderly bun.

At Carla's approach she half turned, still looking out across the gap to the next islet with frowning features. "Why are all the natives staying away?" she asked finally. "They left almost as soon as they got here."

"You can blame me," Carla answered, keeping her voice low. "I had James send them back—told them it was too dangerous to stay here."

"But why? There's no danger the plane will explode now."

"That's not the reason." Carla hesitated. "I wasn't sure whether I should say anything or not—I mean, since there's not much we can do about it—but there was a radio message not long after I reported the crash. I was told that there were containers of atomic materials on the jet. There's a chance the crash could have broken them and contaminated some of the debris."

Maggie Newcombe sucked in her breath. "Blimey! You mean this whole spot could be radioactive?"

"Nobody knows for sure," Carla replied calmly, wanting to avoid alarming anyone, least of all those whose continued help she needed. "But the point is, there was no sense in taking a chance. I didn't want the islanders exposed if it could be avoided."

"Doesn't help *us* much, does it?"

"There are people on the way, with equipment and medical gear to help out. I think we'll be all right." Hoping that the women had been momentarily reassured, she changed the subject. "We have to start a list," she said. "The radio operators who have been relaying messages want to know about the survivors—who made it and who didn't, so relatives can be notified. Do you think we can sort it out?"

Maggie Newcombe searched through the pockets of her uniform and pulled out a folded and crumpled sheet of paper. "I think so. I still have the printout passenger list for the flight. If we can identify all of the survivors, either through questioning them or by checking personal papers, then the rest on the list can be presumed among the dead or missing—" She shook her head suddenly, eyes downcast. "Lord! Listen to me, will you—sounding so bloody official, and here it is people's lives I'm talking about. When . . . when do you want to get started?"

"Right now, if we can," Carla replied. "I made the rounds of the more seriously injured a few minutes ago. I think we can spare a moment for this."

"All right. I know it should be done." Her eyes studied the list briefly. "One thing—we already know for sure about the pilot and copilot."

As they started away from the window, Carla said, "The thing that I still can't understand is how you could have been so far off course."

Jill Laudon shook her head in bewilderment. "It makes no sense. Everything seemed to be going normally."

"It's a complete mystery," Maggie Newcombe agreed. "Of course, in the back where we were, busy with the passengers, there was no way of knowing. One of our girls was up at the front of the passenger section, but she wouldn't have noticed anything either, with the cargo section between us and the cabin. Besides . . . she was killed when the plane broke up."

"It's odd the cabin crew didn't tell you that something was wrong," Carla remarked.

"Yes—odd."

The first of the survivors they approached was the one nearest them—the man in the simple black suit of a minister. He was a puzzle to Carla, not only because of his commanding behavior at the crash site earlier, but also because he did not seem to fit her preconceived notion of how a minister should look. He had the build of an athlete, even if a retired one.

At the moment, the man was sitting near the wall in one of a half-dozen chairs brought into the main room from scattered locations throughout the research facility. He seemed to be meditating, or in prayer, and he did not notice their presence at first.

"Sir—" Carla said finally, touching his shoulder. As he looked up, she continued, "I hate to disturb you, but we're checking everyone against the passenger list, so we can notify the international agencies—there must be a lot of anxious relatives waiting for some word of who's all right."

He smiled faintly, then flinched slightly as the

movement of his features put pressure on the bandage that Carla had applied to his forehead. "I'm afraid I have no relatives for you to contact—there's no family left that I know of. But you might contact my church group in San Francisco. They were expecting me there for reassignment in a few days, and they may be worried."

Carla copied down the name and address of the group, then asked his own name.

"Father Brian Daniels. I've spent the last few years in Southeast Asia, with several missionary posts there."

Out of her own curiosity, Carla probed more than she had to. "And you say you were returning for reassignment?"

"Yes," he said, sighing. "That's the kind way of putting it, really. I was ejected, along with several others. You probably know what's been happening in that region, and it seems some of the new governments there have got it into their heads that American missionaries are all CIA men. Which is nonsense, of course, but then those governments are not exactly known for promoting freedom of religion even under the best of circumstances. I suppose it was a convenient excuse for them."

As Maggie Newcombe made a notation on the passenger list, Carla asked on impulse, "You've been around aircraft before, haven't you?"

"Yes . . . a very long time ago."

"*Make way—*" The voice came from behind Carla and the two stewardesses, and as she turned she saw that Mary Akaru had finished heating up the soup she had been working on over the small hot plate, which was hardly adequate for cooking for a group of this size. The Polynesian woman had portioned out the hot soup into every vessel handy—bowls, cups, and even a few drinking glasses wrapped with napkins.

Mary Akaru brought the tray of assorted cups and bowls first to Father Daniels, displaying a special respect for the man of God. Even as Daniels was accepting his, the young man next to him was already reaching out to help himself to the largest bowl. It was the first sign of life he had shown in hours. He had spent most of the afternoon sprawled in a chair while others did what they could to help. He had shed the jacket of his denim leisure suit during the heat of the day, folding it behind his head like a pillow against the wall.

Carla Jennings was not surprised by his actions—not any longer. She had still not gotten over the way he had shoved her aside in his frantic efforts to get out of the plane, and his total lack of interest in helping anyone but himself had not changed in the hours since the crash. There were any number of words that Carla thought would describe him perfectly, none of them kind.

"What about you?" she asked him, trying to curb the bitterness she still felt. "Your name is—?"

The young man took a careful, inquiring sip from his bowl, then a longer draft of it. Looking up at Carla with a sullen expression, he said, "Copley—Alex Copley. But my super-straight parents made the reservation, so you'll probably find it under *Alexander.*"

Maggie Newcombe glanced down at her list and said, "Check. I'll put him among the living." There was a grudging tone to her last remark that did not go unnoticed.

Yet Father Daniels amended the thought without rancor. "We are *all* lucky to be counted among the living."

There was a cold sneer on young Alexander Copley's lips. "Yeah, only half of the passengers weren't so lucky."

"All the more reason to be thankful," Daniels said calmly, "for those spared by God's mercy."

"Mercy!" Copley slid erect in his seat and leaned forward, staring into his bowl. "If there were any mercy in this world, Father, then we wouldn't have crashed in the first place, and we wouldn't be stuck on this rock in the middle of nowhere."

Daniels said nothing more, but he looked in Copley's direction with a saddened, knowing expression.

Jill and Maggie received their own cups of soup next, and as Mary Akaru continued to pass out the others, Carla moved on around the corner of the room where a third man sat—the middle-aged businessman who had helped Carla and Father Daniels bring out the wood and canvas pressed into service to transport the injured survivors. Carla would have thought that after the day's events, business would be the last thing on his mind. But surprisingly, the man had his attaché case propped open on his lap, studying papers.

"Sir," she said as she approached, "we have to have your name, to check you off the passenger list."

Looking up from his notes, he said, "Peter Benson—Far East Import/Export." He paused while Maggie Newcombe methodically checked her list, looking at her impatiently as he ran a hand through his dark, well-groomed hair. "How long before we're rescued?" he demanded to know. "I've got several business deals that will fold if I don't reach Honolulu by Monday. There's at least a hundred thousand at stake—"

"I don't know when," Carla interrupted sharply. "But I'm sure it will be soon. Many people here need help desperately." She suppressed her annoyance. It was going to be hard enough managing in the hours ahead without adding to anyone's irritability. "I'm sure your corporation will be glad to know you're safe," she added. "Perhaps they can take care of any problems caused by the delay."

"If you knew my partner, you wouldn't be so optimistic!"

Maggie checked Benson's name off her list, and they moved on to the next survivor, a slightly built man whose slim form seemed hardly substantial enough to support the loose-fitting gray suit he wore. His receding hair, fine and jet-black, left a sizable bald area at the top of his head, and his tortoise-shell glasses bore lenses thick and distorted enough to suggest that the man had either had cataracts or some other severe vision disorder.

Carla learned from him three things of interest—the first, that he was Professor Arturo Maca, a biologist from the Philippines who worked in the field of genetics and cellular research. The second item was that he was bound for a science conference in Hawaii, where he was to deliver a major report on his findings. The third was of immediate, practical use, for he knew the identity of the bearded man who had suffered a heart attack earlier—Stefan Lorenz, a Czechoslovakian scientist known to many in the scientific community, whom Professor Maca had sat next to during the ill-fated flight from Manila. Lorenz' destination was also the World Science Conference, and the delay of both men would markedly affect the proceedings. Professor Maca had sustained only minor abrasions during the crash, but his strength seemed almost totally drained by the experience.

The remaining survivor in the room was a cause for more concern, even if not of an immediate nature. He had seemed dazed earlier, after the crash, and Carla had noticed no significant improvement in the hours since. He had no observable injuries, yet he remained remote, staying apart from the others. He could not, or perhaps would not, speak, and Carla was certain the man was suffering from some form of psychological trauma as a result of the crash.

"Does he have identification?" Maggie Newcombe asked.

Carla searched through the man's personal papers and found several credit cards bearing the same name. "Martin Sandersen, if these are his. There's no driver's license, though. Was he traveling with anyone?

Maggie checked the line beneath Sandersen's listing. "Yes, with his wife." She looked up suddenly, gravely, at Carla. "I wonder—was she one of the ones that didn't make it?"

"There's no way of knowing, not until we check all the IDs."

"If she was, it could explain the . . . way he is."

"Yes, I know," Carla said. "Do you remember what she looked like?"

The stewardess frowned in thought, then finally shrugged. "I see a lot of faces in my job, and not for very long either. Some I remember . . . some I don't. Maybe if I see her again, something will click, but . . ." She trailed off with an apologetic look.

"Don't worry about it. We'll do the best we can." She hesitated for a moment, checking her watch. "I think we'd better look in on our friend from Czechoslovakia. Especially now that we know who he is."

Maggie Newcombe followed Carla out of the main room and into the larger room behind it. Before the crash, the room had been used as a temporary clinic, until routine medical responsibilities could be returned to the small hospital at Omoka village on the other side of the lagoon. Before that, it had been empty, an unused remnant of the building's earlier days as the office and storerooms of a profitable trading business. Once, thousands of high-quality natural pearls had exchanged hands in this building—pearls gleaned from the bottom of the sparkling lagoon by divers brave enough to risk the constant danger of sharks. But that was in the past, before the natural pearl market had lost out to the cultured pearls of Asia. The island's only exports now were copra, dried from the broken kernels of coconuts, and mother-of-pearl shell. Even at that, it was a meager existence for the island's diminishing population, which now numbered slightly less than seven hundred.

Now there were twenty-three seriously injured people in this room, some fighting for their lives. One of those was Stefan Lorenz.

Carla bent over his improvised cot, holding her stethoscope to the bearded scientist's chest. She listened for a long while, hearing only too well the irregular sound of the struggling heart. As she listened, she checked the small plastic oxygen fitting which ran from Lorenz' nostrils to the tank beside his cot.

Next to her, Maggie Newcombe stood, her facial muscles taut beneath the surface of her skin. She looked down at the semiconscious man, occasionally shifting her gaze to Carla. Finally she asked, in a low voice, "How's he doing?"

Carla removed the stethoscope and stood erect. Keeping her own voice low, she said, "Not good. There's not much I can do for him. The way he is now, I'd be surprised if he lasted more than a few days ... maybe not that long." There was concern in her voice and on her features. That, and a trace of guilt as well, for Carla partially blamed herself for hastening the attack by allowing Lorenz to help carry some of the injured.

Lorenz stirred suddenly, rousing from the semiconscious state in which his condition and the medication kept him. Carla noticed, and bent close to him.

"It's all right, Mr. Lorenz," she said soothingly. "Help is on the way. We know who you are now, and we can notify your country's government." Carla watched as Lorenz frowned and feebly shook his head from side to side. She wondered if he had understood. "Do you have any relatives we should notify?"

Lorenz moved his lips, silently at first, then again, struggling to form the words in English. "No one ... no one."

Carla placed a comforting hand on his arm, then after a moment rose and motioned to Maggie Newcombe. "Let's start with the others. I want to establish the identity of all the survivors as soon as possible."

The senior stewardess nodded and followed her off. Looking back briefly as she walked, she noticed that Lorenz' hand reached down and probed the space beneath his cot, then stopped as his fingers closed around the grip of his attaché case. Then Maggie had to return her attention to the passenger list as Carla continued to check it against the survivors.

Lying still now, Stefan Lorenz felt somewhat reassured. He had gone to the trouble of getting the case from his seat the last time they had gone back for the injured, just prior to his attack. Its presence under the cot eased his mind, even though something he had told Carla Jennings troubled him.

He had said that he had no relatives—no one close to him to be contacted. It was a lie, of course, and it bothered him that he had to tell it. Lorenz' nineteen-year-old daughter, Katya, was very much alive. She was the only one close to him—dear to him—since his wife's death four years ago. At least, she had been. He still chided himself for his failures—*if only* he had spent less of his time at his work and more of it in countering the effects of procommunist propaganda in the government school system. In the years since his wife's death he had seen, and more clearly now in hindsight, the steady conversion of his daughter. He remembered all too clearly the first, almost innocent disagreements—disagreements that later led to pronounced arguments. And finally, worst of all, the pained and chilling silences. She had gradually become a perfect Marxist supporter of the state. Lorenz could not even trust his own daughter—a daughter who condemned his views on freedom and his belief that scientific research must be unrestrained by the militaristic goals of governments. She was no longer his, really— there was simply nothing left of the child he had loved. There was a shell that vaguely resembled the girl he thought he had known, but inside, there was no heart or soul. It was like the old folk tales of changelings, he thought, brought to ugly reality.

No, he had not told the doctor such a great lie after all, he decided. There *was* no one left to care. As far as he was concerned, Katya was already dead.

Lorenz stirred slightly again, seeking comfort and not finding it. His thoughts drifted back—back to the months that preceded his planned defection. He had known for nearly half a year that the Russians planned to "recruit" him for work within their own national boundaries. As bad as the intellectual repression was in Czechoslovakia, he knew it would be far worse within the Soviet Union. True, he would be granted certain privileges and luxuries not given to others, but even that would last only so long as he continued his work on the project and did not voice his "imperialist" views too often or too noticeably.

The project! He wished he had never begun it. It was a splendid breakthrough, to be sure, and one with immediate value to the space program of any nation. That is what it could have been—*should* have been. But the Soviets' plans for his system were less humanitarian. He knew only too well what use they would make of it, and once all the information was turned over to them, he would be powerless to prevent it. He could not be sure of the Americans' motives, either, but even with his doubts it would be worth the risk.

The last months had been hard. Lorenz cringed, even now, as he recalled the desperation with which he had worked. He had to conclude his efforts before the Soviets expected—had to finish everything before the World Science Conference. The Czech authorities had almost not let him attend the conference. His outspoken views branded him as a threat to the established order, and a high risk if allowed out of the country. But national pride had demanded that the man who held the respect of scientists throughout the world be allowed to attend. The authorities had assumed that with Katya staying behind in Czechoslovakia, he would be disinclined to defect, or to do anything else that would reflect unfavorably on the government of the communist bloc nation. They had been wrong, of course, and Lorenz felt it was ironic that the nature of the regime itself had been responsible for severing the last bond that would have ensured his loyalty.

Lorenz wondered if his colleagues in Prague had yet discovered what he had left behind in the storage closet at the research facility where he worked. It had been such a direct and daring way to smuggle his project and related equipment out of the country. He remembered going back to the facility late at night, on the pretense of doing some last-minute work on his report for the conference. What he had done instead was to carefully remove the side panel of the crate that held the equipment and display materials he was taking to Hawaii the next day. Those materials had already been inspected and approved by the government representatives and the crate sealed and tagged, but the agents had not known that Lorenz had prepared the crate in such a way that one panel could be removed without disturbing any of the official inspection tags or seals. What he was supposed to take along on the trip went into storage, well hidden. Everything connected with his project took its place within the large crate, which was resealed and readied for transportation to the airport.

It had taken almost the entire night, and the physical

effort of it had exhausted him. Lorenz felt a sudden twinge of pain in his chest, a fleeting thing but a fearful reminder. And it served also to renew his regret over the fact that he had been forced to take stimulants during the past month, in order to extend his working hours. He was paying the price now, he knew, and he could only hope the Americans could arrive soon enough to make good their promise.

Something else still nagged at Lorenz' mind—something he knew he should have told someone. Even now his thoughts were confused and murky. He had only a little trouble losing his "traveling companion" at the airport. The government agent had been locked in the men's room long enough to miss the flight from Manila. But there was something else. He seemed to recall that there had been trouble of another kind at the airport—men whom he had been barely able to elude. He half-suspected they were KGB agents sent to detain him, which would mean that the truth had been discovered. But he had not been sure of his suspicions. Even now he was not certain if the whole thing had been real or only some paranoid dream, stirred to life by the aftermath of the crash and the medication that flowed through his veins.

He tried to concentrate on the incident, but for the moment it was a losing battle. Gradually, inexorably, Lorenz slipped back into the sleep that he both desired and feared—a sleep that lapped over him now like the warm waves of the ocean beyond.

When Carla Jennings had finished checking the injured survivors against the passenger list and had transmitted the information for relay to the International Red Cross, she returned to the main room. Alone now, she stood by the open door, looking out into the darkness that had finally enveloped Tongareva.

She felt tired, and the muscles of her back and neck ached. It seemed to her that almost a week's time had been compressed into just a few, nerve-wracking hours. The plane tragedy was a nightmare, a living nightmare, and yet for all its bizarre complications it seemed more real now than the quiet and serene weeks and months that had preceded it.

Carla felt an involuntary sigh escape her lips as she leaned against the doorframe with its peeling paint. The ocean breeze swept past her, stirring the auburn hair that hung about

her face and slender neck. Many times during the past year she had felt that sense of unreality creeping into her thoughts. And more than once she had wondered if her decision to accept the research position here had been too quick ... too easy. The work was important, that much could not be denied. But there had been other grants available, even some in California, and all closer to home than this remote spot.

Perhaps, Carla thought, the choice had been simplified by Tongareva's very isolation. It had offered a kind of self-exile—a safe haven from the storms of feeling that had brought so much pain. When she accepted the job, she had told herself that it represented the kind of beneficial work that mattered most to her. Now, she wondered, perhaps it only represented escape.

A movement caught her eye, and Carla noticed James Akaru walking slowly back across the beach, heading toward the crash site, his improvised drag-litter trailing behind him. Carla was glad that Mary's husband had assumed the responsibility for what had to be the worst task of the day. James Akaru had been working throughout the afternoon, transporting the bodies of the dead, one by one, to the elevated building nearby, a former warehouse. The building was a *pataka,* in the Maori language—a safe storehouse above ground level—and it was important that all the dead be taken there before many hours of darkness had passed—before the rats and coconut crabs began their nocturnal foraging.

Almost all the bodies had been moved into the storehouse, covered by heavy tarpaulins, there to stay until the rescue force could claim them. The thought sent a chill along Carla's spine, and she finally turned away from the open doorway, glad to resume her efforts for those that were still *alive.*

Outside, in the darkness, James Akaru was also glad that his macabre work was nearly done. Although the hard life on Tongareva had made him extraordinarily tough and conditioned, he found that he was bone-tired, and the trips back and forth were becoming more and more of an effort. He could not remember having felt such fatigue. It reached through to the pit of his stomach and radiated out to his limbs, where the skin tingled and occasionally crawled.

He paused on his way to the shattered cockpit section, where the last two bodies waited, and rubbed his arms in the places where the circulation seemed to have slowed. As he stood there, gazing out across the lagoon, he saw something that seemed out of place and disturbing. Reflected moonlight shimmered on the water's surface, shifting with the breeze-stirred ripples. The view was one of great beauty ordinarily, but something marred that image.

Dark forms floated upon the surface of the lagoon, near the spot where the cargo section of the fragmented airliner had settled to the bottom. Some of the silhouetted forms were quite small—hardly noticeable except to the keen eyes of an islander. Others were large, perhaps as much as ten feet or more in length.

James Akaru felt the muscles of his stomach tighten as he recalled the warning about the jet's strange cargo. His face, set in a grim mask all afternoon, now hardened still more as he realized what the floating objects were . . . *the bodies of dead fish and sharks.* . . .

"There is precious little glory to this job, Herb. I've found that out the hard way. And I'm beginning to wonder about the prestige . . ."

William Evans, President of the United States, sat in the Oval Office of the White House, not really looking at the man who sat on the other side of his desk. The room's curtains were drawn against the night and the electric lighting in the high-ceiling office made Evans look older than his years. It was almost midnight in Washington, minutes away from the first hours of Sunday. Only a handful of offices in the Executive Wing of the White House were occupied.

Evans directed his eyes to Herb Ettleman, White House press secretary and a close working associate for seven years. Almost in an instant, his mood seemed to change from sober reflection to mild amusement. "You know, before the election quite a number of my critics were so unkind as to suggest I wasn't qualified for this job." He smiled wanly. "If they only knew how often I've thought they were right."

Herb Ettleman sensed behind the wry humor a note of sincerity. "I hope the tone of your address in Spokane next week will be a bit more upbeat," he said.

"It will be." Evans leaned forward in his chair and closed a folder of memos and notes which had lain open on his desk during the last hour's discussion with Ettleman. Most of the things they had gone over were routine matters. One was not.

"You're going to be getting some pressure from the media," Evans said. "Sooner or later. We have to expect it, and the way it's handled will be of great importance."

"Yes, I know. It's unfortunate, though, that we had to use that cover story about the atomic materials. Air transportation of such materials is a hot issue—with the crash, the press is going to leap at the chance to exploit it."

"It couldn't be helped. We had less than half an hour after the mayday call was relayed to us, and State had to quarantine the area before a lot of unsupervised rescue parties got under way. If the wrong people got on the island first, we'd be out of luck. Besides, considering the cargo on that plane, the danger is nearly as great as if there *were* radioactive materials."

Ettleman nodded in agreement, but clearly he was dreading the inevitable questions. As he started to rise, ready to leave, a knock came at the door. The President's personal secretary had long since departed, and Ettleman knew it must be one of the presidential aides.

Evans was on his feet as Ettleman opened the door. The aide took a step inside, looking past the press secretary to the President.

"Everyone's here now, sir."

"Thank you, Phil—I'll be there in a moment."

"Good night, sir."

Ettleman hesitated by the door until Evans reached it. "I'd best be saying good night as well."

"All right, Herb. I'll keep you advised."

They left the Oval Office and went their separate ways—Ettleman to the corridor leading out of the Executive Wing, Evans to the Cabinet Room a short distance away.

It had always been like this, Evans thought—not the clear-cut polished drama to be found in history books, with wise and noble leaders acting out their roles like the characters in a period play, but rather the uncertain reality of essentially ordinary human beings, caught in situations in which there were no clear-cut answers . . . no rule books to follow.

The costumes had changed over the years, the technical systems and other superficialities. Even the White House itself. The entire Executive Wing in which Evans now walked had not existed until 1902, when Theodore Roosevelt had the structure built in what had been a glassy clutter of greenhouses on the south lawn. It had been rebuilt twice, first in 1910 and then again in 1934. Its offices had served Presidents in two world wars, several "conflicts," and uncounted crises.

The details had changed along the way, as had the scope of the problems to be solved. But not the basic conflicts of the human mind, or the decisions to be reached by men like William Evans. Decisions that no one should have to make, especially in an age when the wrong move could result in worldwide destruction.

Evans felt the full weight of that reality. More so today than usual.

He opened the door to the Cabinet Room and entered, his eyes taking in the collection of faces that turned his way. The expressions on many of those faces were tentative ... questioning.

There was the usual brief exchange of greetings, then Evans said, "I'm sorry to have to call you together at this late hour, but I don't think we can afford to wait until morning. I think most of you already know what's happening ... the danger that we're heading toward a confrontation with the Soviet Union."

Evans paused, studying their faces. None of the other men spoke, each waiting for Evans to continue.

Evans said only, "Please—sit down." He motioned to the long table in the center of the Cabinet Room.

It was not the entire membership of the National Security Council—Vice-President Drew Russell was out of Washington, attempting to aid the campaigns of several of the party's senatorial candidates as well as attending a number of planned official functions, and the Secretary of State was out of the country.

But Under Secretary of State Martin Pretori was present to represent his department, as were the remaining regular members and advisers—Lewis Scoville, Secretary of Defense; Mitchell Hoyt, director of the Central Intelligence Agency; Gen. Eldridge Adamson, a top air force officer and chairman of the Joint Chiefs of Staff. Edgar Matheson, the President's adviser on Russian affairs, was also present, as was Adm. Jonathan Hadley, chief of Naval Operations. A number of departmental assistants and aides stood ready with their note pads and briefing folders.

Evans took his seat at the center of the long table, the

Great Seal and the national and presidential flags behind him along the east wall. The great oval table of leather-topped brown mahogany was still fairly new—a change during a recent administration from the older elongated octagon which had uncannily resembled the top of a giant's coffin. The lighting overhead matched the shape of the new table, warmly illuminating the ivory-beige walls and drapes of green satin.

"Admiral," Evans began as the last of the men was seated, "have you any new information on the *Kiev*?"

"Only a little." Adm. Jonathan Hadley handed out copies of his current report and turned briefly to see that his aide was setting up the proper map on an easel. "The *Kiev* is presently at a position seven hundred and fifty miles east-southeast of Hawaii, continuing at slightly better than thirty-five knots." His aide indicated the position on the map for the others to see. "We presently have four United States naval vessels shadowing the *Kiev*, at a respectable distance. The course it is taking leaves little room for doubt that the destination is Tongareva. Also—" Hadley paused. "Naval Intelligence now has fairly solid evidence that two Soviet submarines originally with the squadron are traveling with the *Kiev*."

"Which may or may not be necessary," Secretary of Defense Lewis Scoville commented. "Admiral, for the benefit of the others, would you describe the *Kiev*'s systems?"

Hadley looked through his notes in the briefing folder and found the appropriate sheet. He glanced at it once, then did not refer to it again. "To our best estimates, the *Kiev* has two twin launchers of the SA-N-3 type for Goblet missiles, and another twin launcher we haven't been able to identify yet. Besides those, the ship has a considerable amount of heavy armament—fourteen guns ranging up to fifty-seven millimeters. There are antisubmarine weapons and advanced electronics systems. And of course the aircraft. Twenty-five fixed wing jets with vertical takeoff and landing capability, and twenty-five Hormone A helicopters. In short, the *Kiev* is smaller than our largest carriers, but it's not to be taken lightly."

Evans said casually, "Isn't all that heavy armament a bit unorthodox for a carrier?"

Hadley shook his head. "It's becoming typical of the Soviet Navy, Mr. President. Besides, technically, the Russians don't classify the *Kiev* as a carrier."

"Even with the aircraft it has?"

Hadley shrugged. "They insist on calling it an antisubmarine cruiser, which is plain old diplomatic hornswoggle. It *is* a carrier and the Russians know it, but the problem is that the *Kiev* was built at the Nikolayev Nosenko shipyard on the northern coast of the Black Sea. Before it could be deployed, it had to pass through the straits of Marmara on its way to the Mediterranean and the oceans beyond. The Montreux Convention banned aircraft carriers in that area. So the Russians pretend it's not a carrier, and everything seems legal!"

There was a look of wry disgust on Hadley's features. A look that Evans ignored.

"The four ships you have following the *Kiev*," he inquired. "Is it possible they can reach the island before it?"

Hadley, resplendent in his dress white uniform, hesitated. "That depends, sir. They did start somewhat behind the *Kiev*, which is cruising at top speed. It *may* be possible to catch up, perhaps even to get there with a slight lead. But if we have to swing wide to avoid those submarines flanking the *Kiev* . . ."

Secretary of Defense Lewis Scoville, a balding, bearish man, leaned forward. His expression was deliberate and firm. "I think we should try it. Even if we can only gain a few miles advantage, it might allow us the chance to set up a blockade—to really seal off the island. Four ships against the *Kiev*—"

"The *Kiev* and two submarines," Hadley reminded. "Still, I would have to agree. Our naval force should be used. I don't think we can afford to be intimidated by the Soviet Navy."

"Whether we can or not is academic," Evans said flatly. "I could not approve of a blockade, under the circumstances."

Scoville controlled his displeasure. "It worked during the Cuban situation."

"And we had a *legal* basis for the action taken during the Cuban missile crisis. The presence of Soviet missiles in Cuba constituted a clear threat to the Western Hemisphere. We had the *unanimous* support of the OAS on the blockade, and the *added* support of most of our European allies. Even the approval of a few nations not normally friendly to the United States." Evans shook his head, then thrust a finger at the map with its markings. "What do we have here? What kind of justifiable threat that we can hold up to the peoples of the world? The man who is the cause of all this intense interest is not even an American national. Morally, the Soviets have just as much right in trying to reach him as we do."

Martin Pretori, Under Secretary of State, seemed somewhat awed by the situation. Harvard-educated, he was younger than the others seated at the long oval table. "However," he reminded them cautiously, "Lorenz freely chose to defect. If the Russians recover him, whether for transport back to Czechoslovakia or, more likely, to the Soviet Union, it will be against his will."

Evans was firm. "That still does not give us complete license to act. Whatever we do will have to be limited . . . careful . . . discreet."

"It will also have to be successful," Admiral Hadley pointed out. "Unless we're willing to sacrifice Lorenz' development to the Russians."

Evans digested the opinions and comments for a moment, then asked, "Just how certain can we be of Lorenz' development? How do we know it's worth the risk?"

The others in the Cabinet Room were silent at first, until Scoville took it upon himself to answer. "Without the engine prototype it's hard to be *absolutely* certain, of course. But from the limited test data already passed along by Lorenz, and from a small sample of the rocket fuel, the implications are enormous. A spacecraft or ballistic missile of ordinary size and fuel volume could double its range. Or missiles of equal destructive power could be reduced to nearly half their present size, with no loss of range. Such an advance could double the firepower of their missile-carrying submarines. Theirs, *or* ours."

"Yes," Evans said. "*If* what he says is true."

Martin Pretori spoke up. "Sir, I've handled most of the details of Lorenz' defection. We've had him thoroughly checked out, both through our own intelligence section and"—he nodded toward Mitchell Hoyt—"the CIA as well. That included psychological profiles of the man and a complete history." Pretori held up both hands in a gesture of mild exasperation. "Everything checks out. Lorenz is a scientist, first and foremost, and there is nothing to indicate that he would lie about his breakthrough."

"Not even to obtain our aid in his defection?"

"No, sir. At least, not in my opinion."

Evans winced inwardly. Opinions were not always to be trusted in making difficult decisions. He wished there were more hard facts. "And there are no other American naval vessels closer to the island?"

Admiral Hadley's look was pained, almost embarrassed. "No, sir. Unfortunately not. The closest ships of the Seventh Fleet are presently near the Solomon Islands—too far to have any chance of reaching Tongareva soon enough. And the only ships of the First Fleet in a position to act are those based at Honolulu, four of which are now following the *Kiev*. If the crash had happened at any other time, there might have been a dozen or more vessels in a better position to act, but as it happens, the timing is against us. But I still believe that our primary effort should be to neutralize the *Kiev*'s effectiveness through the use of *naval* power. As you know, the problems of landing conventional aircraft there are almost insurmountable, and"—he glanced quickly at the chairman of the Joint Chiefs of Staff, Gen. Eldridge Adamson—"I don't think we should pin our hopes on an oversized blimp."

Adamson sat up straight. "The *Grand Eagle* is an airship, not a blimp," he said curtly. "And if necessary, it can take care of itself quite well. It has an excellent chance of reaching the island long before the *Kiev* gets there."

"I agree." Martin Pretori removed his glasses and massaged the bridge of his nose. "When General Adamson came to the State Department early this afternoon and explained the value of the *Grand Eagle* in this type of situation, I immediately agreed that it should be placed on alert and sent on the recovery mission."

Scoville said acidly, "And I still think that should have been discussed first, before the complete council."

"There wasn't time for that," Pretori replied. "Besides, you approved the order as well as the President."

"Yes, of course. I realized there wasn't time to debate the issue then, and I didn't want to rule out any options open to us. But I intended it to be only an alternative answer. The nuclear airship is still somewhat experimental. It doesn't have any track record, to speak of, and we don't know how its systems are going to work in the event of a conflict."

"A conflict," Evans interrupted suddenly, "is exactly what I want to avoid."

There was silence in the room for a long moment, then Martin Pretori raised another point. "Something we must consider also is Lorenz' condition. If we don't reach him soon, it may well be too late. There is a doctor on the *Grand Eagle*, well briefed on Lorenz' medical history. We had already made the arrangements with him before all this happened. I think he may well be Lorenz' only hope."

Pretori received support from an unexpected source—Mitchell Hoyt, the reticent director of Central Intelligence. "He's right," Hoyt said abruptly. "And for another reason he hasn't mentioned. If we want to recover the prototype, which I think is as essential as the plans and research data, then the airship is still our best bet. From the initial report, the jet's cargo section is in the lagoon, roughly eight fathoms down. There are sharks in the area. If we have to go after the prototype under-water—whether by unloading or by cutting through the side to get at the crate—it's going to be time-consuming and hazardous. With the airship, divers will only have to be in the water long enough to attach cables. The entire cargo section of the aircraft can be lifted and taken back within the airship's hold."

"And that's not all that's in the lagoon, is it?" Evans asked.

"You mean the fuel canisters? Yes, of course those are with the prototype," Hoyt said dispassionately. "I suppose that we might eventually succeed in duplicating the formula by break-ing down the small amount of the sample we have left, but still—"

"I was thinking more in terms of the safety of the people on that island," Evans said with an edge of impatience. "The reports state that besides being an extraordinarily power-ful rocket fuel, the substance is also incredibly toxic—almost as lethal as nerve gas—I believe that's the way one of the proc-essing technicians described it."

"Yes, Mr. President . . . so it seems."

"Well? What effect is that likely to have on the people there?"

"It depends," Hoyt replied. "If the canisters leaked any of their contents during the crash, then some of the land area is contaminated. If they have begun to leak the chemical after impact in the lagoon, then the waters of the lagoon itself could be poisoned—although that could take some time. The sub-stance is a solid fuel, in minute granules, and it shouldn't spread quickly in the lagoon. But once suspended in water, the sub-stance could endanger anyone who got close enough to absorb even a small amount through the skin."

"Including our divers?"

Hoyt nodded grudgingly. "Yes. But I think that only reinforces the need to reduce the time those men have to stay in the water. Regardless of any other factors, the canisters are there, now, and they'll have to be removed if the safety of the islanders is to be maintained. The only question left is whether they will be removed by us, or the Russians."

Evans clearly was not happy with the choice. "I know we are committed to some form of action, that much is certain. But we must be careful to weigh the consequences of any steps we take."

"We also can't afford to waver," Scoville said firmly. "If we appear reluctant to act in this situation, the Soviets will interpret it as an indication of weakness. If they can act with impunity anywhere in the world, we may as well throw in the towel. A wrong move that way now will cost us dearly."

"And a wrong move in the other direction may exact a *higher* price. Consider that," Evans said.

General Adamson had a suggestion of his own. "We *could* use conventional aircraft—propeller-driven transports could reach the island before the *Kiev* and drop paratroops equipped to handle the situation. With a force of men already there, it might well discourage the Russians."

"And it might only provoke a conflict." Evans shook his head. "No—I can't permit that. We would have little—if *any*—moral or legal justification for landing a military force on that island. It is a trust territory of New Zealand, and there is *no* clear threat to our national security."

Admiral Hadley shifted uncomfortably in his chair. "Then your decision regarding our naval effort. . . ?"

Evans' eyes focused on the map and the tiny dot that was the island of Tongareva. "I think it would be better if you had your ships pull back. I don't want your captains trying to intercept the *Kiev,* and I don't want them putting undue pressure on the Russians. Direct naval contact might well put both sides in a position neither of us could get out of easily." The President looked back to the others who made up the National Security Council, studying their faces. "For the time being, gentlemen, we are going to follow the plan suggested by the State Department. For now, we are going to have to put our faith in the success of the *Grand Eagle*. . . ."

Minutes later on Tongareva, as the evening darkness deepened, Carla Jennings was interrupted in her tending of the injured as

James Akaru appeared in the doorway, motioning for Carla to join him outside.

"What is it, James?" Carla asked as she descended the stone steps to the ground. "Have you finished moving all of the dead?"

"Yes, ma'am." James Akaru kept his voice low. "There's something you should see."

Carla was puzzled by his manner, but said nothing more as he led her to the raised storehouse temporarily pressed into service as a morgue. Knowledge of its contents gave the familiar building a forbidding aspect as it stood there in semidarkness, partially illuminated by moonlight filtering through the palm trees' fringed foliage. The palm fronds rustled more insistently now, the sea breeze that moved them stronger than it had been a few hours earlier.

"Feels like a storm's coming up," Carla said.

James Akaru seemed not to notice the change of weather. "Yes, ma'am, I suppose."

As he worked the latch that secured the door to the building, Carla thought she noticed a faint tremor in his arms. That, and something odd in his posture. "James . . . are you feeling all right?"

"Fine, ma'am—just tired," he lied. The feeling of fatigue and strangeness that he had felt before was worse, not better. It crept across his skin and danced along his spine in searing twinges of pain, and he was barely able to control his facial muscles. But for all the discomfort and all his fear of what he had seen floating upon the surface of the lagoon, James Akaru was also afraid to voice those fears . . . to have confirmed what he felt he already knew. He would sleep outside tonight, apart from the others, lest there somehow be any danger to them. He regretted bringing Carla out here now, though she would be near him only minutes. He regretted it, but could not avoid it. She had to see—had to know what he had discovered, just minutes ago.

James ushered her into the building, not looking directly at the neat rows of tarpaulin-covered bodies revealed in the peripheral glow of his flashlight. He headed toward the far end of the building, where the last of the bodies to be removed from the wreckage had been placed.

Carla shuddered involuntarily in the presence of the dead. Earlier in the day, when confronted with the visible horror of the carnage, there had been a feeling of revulsion, and then a merciful numbness settled in, allowing her to do her job. Now, there was a different feeling. The visible horror was not present, to be sure, but somehow the still, covered forms were more dreadful in their orderly rows than the chaotic aftermath of the crash.

James Akaru reached the end of the building and stooped beside two forms beneath one tarpaulin. Carefully, as if the movement might disturb the sleep of the dead, he raised the heavy canvas covering and revealed the men beneath.

"The pilot and copilot?" Carla looked down at the bodies, remembering the way she had found them in the fragmented cockpit of the jet airliner.

"Here—closer," James Akaru told her, directing his light full on the features of the two men whose heads were turned to one side. "From this side you see better."

Carla moved to the vantage point James indicated, her eyes striving to make out what had disturbed the islander. Outwardly, at least, the pilot and copilot had been injured only slightly. But of course, the crash impact would have caused any number of internal injuries.

"I don't understand, James—what is it that . . ." Carla's voice trailed off as her eyes focused on something she had not noticed before. At the base of the pilot's skull, just above the back of the neck, there was a small wound, round and almost pencil-sized. The blood had clotted around the opening, partially obscuring it. And barely visible on the copilot's left side, a small blackened hole marred his uniform jacket.

At first, her interest in the wounds was medical, almost academic. Then gradually the full impact of what she saw struck Carla with chilling force.

The crash had not killed them. She knew that now, just as certainly as she knew that the men had not been alive at the moment of impact. And she knew with awful clarity just how they had died. . . .

CHAPTER THREE

"I'm impressed. I really am, so please don't misunderstand. . . ." Paul Brandon stood on the command deck of the

Grand Eagle, surrounded by the tangible wonders of modern technology, yet his expression was one of doubt. His features were colored from below with the glow of instrument lights, and beyond the command deck's reduced lighting only inky blackness could be seen through the wide Plexiglas panels. The main clock showed 9:20 P.M., San Francisco time, although at the moment the airship was roughly three hundred miles out from that city on its course over the Pacific. As he gazed down at the projected map on the illuminated chart table, with General Smalley to his left and the government man, Haddock, to his right, Brandon pointed to the speck of red light that represented Tongareva.

"It's just that the distance seems so great," Brandon continued. "Wouldn't we be better off in a faster aircraft?"

"Of course," Haddock replied. "And that's exactly what we would have used, if the crash had occurred almost anywhere other than where it did. In some of our new, large jet transports we could reach Tongareva in twelve, maybe fifteen hours."

"The problem," General Smalley said, "is what could we do once we got there?" He reached out, his fingers tracing the faintly etched lines of the screen where they crossed the island. Locating the coordinates at the sides of the chart display unit, he then punched up the coding numbers for the spot and hit the key for an enlarged view.

Instantly, the overall view of the Pacific vanished from the chart table's translucent surface. Replacing it was a projected view of the island that nearly covered the display area.

"As you can see," Smalley continued in his easy voice, "despite the island's large diameter, the lagoon is so big that the surrounding landmass is quite narrow. Much of it's covered with coconut palms, and the few open areas are pretty small. And those are occupied with islanders' homes and some business structures. There *is* an airstrip—right here, a little south of Omoka village—but it's not much help. It was built during World War II—landed there myself once—but it hasn't been used much since. Our big jet transports couldn't begin to land there. We've been testing a few new short takeoff and landing transport prototypes, but they haven't got all the bugs out yet."

"I see," Brandon said. He stared at the huge lagoon. "What about seaplanes?"

"The ones we have," Haddock said patiently, "are relatively small, propeller-driven craft—not a great deal faster than the *Grand Eagle*. If we used enough of them, and if we could somehow refuel them in flight, they would still be too risky. The island is surrounded by a coral reef that can rip a plane apart if you hit the wrong spot at the wrong moment. The lagoon isn't free of coral heads either, and even if we could get past the landing problems I'd hate to put the injured survivors through that kind of transfer and takeoff. But in this"—he gestured around himself—"we don't even have to land. We can hover over the island and use the shuttle helicopter."

Brandon was beginning to see the logic of the decision. With more than a score of injured people to be airlifted out—and they'd have to be horizontal, not upright in seats—space would be important. The dead would have to be transported too, and Haddock had said something about recovering a sizable portion of the wreckage for analysis. An oceangoing ship might be able to handle the enormous task and provide the necessary on-the-spot medical facilities. An *airship* could do it faster.

"All right. You make a convincing argument," Brandon agreed. "Now, when am I going to see your hospital?"

"Right now, if you like," Smalley said. He turned to his second officer, Colonel Curtis. "John—mind running things for a while?"

Brandon retrieved his medical gear and followed Haddock and General Smalley back along the short hall to the elevator.

"Once I've seen your medical facility," Brandon said as the door slid shut, "I'd like to be put in radio contact with the people on the island so I can get a report on Lorenz' condition."

"Yes," Smalley replied. "We can set that up easily enough."

"I just hope the treatment he's received so far will be enough to keep him going."

Haddock displayed a cautious optimism. "As it is, we can be grateful there was medical help available. It could have been a lot worse—a *lot* worse. But I think the situation is pretty well under control. From the last report, Dr. Jennings is doing an extraordinary job."

"Jennings?" Brandon's eyes riveted on Haddock. "Dr. *Carla* Jennings?"

"Yes. She's there on a research grant from the World Health Organization."

"I know her. I've . . . worked with her."

"Yes, I know," Haddock replied. "It's in your file."

Brandon fell silent, wondering why the news disturbed him the way it did. The thought itself brought back memories, both pleasant and unpleasant, and the recent past became uncomfortably close once more. His mind was still on those thoughts when the elevator stopped and its door slid back.

They had gone past Deck A, which was entirely composed of crew quarters. Brandon dimly recalled that much from General Smalley's continuing explanation. They were now on Deck B, whose 5,400 square feet of space was shared by three sections.

The wide corridor from the elevator headed back toward the aft end of the ship for a distance of roughly ten feet, where it formed a T with a lateral corridor. A turn to the left, Smalley explained, would take them to the airship's mess facility. Straight in front of them was the door to the recreation room, for the use of off-duty crew members. To the right was their destination—the *Grand Eagle*'s hospital section.

As Brandon turned the corner he had to remind himself that he was in an aircraft, flying almost a mile high over the Pacific, rather than an office building. The walls and flooring appeared to be composed of the same composition material, hard and firm yet slightly resilient. Ventilation came from ducts which beveled the juncture of wall and ceiling, and electric lights behind translucent panels glowed at regular intervals along the sides of those ducts.

General Smalley pushed through the door at the end of the corridor and held it open for the others. They entered the hospital section, which was relatively small, but impressive. Brandon estimated the main area to be thirty by forty feet. Beyond that, through Plexiglas windows that could be curtained off, Brandon could see a fully outfitted operating room, roughly half the size of the first room. The main area held an examination table, a small office adjacent to a room for medical stores, and beds for at least twelve patients—or rather bunks, molded into the plastic walls. Each of the four cubicles on the far side held three such bunks, one along each wall. Curtains that framed the open side of each cubicle could be brought together to render the spaces more private.

"What do you think of it?"

The voice had come from his right, and Brandon turned to see that three people had emerged from the office—two men and a woman. The man in the lead wore over his blue flight uniform the pale jacket of the airship's medical officer. His jet-black hair was only slightly darker than his steely eyes—eyes that were both cool and alert.

"Dr. Brandon," General Smalley started the introduction, pointing out people with a gesture of his pipe, "this is Maj. Donald Shaffer, our chief sawbones"—he ignored Shaffer's wry glare and continued—"and his physician's assistant, Master Sergeant Griffith. Lt. Miriam Lynch, here, is part of our regular crew, and we have two additional surgical nurses along for the mission."

Brandon shook hands with each, wishing he knew more about their professional backgrounds. Dr. Shaffer was close to his own age, slender and intense-looking. Griffith was a large-boned man with crew-cut brown hair and a strong, muscular face, a man who looked as if he might be adept at causing as well as treating injuries.

The nurse, Lieutenant Lynch, was young—perhaps in her mid-twenties—and strikingly pretty, a blue-eyed blonde whose air force nurse's uniform fit in a way that inspired distinctly nonmilitary thoughts.

"You must get quite a crowd down here at sick call every day," Brandon said as he shook hands with her.

"Oh, no, not really," she said. "Only those that really need something. You see, we have a *special* treatment for nonexistent maladies. No one's been brave enough to risk a second dose yet."

"Miriam's right about that," Shaffer said with an amused look. "But whatever else comes up, I think we can handle it here."

Brandon nodded, looking around the impressive hospital section. "It looks like you have everything necessary for the surgery."

"Had most of it on board already," Shaffer explained. "And we brought extra equipment from the base hospital when we left." He glanced around his domain briefly, then back to Brandon, "It may not be perfect, but one thing's for sure—it's the best you'll find at *this* altitude."

"And there's no problem with turbulence?"

Shaffer shook his head. "No, the ship's steady as a rock, even through most of the maneuvering phases. And we'll be in a stable holding position for the surgery."

"Good. I'll want to go over details of the operation with you and your staff sometime soon," Brandon said. "And if we can get in a rehearsal of the technique, so much the better. But the first thing I think we should do—and quickly—is get an electrocardiograph unit up to the command deck. If they have a transmitting EKG unit on the island, we can get current read-outs on the way there."

"They have one," Haddock told him.

"That will help," Brandon said, his look of concern deepening. "But how much it will help will depend a lot on Lorenz' condition."

"Yes," Shaffer agreed. "And lest any of us forget, we're going to have a good deal more on our hands than Stefan Lorenz. There are twenty-two other people on that island in need of treatment—some who will need surgery for problems we can only guess at now."

"Can you handle that many?"

"Not in here, beyond initial treatment. But I've had the recreation room cleared, so we can put the overflow there on cots. We'll keep the most serious cases here, of course. The dead we'll have to put in one of Deck C's storage bays."

Brandon nodded, his look somber as he realized the grim situation that had been suddenly thrust upon Carla Jennings. He hoped he could help ease some of that burden. In a way, he blamed himself for her being there in the first place.

In less than ten minutes they were back on the command deck, in the midst of the control center's varied equipment. Shaffer had come along to add his own medical background to that of Brandon's and was busy positioning the electrocardiograph unit they had brought up while Staff Sergeant Jordan made the necessary connections to the airship's communications gear.

"All patched in, sir," Beth Jordan told Shaffer as she stood clear. "We'll be transmitting over one of the lesser used shortwave bands."

Haddock displayed a disapproving look. "I still wish we had this on a scrambler."

General Smalley nodded. "So do I. But since Dr. Jennings' rig doesn't have that capability, we'll just have to watch what we say." He glanced at Brandon. "Right, Doctor?"

"All right. Just so long as I can get the information I need."

Beth Jordan leaned over the communications console, her dark hair falling softly across her face. She adjusted the power and checked the frequency, then picked up the microphone headset and called to make contact.

It took several times before Carla Jennings' voice came back. Except for minor static, it could be heard clearly through the console's small auxiliary speaker. The voice showed fatigue and worry, and the sound of it touched Brandon like a knife into an old wound.

As he took the headset unit handed him by Beth Jordan, he hesitated, collecting his thoughts. Somewhere out there in the darkness, beyond the great window of the command deck, the Soviet aircraft carrier *Kiev* was cruising toward Tongareva. There was a good chance the officers aboard it were monitoring the radio frequency on which he would be broadcasting. Whether his words would have any effect on the security of the mission, he could not guess. But the Russians were out there. And also out there, at an unimaginably great distance, was Carla Jennings. Brandon squeezed the tiny switch on the headset's microphone and spoke into it. "Carla . . . this is Paul Brandon."

There was a long pause, and Brandon strained to catch any sound in the radio's silence, hoping the signal had not faded. At last, Carla's voice returned, hesitant, questioning.

"*Paul*? I—Are you—I mean, I can't believe it's really you. How did you get in on this?"

Brandon glanced at Haddock. "I was drafted. Look, Carla, I don't want you to think I'm interfering with your handling of things there, but—" he paused, releasing the transmit switch.

"Interfering!" the voice shot back, full of tired irony. "I need all the help I can get, Paul. Where—where are you?"

Brandon ignored the question deliberately. "Help is on the way, Carla. Complete medical assistance will be there, within roughly forty hours. All the help you need, so you don't have to worry."

"Paul . . ." Carla's voice came back through the headset with a trace of anxiety, and perhaps something worse. "There's something I must tell you—"

"Can it wait a moment? I'm very concerned about one of your patients—the heart attack victim."

There was a hesitation, then, "Yes, of course. He's

stabilized, for the moment, but I don't know how much longer he can last. This is more your field than mine, Paul, but his condition is really critical. I don't like the sound of his heart—there's a definite diastolic murmur, and I'm sure the man has had an attack before."

"You're right about the murmur," Brandon answered. "I've been informed of the patient's medical history. He has a genetic valve disorder."

"Then it *is* aortic insufficiency?"

"Yes, although what additional damage there is now is hard to know without the right tests. What treatment have you used?"

"Digitoxin at first, as soon as I was able to," Carla responded. "And of course he's on oxygen—thank heaven the last doctor here maintained a good stock of drugs and supplies."

"You're going to have to reduce the edema."

"I know. I've administered hydrochlorothiazide and spironolactone. But eventually those are going to diminish his tolerance for the digitoxin, and then his heart rhythm is going to get pretty irregular."

Brandon considered it a moment. "I think we can still get there before that happens." He hesitated, then added, "You're doing a good job, Carla. I know you'll give everyone there your best effort. But I want you to make sure you get some rest yourself. You won't do anyone any good if you're out on your feet."

"I'll manage."

Brandon knew it was useless to argue. Carla would put her own needs last as long as there were things to be done for the injured survivors.

"Before we break contact," Brandon said next, "I want to get an EKG relay for your patient. I understand you have the necessary equipment?"

"Yes—I can patch it through the radio here, as soon as I get it hooked up and the leads attached. I'll start now."

A long silence followed, a silence that left Brandon feeling even more remote and aware of the distance involved than he had before. He closed his eyes momentarily, trying to visualize the working conditions at the research facility on Tongareva. He had no idea what it looked like, but assumed conditions were primitive.

After what seemed an agonizingly long period, Carla's

voice returned, melodic even in its weary state. "It's all set up, Paul."

"Good—go ahead." He switched on the electrocardiograph next to the communications console and waited as the graph paper began to unroll, the indicator needles marking straight lines upon its surface.

Then there was a jolt as the signal came through and the device began to record variations in the minute electrical impulses radiating through Stefan Lorenz' heart and system. Both Brandon and Shaffer studied the multiple tracks as the graphs progressed, watching the characteristic signs reveal themselves in the tracks' peaks and valleys.

The signal ended abruptly and Brandon switched the equipment off. He tore loose the graph and held it where both he and Shaffer could read it.

Shaffer sighed, his tone grim. "There's been damage, all right. Quite a lot from the looks of this."

"I know," Brandon said resignedly. "The crash must have aggravated everything."

"I don't suppose a simple valve replacement operation is going to solve much of anything."

"It might have once. I doubt that it will now, but we won't know for sure until we get into the chest cavity."

"So it looks like your new procedure is the only chance." Shaffer carefully folded the electrocardiogram and tapped it on the flat surface of the console. "I can't say the man has much to lose by your trying."

Carla's voice broke in again. "Is there anything else?"

"No," Brandon responded.

"Paul, I . . ."

The brief silence that followed aroused his curiosity. Carla's voice was nervous—almost quaking.

"What is it?"

"There's something wrong," her words came back through the radio circuits. "*Terribly* wrong." Her tone dropped slightly in volume. "I don't think anyone else can hear me here—I'm alone in the radio room."

"What's wrong?" Brandon was aware that both Haddock and General Smalley had straightened and moved closer to the communications console.

"Something we've just discovered a while ago," Carla said softly. "I've had a chance to examine the bodies of the pilot and copilot. Paul—they weren't killed in the crash. They were murdered—*shot*—before the plane hit and broke up!"

Brandon looked around to the other's faces. The expressions ranged from deep concern to shocked disbelief. "Are you sure?"

"Yes. I'm absolutely certain." After a fearful pause, Carla added, "You know what that means—someone on board the plane killed them. Someone who's here now, *on the island.*"

There was a momentary silence on the command deck, then Smalley spoke up. "That would explain the jet's being so much off course. It was hijacked."

"I doubt it was a simple hijacking," Haddock said, his brow deeply furrowed. "Knowing what we do about the plane's cargo, we can't rule out a KGB agent. In either case it's a whole new ball game."

"The hijacker might have died," Smalley offered with grim hope. "He could have been killed in the crash."

"Maybe ... maybe not." Haddock shoved his hands deep into his pockets and began to pace. "Whatever happened on that plane, we can only be sure of one thing—it started after the flight left Wake Island for Hawaii."

Brandon hesitated, then fingered the microphone switch. "Carla, if what you say is the case, the person responsible may not have survived the crash—you may have nothing to worry about." He only hoped he was right. For the moment, his words were intended more to reassure. "We'll do what we can to find out from our end. But be careful, anyway. I'll be in contact again."

"All right," her voice replied. "Out—"

Brandon continued to hold the radio headset in his hand for a while, letting his mind linger on the sound of Carla's voice. Finally, he turned to Haddock, who had stopped abruptly next to him.

"What now?"

"I want a security channel opened," the government man said quickly, imperatively. "Washington has to be made aware of this development at once. And I think there's something else we'd better do as well—I think someone ought to be sent to Wake Island, by the fastest means possible. The answer we're seeking may not be there, but it's a place to start. ...."

The warm waters of the Pacific churned and frothed as the

prow of the aircraft carrier *Kiev* split their surface. It was now 9:00 A.M., and the *Kiev* was still moving at top speed, better than thirty-four knots. It was steadily closing the gap between itself and the island.

Far from the early morning brightness, three men stood watching from one corner of the enclosed hangar deck beneath the top surface of the ship. Electrical illumination revealed the carefully fitted rows of helicopters stored within the hangar deck, and beyond them, the special jet fighter craft.

Adm. Nikolay Bakhirev looked approvingly on at the rows of helicopters, and at the crewmen busily engaged in checking out the craft, loading stretchers and medical gear aboard some of them. Beside Bakhirev stood the *Kiev*'s captain, Konstantin Dashkevich, methodically checking through a clipboard full of duty rosters, navigational data, and information on the status of crash survivors picked up from radio broadcasts monitored the night before. The ship's political officer, Grigorovich, was also with them.

"We should be there sometime late tomorrow, Admiral." Dashkevich said. "The ship itself, of course, will have to stay well beyond the area of the reef, but our helicopters can ferry the injured across the distance."

Bakhirev nodded. "How many may be transported in each helicopter?"

"At least three or four, with several crew attendants."

"Then no more than ten of our craft will be necessary."

"Yes, sir," Dashkevich replied. "Of course we will have to make a second trip, for the remains of the dead."

Grigorovich was growing increasingly irritated at being left out of the discussion. He chose the moment to interrupt. "What about treating the people in our medical facility?"

Bakhirev did not acknowledge him with a look. "That is all being arranged, Captain. I am sure our medical personnel are quite capable of handling everything."

"I was thinking more in terms of Lorenz, sir. He must be kept isolated from the start. His decadent views about our rescuing him might . . . *confuse* the other survivors."

Dashkevich tried to remain patient. "Perhaps. Presuming that he does not expire before we arrive there."

Grigorovich considered it only briefly. "Actually, that might tend to simplify matters," he said dispasssionately. "I seriously doubt that a man whose loyalty to his homeland and allies has been so corrupted will ever be trustworthy again. The report we received on his planned defection shows exactly the kind of traitor he is—he has lied to our representatives, to his colleagues in Czechoslovakia, even to his daughter. His thinking has become too undisciplined, too perverse, for him to have any value."

"That may or may not be," Bakhirev replied. "The man is a Czech and I cannot say that I understand him. But none of this matters. Our orders are clear and specific—we are to recover this Lorenz and the prototype he smuggled out, and we are to ensure his return. Nothing less than that will suffice. Once he is back then it will not be our responsibility whether or not he can be reeducated. That will be left up to the skills of others."

For once, there was nothing Grigorovich could say. The admiral was right. The orders *were* clear, and their mission well defined. Finding himself awkwardly on the wrong side of the discussion, he changed the subject.

"I had best arrange briefings for the crew, since we are going to be in contact with these Westerners. At least they will only be on board until we can transfer them at Tahiti."

"Yes," Dashkevich said, "which will take us only a short way further off course. I think we can—"

His words were sharply interrupted by a buzz and a voice from the intercom on the bulkhead behind them. Someone was calling from the bridge.

"*Captain?*"

Dashkevich went to the unit and depressed the talk switch. "Yes—I am here."

"Captain," the voice repeated, "there is something you may wish to see. Our radar has picked it up and locked on."

"A ship?"

"No, sir. An aircraft, but like none we are familiar with."

"I'll be right up. Keep it under observation."

Dashkevich and the others reached the bridge in a matter of minutes, taking the stairs and companionways that led to the command section, well above the flight deck. As they reached it the man who had called on the intercom, Dashkevich's second-in-command, met them and directed them to the console containing the radar equipment.

"There, sir," the man said, indicating the primary screen as the illuminated band swept along its circular path. At the bottom of the screen, in a location representing the segment of sky to the rear of the vessel, a large blip glowed, fading and renewing with each sweep of the electronic screen. A secondary circuit showed the object's approximate altitude.

Both Dashkevich and Bakhirev stared in mute wonder at the image on the screen. Finally, Bakhirev directed a question at Yakosev, the warrant officer manning the scope.

"Distance—?"

"About three hundred miles, sir."

"But the size of it . . ." Dashkevich blinked. "Are you certain it is not an equipment malfunction?"

The technician quickly changed the circuit to a backup system, even though he knew it was not necessary. "The object and position still confirmed, sir."

Bakhirev considered it a long moment, then asked, "And its airspeed?"

"Over a hundred knots."

"Slow . . . not a jet aircraft," the admiral said. "I had been wondering if the Americans were going to attempt to reach the island by air, ever since their ships fell back and returned to Hawaii."

"But a large aircraft cannot land there on the island," Dashkevich said.

"One wonders. . . . Nothing that large could be a conventional craft."

Grigorovich frowned as he studied the screen. "If it is an American craft, and it *can* somehow land there, then we have a great deal to fear. Even at that speed, it will easily overtake us and reach the island long before we can."

"If, if . . ." Bakhirev said irritably. "There are too many *ifs*. To be able to act effectively, we must know what we are dealing with."

Dashkevich was hesitant. "We cannot be certain they will interfere."

"Their present course can hardly be accidental. It is almost certainly an American craft—and its very presence threatens the success of our mission."

The three men watched the radar screen for another long moment, each following his own thoughts. Finally, Dashkevich turned to his superior officer.

"Your orders, sir?"

"Orders?" Bakhirev said. "I should think they would be

obvious. What we must do is quite simple. We are going to have to investigate our mysterious follower . . . learn what it is and how to deal with it. Yes, we shall investigate, Captain. Just as soon as it comes a bit closer, and within our range. . . ."

CHAPTER FOUR

High over the Pacific Ocean an enormous silver projectile reflected with dazzling brilliance the rays of the morning sun. The nuclear airship *Grand Eagle* cruised through currents of air, the mammoth twin propellers at its stern pushing it forward at top speed. Now almost 2,300 miles out from San Francisco, the *Grand Eagle* had covered more than half the distance to Tongareva during the night.

Its passage through the region was a triumph of effort and technology that no casual observer would note. Systems and materials incorporated within the gargantuan aircraft had not existed a dozen years before, and many were the direct benefits of the American space program.

The largest airship of the preatomic era had been the ill-fated German Zeppelin *Hindenburg,* at a length of 803 feet and a gas volume of over 7 million cubic feet. Its total payload was only a little over 40,000 pounds—just at the beginning stages of performance efficient enough to be of value.

The *Grand Eagle,* half again as long as the *Hindenburg* and with a 50 percent greater diameter, held 25 million cubic feet of helium within its impermeable Tedlar gas cells, with a resultant payload of close to 900,000 pounds. But the advance over the older designs represented more than just an increase in size.

Special titanium-aluminum alloy formed the rigid framework of the craft's hull, a material both lighter and stronger than any previously used in the construction of an airship, and several berylium components were incorporated for further weight reduction. Du Pont Kevlar had been used for the tough outer covering, and within, the walls, floors, and ceilings of the command and quarters decks located near the nose of the airship were formed in honeycomb constructions that were extraordinarily light in weight. Weight saved in the nonessential areas allowed for the full complement of electronics, aircraft, and the weapons systems.

But the most significant factor distinguishing the *Grand Eagle* from the older airships—and from all other types of aircraft, for that matter—was the nuclear reactor located 130 feet back from the middle of the ship, buried deep in the center of the spacious hull so that its very distance from all crew areas was an added, if unnecessary, safety factor.

The Pratt & Whitney reactor supplied energy, through heat exchange systems, to the three turbines at the stern of the ship, the largest of which powered the great counterrotating propellers while the smaller two reduced drag by sucking in boundary layer air along the ship's vast surface and expelling it through vents at the stern. Nuclear fuel for the reactor would last up to two years without replenishment, giving the *Grand Eagle* almost unlimited range.

At that moment, within the great airship, Paul Brandon woke from a dream-plagued sleep and peered about him, trying to clear his vision. Gradually, the outlines of the room came into focus and became familiar—the smooth bottom of the upper bunk above him, the empty bookshelves molded into the wall above his feet, the small writing desk in the opposite corner of the room, and the two molded lockers which rose from floor to ceiling, filling the last remaining corner and adjoining the desk. A pale blue light illuminated the interior, and the digital clock above the door displayed the time in yellow numerals.

That was odd, Brandon thought. He was certain those numerals had been blue when he had at last retired for the night a little over six hours ago, after staying quite late in the command deck's control center awaiting further word from Carla. But now it was 9:50 A.M. and the numerals were bright yellow. He threw back the cover and got up from his bunk, then fumbled with the light switch beside the door. Blinking in the sudden brightness, he looked around the room.

It should not really be called a room, he realized—compartment was a better term. It was small—probably ten feet square counting the enclosed lavatory at the rear of the compartment—but efficient use had been made of the available space, and the area did not feel confining. It was hard to shake the feeling that he was still on the ground somewhere, for there was no sensation of movement and the only sound was of the faint rush of air through the vents. And Colonel Curtis had been right about one thing, Brandon thought—they *had* given him VIP treatment. A private compartment next to General

Smalley's on the command deck, rather than one on the quarters deck below, must carry a certain amount of prestige on the military craft.

Brandon headed for the lavatory and made use of its small shower, despite an aggravating control lever that had to be held down to keep the water flowing. He wondered vaguely where the drain water went, speculating idly that it was probably recycled in some way. (He would learn later that it was filtered and eventually returned to the airship's ballast systems, a series of large, interconnected tanks and pumps which provided balance and stability to the lighter-than-air craft.)

Brandon had brought only the clothes on his back when he boarded the *Grand Eagle*, but someone had managed a fresh supply of underwear and shaving gear, along with a plain flight uniform. Surprisingly, the uniform bore a visitor's ID badge with his name and photo, and a strip of film that Brandon recognized as a radiation exposure indicator. He held up the lightweight garment, briefly considered discarding it, then sighed and put it on. Naturally it was a perfect fit. Tossing his own shirt and trousers into a laundry bag already tagged with his name and compartment number, he prepared to leave.

At the door, he hesitated. Why, he wondered, did the prospect of seeing Carla again arouse such conflicting feelings? Whatever had been between them before was over now. Surely that was true. Carla herself had made it clear by her sudden departure from San Francisco almost a year ago, without so much as a good-bye call or note of explanation. He deserved better treatment than that, he thought, after their work together at the hospital and in Philip Norton's university program. Their work, and what developed from it.

It was a puzzle Brandon could not fathom. They had been as close as two people can be, and yet even now he doubted that he understood Carla. The memory of their last meeting was still burned into his mind, and thoughts that had lain dormant for months became fresh and painful once again.

The recollection grew stronger, the details of it becoming vivid and clear, as if the fateful last encounter had occurred just hours ago. . . .

It was early evening when Brandon had driven over to pick up Carla that day, and the air was crisp and chill in wintry San Francisco. When he walked Carla down the steps of her apartment house and over to the new Corvette Stingray, she had stopped, looking confusedly for Brandon's old car.

"No—*here*"— Brandon indicated the shiny sports car, fresh from the showroom.

She seemed puzzled as Brandon unlocked the door. "Is . . . is this yours?"

"Yes. I just got it."

"What did you do," she asked with a hesitant smile, "win the Irish Sweepstakes?"

"No. But we do have something to celebrate," Brandon said mysteriously. As they got into the car and headed out of the drive in the general direction of Montgomery Street, he added, "I thought we'd go to Ernie's, if that's okay. . . ."

Carla frowned. "It's *more* than okay. But isn't it rather expensive?"

"No arguments, now—if we're going to celebrate, we may as well do it right."

"Celebrate *what*? What's this all about, Paul?"

"All in good time, Doctor . . . all in good time. . . ."

As expected, the dinner at Ernie's, with its continental cuisine, was superb. And by the time they arrived back at Brandon's place, Carla's curiosity had reached its peak.

"Paul, what is happening? All evening you've been looking like a cat full of canary."

Brandon emerged from the kitchen bearing a bucket of ice and a bottle of champagne. "I've been saving this for a special occasion. I think this one will qualify."

Carla sank into the thick-cushioned sofa that faced the television. "You're going to make me drag it out of you, aren't you? After all this buildup, it had better be good."

Brandon sat beside her, placing the champagne on the coffee table. "All right. The news is too good to keep secret any longer, anyway. It's about the artificial-heart project."

The enthusiasm already present in Brandon's eyes became mirrored in Carla's own expression. "Oh, Paul—you've interested someone in your design?"

"The Steinman-Keller Institute, no less," he said triumphantly.

"Great!" She kissed him impulsively, happily, knowing how much the project meant to him. "Do you think they'll do a good job of developing it?"

"I'm positive they will," Brandon replied. "Because I'm

going to be overseeing it." At Carla's puzzled look he continued, "They don't just want my design—they want *me*, too. I've accepted a full-time advisory position with their research facility here in San Francisco."

She pulled away from him slightly, staring into his eyes in confusion. "A full-time position? But what about your work at the hospital?"

Brandon busied himself with the champagne cork. He poured two glasses. "I'm afraid there won't be time for that for a while. I've already notified McCauley and the others that they're going to need another surgeon."

"Do you think you should have done that?"

"Yes, of course. I would have given them more advance warning than that if I had been certain about the position." He paused as they clinked glasses, hardly aware of Carla's sudden diminished enthusiasm. "It's a well-paying job . . . *very*. And I'll be acting as the institute's representative in all matters concerning the new device."

"Representative? Paul, that's not medicine, that's public relations!"

"There's a lot more to it than that," he replied, a slight irritation creeping into his voice. "My main job will be to help them in their research and development . . . I'll be working directly with their engineers."

"But still it means you'll be leaving medicine . . . not working with *patients.*"

"It has to be that way if I want to develop this project the way it should be done. And you know how important the project is to me."

Carla started to speak, then hesitated, seeing the unassailable enthusiasm still glowing in Brandon's eyes. Finally, she said only, "I think maybe we should talk this over."

"We'll talk about it in the morning, while you're taking me to the airport."

"The airport?"

"They want me to meet the senior executives at Steinman-Keller's main office in New York, and see their facilities there. I'd take you along, but the institute is flying me there in its private jet."

"I . . . I couldn't go anyway, Paul. I have patients to see at the hospital tomorrow."

Brandon frowned at his own forgetfulness. "Yes, of

course, I should have realized. Anyway, I won't be gone more than a week. And when I get back," he said tenderly, taking her into his arms once more, "we'll take a look at that apartment over on Telegraph Hill. I can afford it now, and besides ... everybody's been telling us what a great couple we make. It's time we made it official."

"Paul, I..." She hesitated, her chin resting on his strong, firm shoulder. Her expression was troubled, and her voice bore a trace of sadness as she spoke again. "Are you so very sure this institute position is the way you want to go with your life?"

"Yes, of course. The opportunity is too good to pass up. Don't worry. Before long, we'll have everything we want."

"I still think we should talk about this, Paul."

"In the morning, I said." He kissed her gently, sheltering her with his arms, trying to chase away the doubts lingering in her eyes. "We can talk all you want then. ..."

But on the trip to the airport the next day, Carla was strangely silent, and when Brandon called her apartment from New York, she was always out. The week passed slowly enough, despite a busy schedule of meetings and tours and the unavoidable cocktail parties. By the end of the week he was bone-tired and eager to get home.

There was no one to meet him at the airport. Brandon caught a cab into town and wearily unloaded his suitcase at his apartment. He was about to leave again when he saw the key lying on the television console. It was the spare apartment key he had given Carla some months ago. Calling the hospital, he discovered that she had not been there in several days. A hasty, anguished call to Carla's apartment house manager only confirmed his worst fears. She was gone. Packed and moved out, without so much as a forwarding address, a message, or anything.

Brandon hung up the receiver and stood for several long moments in the silence of his apartment, staring down at the key in his hand. He had gripped it so hard while telephoning that the zigzag edge had left a reddened impression in his palm.

Turning explosively, he threw the key the length of the room, where it chipped a bit of plaster from the wall before clattering noisily to the floor. Almost in a daze, he walked over and sank wearily into the sofa, eyes shutting out the emptiness that surrounded him. ...

Whatever might have been between them had ended, abruptly and unexplainably. Thinking about it again now made things no clearer. Brandon forced the thoughts from his mind and opened the sliding door. Leaving the compartment, he latched the door behind him and started down the hall. He had just reached the intersecting corridor which led to the control center when the double doors at the end opened and Stewart Gardner emerged, heading toward him.

Gardner's normally sober features allowed a brief smile at the sight of Brandon's flight uniform. "Good morning, Doctor. You know, you don't look half bad in air force blue—"

"No remarks, please, Colonel. This is purely temporary." Brandon held up the laundry bag he was carrying. "Have any idea where I'm supposed to deposit this?"

"Sure. I can show you on the way down to the mess hall if you like. I'm heading there myself."

Brandon glanced anxiously past him at the closed doors of the control center. "Has there been any further word from the island?"

"Not a peep. I was down here when the blue shift personnel went off duty, and there haven't been any more radio messages at all."

"Blue shift?"

"Right." He saw Brandon's puzzled look and explained. "Someone had the idea of having different-colored numerals on our clocks for each of the three duty shifts, and in the last month or so during testing, we've got in the habit of calling the shifts by their colors."

Brandon thought back to the digital clock in his compartment. "So, we've just started the yellow shift?"

"Right. And the next one, the red, goes from four P.M. till midnight."

"Makes sense, I guess." Brandon sighed. "All right, I may as well go down to breakfast while I can. Some of us may end up working a tricolor shift before this is over."

"I imagine so, sir."

They turned and headed for the elevator. Inside, Gardner pressed the button for Deck B and the door whisked closed. When it opened again, Gardner led the way out, to the right, and pointed to a wall panel marked with the word *Laundry*. Brandon pushed the panel in and dropped his parcel inside, then walked on with Gardner, turning left at an intersecting corridor until they reached the airship's mess facility.

The chamber was surprisingly spacious, and natural sunlight streaming in through several view ports in the sloping far wall brightened the area. Yellow wall paneling added to the cheery aspect, and the scent of hot food in the air stirred Brandon's appetite despite his concern over Carla. He realized he had had nothing to eat in the past twenty-four hours except for a hastily gulped sandwich in the command deck the night before.

He followed Gardner to the counter at the near end of the mess hall. As he drew nearer, Brandon was surprised at the apparent lack of steam tables to keep the cooked food hot . . . and for that matter, the apparent lack of *food*.

"Yes, sir?" A young aircrewman in white mess garb stepped up to the other side of the counter.

"Eggs and ham," Gardner told him. He turned to Brandon. "You want the same?"

"No—thanks. Have you any hot cereal?"

"Yes, sir," the aircrewman responded, stepping quickly back to the rear counter where several racks were located next to three microwave ovens.

Brandon watched as the man pulled two parcels from the racks, each with a different color-coded edge, and began to cut through the heavy, sealed covering that appeared to be a kind of metalized Mylar film. The aircrewman removed the wrapping and added water to one of the plastic trays, then put both into one of the special ovens and activated it.

"Isn't . . . isn't the food refrigerated?"

"No. The menu we have on the *Grand Eagle* requires mostly fresh foods," Gardner explained, "but the weight of refrigeration equipment necessary for all our stored rations was considered too great—for that matter, so was the traditional cooking equipment. So we use microwave, and the dishes are all prepared at our base, hermetically sealed, and irradiated to prevent spoilage."

"*Irradiated*," a voice said ominously behind them, and both Gardner and Brandon turned to see S/Sgt. Elizabeth Jordan standing a few feet away. She had approached them almost soundlessly, and now leaned closer to Brandon, blue eyes flashing. She spoke in a low, conspiratorial tone: "There's a nasty rumor on board, Doctor, that if the reactor doesn't make us all sterile, the food *will*." She smiled. "Of course, there's not a gram of truth to it, so I wouldn't worry if I were you. . . ."

Gardner regarded the young woman resignedly, then said "Dr. Brandon—Beth Jordan, one of our best communications noncoms. But I guess you've met, haven't you?"

Brandon nodded in her direction, then turned as the aircrewman brought the two fully heated food containers forward on molded trays, to which had been added coffee, water, canned fruit juice, and plastic utensils. On Gardner's was a container with a moderate-sized ham steak and a mass of scrambled eggs. Triangles of toast filled the corner, as they did in a separate section of Brandon's own tray, next to the now steaming section of hot cereal.

Beth Jordan put in her own order and soon joined Gardner and Brandon at one of the tables, swinging out a legless seat that was pivoted to one of the table supports. There was, as Gardner explained, no separation of officers and enlisted personnel in the airship's mess facilities. It would have served no useful purpose, and besides, on the experimental craft the special crew was too tightly knit for such a restriction.

"At least the coffee's not instant," Brandon said with relief, swallowing another sip.

"A minor concession for the sake of morale," Gardner admitted, then looked toward Brandon's tray. "Don't you like eggs, Doctor?"

"Sure. But as a heart specialist I've seen the results of too much cholesterol more times than I like to think about."

"Please—" Beth Jordan blanched, a forkful of eggs nearing her own mouth. "Breakfast is one of the few things I look forward to."

As she momentarily glanced toward Stewart Gardner, Brandon thought he caught something in her look—a brief shade of expression, something that suggested Jordan thought of the senior flight officer as more than just a fellow crewmember. Considering his own life, Brandon admitted to himself, he was probably not the best judge of human emotions, but still he would be willing to bet that Beth Jordan was in love with Gardner. Whether Gardner knew it himself or not was harder to tell.

"How much longer before we reach the island?" Brandon asked.

Gardner glanced at his watch. "With luck, maybe twenty hours or less. The wind currents have favored us so far—they will till we get closer to the equatorial region—and we've been making at least a hundred and twenty miles per hour, about three times the top speed of the *Kiev*. We get data constantly from weather satellites as well as from home base, so we can choose the best course pretty far ahead of time. There's some indication of a tropical disturbance building up south of the island, but otherwise I'd say we should have a pretty good flight—"

Abruptly, almost as if mocking his words, a loud sound reverberated through the deck—a high-pitched staccato electronic whistling, commanding attention. Simultaneously, lights flashed over the doorway of the mess facility.

Tensing, Brandon snapped, "What is that?"

"We've just gone on *yellow alert*," Gardner said quickly, pushing up from the table and deserting his breakfast tray. "I've got to get to the command deck!"

As Gardner ran from the mess facility, several others there left hurriedly to assume their predesignated positions. Brandon followed close behind the air force officer, trotting to keep up. He heard Beth Jordan running behind him.

His first thought was that somehow, something had gone wrong which posed a threat to the people on the island—and Carla. But there was no point in speculating without information.

In seconds they were on the command deck, hurriedly entering the control center. Gardner immediately took up a position behind his two junior flight officers, who had already taken the ship's controls off automatic status. Yellow alert lights still pulsed here in the control center as well.

Brandon stopped next to the government man, Haddock, who was conferring with General Smalley before the bank of television monitors that displayed all sectors of the sky and the sea below.

"What's wrong?"

Haddock turned to him, his features taut. "Maybe nothing," he said softly. "And maybe everything. We've got company . . ."

Brandon looked at the screen to which Haddock had pointed, studying it for a moment before he noticed the speck of light moving slightly to the right. "What is it?"

"A Soviet jet," General Smalley answered, punching up another circuit that magnified the image. "The *Kiev* is still about a hundred and eighty miles ahead of us, but they've sent one of their birds back for a look."

Brandon continued to watch as the jet drew near. It began to bank slightly, making a wide circle around the massive airship. The image was soon lost from one screen, only to appear on one covering another sector. This process repeated itself as the plane continued its arc, finally beginning another turn around the huge aircraft.

Approaching the group, Lieutenant Colonel Foster—an officer Brandon had been introduced to briefly the night before—studied the television display screen with hawklike eyes set deep in a narrow face.

He finally looked toward General Smalley. "Shall I scramble the Harriers, sir?"

Smalley chewed on the end of his pipe for a moment, watching the screens. "No," he said at last. "Not yet, anyhow. We probably gave them quite a start. It's only natural they'd want to look us over. There's no need to chase him off yet, and besides, for the moment I'd just as soon they didn't know we're carrying fighter craft."

Foster looked unconvinced, but said only. "Understood, sir."

The men watched as the jet still circled, and then abruptly, as quickly as it had appeared, the jet banked away from them and headed back the way it had come. It faded from view in another few minutes.

"Just a look," Smalley said quietly, puffing on his meerschaum. "And for that matter, I wouldn't mind a look at *their* hardware."

Haddock considered it. "I'm sure Naval Intelligence has a photo file on the ship, General. I could relay the request through the State Department, if you wish—"

"No, that could take awhile," Smalley said in his easy drawl. "Besides, Mr. Haddock, we in the Air Force are not entirely without resources. . . ." He looked up into the alert gaze of Colonel Curtis, who was standing close at hand. "John, how long would it take for one of our RPVs to reach the *Kiev?*"

"One of our fast recon models? Not long, sir."

"Get it started then. And take us off alert status."

Curtis headed back toward the rear of the control center, the others following. There, located just in front of and slightly between the two L-shaped banks of computer equipment that spanned the width of the command deck on both sides of the main doors, four semienclosed consoles were waiting and ready. At each one were seated two controllers, an officer and an NCO. These eight men were technically under the supervision of the airship's weapons control officer, Major Tate. From these four consoles, two on each side of the main aisle, a variety of the airship's RPVs—remotely piloted vehicles—could be launched and guided through their mission.

Curtis chose Control Console Three, instructing the captain and master sergeant there to activate their equipment. "We'll use the modified BGM-34C, recon mode."

"Yes, sir."

The master sergeant tapped out the coding sequence that would open circuits to the RPV bay at the bottom of the airship's hull, 360 feet back from the nose. At once, television monitors mounted within the tall console came to life. One showed the interior of the RPV bay from a high angle, its interior brightening as the bay doors slid open. Amid a maze of catwalks and machinery, a multitude of RPVs of varying types waited, some secured in storage racks, others ready to be launched.

Pressing another control button, the master sergeant watched the main television monitor as one of the small, pilotless aircraft was extended downward at the end of its launching arm. The RPV was a Teledyne Ryan BGM-34C. Initial testing had been done at Edwards Air Force Base, where the *Grand Eagle* had been constructed, and it had been relatively easy to modify it and other RPVs for use by the giant airship. Twenty-six feet in length, with a wingspan of fourteen and a half feet, the BGM-34C looked like a small jet fighter—which indeed it could be in its weapons mode. A greatly advanced version of the Firebee I drone, it was in reality only an intermediate design—a half step in the development of a low-cost, multi-mission RPV. Depending upon which modular nose section was used, the RPV system could be used for reconnaissance missions, electronic countermeasures, or even strike missions. This particular craft was outfitted with reconnaissance gear.

As the launch arm locked into place, indicator lights flashed on the control console. On the computer printout screen, white letters against a blue background spelled out the prelaunch data:

```
FUEL PRESSURE                        + + +
ELECTRICAL SYSTEMS                   + + +
GUIDANCE SYSTEMS                     + + +
    FLIGHT REFERENCE COMPUTER        + + +
    INTERFACE COUPLER                + + +
    MANEUVER PROGRAMMER              + + +
    BACKUP AUTOPILOT                 + + +
    CONTROL SERVOS                   + + +
    GYROS                            + + +
        PRIMARY VERTICAL             + + +
        BACKUP VERTICAL              + + +
        PITCH                        + + +
        YAW                          + + +
        ROLL RATE                    + + +
    AIR DATA COMPUTER                + + +
    AIRCRAFT STATUS  SENSORS         + + +
DESTRUCT SYSTEM TEST                 + + +
RECON SYSTEMS                        + + +     STANDBY MODE
COMMAND CIRCUITS                     + + +     OPEN
RECOVERY SYSTEMS                     + + +     STANDBY MODE
```

Had any pulsing zeros shown up on the screen where the plus signs now were, it would have been a signal that one or more of the systems were not functioning. With no zeros, everything was operational.

The control officer glanced up at Curtis and Smalley. "Ready for launch, sir."

As Smalley nodded, the control NCO opened circuits which patched the console equipment into the airship's main radar and allied sensors network, which would accurately direct the recon RPV toward the *Kiev*. He depressed the button that ignited the RPV's 1,920-pound turbojet engine, waiting a moment as the indicator lighted, showing that the engine had caught and fired. Then, with his right hand poised near the manual override controls, he hit the launching disengage switch.

"The bird's free, sir."

Beneath the great airship, the jet RPV dropped from the bracket that held it, losing altitude but steadily pulling away from the airship as its engine gained increased thrust. Its form was sleek and powerful, with swept-back wings and small delta fins at the ends of its rear stabilizers. Its rudder, high and tapered like a shark's fin, made minute corrections as the robot plane started on its course.

On the command deck, Paul Brandon watched with interest as the RPV came into view from under the airship's nose. It sped straight ahead, reaching its peak velocity of close to seven hundred miles per hour, and quickly vanished from sight. Looking back to the control console, Brandon saw that the main television monitor now showed a different picture—one relayed from the RPV's own scanner. Flight data continued to show on the computer printout screen, and an auxiliary display screen incorporated in the control console depicted the position of the RPV in relation to both the *Grand Eagle* and the *Kiev*.

"Pilotless planes," Brandon mused out loud, "Something like that could really reduce casualties."

"That's the main idea," General Smalley replied. "That and the cost factor. Manned aircraft are getting to be almost too expensive to use. Of course, there are still times when plain ol' seat-of-the-pants flying is unbeatable, but these RPVs are handy to have around. We used them quite a bit in Vietnam, for surveillance and other missions."

In just a little over fifteen minutes, the Soviet aircraft carrier *Kiev* came into view on the television monitor, at the edge of the image relayed from the RPV's nose camera. The RPV was being maintained at an altitude of two thousand feet, on a course one mile east of the *Kiev*'s.

"Within range, sir," the control officer reported.

"Take her down to a thousand feet," Smalley ordered. "Straight flyover."

The control officer reprogrammed the guidance circuits. "Done, sir. Beginning approach in six seconds."

Smalley and the others waited, watching the television monitor as the image changed, tilting as the nose of the craft dipped. The RPV banked briefly, bringing it directly in line with the *Kiev*'s course, and leveled off at a thousand feet altitude. The Soviet aircraft carrier grew larger on the monitor's screen, seeming to rush toward them as the RPV closed the gap.

"Cameras on, sir—all systems working."

Within the RPV's forward fuselage, rapid-sequence high-resolution cameras were whirring, recording on special low-grain film whatever passed beneath them. A third camera—a television unit—was tranforming the same images into complex electronic signals and transmitting them back to the *Grand Eagle*'s high-speed video tape recorders and to a secondary monitor on the control console. Still moving at close to seven hundred miles per hour, the RPV completed its flyover of the *Kiev*'s 925-foot length in nine tenths of a second, photographing the ship from stern to stem.

"Bringing her back, sir." The control officer tapped in new guidance commands, watching the monitor and position indicator as the RPV banked quickly to the left, swung wide, and looped back in the direction of the *Grand Eagle*.

"While we're waiting," Smalley said, "let's see what we got on the video tape system."

"Rewinding now, sir." While the officer next to him concentrated on the returning RPV, the master sergeant keyed in the video replay circuit.

At once, the image reappeared on the secondary monitor screen as the RPV's pass over the *Kiev* was repeated, this time in slow motion. The image was not quite sharp enough for a detailed analysis of the carrier's hardware, but good enough to give some idea of what they had stored in the RPV's film canisters.

At first there was only a view of the ocean's rolling surface, with white water left in the *Kiev*'s wake. Then the afterdeck of the ship came into view at the top of the screen. The angled flight deck was clear of aircraft, although what appeared to be the jet that had circled them earlier could be seen on the flight deck's forward elevator, disappearing into the hangar deck. The ship's radar and other electronics array could be seen only in limited detail, but the positions of the heavy guns and missile launchers stood out clearly. And one other thing stood out as well—despite the reduced speed of the video replay, the forms of sailors could be seen running to combat-ready positions at widely dispersed points across the *Kiev*'s expansive surface.

General Smalley studied the image and the running figures, an impish grin lighting his features. "I'd say we gave them something to think about, gentlemen."

As the carrier's image finally disappeared from the screen, the control officer asked, "Standard recovery procedure, sir?"

Smalley's grin lessened as he considered it. Standard recovery procedure for the RPV was to increase its altitude and let it go into an unpowered glide. The craft's flight control equipment would be switched to battery power, and its parachute would be deployed for a midair pickup by helicopter. Normally, that would be the best method. Now, however . . .

"Can't afford to," Smalley said flatly. "We can't launch the helicopter at the airship's present speed. We'd have to slow almost to a standstill, and that would cost us time."

Col. John Curtis knew what he was thinking, but doubts showed on his features. "We haven't really tested the in-flight recovery technique."

"I know, John. But we're going to have to try it sooner or later. Now's as good a time as any."

Curtis did not argue. He turned to the two controllers. "Set it up."

In moments, the RPV's guidance system was reprogrammed to return it to the area of the airship and continue past, then make a wide arc which would bring it around again, approaching the *Grand Eagle* from below and behind. A flyby directly beneath the great craft would involve some element of risk, to be sure, but theoretically the on-board computers would guide it with responses quicker and surer than human reflexes.

From the interior of the RPV bay two hydraulic arms extended down until they reached a full twenty feet beneath the airship's lower hull. A wide cross-bar joining the ends of the arms held a mass of woven nylon cables—pliant, yet strong as steel. At the touch of a control on the command deck, electromagnetically triggered clamps released and let the mass of cables open out into an interlocked grid which hung another thirty feet down. Tie cables attached to all four corners of the net ran loosely up to a connection with a heavy common cable indirectly linked to the bay's winch. In the center of the hanging grid, a large circle of metallic fabric marked the target area.

"Completing the turn, sir."

Smalley watched the double images with concern—one screen had been switched to the lower hull camera, which showed the approaching RPV and the waiting recovery net; the other, the main screen, showed the mammoth airship from the viewpoint of the RPV itself.

On board the RPV, the craft's visual circuits had already locked onto the target circle's bright metallic surface. As the robot craft rocketed nearer, the guidance system made minor adjustments to keep it from straying off the correct approach path.

"Engine throttled back," the control officer said aloud. "Ready to shut down."

"If you miss," Smalley said, "and you can't restart the turbojet, we won't have a second chance."

The control officer knew it, only too well. But for the moment, he was more concerned about the possibility that the RPV might accidentally be deflected up, against the airship's hull.

His hand stayed near the manual override controls. Even without jet power, the RPV's control surfaces could be operated. The officer watched as the indicator flashed, signaling turbojet shutdown. The RPV responded to the loss of power, adjusting its control surfaces to maintain altitude and direction.

Even as the speed diminished, it took only seconds for the small craft to pass beneath the hull's considerable length, hurtling on toward the grid of cables. The target circle grew large within the main monitor's screen, and then abruptly the image blurred as an explosive force caused the RPV to shudder.

Automatic systems had tracked the approach of the craft to the grid, and had at the precisely correct moment fired the RPV's forward thrust jet. The sudden, forward-directed energy cut the craft's momentum almost in half, so that at the moment of impact it was going only forty miles an hour relative to the airship, which was continuing at top speed.

The RPV hit the cable grid almost dead-center and became enveloped in it, tearing it free of the breakaway mountings which had held it. Cable played out with a screaming whine through heavy-duty nylon pulleys, easily at first, then more slowly as drag pressure was exerted through braking devices. The RPV's forward momentum carried it almost even with the nose of the airship before the force had been spent.

As the craft began to lose altitude and drop oceanward, the cable braking devices locked firm. The cable grid tightened around the now quiet RPV and it swung slowly, suspended beneath the *Grand Eagle*. In the next moment, the power winch began to reel in the expended cable with its dangling burden. The netted RPV moved steadily up toward the open bay.

On the command deck, General Smalley set his meerschaum firmly in the corner of his wide grin. "Got it! Good recovery, men . . . *very* good. Now let's get those film canisters out and processed, so we can have a good hard look at our competition. . . ."

At that moment on Tongareva it was 10:15, a full day after the jet crash, and peace had settled about the wreckage-dotted northern shore. The heart-stopping squall of the crash seemed a distant memory now in the quiet solitude of the remote island, and the steady sea breeze had lulled, creating a heightened sense of calm. Even the shattered airliner's fragments seemed oddly a part of the tropic landscape as they gleamed in the morning sunlight. But if there was now peace on Tongareva, it was a peace concealing a less obvious, lurking form of danger.

Carla Jennings knelt beside the cot in the small private room at the far end of the primitive medical research facility. The room had been set aside for the use of Mary Akaru, for brief afternoon naps and for sleeping over on the few occasions she did not journey back at day's end to her own house near Omoka village. But now her husband, James, lay on that cot, sometimes shaking it with the violence of the muscular spasms that racked his body. His features periodically contorted as the muscles of his face twitched involuntarily, and his entire torso glistened with sweat.

Carla moved the bell of the stethoscope to another spot on his chest and studied the sound of his labored breathing.

"What is it—what's wrong with my James?" Mary Akaru looked down at the twitching form of her husband with red-rimmed eyes, her expression grave. "Tell me please, Dr. Carla."

"How long has he been like this?"

"I don't know," Mary wailed. "Maybe half the night . . . maybe longer. James did not want to stay here last night. I don't know why, but he slept outside, away from the building. When I went out this morning, I could not find him. He had walked very far into the grove of coconut trees." Her words tumbled out rapidly, her tone a mixture of fear and perplexity. "He did not *know* me, did not know where he was or what he was doing. I helped him back. Can you do something? Can you make James well?"

Carla stuffed the stethoscope back into her bag. "I wish I knew what was wrong with him, Mary."

The Polynesian woman's features became taut and her eyes rolled in the direction of the lagoon. "It is *makutu*, bad magic," she said softly, "the death that came with the aeroplane—what they warned you about on the radio!"

Carla hesitated, frowning. "I'm not so sure. The symptoms aren't like radiation sickness. They're not like anything I've encountered before." She sighed, still feeling the exhausting effects of the day before. She had managed to get only a little rest during the long night, between checking Lorenz' condition and tending the other seriously injured survivors. And now this ... Mary Akaru and her husband were the closest to Carla of any of the islanders. And now, the first time they really needed her medical skill, she was stumped, not even knowing the cause of the strange illness.

She stood, eyes still on James's quaking form. Almost to herself she said, "I wish Paul were here. He might see something I'm overlooking."

"This man, this Dr. Brandon," Mary said. "You say you know him?"

"Yes ... very well." There was a momentary recollection of the doctor and the man; the warm touch of his hands upon her face and his determination to accept the position at Steinman-Keller the last time she had seen him. "I should make radio contact again, Mary. And maybe they can tell me something that will help James."

Carla left the small room and headed back through the building. She had to pass through the main room to reach the part of the facility where the radio was kept, and her movement attracted the curious gaze of several of the people there. From the other section came the moans and mutterings of some of the more seriously injured, delirious from the effects of the crash and the pain-numbing drugs that kept them barely comfortable. Carla had already made her rounds a half-dozen times during the course of the morning. A few of the survivors were still very close to death, and she could do nothing more for them until help arrived.

She reached the radio room and switched the equipment on. The power generator had been going almost continuously since the crash, supplying energy for the lights and some of the equipment. She should have had enough fuel to last until the next shipment arrived with the other supplies due next week. Now it would not last that long.

She triggered the microphone. "This is ZK1DL, Dr. Carla Jennings, calling USAF NA1 and Dr. Paul Brandon . . . Paul, are you there?" She waited a long moment, then called again. "Paul, this is Carla. Are you monitoring?"

There was another moment of silence, then a brief crackle of sound followed by an unfamiliar female voice. "We read you loud and clear, Dr. Jennings. Please stand by. . . ."

After several seconds the voice she had wanted to hear came over the receiver. "This is Paul, Carla. I've been waiting for you to make contact."

"This is the first chance I've had, Paul—there's been so much to do—so many people to look after." She hesitated a moment, trying to collect her thoughts. "Paul—*where* are you? I don't understand what's going on. Over."

There was a brief pause. "I guess I can tell you now," Brandon's voice answered finally. "I'm on an experimental aircraft, Carla. I can't tell you much about it, except that it has complete medical facilities and will be able to airlift everyone out and back to civilization. We should be there in another twenty hours . . . maybe sooner. And I should warn you, there's a ship also heading for the island. A Soviet aircraft carrier. We should reach you well before it does, but should anything go wrong, I'd rather you were prepared."

Carla frowned at the radio apparatus before her. "Prepared? Prepared for what? Warn me about what?"

"They're interested in more than a rescue mission. For that matter, so are we." Brandon's voice sounded strange. "They want Lorenz. A lot. For reasons I can't explain to you yet. How is he doing, Carla?"

"His condition is still stable. I just checked him a while ago. But he'll have to have help soon—more than I can give him."

"Yes, I understand. We're doing the best we can. Is Lorenz cyanotic at all?"

"His lips were blue initially . . . some loss of color in the fingertips. But that's been almost totally reduced since he's been on oxygen."

"Good. Just do what you can to keep him comfortable, and hope his system's strong enough."

Carla hesitated briefly, then transmitted again. "Paul,

there's another problem—a serious one. One of the islanders here, the husband of my assistant in fact, is violently ill. We're afraid, especially after the warning about the plane's cargo, that there's a connection."

"What are the symptoms?"

"They don't seem right for radiation sickness, Paul. Almost continuous muscle spasms and profuse sweating, some vomiting. But there's no fever ... no sign at all of bacterial infection. If anything, the man's temperature is a few degrees lower than normal." She paused. "Paul, I must know. Is there a danger of contamination to the others? Should I take any precautions?"

"I don't think so." There was the faint sound of another voice in the background, and Brandon relayed the question. "Was the man in the lagoon, near the area of the wreckage?"

"Yes, he was. God forgive me, but I sent him down there, to see if anyone was trapped in the wreckage. I didn't know it was a cargo hold then, or what was in it."

"It's all right, Carla. You couldn't be expected to know." There was a pause, stretching into a worrisome silence.

"Are you still there?" Carla transmitted.

"Yes—sorry," Brandon replied. "I was getting a second opinion on it. Do you have any atropine?"

"Yes. But I've been afraid to use it, not knowing exactly what I'm dealing with."

"Try it. I have it on good authority that the problem is a kind of chemical poisoning. There's some form of toxic substance in the lagoon as a result of the crash. It can be assimilated directly through the skin, and it attacks the nervous system. The fact that your man's still alive indicates he got a rather dilute dose of it. His system may be able to fight it off. But I still couldn't guess at his chances."

"I understand," Carla replied, grateful for some idea of what was wrong with the man, yet still wishing she had more optimistic news for Mary Akaru. The sight of the long cable connecting her radio gear with the electrocardiogram unit in the other room reminded her of another responsibility. "Paul—do you want another EKG on Lorenz?"

"Yes. It wouldn't hurt to compare it with the previous one. Do you have to set up the equipment?"

"No, I've kept it connected. I've had the unit on, monitoring his heart activity so that the alarm circuit could alert us if he should go into arrest. I'll start transmitting at once."

She flipped a switch on the small control unit which patched in the EKG signal through the shortwave transceiver. She left it on, broadcasting across the thousands of miles to Brandon and the others, for a full minute and a half. Finally turning it off, she transmitted, "Did you get it?"

"Yes," Brandon responded. "It looks about the same. There may be some deterioration, but it's hard to tell."

"Paul, is there anything else you can tell me about the . . . the matter of the pilot and copilot?"

There was a brief silence, then, "We haven't found out anything yet, but we're still checking. Remember what I told you last night—the problem may have been resolved in the crash. But stay cautious. And contact us when you can."

"All right. I'll call again a little later. Out for now." Carla switched off the equipment, but remained at the desk for a moment, her mind still on the sound of Paul Brandon's voice. He had seemed so businesslike, so routine. So . . . impersonal. Perhaps he was only trying not to alarm her, but if he truly had concern for her safety, he was certainly keeping it subdued.

She got up from the desk and turned for the door—then froze abruptly as she saw that someone was standing there, just within the doorway. It was the young man who had been so troublesome—Alex Copley. How long he had been standing there she could not guess.

"Is there something you wanted?" Carla asked flatly, wondering how much of the conversation he had overheard.

Copley's posture was tense and impatient. "Just when is that rescue party going to get here? They can't expect us to sit here on this stinking island forever!"

"Help is on the way. This isn't an easy place to reach quickly, by air or sea."

"Well, when, then?"

"By morning, probably."

"*Morning!*" Copley half shouted. "You mean tomorrow?"

"Yes."

He jerked his eyes heavenward, shaking his head, a loud hiss of breath escaping from his tensed lips. Turning abruptly, he strode out of the room, almost knocking over Jill Laudon in the hallway as he headed for the outside door.

As Carla reached the hall, the young blonde stewardess was looking over her shoulder at Copley's departure. As her eyes swung around to meet Carla's, she sighed, shaking her head slowly. "Maybe I shouldn't say it about a passenger, but that one's a jerk. A twenty-four-carat gold-plated jerk. Guys like that make my job a real pain in the neck."

"I can imagine." Her eyes searched Jill's features. "You were asleep earlier when I came by. How are you feeling this morning?"

"Better," the girl replied. "The rest helped a lot, even though I dreamed about the crash once, and woke up pretty shaky. I'm all right now, though."

"Good." Carla bent to examine Jill's leg, where the long line of coagulated blood had begun to narrow somewhat. "This is looking better. I really think it's going to heal up nicely."

"Are you sure?" Jill asked, looking down at the mark. "You wouldn't just say that—?"

Carla smiled reassuringly. "No—I mean it." She put an arm around the girl's shoulders and steered her back to the main room. She added, her tone more serious, "Now I've got to prepare an injection for James—he's quite ill. You can come along if you like. I may need help holding him steady."

Minutes later, in the small room on the building's far side, Jill looked on in mute horror as James Akaru still writhed upon the sweat-soaked cot. Carla plunged a hypodermic needle through the rubber stopper of a sealed vial of liquid and withdrew a carefully measured amount. She checked the level of fluid in the transparent cylinder and voided the air in the needle, then bent over James's trembling form.

"Hold him, please."

Mary Akaru held his shoulders down from behind while Jill threw her own slight weight into the task of pinning his arm in place. It was not easy—James Akaru's powerful body struggled with a will that was not his own.

Carla quickly disinfected the area above his elbow and made the injection, then taped a fresh piece of cotton over the puncture.

She straightened, signaling for the others to release their hold. Watching carefully, she waited for some sign that the drug would take effect.

Seconds went by, became minutes—long minutes of wondering if the medication was the proper one, if it had been administered soon enough to do any good—then, gradually, the muscular spasms began to lessen and subside. In another moment, Akaru's tense form relaxed, his breathing becoming slower and more regular.

Mary looked anxiously at her husband, then up at Carla. "Will he be all right now?"

"He'll be better, I think," Carla said. "We'll just have to wait and see if he's strong enough to fight off the poison in his system."

Jill's gaze fixed on her, a strange look. "Poison . . . ?"

"A toxic chemical of some kind, from the wreckage in the water."

"But not . . . radiation poisoning?"

"No, not according to the rescue team heading here," Carla said softly. "And we can be thankful for that at least." She watched James a moment longer, then turned and walked a few steps away. "I should have noticed sooner! He was behaving strangely last night, but I thought he was just nervous about what he had found—" She clipped off her words, conscious of Jill's presence.

The girl frowned. "What are you talking about?"

Carla hesitated. She was reluctant at first to explain, but she felt she could trust Jill. Besides, it might be better if the girl knew something of the danger they faced.

"It was about the pilot and copilot," she began carefully. "James showed me their bodies last night . . . what he had discovered. They didn't die in the crash, Jill. The men . . . they were both shot."

The girl's expression was a mixture of confusion and horror. "Shot?" she said, the word hollow and small within her mouth.

"Yes. We think there must have been a hijacker on the plane. For some reason, he killed them just before the plane crashed."

"And that's why we're here . . . instead of Hawaii?"

"Apparently so."

Jill gazed off into space, her eyes moist. "You know, I'd flown with those men before a few times. The copilot was a nice guy, really nice, but kind of fiesty. Not the type to take a hijacking passively. I remember, he said once that a flight crew should try to jump a hijacker, if the chance came, rather than risk the possibility he might kill everyone."

"That's not airline policy, is it?"

"No . . . but when something like that happens, policy

doesn't mean a lot." After a moment, her eyes widened as the awful implication of the news struck home. "Then the one who killed them—" She paused. "He's here, with us, on the island. . . ."

"Yes," Carla replied. "Unless he was killed in the crash, which is possible. And perhaps I shouldn't say *he*. I suppose it could have been a woman."

"Is there any way we can find out who it is?"

"I don't know. The authorities are investigating, but it may not be easy." She was silent a moment. "We can try to learn what we can about everyone, I suppose, but that could be risky. I didn't see a gun in the cockpit, so whoever killed the two men probably still has it."

"Yes," Jill agreed, but added, "unless the person fell into the ocean when the plane first broke up."

"As I said, it's possible. But I don't think we can afford to count on it." Carla turned and approached the still form of James Akaru, bringing her stethoscope to his chest. She listened, and was relieved at what she heard. James's breathing and heartbeat were slow and steady now. It would take time, but there was a good chance his system could resist the toxic substance which had very nearly killed him. His illness was doubly unfortunate, though. Carla would have felt better having the powerful islander well and in a position to help.

"Mary," she said finally, "stay with him . . . let me know if his condition changes any."

Mary Akaru nodded gratefully, close to her husband's cot. "Yes, Dr. Carla. Thank you. Thank you for helping James."

Carla smiled and patted Mary's arm, then left the small room and headed back to the main area.

She hesitated in the doorway for a moment. Not counting Jill, who had followed her back, there were only three of the crash survivors in the main room. Martin Sandersen, the man who remained mute, was still in one corner in almost the same position she had last seen him. He had spent hours staring off into empty space, and had shown no improvement since the crash. He would need psychiatric help—Carla was sure of it. By checking the passenger list the night before, she and Maggie Newcombe had determined that Sandersen's wife had indeed been among those killed in the crash. She wondered if he knew. If not, and the state he was in was only a result of the crash, then the tragic news might drive him closer to the edge.

Professor Arturo Maca was also in the room, reading a copy of *Scientific American* salvaged from the personal belongings he had carried on board the jet. Carla could not bring herself to consider this slightly built and scholarly-looking man as a possible hijacker. The third man was Father Brian Daniels. He had helped with some of the work this morning, but at the moment he was sitting alone, head bowed and hands interlocked, apparently in prayer. Carla had vague doubts about him, but nothing solid enough to justify considering him a hijacker and a murderer.

She heard sounds on the steps outside and looked around to see the businessman, Peter Benson, entering the building. The man seemed even more out of sorts than usual, and as he neared Carla and their eyes met, he cocked a thumb back over his shoulder. "That young man out there has a lot to learn about respect! It's impossible to get a decent answer out of him."

"You mean Mr. Copley? What's wrong now?"

Benson cooled a little. "Oh, nothing significant, I suppose. It's just that I saw him starting over toward the wreckage, to poke around I guess, and I asked him what he thought he was doing, considering the warning we'd been given." His eyebrows raised slightly. "The answer he gave me is not fit for your ears, Doctor, but I can assure you that if he were *my* son I'd either straighten him out or kick him out."

"Perhaps. Maybe we should feel sorry for his parents."

"I don't. You only get back what you put into something. They'd be wise to write him off as a bad investment."

Carla was not inclined to debate the aspects of child-raising. "You say he was heading for the plane?"

"Yes," Benson replied. "Maybe it's just as well . . . I don't suppose he can do any damage out there."

Carla leaned forward, trying to see Copley through the window. She still wondered if he had been listening in on her radio contact with Paul. Despite his unpleasant manners, it was hard to imagine him capable of murder. He was so young. . . .

"Miss Jennings—Doctor—" Benson interrupted her thoughts. "When are we going to be rescued? If I'm not back in Honolulu by the close of business tomorrow, I could lose a fortune! Why aren't the authorities here yet?"

"They're doing the best they can," Carla said, answering the question that had been asked of her too many times this morning. "Do you want to have a message relayed by radio to your company?"

"No." Benson continued to fume. "That would do no good. The signed contracts I'm carrying must be delivered to the distributors' representative in person, or else the deals may fall through."

"To be honest, I don't really think you'll be able to get back in time, Mr. Benson. But I'm sure, considering the circumstances, the people you're doing business with will—"

The abrupt and nerve-shattering sound of a high-pitched scream cut her words short. Carla whirled in the direction of the sound, facing the door that led to the back room, where the more seriously injured survivors were confined. For a moment she froze, but in the next instant her professional training overcame that fear and she ran for the door to the room.

She was met in the doorway by Maggie Newcombe. The senior stewardess was pale. Her voice quavered, and her Australian accent was more pronounced.

"You'd better come quick. It's one of the women." She led Carla back to the middle of the section, but did not need to point out who had screamed. The bandaged woman was hysterical, crying and gasping, eyes wide and full of horror. She was staring at the man in the improvised cot adjacent to hers—a man whose own staring eyes were fixed, unseeing, on the rough timbers of the roof above.

"Oh, no . . ." Carla's mouth went dry. One look at the man's still form, his slack jaw, told the story. He had sustained the most serious internal injuries during the crash and had been barely hanging on since. The struggle was over now. "When did this happen?"

"I don't know. Couldn't have been too long," Maggie replied, her voice still unsteady. "I was just in here, seeing if I could help anyone, when the woman screamed."

Maggie Newcombe watched in silence as Carla checked the man, methodically looking for signs of life, then finally pulled the sheet up over the man's head. Maggie put her hands on the hysterical woman's shoulders, trying to calm her.

"She'll need a sedative," Carla said wearily. "The medication I gave her earlier is wearing off now, and this happening so close to her was just too much." She moved quickly to the cabinet in which the medical stores were kept and withdrew a hypo and a vial of fluid. When she had finished with the injection, Carla said, "She'll rest easier now. She's not as badly hurt as some . . . she should be all right."

Carla stood in silence for a long moment, then sat down on the edge of the crate supporting the dead man's cot. She leaned forward suddenly, her eyes closing as moisture rose within them. The others had been bad enough, the ones already dead after the crash. This one had been different. Despite his slim chances, he had still been alive, and in Carla's care. The deaths of the others had been horrible, but this one brought a sense of defeat.

A firm hand lightly touched her shoulder and Carla jumped. Then she looked up, into Father Daniels' gaze.

"You did everything you could, you know," Daniels told her softly. His low voice was firm, yet soothing. "The weight of the living is so great, Doctor. Do not take up the burden of the dead as well."

The words very nearly triggered an onrush of tears, but she could not afford that kind of release. Not now, not here among the others. She was their only source of comfort and security after the trauma of the crash, and she was determined not to break down before them.

Carla got to her feet, blotting the moisture away from her eyes with the back of her hand. Her gaze drifted again to the still form beneath the sheet.

"It's impossible to practice medicine and not lose a patient sometimes," she said finally. "But that doesn't make it any easier."

"I know," Daniels said, his voice still low. "And you can't afford to stop caring. But don't let the burden of those that you can't help accumulate. That can be deadly. I know because I watched it destroy a friend of mine, a surgeon in the Air Force. He couldn't cope with the casualties, those that could be recovered from the planes that were shot down. He was dead, inside, a long time before the drinking killed him."

Carla looked at him suddenly with dawning realization. "The Air Force . . . that's why you know about planes, isn't it? You were in the Air Force—"

Daniels' look became more remote, as if he realized he said something he should not have mentioned. "Yes . . . I was. About nine years ago." He hesitated, with some effort overcoming his reluctance. "I was a pilot—what I had trained for, planned for all my life. I flew a lot of bombing and recon

114

missions in Vietnam—nothing extraordinarily harrowing, but after about a year of seeing the aftermath of war I didn't really care whether our side was right or not. The amount of human misery was the same, regardless." He paused again, briefly, remembering. "They let me resign my commission. I returned to the States and more or less wasted a year of my life going nowhere. The church was the only thing that kept me from ending up like my friend. When I accepted the call to the ministry, it was really a second chance for me."

"And you volunteered for a missionary post in Southeast Asia?"

"Yes. I *care* about the people there. And I guess I wanted to try to balance things out."

Carla studied his face for a long moment. "I guess I can understand that." Her eyes turned away from his. "Maybe better than you realize."

When she looked at him again, his lips were moving in a silent prayer as he stood at the foot of the dead man's cot. After a long moment Daniels raised his head. "He'll have to be taken out."

"Yes. It should be done now."

"I don't mind doing it, if I can get some help."

"Of course," Carla replied. "You know where the storage building is?"

Daniels nodded. Carla looked toward the door, where Jill Laudon and Peter Benson stood looking in. Both were grimly silent.

"Mr. Benson," Carla called out, "could you give us a hand?"

The businessman hesitated only a moment, then came forward. At Carla's direction, he moved to one end of the covered stretcher. With Daniels at the other end, the stretcher was lifted from the crates which had supported it and carefully moved into the aisle and out of the room.

Carla watched as the men left, grateful for their help. The more she came to know these people, these strangers thrust into her life, the harder it was to believe that any of them could be capable of murder. The more she thought about it, the more she doubted that the hijacker had survived the crash.

Her prime suspects thus far had been Daniels and young Copley. Daniels' knowledge about aircraft seemed satisfactorily explained now, and even Copley at his worst still seemed more the spoiled brat than the cold-blooded killer. Besides, she was certain Copley had been in the rear of the crashed jet when she had first approached, and almost equally certain about Daniels. It seemed next to impossible that anyone could be in the cockpit one moment, killing the pilot and copilot, and then in the moments before the crash return to his seat unnoticed. Especially with the cargo compartment in between.

There had been a hijacker—that could not be doubted. But of the surviving passengers there was simply no one who fit the part. Paranoia would do no one any good, least of all Carla. Her concentration was more urgently needed by the injured. And one among them, especially.

Carla headed back toward the head of the row of cots, to the corner where one cot had been curtained off with sheets. A separate room would have been better for Stefan Lorenz, but she had wanted to keep all the injured close together.

She pulled back the edge of one sheet and entered the sheltered corner. Lorenz was asleep, still under the influence of the medication and his weakened condition, and had not heard the commotion of a few minutes ago. It was just as well, Carla thought, for excitement was one thing Lorenz did not need.

Carla checked his pulse and breathing. They were about the same, and if they had not improved, at least they had not worsened appreciably. She checked the connections to the oxygen tank and made sure the tubing had not become entangled. Everything seemed in order.

She was about to leave when her foot struck an object beneath Lorenz' cot, something nearly hidden by the drooping edge of the sheet, which was too wide for the narrow cot. Carla bent down and felt for the object. Her hand grasped the handle of a case of some kind, and when she raised the sheet's edge for a better view, she recognized the object as the attaché case brought out of the wreckage by Lorenz.

But something was wrong—drastically wrong. The attaché case had been closed before, and apparently locked. Now it was sitting open beneath the cot, its latches sprung and bent out of shape. The contents of the case were in a state of complete disarray, half spilled out onto the floor. Someone had gone through the contents hastily, searching. And it had happened within the last hour.

Carla felt a chill along her spine as she recalled Paul Brandon's warning about Lorenz and the Soviet ship on its way.

For the ransacked case proved one thing beyond any further doubt—proved it with frightening clarity.

The mysterious hijacker was not dead.

Paul Brandon stood on the command deck of the *Grand Eagle,* next to Haddock and General Smalley, waiting impatiently as the two men studied an array of reconnaissance photos spread across the top of the chart table. It was noon now in this part of the Pacific, and the immense airship had not only closed the gap between the *Kiev* and itself, it had passed the Soviet aircraft carrier and was leading it by a distance of several miles, increasing the lead with each passing minute. They were flying on a steady course roughly twenty-five miles to the *Kiev*'s port side, a precaution ordered by Smalley after intelligence information relayed from Washington confirmed the fact that the carrier's Goblet missiles had a slant range of twenty miles.

Some of the enlargements showed the *Kiev*'s systems and weaponry in incredible detail, and Brandon could not help but marvel at the recon RPV's photographic system. One greatly enlarged shot was clear enough to make out the rank and insignia of several sailors on the ship's deck.

"They're going to love these in Washington," General Smalley said with a broad smile. "Pity their planes aren't on deck."

Haddock raised an eyebrow. "I think we can be glad they aren't."

Brandon could wait no longer. For the past hour his mind had been troubled by certain questions, questions in need of answers.

"Mr. Haddock," he said, his voice low but imperative. "I don't think you've leveled with me completely. There are still things that just don't add up."

Haddock's reply was also kept low. "If you're talking about the matter of the radiation warning, I've already explained the need for the cover story—"

"It's not just that. There's more." Brandon paused, his eyes hard and searching. "This toxic chemical the jet was carrying, with which you seem so familiar—what is it? What's its connection with Lorenz?"

"It's nothing for you to be concerned about—"

"It's nearly killed a man! And if it's a danger to the

others on that island, then it certainly *is* a cause for concern."

Haddock studied him for a long moment, seeming to weigh the matter, and also seeming to evaluate Brandon's resolve. "All right. I suppose it will do no harm." He sighed. "The chemical is actually an advanced and highly exotic solid fuel, to be used as a propellent in missiles and spacecraft. Lorenz developed it, for use in a new rocket engine of his own design. It's incredibly efficient—better than anything currently in use on either side, or anything even in the planning stages. Lorenz managed to smuggle several canisters of the fuel out of Czechoslovakia—all that he had produced."

Brandon hesitated. "And that's why the Russians are interested?"

"Yes . . . they want Lorenz, the fuel, and the prototype engine he designed, which was also in the jet's cargo hold. But you needn't worry about further contact with the chemical. The only contact so far occurred before the warning reached them."

"A misleading warning—"

"But an *effective* one, for our needs," Haddock said flatly. "Don't chastise us for being devious, Doctor. We didn't invent the ground rules."

Brandon was silent a moment, framing his words carefully. "There is one other thing," he said finally. "It's occurred to me, later than I like to admit, that the fact that I know the doctor on Tongareva is more than mere coincidence. Am I right?"

Haddock diverted his eyes. "There was . . . some element of choice."

"What do you mean, choice?"

"I mean," Haddock said irritably, "that you were not the only doctor contacted when the initial plans for the defection were formulated." He hesitated, studying Brandon's features. "We had to—the matter was too important to allow no backup. Two other cardiovascular specialists were approached, in the same way we approached you last month. We preferred your capabilities from the start. And when we learned that Dr. Jennings was on the island, the choice was made for us. You've worked together, you know each other, there was every reason to believe you'd work well as a team on this mission."

Brandon studied him, trying to gauge the intent of Haddock's explanation as well as the words that formed it. "Are you sure that's the only reason? Are you sure you weren't thinking of it as insurance—using my friendship and concern for Carla as a way to ensure my continued cooperation?"

Haddock was silent, offering no answer. His features were firm and expressionless, an unyielding mask as impenetrable as stone. And yet in that silence, there was an answer of sorts.

From behind them, Colonel Curtis called out. "General!"

Smalley turned, his movement breaking the tension between Brandon and Haddock. "Yes, John?"

"Sir, radar indicates an aircraft has taken off from the *Kiev*'s deck."

Smalley moved to a position alongside Curtis, behind the radar systems tech sergeant. The two officers watched the glowing screen.

"One of their VTOL jets?" Smalley inquired.

Curtis quickly scanned the readouts from the tracking indicators and infrared sensors. "Could be a jet. Hard to tell, though—the infrared signature could also be that of one of their turbine helicopters. Maneuvering doesn't tell us much yet, but from the speed I'd say it's most likely a copter."

They continued to watch the complex display screens of the radar and allied sensor equipment as the minutes passed. As the unknown craft drew near, Smalley and Curtis returned to the forward area for a look at the television monitors. Smalley keyed up a telephoto view from one of the cameras on the airship's starboard side. The image flipped once, then sharpened into a clear shot of the Soviet aircraft.

"You're right, it's a Hormone A," Smalley confirmed, using the NATO code designation for the helicopter, a Kamov Ka-25.

It was a medium-sized antisubmarine helicopter of the Soviet Naval Air Force, fat and stubby in its appearance, with large, double contra-rotating blades above and no tail rotor. Landing gear was fixed, extending well out from the craft's sides, with inflatable pontoons surrounding the wheels. The large and bulbous radome extending beneath the nose gave the odd appearance of a chin, jutting out from a round, staring face.

"You see any weapons systems on that thing?" Smalley asked.

Curtis leaned over to study the image. "No, sir—no

air-to-air weapons pods visible. I think all they're designed to carry are torpedos for use against subs."

"So I've heard."

"And yet, there seems little reason for them to come up just to look us over again."

"Maybe." Smalley chewed on his pipe. "And maybe one of their senior officers wanted a closer look. I know *I* would."

The helicopter drew nearer, staying even with the massive airship. It was less than 150 yards away, keeping pace but doing nothing at all alarming.

Haddock kept a watchful eye on the television monitor. "I hope we can avoid any kind of . . . misunderstanding. We don't need any riled feelings that will further complicate things."

"I understand State's position," Smalley acknowledged. "I just hope they understand the situation out here."

Curtis asked, "Evasive action, sir?"

"No, hold true to course," Smalley said. "They're not going to chase us off that easily."

The Soviet helicopter drifted back, slowly losing its lead, passing gradually along the length of the airship but still keeping at least minimal distance. It began to seem that it would merely conclude its reconnaissance and swing back to the deck of the *Kiev*. But when it reached a position near the tail of the great airship, it did not drift further.

In the next instant its purpose became known—but *too late*. Although it did not show up clearly on the television monitors, the entry door on the cabin's port side slid back swiftly. A marksman of the *Kiev*'s Naval Infantry unit positioned himself behind a large-caliber machine gun on a jury-rigged mount and took dead aim at the huge double propellers at the *Grand Eagle*'s stern. With the blades of one rotor in his sights the man triggered the weapon, sending a long burst of explosive rounds directly at them.

The first few rounds missed, leading their target by too great a margin. But the next ones hit their mark, chewing through two of the blades just as the marksman completed his abrupt pass.

Fragmenting, the huge rotor lost two of its blade sections, the severed ends thrown violently out to the sides before starting their tumbling drop to the sea below.

The Soviet helicopter swung away at a dangerous angle,

speeding off even as alarm systems on the *Grand Eagle*'s command deck erupted into life. Shrill klaxons blared their warning throughout the great ship, light panels in every corridor and compartment flashing two words imperatively, again and again—

RED ALERT, RED ALERT, RED ALERT . . .

CHAPTER FIVE

The pale blue government car sped along Arlington Memorial Bridge, barely keeping within the posted speed limit. Traffic was light, as it generally was on Sunday afternoon.

Seated in the back, Gen. Eldridge Adamson checked his watch. It was 4:15, only scant minutes after the message had come into the Pentagon's air force communications center, relayed through radio and ground systems set up at the beginning of the mission. Adamson had informed the President at once upon decoding the message, and was even now heading for the White House.

In the briefcase on his lap were copies of that decoded message. Less than a full page of information, brief and sketchy . . . alarming in its lack of details.

Adamson had already set up the machinery for putting air bases in the Hawaiian Islands and other locations on standby alert. For the moment, nothing more than that could be done without President Evans' approval.

Within minutes the car reached East Executive Avenue, approaching the White House. Adamson waited anxiously as the vehicle pulled to a stop, still gripping the briefcase in his lap. As he emerged from the car, he saw a second government limousine pull in next to his.

The doors on the second car swung open smoothly and Secretary of Defense Lewis Scoville emerged, bundled in a topcoat, his bald head bare. He was followed out by Mitchell Hoyt, the CIA director. Martin Pretori, Under Secretary of State, came around from the other side of the car. The three men joined Adamson as he headed for the Executive Wing, walking quickly in a loose-knit formation.

Nearest to Adamson, Scoville said, "We thought we'd better avoid having a large group of cars arrive here at the same time. I understand that Matheson and the admiral are already here."

"Good," Adamson replied. "I don't think we'll have any trouble getting a consensus."

Scoville's gaze was straight ahead, his look grim. "I hope you're right."

The Cabinet Room looked somewhat different now. Afternoon sunlight was slanting in through the arched windows which faced the rose garden, casting a more mellow glow upon the room's interior. The maps and special charts were still there on their easels from the midnight meeting just sixteen hours earlier. Admiral Hadley was waiting, as was the President's adviser on Russian affairs, Edgar Matheson. Several aides were arriving from other parts of the building, checking everything and bringing in new data. The only noticeable exception from the night before was the absence of Evans himself.

A few minutes elapsed and Scoville began to look about expectantly. Under his breath, he said to Adamson, "Where *is* the President?"

"It can't take long," the air force officer said. "When I called from the Pentagon, he was in his office, talking with someone, I think."

Adamson put his briefcase on the long oval table in the center of the room and opened it. He removed the copies of the emergency message received from the *Grand Eagle* and spread them around at key points along the table's edge. Then he waited, as impatient as the others.

In the next moment, William Evans appeared, striding into the room with the same calm reserve that had always characterized him. His look was sober as he nodded to the others. This time there were no casual greetings, no exchanges of cordialities.

Evans went directly to his place at the table, but remained standing. Picking up the copy of the emergency message, he read it over carefully, then looked to General Adamson.

"This is all?" he asked, concern deeply etched upon his tired features. "No real idea of the extent of the damage—nothing about casualties or anything?"

"We're still waiting for further word, sir. I've arranged for any follow-up messages to be transmitted directly to the White House communications center." Adamson paused. "All we can be certain is that the Russians have made an unprovoked attack on the *Grand Eagle*. It's stopped dead in the air, and will soon be outdistanced by the *Kiev*."

Evans looked over the message once more, then threw it down on the tabletop. "This is exactly what I wanted to avoid!"

Secretary of Defense Lewis Scoville nodded solicitously. "The question is now, sir—what are we going to do about it?"

Admiral Jonathan Hadley was quick to respond. "They've already made the first move, Mr. President—we can't be accused of precipitating an action. The Russians have already assumed that responsibility."

Evans looked at the naval officer long and hard. "And your recommendation is—?"

"The ships we had shadowing the *Kiev*," Hadley explained. "Our carrier-based aircraft are still within range—they could reach the Soviet vessel in thirty to forty minutes. They could drop charges that would stop the *Kiev* cold."

"And then what?" Evans demanded. "The Soviets would feel compelled to divert their other surface vessels to the area to support the *Kiev*."

"We could match them, sir," Hadley said calmly. "Ship for ship, if need be."

"And how far would it go? Are we talking about World War III, gentlemen?"

Scoville let an interval of silence go by before replying, "Mr. President, we *do* have to do something."

"Yes, of course," Evans relented a degree. "But I want to remind you all that our choice of action is highly critical." He thought for a moment, then pulled out his chair and sat down, motioning for the others to follow suit. He looked to Adamson, chairman of the Joint Chiefs of Staff. "General, what's your opinion?"

"As far as any direct action against the *Kiev*, sir, the aircraft and weapons systems on board the *Grand Eagle* are a good deal closer than the admiral's ships."

Evans shook his head. "And using them against the *Kiev* could be just as deadly a mistake. No—the airship can and must defend itself from here on out, but I will *not* have it launching an offensive attack against Soviet forces."

Evans was silent a long moment, his keen eyes searching through the various briefing papers and charts. Finally, he looked up at Under Secretary of State Pretori. "Martin, I want you to get the Soviet ambassador on the line . . . immediately."

"Yes, sir." Pretori left his seat and headed for the phone. The switchboard would connect a special line to the Soviet Embassy at 1125 Sixteenth Street, NW.

Even as Pretori began speaking on the phone, an aide entered the room and approached Mitchell Hoyt. Getting his attention, the man handed Hoyt a sealed folder, then departed.

The taciturn director of Central Intelligence broke the seal on the document and opened it. He read through it quickly, a reflective frown forming upon his features.

"Peculiar," he said, almost to himself. Then, looking up at the others, seeing their attention focused on him, he said, "I've just received word from one of my operatives in Tahiti. He reported on something strange—it may have nothing to do with this matter in the Pacific, and then again, it may explain a great deal."

"What is it?" Evans asked.

Hoyt folded the document and, almost reluctantly, extended it to Evans. "It seems the police in Tahiti have something of a mystery on their hands. Five of their officers, attached to airport security duty in Papeete, disappeared yesterday, shortly before the time of the crash on Tongareva. They've been found, in a locked storeroom at the airport."

Scoville asked, "Alive?"

"Yes, but bound and gagged, and rendered practically comatose by the use of some drug." Hoyt paused. "There are two things of interest—the first, all five men had been stripped of their police uniforms. Everything but their underwear and shoes. The second—and this is of particular interest to us—is the fact that all five were rendered unconscious by use of the same drug, by injection."

Evans looked up from the report. "How is that possible?"

Hoyt shifted in his seat. "There is a device, in use by the Soviet KGB—an air-pressure gun small enough to be concealed in the hand. It can fire any chemical, poison, drug, what have you, directly through the skin, even through clothing. It is not the kind of device an ordinary criminal would have or use."

Evans considered it. "So presuming that Russian agents were involved—why? What connection would it have?"

"Maybe none," Hoyt said, getting up from his seat and moving to the large map of the Pacific that stood along the near wall, blocking the middle section of bookshelves. Picking up a long straightedge and a marking pencil, Hoyt carefully drew a line upon the plastic-coated surface of the map, extending from Wake Island all the way down in a diagonal path to Tahiti. When he had finished, he stood back so that the others could see. "You'll notice," Hoyt said simply, "that Tongareva falls almost precisely on the line, roughly six hundred miles short of Tahiti."

There was a moment of silence, then Evans said, "The plane—it was being taken to *Tahiti*, then?"

"It's a strong possibility, Mr. President. We know now that there was a hijacker on board the jet, presumably a Soviet agent, and it makes sense that if they had a plan to prevent Lorenz' defection, they would try to divert him to a more or less neutral country. French Polynesia would fit their requirements."

"So then," Evans reasoned it out, "all they had to do was meet the plane when it landed, in the guise of local police, and take the so-called hijacker into custody. And of course, detain Lorenz and his equipment."

Hoyt nodded, a certain look of admiration on his features. "It probably would have worked, too. Lorenz could have been quietly returned to Czechoslovakia, for 'reasons of health,' and the local authorities would have been left wondering what happened to both the hijacker and the police impersonators. But of course, the plane never reached Tahiti. Why not, we can only guess."

From the door came a voice, interrupting further discussion on the matter. "General—"

One of Adamson's aides sought his attention, then entered quickly. "Sir, we've received that update you wanted. It's been decoded and checked."

"Thank you." Adamson took the report and dismissed the man, then began reading through the new information. Finally, he faced the President and the others. "It may not be quite as bad as we feared—damage is limited to the propellers at the rear of the craft. There are no casualties, and for the moment at least, no indication that the Russians intend any further aggressive action."

"Thank God for that," Evans said softly. "Apparently they just wanted us out of the race."

"We're not really out of it," Adamson corrected.

"Repairs will be under way shortly, and it's possible that the *Grand Eagle* will be able to continue its mission within two hours."

"In that time," Admiral Hadley spoke up suddenly, "the *Kiev* will have gained an extra eighty miles, and retaken the lead."

Adamson reminded him, "It's a lead we can recover."

"I still think we need a better balance of power out there—something potent enough to make the Russians think twice about risking another contact like that."

"Admiral," Adamson said with a tinge of irritation, "the *Grand Eagle* has what it takes to send the *Kiev* to the bottom, if necessary. It's not one of the Navy's World War II recon blimps. It's a fully armed, fully operational airship."

"I suggest you try to convince the Russians of that."

"That's enough," Evans said shortly. At his words and stern look, the two officers ceased their debate, falling silent. "The problem is—how do we go about achieving our goal *without* starting an international conflict entirely out of proportion to the benefits we might hope to gain?" He paused a moment, looking toward the Under Secretary of State, who was still on the phone. "Martin—what's happening with that call?"

Pretori gestured for another moment's patience, the phone handset still clamped tightly to his ear. Finally, after several long moments, Pretori made a reply and hung up the phone. With a deeply disturbed expression, he returned to the table and the others who were anxious for an explanation.

"What's the problem?" Evans asked.

"I think they're going to be difficult, sir," Pretori replied. "I couldn't speak to the ambassador himself—he's *allegedly* tied up with something critical at the moment, and is not available for comment."

"I'll bet!" Scoville huffed.

Pretori continued. "I was able to speak with one of his aides, though. And they're playing it very cool—they claim to have no knowledge of any incident in the Pacific. According to them, the *Kiev* is only on maneuvers, and they know nothing at all about the airship."

"They're lying, of course," Mitchell Hoyt commented. "We already have proof that the Soviets have contacted the government of New Zealand, telling them the *Kiev* is involved in a rescue attempt."

"And they may well end up changing their story to us,"

Pretori said with a shrug. "I had the feeling that the man I spoke to was reading from a rather hastily prepared statement given him by someone else . . . perhaps even the ambassador."

Evans gave it thought, finally turning to Edgar Matheson, who had been silent thus far. Looking like a retired business executive, with thinning gray hair and pale, spotty complexion, Matheson had spent five years in Moscow as American ambassador and was considered one of the foremost authorities on Soviet policy.

"Edgar—what do you make of this?" Evans asked. "Do they really think they can simply bluff their way through this matter?"

Matheson kept his relaxed pose, his clear eyes focused not on the President but rather on the tabletop before him. He took a deep breath before he spoke. "I . . . I believe that's only a staying move—something to give them time to think. And we should consider the possibility that there's been some kind of, ah, communications foul-up—that the officers of the *Kiev* have misunderstood their authority to act."

Lewis Scoville fumed with ill-concealed anger. "Mr. President, I think they know *exactly* what they're doing, and I think Moscow does as well. And I also think that if we don't take appropriate steps *now,* they will act again to threaten the safety of the airship and its crew. And next time, the consequences may well be worse."

"I tend to agree, sir," Admiral Hadley said firmly.

Adamson nodded also, less adamantly, but with no less concern. Only Martin Pretori and Edgar Matheson seemed reluctant to follow the others in their view.

William Evans studied the faces of the men around him, weighing his own thoughts carefully. Finally, he said. "No—we will not engage in open warfare. I can't allow that. The *Grand Eagle* shall have the authority to protect itself with whatever means are *necessary*—and General Adamson, I want you to issue orders to that extent—but I will not sanction offensive action directed against the *Kiev*. That is only acceptable as the very last resort, should it be necessary to protect the crew of the airship. And if it should come to that, gentlemen," Evans added soberly, "then we had better be prepared for the worst. . . ."

At that moment, high over the vast Pacific, the nuclear airship

Grand Eagle hung motionless in the air, a wounded giant with one of its great double propellers mangled beyond use. The enormous airship was drifting very slowly but steadily off course, and there was only the sound of the wind to break the silence that engulfed it.

On the command deck, there was a flurry of activity. Crew members continued to check and double-check emergency evacuation equipment and procedures. If for any reason it should become necessary to abandon the *Grand Eagle,* there were parachutes and paragliders stowed in the compartment surrounding the lower emergency hatch, directly below the command deck's forward section. Inflatable life rafts were there also, for ditching at sea, and they were equipped with provisions and radio beacons.

General Smalley stood before the main television monitors at the front of the command deck's control center, surveying the damage to the propeller on one of the screens. The camera that afforded the view was mounted just behind the top fin of the immense craft, its lens peering through a clear blister. Next to Smalley stood Colonel Curtis and Senior Flight Officer Stewart Gardner.

The image on the screen showed the damage clearly. The first propeller of the double set was the one that had been hit. Each normally had three blades radiating out from its hub, but the first now was missing two, with only the shattered stubs remaining.

"I know we'd planned for this possibility," Smalley was saying, "but if either of you have any doubts that we can manage it, now's the time to speak up."

Curtis considered it briefly, eyes still on the television image. "No, sir—I think we can do it. Under the present circumstances, it's going to be risky. But I don't think we have any choice."

"All right," Smalley agreed. "Then we'd best get started."

"Yes, sir. I've already alerted the repair crew. They're on their way now."

As Curtis made a final check on equipment status, Stewart Gardner conferred briefly with his two junior officers at the helm of the great airship, then turned and started out of the control center. As he reached the outer hall, heading for the elevator, S/Sgt. Elizabeth Jordan caught up with him.

"Colonel—"

Gardner turned and faced her. "Yes, Beth?"

For a moment the young woman looked at Gardner's expressionless features, afraid to speak. Then finally, she said, "Do you have to go up in the helicopter?"

"Yes, of course. Look, the general needs Colonel Curtis here with him. If those Russians should try anything else, we need the top command officers right here on deck. Besides, as long as we're stalled, there's not much I can do at the helm. Out there, I can at least see what has to be done. Supervising the repair is my responsibility."

"I know, but . . ." She hesitated. "It's just that I know the risk involved—working so close to the ship. If a gust of wind should blow the helicopter against the top fin—"

"That shouldn't happen . . . the air currents should be pretty steady."

As he started to turn again, Elizabeth Jordan reached out and touched his arm. He looked at her hand upon his sleeve, and for a brief instant, there was the recollection of his wife's hand, touching him that way. It was a memory that hurt.

"What is it, Beth?"

"I . . . Colonel . . ." she said, suddenly uncertain of herself, but having to try. "Stewart—be careful."

She had never called him by his first name before, and he was not prepared for the note of personal concern in her voice. "Of course I'll be careful. I care too much about this ship to foul things up."

"I just . . . I just wish you'd care more about yourself," she said softly, abruptly turning away from him and heading quickly back down the hall to the control center.

Gardner hurried on into the elevator and started down to Deck C. He had an uncomfortable feeling there was something he should have said to reassure her, but he had no idea what it might have been. The feeling still nagged at him as he reached Deck C, but he forced it from his mind.

He quickly passed between the two storage bays and entered the corridor stretching back toward the middle of the airship, trotting along its 270-foot length. The car of the main elevator was waiting, and he took it up to the top of the hull, emerging in the upper missile room. From there it was only a short way to the helicopter hangar.

As he entered that chamber, he saw four of the ship's

flight mechanics busily unloading cables and releasing two replacement rotor blades from their mountings along the hangar wall. The propeller blades were made of a tough, reinforced honeycomb material, just as the helicopter's own blades were, but despite their relatively light weight, it still took three of the mechanics working together with a pneumatic lift to position the blades where the cables could be attached.

Gardner headed for the helicopter pilot and copilot, who were already suited up and putting on their flight helmets. Approaching Captain Lee, he said, "Have you got the procedure down?"

"Yes, sir, by the book," Lee replied, making a final adjustment on his flight uniform. "But to tell the truth, I feel a lot better in my jet than I feel in that whirlybird."

"I know," Gardner said. "But you knew the Harrier crew would have to double as helicopter jockeys when you signed up for this project."

"No complaints, sir," Lee said with the trace of a grin.

The chief mechanic approached, examining the fastenings on a special harness. Concern etched his rough-hewn features.

"I sure hope whoever designed this thing knew what he was doing," the man said.

"Have you checked the cables?" Gardner asked.

"Yes, sir. First thing."

"All right—let's get it going."

Gardner quickly stepped up into the Bell UH-1N helicopter and fastened a lightweight harness around his waist, one secured to the inner framework of the ship. Picking up a spare flight helmet, he put it on and adjusted the position of the microphone before his lips.

He gave a signal to one of the flight mechanics, and the man activated the hangar doors above, watching as the large panels rolled aside along their channels. Raw daylight poured in, for the sun was nearly directly overhead.

In the next instant, the lift platform that supported the helicopter started up, raising the small craft to a position above the airship's outer surface. As soon as it was locked into position, the pilot released the rotor lock and started the engines.

The clamps that held the craft tight to the lift platform were not released until the rotor was whirling at just above idle speed and everything seemed stable. Then with a loud snap the clamps freed their grip and the helicopter hovered above the open hangar, shifting slightly as the pilot readjusted for the air currents playing across the top of the airship.

Cables dangled down into the hangar's interior, and one of them was fastened to the first replacement propeller blade, fixed at its center of gravity with a special bracket which gripped the blade's edges. The second cable reached down to the harness worn by the chief mechanic, and as Gardner waved a signal at him, the man took up a position near one end of the thirty-foot-long blade.

It was an awkward and risky procedure, but the only one found to work well in static tests on the surface of the desert at Edwards Air Force Base. To keep the long rotor blade from turning uncontrollably as it was being moved, the mechanic had to grip with his arms and legs the end that was to be connected to the propeller hub. With his own cable in effect steadying the blade, he could guide it into position.

Beginning the ascent with the utmost care, the pilot brought his helicopter higher, raising the dangling blade and mechanic slowly out of the hanger. A radio-equipped flight helmet protected the mechanic's head from the force of the downdraft and put him in contact with the helicopter crew. On the back of his harness was a tank of compressed air, with a hose leading to a pneumatic wrench hooked to his belt. As the helicopter drifted back, past the brilliant reflections from the *Grand Eagle*'s upper surface, the waters of the blue Pacific came into view, nearly a mile below.

"Steady as she goes, sir," the mechanic's voice rasped in Gardner's helmet. "It's a long drop."

Swinging there at the end of the cable, wind whistling past his helmet and dazzling sunlight barely suppressed by his visor, the mechanic fought to keep the end of the blade within his grip. Above him, the helicopter appeared to be dangerously close to the airship's massive top fin. Even a brief contact with the spinning rotor blades could send the helicopter plummeting down to the sea below.

Above him, Gardner leaned partway out the open door of the craft, peering down at the dangling man. Moving slowly toward the pointed end of the airship, the blade was nearly in position next to the first propeller hub. The remaining intact blade had ended up pointing down, so fortunately the shattered sections were in a relatively good position for the approach.

But for some reason, the pilot appeared to be having trouble keeping the craft in position above the hub. Gardner spoke into his helmet mike.

"What's the problem—can't you keep it steady?"

The pilot's voice came back, "It's hard, sir. The airship is drifting quite a bit. The wind isn't affecting us as much, and it's going to be tricky staying with it."

"We're going to have to."

"I know, sir." There was a slight pause. "It would be easier if we were both heading into the wind."

Gardner considered it, estimating the airship's capabilities in its current state, virtually without forward propulsion power. Or was it?

Gardner switched to the main ship's channel and contacted the commo console. Elizabeth Jordan's voice answered.

"Beth—switch me through to the helm, quickly!"

"Yes, sir." There was a certain flatness to her voice, and Gardner wondered briefly if he'd said or done anything to hurt her feelings. The thought vanished as one of his junior officers replied.

"Here, sir."

"I want you to use the thrusters to head the ship into the wind—clear it with the general."

"At once, sir."

There was a brief pause, then the man's voice returned. "We have the general's go-ahead. Beginning forty-five-degree turn to the west, commencing in fifteen seconds."

Gardner switched back to the helicopter's commo channel. "Captain, take us up, clear of the tail. The ship's turning. Follow it around into the wind, and for our mechanic's sake, keep it *steady*."

"Will do, sir."

Gardner braced himself as the helicopter rose slightly, moving clear of the aft end of the great airship. No sooner had they reached a safe position than the turbo thrusters located at the top and bottom of the airship's ends revved up. The ones near the nose directed their force to the port side, the rear thrusters to the starboard side. Gradually, the immense craft began to turn, pivoting as it slowly swung around into the wind. But even with its reduced profile, there was still too much drift.

Gardner said to the pilot, "Get us back in position." He

switched back to the ship's channel. "Helm—is General Smalley near your console?"

"Right here, sir. Putting him on."

Smalley's easily identifiable drawl came through his helmet. "What is it, Gardner?"

"Sir, I'd like to start the secondary turbines, the ones that suck in the boundary layer air. I think the air being expelled through the vents at the rear might exert enough force to keep the ship from drifting."

There was silence for a moment. "It might work. But there's going to be some turbulence back there if we do."

"Most of it will be under the stern, away from us."

"All right. It's worth a try."

Gardner instructed the junior officers at the helm to key the control circuits for separate operation of the secondary turbines, then waited for those orders to take effect.

It did not take long. With a faintly audible whine, the two smaller turbines, each with a thousand horsepower, started up, forcing air pulled in through the outer surface of the hull out from vents just beneath the horizontal fins. But as their power increased, an unexpected side effect placed them in sudden danger.

The force of the expelled air moving across the airship's propellers started them turning, like a breeze across the blades of a fan. The hub only turned a partial revolution before locking again, but in that turn one blade of the second propeller sliced dangerously close to the dangling mechanic, barely brushing the end of the replacement rotor.

Gardner fairly yelled into his microphone—"Freeze that turbine! I don't want those propellers spinning on us back here!"

"Working on it, sir," his junior officer reported back. "There's a maintenance technician in the aft end, checking for damage."

"Well, tell him to secure the locking brakes, manually, if necessary. But rotate the hub electrically first, to bring the two damaged blades up into position again."

"Roger."

They waited, high above the wind-tossed waves, until the propeller hubs had been returned to the proper position. Once they had, and Gardner had been assured the turbine was locked, he directed the helicopter pilot to move in slowly, using the copter like a flying crane to lower the new blade into place.

Reaching out to steady himself as the propeller hub drew near, the suspended mechanic worked himself into a position where he could reach the mounting brackets that held the old, damaged blade section secure. The brackets themselves were nearly as large as a man's torso. They were fastened permanently to the hub with large bolts that would unscrew far enough to permit the bracket to release the blade end.

The end of the replacement blade was resting on the narrowing end of the hull now, and the mechanic braced his knees against the reinforced surface. Bringing the pneumatic wrench around to the bolts on the hub brackets, he began to turn them out one by one.

The damaged blade shifted slightly, repositioning itself as the pressure upon it was released. When the last bolt had been backed out and the bracket was clear, the mechanic braced himself more firmly and reached out with one foot, kicking at the end of the old blade.

Shuddering briefly, the propeller section sprang free of the mounts that had held it and tumbled end over end toward the sea. It almost disappeared from view before reaching the ocean's surface.

The mechanic gave a slight shudder of his own, then said into his helmet mike, "Take us up a little, sir."

Gardner did not have to relay the message. But he watched alertly as the pilot moved the helicopter slightly higher, allowing the replacement blade to raise above the mounting bracket.

The blade came up level, the mechanic still gripping one end even as he himself dangled from a cable. Gardner estimated the angle needed to bring the end of the blade into position against the hub, then carefully activated the electric winch that controlled the cable connected to the man's harness. Slowly feeding out line, the mechanic's weight gradually brought the end of the new blade lower, nearing the hub.

Great skill and caution had to be exercised in the next step, for if the mechanic made a wrong move, allowing the blade end to slip too quickly into the recessed spot behind the mounting bracket, his hand could easily become pinned between the titanium-aluminum surfaces—pinned, or worse. The blade end had to mesh precisely within the bracket's opening, or else the mounting device would not clamp down and secure the blade.

Grasping a handhold on the outer surface of the large propeller hub, the man pulled himself and the blade closer still, carefully guiding the end into position. When at last he was certain that it was set and caught, he brought the pneumatic wrench back around and began tightening the bolts. He double-checked each one before releasing his hold on the hub.

"It's secure, Colonel," the man's voice came over Gardner's helmet earphone. "Move me out a little—I'm going to release the blade cable—"

Working his way along the length of the new blade, he reached out for the device that secured the cable. The clamps that gripped the blade were geared to a central point where a shaft protruded. Slipping the air wrench over the end of the shaft, he triggered it, causing the clamps to extend and free the blade.

His work done, the mechanic reclipped the wrench to his belt and grasped the loose cable and clamp, carrying it along as Gardner activated the winch, reeling him back up to the helicopter. As he finally reached the open hatch and climbed into the cabin, Gardner helped him aboard and gave him a grateful slap on the back.

"Perfect. No one could have done it better," Gardner told him.

The man raised the visor on his helmet and used his sleeve to blot away the sweat on his face. "Thanks, sir. Now I guess we'd better head back to the hangar and pick up the other blade."

On the command deck, General Smalley seemed visibly relieved that at least one of the replacement blades was now secure. Near him, Paul Brandon studied the image on the television monitor with a certain grim awe.

"That's not the kind of job you'd want to do often," Brandon told him.

"We didn't expect to," Smalley replied. "The useful life of those blades is normally enough to last until a routine maintenance visit at the base. Once we begin our regular patrols, we won't be making return visits often."

The remark reawakened Brandon's interest in the true purpose of the airship. "Patrols?" he said.

Smalley looked at him for a moment, perhaps wondering if there was any harm in discussing the purpose of the program. "Come on," he said finally. "There's something I'll show you."

The general led him back, beyond the doors of the control center to the first compartment on the left, the space that served as both office and private quarters for the *Grand Eagle*'s commanding officer. The compartment was tidy and its furnishings simple and well ordered. There was only one bunk and one locker, leaving more wall space for a medium-sized desk.

On that desk was a small model of the airship, encased in a Plexiglas box secured to the desk top, and the walls bore numerous photos of past commands, and a few prints of old airships. Smalley gestured toward a wall map depicting the world. Sectors had been marked off, dividing the sea and land areas into near-equal amounts.

"The *Grand Eagle*," Smalley began, "is more than just my private dream, although I must confess this old farm boy has been dreaming about airships since the days when they still used hydrogen. No, it's much more than that. It's the prototype of a whole squadron of such craft, to be built at our home base in California, *if* testing on this one works out as expected."

"Why so many?" Brandon asked.

"To cover a wide area. With at least six of these craft on regular patrol around coastal areas, there will always be tactical aircraft available for use at a moment's notice, almost anywhere we might need them. Also defensive missiles for use against enemy aircraft or rockets that might be used against the United States or any of our territories or our allies. And above all, a series of airborne command posts that almost never have to touch down or refuel—a complete control center with more electronics gear, computer systems, and radar systems than you could ever put in a conventional aircraft. Complete facilities for relaying on-the-spot information back home. And if necessary, we can stay back out of range of a hot spot and let our RPVs do the work for us."

"In anything this large and slow-moving, wouldn't you be an awful easy target?"

"No more so than a remote land-based installation," Smalley replied confidently. "Besides, for anything to bother us, they have to get within range first. The *Grand Eagle* may be big as a dinosaur, but it also has *teeth*."

Brandon took it all in with interest. Even if he was not greatly interested in military matters, he could still see the potential of such craft.

"And let's not forget emergency missions like this one," he suggested.

"Exactly," Smalley said. "And when we're not concerned about extra payload, we can normally carry heavy equipment which can be used to clear an airstrip in a remote area so that regular heavier-than-air craft can go in. And there is one other consideration."

"What's that?"

"The fact that we're steadily losing air bases around the world," Smalley said soberly. "We have only a few in Asia now, and there are several in Europe which may be removed. Of course you've heard about Portugal and the Azores base. I'm not saying that far-ranging nuclear airships are going to be the answer to our problems, but they *will* be a valuable addition. And with this prototype completed now, the cost of the next ones will go down considerably. Civilian applications are inevitable."

Brandon reflected, remembering some of his own aspirations and dreams. "I'm beginning to understand your enthusiasm, General. And I rather envy your ability to achieve what you want. That's no small accomplishment in itself. Believe me."

"It took awhile. I knew something like this project—this ship—was inevitable. I'm just glad I lived to see it."

Brandon smiled back, beginning to understand just how much the *Grand Eagle* meant to Smalley. They headed out of the compartment, starting for the control center.

"Thank you, General," Brandon said sincerely.

"For what?"

"For letting me in on all this."

Smalley acquired a wry look. "Well, Doctor, I reckon if the government can trust you with Lorenz' life, I can trust you with a small bit of classified information."

Brandon faked ignorance. "What information is that?"

Grinning broadly, Smalley slapped him on the back. "You got the picture, Doc! Come on—let's get back and see how they're doing with the repairs."

It was 1:55 P.M. when the second replacement blade was finally installed and checked, and the helicopter was back safely within its hangar. Heads turned on the command deck as Lt. Col. Stewart Gardner pushed through the double doors at the rear of the control center and walked quickly to the helm.

General Smalley intercepted him. "Good work, Stewart—your idea about using the secondary turbines cut our drift rate almost to nothing. We could have been a lot farther off course than we are. How are the rotors—are we in flying shape again?"

"Yes, sir," Gardner told him. "But if we have to go through that again, we may just have to recruit a new chief mechanic."

"Don't worry. Nobody's getting that close a *second* time!" He turned to Colonel Curtis. "John—have Tate put our defense systems on ready alert. If anything else lifts off the *Kiev*'s deck, it's going to have one deuce of a time getting near us. I don't want them close enough for a good visual sighting!"

"Understood, sir," Curtis replied, then headed his tall and lanky form toward the weapons systems officer to relay the order.

Stewart Gardner was slipping into the senior flight officer's seat, wasting no time in putting the *Grand Eagle*'s flight circuitry back on operational status. At the touch of a button, servos at the rear of the ship released the braking locks that had held the rotor shaft immobile. He carefully checked the display screens which showed the status of the turbines and the reactor readings. Everything seemed in order.

Gardner slipped on his operations headset and announced to the others, "Leaving stable hold—prepare for forty-five-degree turn."

He watched as the computers quickly flashed the necessary information on his screen, filling in the flight data for resuming course to Tongareva. Fingers crossed, he keyed in the electronic commands to start the main turbine. Looking up at the monitor in the bank overhead, he watched the image as the giant twin propellers began to spin. When he was sure they were going to function without further problems, he brought their speed up to full power, simultaneously adjusting the angle of the ship's rudder planes.

The view through the huge main window of the control center began to swing about to the right as the immense airship began to move forward, its control surfaces bringing it back in line with a south-southwesterly line of flight. Gardner checked the airspeed indicator, encouraged as the digital readout continued to increase. It would take perhaps another ten minutes before they were at maximum cruising speed, but it would not take long after that to overtake and pass the Soviet aircraft carrier that was still plowing through the ocean ahead.

Gardner turned to Smalley, who was still standing nearby. "We're back in business, sir. Under way, and approaching normal speed."

Smalley stared out at the horizon intently. "Outstanding. I guarantee you we're going to reach that island. And if the Russians think we're going to be an easy mark the next time, then they've got another think coming. . . ."

"What are we going to do?"

Carla Jennings was not sure she had an answer to Jill Laudon's question. The young stewardess stood nearby in the small radio room, an anxious look on her face. Maggie Newcombe's features were also drawn and tense. It was 1:30 P.M. on Tongareva, but the bright daylight did not dispel the feeling of menace.

The three women were there by the radio set, the door to the room closed to ensure privacy. Carla had brought them together to tell them what she had found—Lorenz' attaché case broken into and the contents ransacked—and the horrible implication of the discovery.

"Well," Carla began, "at least there's no longer any question whether the hijacker—the murderer—is among us. The only question now is . . . *who*?"

"Not a cheery thought," Maggie responded.

"I think it would be a good idea," Carla suggested, "if at least one of us was in the main room, awake and alert, at all times tonight."

"After what you've just told us," Jill Laudon said, "I don't think that will be too hard."

"It's possible that, whoever it is, he won't do anything else—anything that might expose him. But we're still going to have to be extremely careful."

Jill frowned. "You realize, from what you've said, it's not just a criminal or nut we're talking about. If someone is really after that Mr. Lorenz, then it must be a regular spy of sorts—a pro. How are we supposed to handle someone like that?"

"I don't know," Carla replied soberly. "I'm not sure we can, and maybe we don't have to. If we can just hold out

until help arrives, then we won't need to do anything."

"But what if help doesn't arrive?" Maggie said worriedly.

Carla shifted her eyes away, starting to pace. "It will." She walked aimlessly about in the small room for several long moments—moments of worried silence. Finally, she tried to clear her thoughts. Checking her watch, she said, "Jill, I hate to ask you this, but would you mind seeing about fixing something to eat for the others? It's after lunchtime. Mary's been worried sick about James, and I don't have the heart to ask her to leave his side right now."

Jill started for the door. "No, I don't mind. It will give me something to do. And Lord knows I've had enough practice serving meals."

"Can I help with anything?" Maggie asked Carla.

"Well—maybe it would be a good idea if you stayed in the main room for now. Not just to keep an eye on things, but in case someone in the other section needs anything. I'll be in to check the patients again in a little while, but right now I have to make radio contact with the rescue party."

"Sure," Maggie said, with a trace of anxiety still in her voice. "I'll do my best."

Carla waited until both were gone, then closed the door again and went to the radio transceiver. She switched the set on and waited a moment, then picked up the microphone and depressed the transmit switch, calling as she had the last few times to establish contact with those on the way. Again, as before, a woman's voice answered, and then after another moment Paul Brandon's voice came through clearly.

"Carla—is everything all right?"

She hesitated, then replied, "I've got mixed news, Paul. Some of it bad. Very bad." She paused, trying to steady her voice. "We've lost one of the injured . . . a man who had some bad internal injuries. The others are still managing, but for how long I honestly don't know. If you were here now, it wouldn't be a moment too soon."

"I wish we could be there sooner," Brandon's voice replied. "But as it is, we may be a few hours later than I told you before. We've had . . . ah, some mechanical trouble here, and it had us stopped for a while. But it's fixed now, so don't worry. Now what's the rest of it?"

Carla glanced toward the closed door of the radio room, somewhat nervously. "It's about our problem here, Paul—our mystery man, or whatever. He's definitely among the living. Lorenz' attaché case has been gone through, sometime this morning. There's still no clue as to who we're dealing with, and to tell you the truth, I couldn't really point a finger at anyone."

There was silence for a moment, and for a fleeting instant Carla felt a twinge of panic. Then she realized that they were probably discussing the information. In the next moment, the reassuring sound of Brandon's voice came back.

"We understand, Carla. Listen—I want you to tell me what you can about the people there—descriptions, anything that might help. There are people in the States checking on backgrounds. Maybe we can turn up something."

"All right. We may as well start with the least injured," she said, then began to describe those currently in the main room. She told him of Alex Copley's behavior and belligerency, of Father Daniels' past with the military, of Peter Benson's business worries. She described Professor Arturo Maca as well, and Martin Sandersen, the silent and withdrawn man. She even described a number of those injured survivors who might conceivably be able to move about sufficiently to have reached Lorenz' case. But she was still left with the awful feeling that none of those described really seemed a likely killer.

When she had finished, Brandon replied, "All right, Carla, we'll do what we can. Every resource available will be used on this matter, believe me." There was a long pause, then Brandon surprised her by asking, "Carla—do you have a gun there?"

"A gun—? Yes, I think so. Why?"

"It might not be a bad idea to keep it handy. Just in case."

She frowned, then transmitted, "Paul, I don't know if I could use a gun against anyone—it's against everything I've ever been taught."

"I'm not saying you have to use it. Just have it handy as a way of discouraging trouble. And remember, the person we're talking about is a professional killer. If necessary, Carla . . . well, just keep it handy and be careful."

"All right. It's in the desk in my room. I'll check it when I get a chance."

"How is Lorenz doing?"

"About the same," Carla replied, "But I hope you mean what you say about having complete medical facilities on board that plane or whatever it is, because there won't be time to just transport him to a facility somewhere else. Over."

"We have what we need. It will be all right." Brandon hesitated, then asked, "How about you—are you managing all right?"

She almost laughed, then caught herself, for she felt it was a laugh bordering on hysteria. She fought back the feeling. "I . . . I'm all right. I'll be better when you get here, with the medical supplies and equipment."

"It won't be much longer. I promise."

"Is there anything else?"

Again a silence. "No, I think that's all for now, but contact us when you can—keep us advised. And Carla—"

There was a gap, and she transmitted, "Yes, Paul?"

"Nothing . . . never mind, I'll be seeing you shortly."

"All right. Out."

She switched off the radio gear and made a mental note to check the generator sometime within the next hour. It must be almost out of gasoline and would need refueling if the equipment was to be operative. She hoped the fuel would last.

Carla left the radio room, pausing to place a padlock on the plain wooden door. She had never found it necessary to lock anything in the building here on Tongareva before, but now, with the ever-present danger of an unknown killer, she was not about to risk possible damage to the only link she had with the outside world.

She returned to the main room, where Maggie Newcombe waited, unobtrusively keeping an eye on things. Several of the men were pacing, stretching their legs and walking off their impatience. Carla studied them without staring. She wished she could rely on one or more of them in case the mysterious killer should make another move. But which of them to trust? For the moment, at least, she dared not tell any of them what was happening, for to confide in the wrong one could well be a deadly mistake.

Of them all, Father Daniels might be the most help. If, that is, she could trust him.

Carla walked past Maggie Newcombe and into the rear section of the primitive research facility, to check once more on the condition of those in her charge. Some of the dressings needed to be changed, and at least two of the survivors needed fresh IV bottles of plasma. It was another fifteen minutes before she worked her way back to the end of the room, checking on Stefan Lorenz, a man who worried her the most of all her charges, and who, she knew now, was the indirect cause of most of the problems besetting her.

Lorenz was still holding on to life, but still balanced precariously between a stable condition and complete heart failure. If anyone could help him, she knew Paul Brandon could. For both their sakes, she hoped he would reach them soon.

Carla started out of the rear section and was about to check on Jill's efforts in preparing the already-late lunch she had asked her to start, when she remembered Paul's warning and his suggestion about the gun. The thought still disturbed her, but seeing at least some logic in it, she headed for her own room, down the hall from the main section.

The gun—a small-caliber pistol—was not truly hers. It had been among the personal belongings left behind by the resident doctor. When he had died, she had not shipped the pistol back to Rarotonga with the other things. Although not sure why, she had kept it there at the facility, tucked safely away in the desk drawer, with no bullets left in the cylinder. It might not be much protection against someone trained in the arts of deception and death, but it would be better than nothing.

Entering her room, she closed the door behind her after checking to see that no one was in the hall. Going to her desk, Carla opened the top drawer on the right and began pushing back personal papers and keepsakes that cluttered its interior. The pistol had been left near the back, under a small photo album with pictures from a past now very remote and unreal.

She searched through the rear of the drawer for another full minute, then, almost frantically, pulled the drawer free of the desk and dumped its contents on the bed.

Spreading everything out, so that nothing could be hidden by other material, her disbelieving eyes sought the barely-remembered form of the small handgun. But the truth could not be avoided.

Carla straightened, her face freezing into a mask of grim realization. The gun and the loose bullets were simply not there. They were gone ... gone, because someone had taken them. ...

CHAPTER SIX

"**C**aptain—the airship is moving again," the young warrant officer, Vasiliy Yakosev, said from his position before the bank of radar equipment on the bridge of the Soviet aircraft carrier *Kiev*. "It seems to be moving at close to its top speed."

Konstantin Dashkevich studied the glowing image in frowning silence. Behind him, Rear Adm. Nikolay Bakhirev looked on with disbelief.

"Impossible," Bakhirev said softly. "They could not, with their propeller disabled."

Dashkevich had less trouble accepting the obvious truth. "Clearly, they had the means to repair the damage."

Bakhirev glanced at the bridge's main clock. It was a little before 1500 hours, or 3:00 P.M. To the radar man he snapped, "Distance?"

"Less than twenty-one miles, Admiral."

"Then they will overtake us in another fifteen minutes. And they can still reach the island ahead of us."

"So it would seem, sir."

Bakhirev turned away from the equipment and walked slowly toward the chart table. He unlocked the drawer and brought forth his code book, then began drafting a message to his superiors at the *Kiev*'s home port of Petropavlovsk. A message informing them of the airship's continued threat to their mission and ending with a request for clarification of their authority to act and of the responses deemed necessary.

When he had finished the message and encoded it, he handed it to Dashkevich. "Have this transmitted at once."

"Yes, Admiral." Dashkevich relayed it to the radio man and returned to the area of the radar console, where Bakhirev had resumed a position.

The admiral viewed the radar blip with growing anger. "How dare they attempt this kidnaping . . . this theft. Do they really think they can intimidate a vessel of the Soviet Navy with a mere bag of gas?"

It was a rhetorical question and Dashkevich did not attempt an answer. Instead he asked of Yakosev, "Will its present course still keep it beyond missile range?"

The man checked his readings. "Yes. Captain—just beyond."

Bakhirev nodded. "It is to be expected. They are not fools." He paused briefly, his mind working behind the outward calm of his cool gray eyes. "No matter—the shipboard missiles would undoubtedly inflict more damage than is necessary to achieve our end."

"Yes," Dashkevich agreed, though with other reasons in mind. "One wonders what the Americans' response would be if we were to make a more direct attack on their airship. Even if sent from Hawaii, American jets could reach us in a matter of hours . . . a small missile in even less time."

"Yes, one wonders," Bakhirev said oddly. "Three hours have passed since we disabled their propeller, yet there has been no apparent response. Intelligence information relayed from Petropavlovsk confirms that no military craft have been sent out yet. Perhaps they do not feel their position is strong enough."

"Perhaps," Dashkevich echoed.

"Whatever their particular reasons may be, they certainly cannot be allowed to interfere in this matter." Bakhirev hesitated, then inquired, "Who are your four best pilots?"

The *Kiev*'s captain considered a moment. "Korsh, Pacheko, Tevosyan . . . and yes, Zheltov."

"I want them alerted, and their jets ready. You had best contact the hangar officer and have his crew on standby."

"Yes, Admiral. And the pilots' orders?"

"Those will depend on what we hear from Fleet Command."

Dashkevich set about the duties given him, and within moments members of the hangar maintenance crew were scurrying about, checking the fuel and weapons systems on four of the twenty-five jet aircraft stored beneath the flight deck of the great ship.

They were advanced versions of the Soviet VTOL jet that had been given the NATO code name of "Freehand," and their appearance could only be described as ominous. Powered by twin turbojet engines located within the lower fuselage, the forward air intakes formed a single wide-mouth O that resembled the gaping maw of a manta ray, and the planes' bulky forms almost suggested there was muscle beneath their smoothly rounded aluminum skin. A ten-foot-long nose probe with reaction control nozzles gave each jet an added look of menace.

Each plane was resting primarily on two wheel units—one at the nose of the ship and a twin-wheel main unit just behind the wings. Balancer wheels at the wing tips kept the ship stable. At a length of just over fifty-seven feet and a width of twenty-seven feet, the planes had to use the larger forward elevator up to the *Kiev*'s flight deck.

Power from the turbines could be diverted downward, exhausted through vectored-thrust nozzles beneath the ship to provide verticle lift for takeoffs and landings, and for flying at low speeds. Beneath each swept-back wing was mounted a sixteen-round rocket pack, and the large tail fin had its ventral fins mounted high. The cockpit was located high in the fuselage, above the turbines, and as with most fighter craft of its type, had room only for the pilot. Hinged panels near the nose and tail of the plane's underbelly were fully extended, to prevent re-intake of exhaust gases during vertical takeoff and landing, and to shield the landing gear from the considerable heat directed downward. They would be retracted once in flight.

For the moment, the maintenance crew ignored the covered object parked near one side of the expansive hangar deck, its boxy form shrouded by a dark tarpaulin tied securely in place. Six feet wide, nearly as high, and a bit over fifteen feet in length, the device had low sturdy wheels for transporting it and extendable locking pins which would secure it to recently added mounting plates located in several spots on the ship's upper deck. When the time came to move it, it would be towed to either the forward or rear elevator by one of the same small tractor units that moved the jet aircraft. For now, it was merely an extra bit of cargo filling a corner of the hangar.

A full half hour passed. And on the bridge of the *Kiev* Admiral Bakhirev waited anxiously for some reply. He stood near the communications console as the carrier continued its steady progress across the Pacific, in what now threatened to be a losing race to Tongareva.

Captain Dashkevich stood by his side, finally interrupting the long silence with a question. "Our contact on the island—how shall we identify the person?"

Bakhirev hesitated, his thoughts elsewhere. Then he replied, "Our instructions state that the operative will use a code phrase for identification purposes. We have been provided with both that phrase and the correct response."

"It seems an unnecessarily complicated procedure."

"Perhaps," Bakhirev said, raising an eyebrow. "But don't let Grigorovich hear you say so."

"*Sir*," the young officer at the communications equipment said abruptly, "we're receiving a message from Petropavlovsk . . . in the special code."

Bakhirev turned quickly to face the equipment, waiting as the sheet emerged from the radio-teletype unit. The lieutenant tore it free and handed it to him.

There were only a few short lines on the sheet, following the codings which identified the source of the transmission. The admiral set about decoding it at the chart table. It did not take long.

"Confirmation of orders originates from the Defense Ministry," Bakhirev said softly.

"And those orders—?" Dashkevish inquired, sober-faced.

"Here—" Bakhirev handed him the decoded sheet, waiting as the captain read the instructions which were so brief and yet so clear:

CONTINUE ON COURSE . . .

RECOVER LORENZ AND THE PROTOTYPE . . .

STOP THE AIRSHIP . . .

Dashkevich looked up from the sheet. "The instructions regarding the airship do not specify *how*."

"Unnecessary," Bakhirev said flatly. "We know how. All that we need is the proper moment. . . ."

Less than an hour later, the nuclear airship *Grand Eagle* had passed the *Kiev* and was now approximately forty-four miles ahead of the Russian carrier. Even without the favorable winds that had assisted the craft during the first half of its journey, the airship was still managing a ground speed of about one hundred miles an hour. The time in this part of the Pacific was a few minutes past 4:00 P.M.

As the enormous silver projectile cruised nearly a mile above the ocean waves, a tiny craft, hardly noticeable compared to the immense scale of the large one, approached the *Grand Eagle*. As it neared the tail of the great airship, its control surfaces made minor adjustments, bringing it up to an altitude just thirty feet below the airship's gleaming underside.

The tiny craft's approach was slow compared to the jet

RPV which had been used earlier. Its size was also markedly different, for its overall length was only six feet and its wingspan a mere seven feet. The mini-RPV was delta-shaped, with a pusher propeller mounted above and slightly to the rear, and the entire fuselage was formed of fiber-glass-surfaced plastic foam. Its total weight was only a little over 125 pounds.

As it continued its flight, it was automatically guided toward a recovery net extending from the RPV bay of the airship, a net similar to the one used to handle the BGM-34C, but smaller. Its engine, virtually noiseless, shut off the instant the tiny aircraft struck the net. Within another minute, even as the first mini-RPV was being drawn up into the open bay, another of the small craft was being swung down into position upon a guide rail, which ran forward for a length of thirty-five feet from the end of the RPV bay along the underside of the airship.

The mini-RPV's engine was running as it locked into position. Radio signals from the command center's control console quickly brought it up to full power, and at the touch of a button an abrupt burst of compressed air sent the craft speeding along the launch rail. At the end of the rail it disengaged and continued on its own, flying in a wide arc which carried it back in the direction of the Soviet aircraft carrier *Kiev,* where yet another of the tiny craft still circled, maintaining a continuous vigil above the surface ship.

On the command deck of the *Grand Eagle* Paul Brandon approached the government man, Haddock, standing near the communications console with General Smalley. Brandon glanced at a number of facsimile printout sheets which the others were examining.

"Have you received photos of the survivors?" he asked.

"Only a few so far," Haddock replied, turning slightly. "Even with all the different agencies involved, it hasn't been easy tracking them down." He extended the three facsimile sheets to Brandon. "They're not very good. There's one of Professor Maca, from a newspaper clipping that's fairly recent, and one of the exporter, Peter Benson, from an old copy of a passport photo. There's a police photo of Alexander Copley from a drunk driving arrest, taken shortly before he took off on his overseas jaunt. But aside from those, and some photos of the crew we're expecting in the next half hour, there's nothing."

Brandon studied the somewhat murky reproductions,

silent for a long moment. "These seem to match the descriptions Carla gave us, but it's hard to be certain."

"Yes, I know. And unfortunately, we can't transmit them to the island without the proper equipment there to receive it. Even if we had the complete set, they wouldn't be of immediate help."

"We need to do something," Brandon replied, handing the photo-sheets back. "After that last report from Carla."

"Yes, the gun," Haddock said. "We have to assume it was taken by the Soviet agent." He paused for a moment, seeming to consider Brandon's concern. "I doubt that there's any immediate danger, Doctor. Being outnumbered as he is on the island, I suspect the agent will keep a low profile until either we or the Soviet ship reach Tongareva."

"Do you have any doubt we'll reach it first?"

"Just stating what the man's likely to do."

Brandon looked out through the wide forward window of the command deck, his eyes grimly scanning the horizon. "I wish we were there now."

Before Haddock could reply, one of the circuits buzzed on the communications console and S/Sgt. Elizabeth Jordan switched the channel to the console's intercom. The voice of the airship's senior medical officer, Maj. Donald Shaffer, came through.

"Is Dr. Brandon there?"

Brandon leaned closer to the intercom. "Right here."

"Good," Shaffer's voice replied. "We're ready when you are, Doctor."

"I'll be down in a minute." Brandon nodded to Smalley and Haddock and headed for the corridor at the rear of the command deck. He took the elevator down to Deck B and made the short walk to the airship's medical section.

Shaffer was waiting in the doorway as he approached, and ushered him in. "Will you need to use the surgery, or will my office be satisfactory?"

"Your office will be fine, if we can get everyone in."

Shaffer nodded as he headed toward the right side of the medical section and the small office that was located in its far corner. "I've already brought in some extra chairs."

Brandon had already met two of the people in the office the night before—Shaffer's assistant, Griffith, and the nurse, Lieutenant Lynch. The two OR nurses who had been brought out from the base hospital at Edwards were present now, seated at the far end of Shaffer's desk.

Brandon located his equipment and the medical bag he had left in the office, and in a minute had unfolded a set of diagrams out across the desk top. "For now, I just want to outline the procedure. We should have time for a rehearsal later, if necessary."

As he removed the mechanical heart device from its protective case, the others leaned forward to study it more closely. Still sealed in two layers of sterile transparent plastic covering, the device was almost identical with the model displayed by Brandon during his talk at San Francisco State University.

"The unit is actually designed to serve as a total replacement for a failing heart," Brandon began. "However, in the case of Stefan Lorenz, what I want to do is leave his own heart intact with its own supply of blood unrestricted, and implant the mechanical unit alongside, where it can take over the work of pumping blood to the rest of the body. That way, there's at least the chance that Lorenz' own heart could regenerate to the point where corrective valve surgery would be successful." To Shaffer he said, "Would you concur?"

The dark-haired medical officer did not hesitate. "Yes. I think that's the best way to go, under the circumstances."

"All right. Then let's go over the procedure, step by step. . . ."

At that moment on the command deck, Colonel Curtis came forward from the area of the RPV control consoles. His frown and quickened pace let General Smalley know something was wrong even before he spoke.

"What is it, John?"

"The RPVs," Curtis said quickly. "The two small ones we've had keeping an eye on the *Kiev*. We've lost signals from both—apparently they've been shot down by the ship's anti-aircraft guns."

Haddock did not seem surprised. "It's a wonder their radar didn't pick them up before this."

Smalley disagreed. "Those plastic foam RPVs aren't easily detected by radar, and their engines don't register much on infrared either. They must have made a visual sighting."

Curtis asked, "Do you want others launched, sir?"

Smalley considered it. "No. It was just a precautionary measure anyway, and we're about out of range for using the slower craft. Besides, they're on to us now."

Ten minutes passed in relative silence, then from the man at the radar console came a sudden shout. "Sir—we're picking up bogies, just up off the deck of the *Kiev*!"

Curtis and Smalley moved quickly to the console, with Haddock close at their heels. Smalley asked, "How many?"

"Four, sir. Heading this way."

Smalley studied the screen which displayed tracking data on the unknown craft. "They're moving slow, but picking up speed."

"Helicopters?" Curtis asked.

"Somehow I doubt it. Can we get them on camera?"

They turned to face the large monitors near the front of the command deck. Long, tense minutes passed before the aft cameras with extreme long-range lenses finally focused on the four approaching craft. The magnified view left no further doubts.

"Put us on *red alert*," Smalley snapped, "those are fighters!"

CHAPTER SEVEN

Alarm klaxons sounded through the great airship as the Soviet jets made their approach. There was barely time for the *Grand Eagle*'s personnel to reach their stations, but all those assigned to man the ship's defense systems were already on the command deck, on standby alert since contact with the Soviet helicopter.

Red lights glowed on every control console, and equipment ordinarily dormant was now on full power. Taking up a position at the center of the deck, General Smalley faced forward, eyes fixed on television monitors which showed the Soviet aircraft.

"Do you have those on master tracking yet?" he snapped.

"Locked in, sir," the weapons control officer, Major Tate, assured him. ·

"Arm the missile systems."

Tate slid back protective panels over the main control switches and activated them. Instantly, at three locations around the *Grand Eagle*'s central hull, special hatches rotated inward, revealing massed banks of missiles in their launching frames. In the two lower facilities, in launchers that would in use be extended out a dozen feet beyond the airship's hull, long air-to-ground missiles reposed. They were long-distance models, capable of striking targets several hundred miles away. But the missiles now armed and ready for launch were much smaller, air-to-air missiles whose primary purpose was the defense of the massive airship.

"Missiles armed, sir," Tate announced.

Smalley continued to watch as the Russian jets swept past at a respectful distance. They were in a tight formation, almost as if they were demonstrating their skill at one of the air shows at Domodedovo or at Tushino Airport in Moscow.

At Smalley's side, the government man, Haddock, stared at the monitors with tight-lipped concern. His eyes shifted down as the jets became visible through the front windows of the command deck.

"What are they up to now?" he said irritably. "Surely they're not foolish enough to—"

"Whatever it is, we'll find out shortly," Smalley said quickly. "At least we're not unprepared this time."

Virtually all eyes were on the Soviet jets now, still visible at a good distance from the nose of the *Grand Eagle*, and somewhat to the starboard side. Abruptly, the jets banked, beginning a wide turn. Still holding their tight formation, the four silvery craft rocketed around in the direction of the airship, heading straight for its nose at top speed.

At the weapons control console, Major Tate waited anxiously with his fingers poised over the buttons that would commit the ship's automatic control systems to full defense mode. It was an action not to be taken lightly, for once committed, the defense systems would track and destroy any craft identified as hostile.

"Orders, sir?" Tate asked.

"Just hang on," Smalley said coolly. "That doesn't look like a fighting run they're making—their ships are too close."

Tense seconds crept by as the jets continued their approach. The flight crew of the *Grand Eagle* had worked with the general for nearly a year now, and all had faith in his ability. That faith was being tested now.

Then, as the Soviet craft reached a point nearly a thousand yards from the *Grand Eagle*'s nose, they pulled up, roaring well above the airship. The monitors showed them continuing past for another few thousand yards, then they began a wide, banking turn that brought them well out and around the airship's starboard side.

"Trying to scare us off, I guess," Smalley said. "But we're not going to back down that easily." Turning to the communications console, he directed, "Transmit on their usual frequency—tell them we won't allow another close pass like that."

The commo officer nodded, opening the appropriate circuits. The message was repeated several times, with a more than adequate pause allowed for a response. Finally, the officer turned back to Smalley.

"They're just not answering, sir. I've broadcast on all their standard frequencies."

Smalley seemed to expect it. "As long as they've heard us."

The Soviet fighter jets were circling the airship now, always staying at least five thousand yards out. As they began to make their second loop, the communications officer called out suddenly.

"No reply yet, sir, but the jets *are* in communication with the *Kiev*."

"Is it intelligible?"

"Negative—they're using some kind of scrambling system."

"Tape it. Maybe the computers can sort it out later."

For the next several minutes, the jets continued their circling. Then, as they neared the point of their turn that brought them nearly even with the airship, they began to change formation, fanning out to allow more distance and with one jet clearly in the lead.

Smalley studied the monitors. "Now we can expect trouble."

Haddock eased closer. "Can we avoid a direct strike against their jets?"

"That's not entirely up to us."

"You know what I mean," Haddock said quickly. "We don't want this thing escalating."

"It also won't do world peace any good if we allow

ourselves to be shot down!" He glared chillingly at Haddock, but finally relented somewhat. At Major Tate he snapped, "Key the system in for Code 2 defense mode."

"Affirmative, sir."

Behind them, Paul Brandon came through the doors at the rear of the command deck's control center. He had taken the elevator up from Deck B as soon as he could after the alarms had sounded. He hurried toward Smalley and the others.

"What's happening?" he asked.

"The Russians are pressing their point," Smalley said soberly. "And we're about to find out just how well protected we really are."

Even as he spoke, the lead jet broke away from the others and banked left, coming directly at the sleek airship's expansive side. The remaining three jets peeled off at different angles, putting even more distance between themselves.

"Systems tracking," Tate said flatly, his eyes riveted to the screens and visual displays of the weapons control console.

With only a little over three thousand yards remaining, the Soviet jet fired a rocket from beneath its swept-back wing. An instant later, the pilot of the craft pulled up quickly, climbing high and away from the airship. The rocket sped on, straight toward the side of the *Grand Eagle*, where its explosive power would surely rupture one or more of the airship's gas cells and damage the main structure. *If* it were allowed to reach its target.

From the first instant of its launching, the rocket had been locked into the *Grand Eagle*'s tracking systems, all of which were coordinated by the main computer. Data on the rocket's speed and trajectory, as well as such factors as the airship's own movement, were processed and analyzed, all in less time than it took the human eye to blink.

A small defensive missile in the bank of projectiles located at the airship's upper launch facility fired, its speed faster than the approaching rocket. At a point less than two thousand yards out, the missile homed in on the rocket and detonated in a bright flare of orange light. A lingering cloud of dark smoke marked the spot for several moments, then was left behind by the airship's forward progress. The sound of the concussive force, a dull *whump* that seemed detached from the explosion itself, was barely heard in the airship's control center.

"So far, so good," Smalley said. To Haddock he added

"Perhaps now you'll understand the situation a bit better. That rocket could have crippled us."

Haddock made no reply. And had he chosen to there would have been no time.

From his console, Major Tate announced loudly, "Another one's coming in! At nine o'clock!"

Swinging toward the airship's port side, the second jet began an approach similar to the first, launching one round from the rocket pack beneath one wing, then pulling away abruptly.

Again the *Grand Eagle*'s tracking systems locked onto the approaching rocket, the automatic circuits launching a missile from the lower left side to intercept it. Again, a successful detonation, and another black cloud drifted away to the rear of the ship.

Immediately, the remaining two jets swept around and dropped, joining forces as they made a low approach from below the airship's starboard side. In the next instant, it could be seen that it was a coordinated effort, for the first two jets had finished their upward spiral and were banking, starting a plummeting dive that would carry them toward the upper surface of the *Grand Eagle*'s hull.

The jets came as near as the pilots dared before pulling away, and this time instead of merely one rocket screaming its way toward the airship there were eight—two launched from each jet.

On the command deck, Tate monitored the functioning of the automatic systems, ready to key it in for Code 1 defense mode at Smalley's orders. Beads of perspiration appeared on Tate's forehead. If it had been entirely up to him, he would have preferred to take out the attacking jets at the start.

Defensive missiles were fired, four from the upper launch facility and four from the airship's lower facility on the starboard side. Only the unimaginable speed of the complex radar and computer system could have tracked and detonated the eight incoming rockets simultaneously. Yet eight balls of orange flame erupted almost at the same instant, nearly surrounding the *Grand Eagle* in their glare. The concussion waves throbbed out across the gap, making the hull's outer covering vibrate like the skin of a taut drumhead.

Still watching the monitors, Smalley seemed unmoved by the spectacle. Paul Brandon studied him, marveling at the officer's apparent calm.

"How long can we hold out that way?" he asked.

"They'll run out of rockets a long time before we will," Smalley replied. Still, with an expression hard to decipher, he turned to the communications console. "Transmit a message to Edwards—scrambled—advise them of what's happening."

"Yes, sir."

A minute passed, with no further action from the Soviet jets. They maintained a loose-knit formation some six thousand yards from the airship.

"What are they up to?" Haddock asked nervously.

"It appears they've discovered how little they can do," Smalley said with a certain grim humor, "and now they're sitting back, thinking on it."

The men watched as the Soviet jets banked once more and headed northeast. They almost appeared to be giving up and returning to the *Kiev*. That impression did not last.

"One of them's leaving formation." Major Tate confirmed what was suddenly apparent on the deck's monitors. "It's swinging wide, coming around toward the tail of the ship."

"Another pass?"

"Maybe," Tate said. Then he almost shouted, "It's coming *directly* at the tail!"

Smalley moved quickly to the weapons control console, with Haddock virtually at his heels. The general leaned forward, looking at the instruments, then at a computer-generated diagram of the airship which depicted the *Grand Eagle* from top and side view, with the location of the missile launchers indicated by glowing dots of light. From the angle of the approaching fighter craft and the information already displayed on the screen, the truth was already clear.

"He's going for the rotors. And that's our least guarded area."

Brandon studied the image. He did not have to be an aeronautical engineer to appreciate the fact that it was exceedingly difficult for missiles to be fired straight back along the sides of the airship. The massive bulk of the ship and its tail fins effectively blocked the aim at any target approaching from the rear on a straight line with the ship.

"What kind of range can we allow?" Smalley asked quickly.

"If he doesn't launch his rockets until he's within twenty-five hundred feet of us, we won't have a chance of knocking them out. Not with our missiles, and not with our ALW system either, since it's line-of-sight."

Smalley's initial decision was quick. "Evasive action!" he shouted at Gardner. "Cut power and bring us around!"

Lt. Col. Stewart Gardner responded instantly, throttling back the turbines from his console near the great windows of the airship. His mind was already aware of the main problem— there simply was not time for the ship to be turned by using the massive control surfaces at the rear fins. The servos would not angle them fast enough. So instead his hand shot out to the controls for the turbo thrusters. There was no chance to program them through the flight control computer for a measured and smooth adjustment. He struck the manual circuit buttons for the port/forward and starboard/aft thrusters, switching on full power.

There was an agonizing second of inaction, then the great airship began to swing about as the turbo thrusters at the ends of the craft pushed it around. The change was slight—only a difference of perhaps twenty-five degrees—but it was enough for the missile facilities on the airship's starboard side to be lined up on the rapidly approaching jet.

It was a fact not overlooked by the Soviet pilot. He immediately pulled up, calling off his strike run and rolling to the left, heading out of immediate range.

"Two more, on the way," Tate called out sharply. "And from the rear again, but each at different angles."

Smalley studied the glowing tracking image. The jets were indeed approaching with different trajectories, one a few thousand feet ahead of the other.

"We can't keep this up," Tate said quickly. "If we turn again, one of them is still going to be in position. And we can't handle their rockets at that angle."

"Then we'll have to take out the plane."

Haddock frowned. "If their pilot dies—"

"We'll do it my way," Smalley interrupted. To Tate he ordered, "Switch in the ALW system. Lock in on the lead jet."

"Affirmative, sir." Tate triggered the dual controls that activated the ALW, a note of grim hope in his voice. It was probably their only chance, even though the airborne laser weapons system was still virtually untested in combat situations.

As the circuits were opened, high-voltage current from generators driven by the nuclear-powered turbines flowed into the system, ready to energize the exotic equipment which had been installed with the greatest security restrictions of anything aboard the airship.

"Keep the turbo thrusters going," Smalley called out to Gardner. "A few degrees is all we need for the first one."

There were three of the greatly advanced laser devices incorporated within the *Grand Eagle*'s weapons systems. One was mounted near the center of the missile arrays at the hull's peak, the other two at the lower port and starboard missile facilities. All three were hybrid systems—part electrical discharge lasers and part gas dynamic lasers. The frequency of coherent light emitted had been chosen particularly for its strength and long-range transmission through atmosphere.

The laser units were bulky and unglamorous in appearance, each weighing nearly six thousand pounds in total equipment. Only an airship like the *Grand Eagle* could have carried them aloft and supplied the electrical power necessary to operate them. The units themselves could not be moved, the actual aiming and final focusing of the intense beams being accomplished by multipivoting mirrors of dense, highly polished alloy. The mirrors were controlled by quick-acting electric motors and gearing, and beneath the bright surfaces was embedded the conduit of cryogenic systems which helped cool them from the incredible heat generated by the beams they reflected.

Main tracking fed the approaching jet's coordinates to the laser control system. On the ALW circuit's targeting screen, a glowing circle marked the point of aim on the jet's simulated form. That circle was dead center on the craft's fuselage.

Smalley was well aware of the effect such a direct hit would have on the pilot. Picking up the display unit's "electric pencil," a small metallic rod connected by cable to the computer section, he hit the reprogramming button and touched the rod to the screen's surface in two places, once on each side of the plane's fuselage.

"Range?" he demanded.

"The lead jet," Tate replied, "four thousand feet and closing."

Smalley looked to the visual display screen which showed the angle of the airship relative to the approaching jet's trajectory. That angle was changing slowly.

"Are we clear yet?" he demanded, his tone becoming imperative for the first time.

"Lasers one and three are tracking, sir. Automatic fail safe should disengage in three seconds."

"Override manually and *fire*!"

Tate's hand flashed to the manual controls and struck down hard on the firing buttons. Immediately, normal lighting within the command deck's control center and throughout the rest of the airship dimmed to a weak glow as additional electrical power was drawn from the main system.

From laser one at the top of the ship issued a narrow beam of light, dazzling in its brilliance, passing almost straight back beyond the ship. From laser three came a second beam, passing dangerously close to the starboard fin, missing it by no more than twenty feet. There was an attendant humming crackle of sound as air molecules along the beams' paths were ionized by the sudden intense heat.

At a distance of 2,600 feet, the pilot of the approaching jet saw the flash of the twin beams and was startled enough to hesitate in firing his remaining rockets. In another instant there was no chance to do so.

The two beams focused on the leading edges of the jet's wings, a short distance out from the cockpit. The *Grand Eagle*'s tracking systems held the beams on target with near-perfect aim.

There was a brief instant of fiery incandescence as the metal of the wings was super-heated by the lasers' concentrated energy, then that metal began to vaporize, a molten path cutting through the outer surface and internal control systems.

In the space of two brief seconds, both wings were severed from the plane's fuselage. Ripping back and away from the jet, they plummeted down toward the waiting sea.

Going into a shallow dive, the wingless jet shot on, soon passing beneath the airship in its steady descent. From the image on the monitors, it appeared for a moment that the pilot was attempting to stabilize his craft by diverting power to the VTOL nozzles beneath the fuselage. But it was quickly apparent that the damaged craft could not limp back to the *Kiev* on VTOL power alone. Still descending, the pilot chose to eject, his parachute fluttering open even as the jet continued its roaring dive. Then, with a great explosion of sea spray, the craft impacted in the water, quickly disappearing beneath its glimmering surface.

Smalley shifted his gaze from the monitors back to the

visual displays on the weapons control console. "What's the angle and range of the second jet?"

"Three thousand feet and closing," Tate told him. "Same approach pattern. No, wait ... he's changing. He's pulling up."

Smalley watched as the approaching jet climbed high above them. In another second it made a rolling turn and headed away from the *Grand Eagle,* finally joining the two remaining jets. "Looks like they're heading out of range for a while. That gives us the time we need." He turned toward Lieutenant Colonel Foster, whose position adjacent to the weapons control console gave him quick access to much of the weapons data. "Foster—scramble the Harriers. Let's give our comrades out there an escort home before they get any other ideas."

"With pleasure, sir." Foster slipped on a headphones and mike unit, his hawklike eyes alert and eager. He triggered the alert button.

Four hundred and thirty feet back from the nose of the airship, on a deck well within the interior of the lower hull, alarm bells rang. The deck served as a maintenance area for the special jet aircraft in the bays below, and along one side of the first section were the quarters for the fighter pilots, so that they could quickly reach their craft. Captain Lee, the group's flight leader, and the others were already in their flight gear—had been since the red alert had first sounded.

Now these men ran past the repair equipment and parts storage areas to a spiral staircase which descended to the aircraft bays. The launch crew were already at their positions, and the senior NCO was in the process of activating the bay doors.

Honeycombed catwalks ran around the sides of each bay section and gave access to the six aircraft stowed within—aircraft suspended by special latch devices hooked to long crane arms that would swing down. The center jet in each bay was hooked to an arm that would swing forward, while the others pivoted out to the sides.

In a moment the pilots were in their cockpits, sliding the canopies forward and locking them in place. At once the pneumatically operated cranes began to lower the jets, extending them through the now open bay doors.

The six advanced model Harriers came into view below the *Grand Eagle,* their engines starting. The vertical takeoff and landing light-attack jets were a joint project of Britain's aircraft manufacturer Hawker Siddeley and America's McDonnell Douglas. Their wingspan was just over twenty-five feet, their length just over forty-five feet. The lead craft, a two-seater, was ten feet longer than the rest.

Sleeker than their Russian counterparts, these VTOL jets still operated in basically the same way, although instead of two turbojets there was only one turbofan engine in each plane—a Rolls-Royce Bristol Pegasus. As with the Soviet Freehand-type craft, power diverted from the main exhaust could be vented downward for vertical lift. The United States Marine Corps already had over a hundred of the advanced, multi-purpose craft when the Air Force ordered a number of them, specially modified for use with its airship project. A VTOL jet was the only type of modern fighter craft that could be launched and recovered from an airship, though this had not been true in the days of piston aircraft. Shortly before the beginning of World War II, two United States Navy airships, the *Akron* and the *Macon*, both carried a complement of four Curtis F9C Sparrowhawk biplanes, used for scouting purposes. The relatively slow speed of the biplanes could easily allow them to hook onto a trapezelike framework which brought them in and out of the storage bay of each airship. The advent of the jet age ended such possibilities, until the development of vertical takeoff and landing technology.

Now, beneath the *Grand Eagle*, six Harriers hung suspended, their jet engines whining into life. The pilots' radio links to the command deck and Colonel Foster were open, and in the lead jet Captain Lee announced—

"Flight Leader to Eagle—we're ready for disengage."

"Roger, Flight Leader," Foster's crisp voice came back through six helmet headphones. "You're cleared."

Each of the pilots increased power, balancing the weight of their craft until they were no longer dependent on the crane arms for support. In each jet, the pilot poised his finger above a switch that would release the latching mechanism securing it to the end of its crane.

"Free on count," Captain Lee said on the common radio link. "Three . . . two . . . one . . . *disengage.*"

Simultaneously, the six VTOL craft came free of their cranes. For a second, they hung there beneath the airship, testing the feel of their controls and the power of their engines. Then, on command from Lee, the six jets dropped, gradually diverting power back to the main exhaust. Picking up forward speed now, they banked in the direction of the Soviet jets, maintaining a wide twin V formation.

On the command deck, General Smalley watched the Harriers depart and cautioned Colonel Foster, "Tell them to give those boys a good chase, but not to get within range of the *Kiev*. There may be a welcoming committee waiting."

"Will do, sir."

Smalley turned back in time to notice an object appearing briefly on the below-ship monitor. The downed Soviet pilot was bobbing on the surface of the ocean, barely visible but for the bright orange flotation device he had inflated.

"One of their helicopters can pick him up in a little while," Smalley remarked, a faint smile coming once again to his lips. "Maybe a dunking will improve his manners. *Gardner*— get us back on a true course. We've got an island to reach. . . ."

Minutes later in Washington, D.C., it was 8:30 P.M., and a light snowfall that had begun late in the afternoon was continuing. Herb Ettleman could still see the flakes' sporadic passage outside his apartment window as he dialed his telephone. The White House press secretary had just returned home from an update briefing with President Evans when he'd gotten the message to phone Archer Grant. There were many things Ettleman would rather have done, but Grant was probably the most influential of the networks news representatives in Washington.

Even after two years, there were times when Ettleman still felt uncomfortable in his job. It was true that he had worked with Evans somewhat during his senatorial days, and then during the campaign, but it was really not that long ago that he was on the other side of the fence, so to speak—a working newsman himself. His boyish face kept him looking younger than his thirty-eight years, despite a distressingly receding hairline, and unlike some of his predecessors he was generally well liked among the members of the news media. What he found harder to adjust to were the intangible differences, the constant little reminders that he was now considered part of the political establishment. He was no longer a seeker of answers but instead dispensed them, and then only those that were officially sanctioned. The change in attitude, even in those whom he considered friends, was marked and gnawingly unpleasant. Ettleman gave a halfhearted shrug and concentrated on the dial. The problems came with the territory.

The phone rang once and then clicked, and Archer Grant said, "Hello. Grant here."

Herb smiled. "Ettleman here," he said. "What can I do for you, Archer?"

"Oh, hello Herb. Sorry to hit you with business on Sunday, but it seems I have sort of a technical problem."

"Technical? How can I help in that area?"

"I'll explain." He paused, then went on. "You see, Herb, our network has a film crew on a plane en route to Tahiti. In fact, they should be landing there in a matter of minutes. We had a charter plane waiting to fly them on to Tongareva, so they could film the site of that jet crash. The problem is, the authorities found out about it and permission for the flight has been refused. The pilot's not about to lose his license over the matter, and we're stuck. From what I've been able to find out, the same thing has happened to one of the other networks and both the AP and the UPI crews too."

Ettleman shrugged. "If you know all that, then I'm sure you're aware of the reason."

"I know the reason we've been given—the area's quarantined because of radioactive materials. But surely there's no risk in a mere flyover, is there?"

"I really don't know," Ettleman said. "Have you spoken to anyone at the FAA?"

"Yes, and we've been getting a lot of run-around. I'm wondering why."

"I can't tell you more than I know."

Grant snorted. "I'd be willing to bet you're saying a lot *less* than you know about this. And I can't help but wonder if there's something going on out there that the administration doesn't want on the evening news. Something about the fact that American nuclear materials are still being shipped on commercial airlines, maybe?"

"What makes you think they were American nuclear materials?"

"Well, aren't they? I mean, there's been no other source identified, and all the government agencies are being very cagey about handing out information. It all adds up."

"Really?" Ettleman said smoothly. "Perhaps you

shouldn't try adding when some of the numbers are missing, Archer."

"Then you do admit that there is information that's been withheld?"

"Of course not. I'm only going by what you've told me—that you're short on facts."

Grant fell silent, and Ettleman wondered if he was reappraising his tactics. In a few seconds Grant spoke again. "There's something else . . . something that didn't make it into this morning's paper," he said. "In California there were a few reported sightings of an unusual aircraft, heading out to sea. Would that have anything to do with the rather sketchily described rescue attempt we've been told about?"

Ettleman was beginning to wish the President had not been so keen on maintaining a look of normal operations. He would have preferred keeping a low profile for the next few days.

"Let me ask you this," Ettleman said finally. "If we did have an experimental aircraft out there, a *classified* military craft on the rescue mission, could you understand the reasons for only limited information being given out?"

Grant considered it. "You're saying that's why we've been denied access to the area?"

"I'm not saying anything. Just sounding you out. Do you realize the spot you could put us in? In that remote area the rescue operation is going to be difficult enough."

"I'll give you that. It's going to be difficult, all right. It's also going to be a whale of a news story, and I resent being kept out of it."

"Frankly," Ettleman replied, "an aerial view of the wreckage wouldn't be all that dramatic. And since that's all you said you were planning . . ."

Grant sighed, sensing he was in a losing battle. "Okay, Herb, you win. But don't expect me to give up on this."

"You've got your job to do and I've got mine," Ettleman said. "But when there's a story, I'll see that you get it . . ."

In the White House at that moment, President William Evans sat behind his desk in the Oval Office, the handset of a very special red telephone clutched to his ear. For the moment there was only silence at the other end—a long silence that had followed the initial answer by an on-duty aide.

Evans glanced at the clock on his desk. It was now almost 9:00 P.M. in Washington, D.C., and Evans knew from quick calculation that it was about 5:00 A.M. in Moscow.

On the other end of the line there was suddenly the sound of a man clearing his throat, followed by an inquisitive reply—

"Da—? Yes?"

"Sorry if I woke you," Evans said brusquely. "I presume you are aware of the situation in the Pacific?"

There was a momentary silence, then Aleksandr Shenikov replied, "I have not been sleeping. And yes, I am aware of the situation you describe."

The Soviet Communist party leader's words were heavily accented, but there was no hesitancy in their choice. Although Shenikov invariably used a translator at official meetings with international leaders, his command of English was quite good.

Evans said, "I am concerned about this friction between our two nations. I would hate to see this develop into something we would both regret."

"I share your concern. But there is a most obvious solution to this problem."

"Then I would appreciate your enlightenment."

"It is simple," Shenikov said. "The presence of your airship is the inflammatory element. Withdraw it from its present course and mission, and there will be no further *friction*, as you say it."

Evans face held a wry smile, and the tone of his voice reflected it. "The same could be said of your aircraft carrier. And as far as our airship being the inflammatory element, may I remind you that it was the *Kiev* that initiated hostile action against our craft, which is engaged in a rescue mission."

"A rescue mission? Perhaps. But it was your airship that destroyed one of our jet aircraft and endangered the life of a Soviet pilot. You cannot deny that."

"The action that was taken was purely defensive. We have taken no aggressive actions against the *Kiev*."

"We are dealing in semantics now," Shenikov chided.

"I think not," Evans said firmly. "And your pilot was deliberately spared. He could have been destroyed just as easily as his plane."

"It would be unwise in the extreme to cause the death of a Soviet citizen."

"It would be equally unwise to risk the deaths of Americans. Your pilot's attempt to disable the *Grand Eagle* could easily have resulted in fatalities."

"*Could have* ..." Shenikov said, his voice rising. "But we are not dealing with possibilities, we are dealing with facts. And it is a *fact* that your military craft and personnel are under orders to kidnap a Czechoslovakian national who has great value to his homeland and its allies. We cannot allow that to happen."

"And we," Evans stated firmly, "do not intend to allow a man to be involuntarily returned to a country he freely chooses to leave." The President paused, then his tone became less formal. "I think we both know what's at stake here, as well as each other's intentions, without the rhetoric. What concerns me the most is the danger that hostilities between our two craft will escalate to the point where real damage *is* done, and lives are lost. That could push both of us toward a much graver conflict than either of us desires. My military leaders are already in favor of some form of action in light of the attacks launched against the airship."

There was a slight pause, then Shenikov said slowly, "Yes ... the leaders of the Defense Ministry are of a similar mind."

Evans thought he sensed in Shenikov's words and tone a strange fellowship of command, as if the Soviet leader was in much the same position as he himself. Despite their ideological differences, Evans knew they were both bound as much by the personalities and mentalities of those around them as by the official policies of state.

"Is there no solution then?" Evans asked.

"I can see none that would be satisfactory to both our nations," Shenikov said. "I cannot and will not counter the orders concerning the *Kiev*."

"And I will not rescind the orders concerning the mission of the airship." Evans paused, then inquired carefully. "Is it possible that this problem could be kept contained ... *limited* to the craft and personnel already committed?"

Shenikov did not answer immediately. When he did, his own words were as cautious as Evans'. "I do not know. What you suggest may be possible. But only if this problem, as you call it, does not come before the eyes of the world."

"I think that can be avoided."

"You understand that I can make no promises ... ?"

"Yes. Neither of us can."

"Then we must trust to our mutual desire for peace, and our abilities as statesmen."

The conversation over, Evans hung up the phone and remained seated behind his desk for a full minute, reflecting on what had been said and on the possible consequences of his unspoken understanding with Shenikov. Evans knew better than to place blind faith in the Soviet leader's words, but from his several meetings with the man he had the impression that Shenikov was at least sincere in wishing to avoid a serious confrontation with the United States.

Finally, Evans rose wearily and left his office, heading once more for the Cabinet Room. The other members of the National Security Council were still present, and had remained almost continuously since the afternoon meeting. Passing a mirror in the hall, Evans paused briefly to study his features. He hoped the others would not notice his slight pallor, or the shadows beneath his eyes. Sighing, he walked on. The hours were ticking away, and there seemed so very little time left to resolve the problem. As he reached the door, Evans steeled himself for the questions he knew would come.

Entering the room, he approached Mitchell Hoyt, the Central Intelligence Agency's director. Hoyt still had his coat on, even though several of the men in the room had long ago abandoned the appearance of a formal meeting. Cigarette smoke hung in the room, and the feeling of muted tension that gripped the men there was every bit as tangible. A photo lay on the table before Hoyt.

Evans picked up the photo and examined it. It was a rather murky shot of a man's face, the staring eyes and open mouth suggesting a corpse. "What is this?" Evans asked.

"It just came in on the wire from Wake Island," Hoyt said. "The body was discovered there, stuffed into a refuse drum in a storeroom near the Trans-Pacific facility. We have no identity established yet, but we're working on it."

"And copies have been transmitted to the *Grand Eagle*," Martin Pretori added.

"Good."

Both Lewis Scoville and Gen. Eldridge Adamson approached Evans. The Secretary of Defense was the first to speak.

"Did you talk to Shenikov?" Scoville asked bluntly. "Did you make him aware of the responses we must take in view of the open attack on the airship?"

"Sir," Adamson began, "may I send new orders to the *Grand Eagle*, so that they are not restricted to a defensive posture?"

To both men, Evans said evenly, "I have spoken to Party Leader Shenikov about the situation. And no. the *Grand Eagle* shall remain under its present orders."

Adamson looked amazed. "But I thought ... surely after what's happened—!"

"The orders *stand*. Now bear with me. I shall try to explain. And I hope my counterpart in Moscow will have equal success. ..."

CHAPTER EIGHT

On Tongareva two hours later, it was a few minutes after 6:00 P.M., and the slanting rays of late afternoon sunlight were fading into their final fiery glow before evening. To the south, there was another kind of darkness approaching as dense and ominous storm clouds spread along the horizon. The disquieting wind that had been present the night before was picking up again, carrying the tang of salt spray with it and setting the coconut palms in motion, making them seem agitated and full of worried whisperings.

In Mary Akaru's room at the far end of the medical research facility the sound of that wind was muted by closed windows. Carla Jennings ignored it, concentrating instead on the sound of James Akaru's pulse as she listened with her stethoscope. Behind her, Mary moved to a small electric lamp in the corner of the room and switched it on, dispelling the encroaching darkness.

Carla was kneeling beside the cot on which James rested quietly now, his body limp and still except for his slow and steady breathing. As she took the stethoscope away, James Akaru's eyelids fluttered open and his head turned to face her.

"Dr. Carla ... ?"

"He's conscious now," Carla said to Mary even as the Polynesian woman approached her husband's cot. To James, Carla said, "How are you feeling?"

"Tired ... so tired," he said weakly.

Carla patted his arm reassuringly. "Your muscles have

been fighting against each other, because of a chemical that's in the lagoon. The worst of it has passed now. You'll be feeling better when you get your strength back."

"I hate to be a burden."

"You're no burden, James. You and Mary have helped me more times than I can count, so don't worry about it. Just relax and let me help for a change."

Carla rose and moved away from the cot. Mary Akaru pressed her hand, and the friendship and gratitude that shone on the Polynesian woman's face seemed to compensate for all the anguish of the past thirty-three hours.

"It is all right that I stay here?"

"Yes, of course," Carla told her. "Jill and Maggie can help out with the food, so you don't have to worry about that."

Mary nodded her head in appreciation, then quickly turned back to her husband as Carla left the room.

As Carla walked down the hall toward the main part of the facility, the pleasant scent of hot food greeted her. She stopped at the door of the small kitchen and found Jill Laudon standing before the hot plate, stirring a pot into which had been emptied the contents of a half-dozen cans of beef stew. The girl looked a bit bedraggled, but glanced up at Carla with a smile, brushing a loose strand of blonde hair from her eyes.

"How's Mary's husband doing?" she asked.

"Better now. I think he'll be all right."

"Good. Seeing him that way had me worried." Jill returned her attention briefly to her stewpot. "This may be the last of the regular meals. We're almost out of canned goods."

Carla frowned, looking toward the depleted shelves. "Already? I thought we had more than that."

"We may have," Jill replied, casting a sour look in the general direction of the main room. "I seem to remember a few cans of deviled ham and a couple of other things that aren't here now. I think somebody's been pilfering."

Carla thought a moment. "Alex Copley?"

"I'd be willing to bet on it."

Carla shook her head, sighing. "Maybe I should have locked this room as well as the one the radio's in."

"I wouldn't worry about it now. There's not much left to steal."

"Well, if we run out before help gets here tomorrow, I may be able to get some tuna from the islanders."

"Canned?"

"No ... fresh." Carla smiled at Jill's grimace. "Don't worry—I can clean it. Oh, and don't throw those empty cans away. The islanders sometimes use the metal for odds and ends."

Jill said soberly, "There's a better supply of metal down on the beach."

"The wreckage? Yes, I suppose so. And don't think some of that won't be used. Some of the islanders here still have aluminum combs made from the fuselage of a Liberator bomber that crashed here during World War II."

"A plane crashed here then, too? Who says lightning never strikes twice in the same place!"

"There are some differences," Carla said softly.

"Yes." Jill fell silent, stirring the stew before her. A worried look returned to haunt her normally cheerful features. "This whole thing's bad enough without having a murderer among us. And there's just no telling who it could be."

"No telling," Carla echoed, her own mind troubled once more by the threat that still hung over them all. "Even knowing now for certain that the person is still alive, and watching everyone for any clue, I still don't know who to suspect."

"I know what you mean. Sometimes I'm not sure if I *want* to find out, but I guess we should try. Maybe if we—"

Jill's words halted abruptly and her eyes focused at some point over Carla's right shoulder. Tensing slightly, Carla turned and discovered one of the male passengers standing directly behind her.

"Father Daniels—what ... what are you doing here?" she blurted out.

"Just going back to see how your helper—James, is that his name?—was doing." Daniels seemed calm outwardly, but he looked concerned. "What's all this about a murderer?"

Carla glanced briefly to Jill, whose fingers turned white as they gripped the stirring spoon harder. She looked back to Daniels, her thoughts racing.

Daniels noticed their hesitancy. "Forgive me for eavesdropping, but I couldn't help hearing what you were talking about. Were you serious? Is there really a killer here on the island?"

"We ... we didn't want to alarm anyone," Carla said finally. There was no way to avoid the matter now, with

Daniels at least. "But yes, there was a hijacker on the plane."

"A hijacker!" Daniels seemed surprised. Whether the emotion was genuine or not was difficult to tell. "Is that why we crashed here?"

"Apparently. The pilot and copilot were both killed before the plane crashed. Shot."

"How horrible. And you think this person is still alive?"

Carla nodded. She glanced toward Jill, but the young stewardess seemed to understand that she was to say nothing beyond what Carla had already explained. Looking back to Daniels, she added, "The problem is, we don't know who. Can't even guess."

"Have you alerted the authorities?"

Carla weighed the answer a moment, th . said, "Yes, I transmitted the information I had. After you've all been rescued, there'll have to be an investigation of some kind."

"Yes, of course. But that doesn't help matters much for the time being. What did you plan to do?"

"There isn't much we *can* do, outside of just keeping our eyes open and watching for signs of trouble."

Daniels nodded, silent a moment. If he sensed that they were suspicious even of him, he said nothing about it. "I'll do what I can to help. And if there's anything you can think of, let me know."

"All right," Carla agreed calmly, conscious now that her heart was beating a good deal faster than it should.

"You're sure there's nothing to indicate who it might be?"

"I wish there was," she told him truthfully, then as he started to walk away she added, "And Father Daniels—"

"Yes?"

"Please . . . don't tell anyone else about this. There's no need worrying them all."

"I understand." He gestured down the hallway. "Do you think James would mind a visit?"

"No. I think he'd be pleased you're concerned. If he isn't sleeping, you might talk to him for a while."

Both Carla and Jill were silent while Daniels' footsteps faded in the hall. Jill brought a trembling hand to her throat, then spoke.

"When I saw him standing there, I almost *died!*" she said, keeping her voice low. "Do you think we have to worry about him?"

"I don't know," Carla replied. "He's been a help in so many ways, and I'd really hate to think he's the one. But I don't know. We can't afford to rule out any possibilities."

"I guess not."

"Jill—do you happen to remember where he was seated in the plane?"

The girl closed her eyes a moment, trying to visualize the interior of the ill-fated jet. Finally, she gave up.

"I can't recall. Maybe Maggie would. She's got the passenger list anyway."

"I think we ought to check," Carla said softly. "Can you leave the stewpot unattended for a moment?"

"Sure—for a minute."

They both headed for the main room. There were only four of the crash survivors present—the businessman, Peter Benson, Professor Maca, Alex Copley, and Martin Sandersen, the silent man who still had not spoken. Maggie Newcombe was just visible beyond the door leading to the room with the seriously injured patients. She turned as Carla and Jill approached.

"Is everyone all right?" Carla asked.

"Yes, things are quiet for the moment."

"That's good. Tell me," Carla lowered her voice slightly, "do you remember where Father Daniels sat in the plane?"

"The minister? I think he was up near the front, but let me check—" Maggie pulled the passenger list carefully from her pocket and unfolded it. She scanned the first few lines of printed names. "Yes, here it is. He was up in the fifth row, an aisle seat. That's pretty close to where the plane broke up."

Carla considered it a moment. She wondered if he could have been in that area and made it through the crash with nothing more serious than the gash on his forehead and the cuts on his legs. Almost everyone else sitting that far forward in the passenger compartment had been seriously injured or killed. It was possible, of course, that Daniels could have escaped the fate of the others. Stranger things had happened in plane crashes and automobile accidents. And yet . . .

And yet the wounds could have another explanation. The gash could easily have come from a fight with the copilot in the cockpit, and the cuts on his legs might have come from climbing down from the shattered front section, for Carla well remembered the twisted prongs of metal that stuck out from the broken fuselage.

"Do you remember," she asked of Maggie, "whether you saw him in his seat during the last part of the flight?"

Maggie thought a few seconds, then said, "No, I really wasn't paying attention. Jill and I were in the back, and one of the other girls was taking care of the front section." Maggie paused, studying Carla's face. "Why? Do you think he might be the one?"

"Maybe . . . maybe not," Carla said. "I just wanted to get things clear in my mind. Thanks, Maggie."

Jill Laudon said, "I'd better get back to the hot plate—I don't want to ruin dinner."

"All right," Carla told her. "Let me know when it's ready and I'll help you serve it."

As Carla watched the blonde girl head back for the kitchen area, she became aware of the fact that someone else was also watching Jill's departure. The young man, Alex Copley, stared until Jill disappeared from sight. Something about him seemed different now.

She briefly considered confronting him with her suspicions about his food pilferage, but finally decided against it. It would accomplish little, and there were better ways of making sure nothing else turned up missing.

Carla was about to turn away and resume her routine checks of the injured when it suddenly struck her what was different about Alex Copley: he was wearing a fresh change of clothing. His leisure suit was almost the same as the one he had on before, but there were differences beyond the fact that this one was clean. His shirt was of a different color, as were his socks, the tops of which were visible as he sprawled forlornly in one of the few chairs.

Carla approached him, her curiosity aroused. Catching his eye, she said, "Clean clothes, Mr. Copley? How did you manage that?"

The sullen-faced young man looked up at her for a moment, as if considering whether to bother with an explanation. Finally, he shrugged and answered, "I found my suitcase in the wreckage this morning. It didn't get busted up, so I brought a few things back."

Carla thought back and remembered Peter Benson telling her he had seen Copley poking around in the wreckage earlier. Now it seemed there was a reasonable explanation for it. Perhaps.

"You really shouldn't go near the wreckage," Carla told him. "It could be dangerous."

"You're just like all the rest, aren't you, Doctor Lady."

Carla frowned. "What do you mean?"

Copley straightened a little in his chair. "If it wasn't my parents telling me what *not* to do, it was teachers. Or the police and judges. Everybody likes to play the big shot!"

"Including you?"

He opened his mouth as if to snap back a sharp answer, then settled for a silent glare. Considering his usual behavior, his restraint now was almost surprising.

Nearby, Professor Maca stopped his pacing and approached them. He gave a quick and disapproving look to Alex Copley, then spoke directly to Carla.

"Have you heard any more news—when we will be rescued?"

"All I know," Carla told him, "is that the rescue team is on the way, and should be here sometime tomorrow."

Maca glanced away, sadly shaking his head. "Ten years of work on my research, and now, when I'm ready to present my findings to the World Science Conference, something like this . . ." He looked terribly distressed, then in the next moment seemed to think better of his words. "But this tragedy overshadows my own inconvenience. Forgive me, Dr. Jennings, if I seem to be thinking only of myself."

"I understand," Carla said, and her look took in Alex Copley as well. "After what's happened, we're all on edge."

Professor Maca nodded tiredly and walked away.

One thing, at least: Of all the varied people who might be responsible for the crash, Carla felt certain that the professor was beyond suspicion. His small, slight form in its loose-fitting suit seemed incapable of violence. Carla had not been able to confirm his story with Lorenz yet, but apparently the two scientists had been seated side by side throughout the entire flight. And there was nothing in the man's actions so far to cast any doubts on his identity.

Carla sighed, wishing she could be as certain about the others. . . .

The *Grand Eagle* was nearing the equator at 7:00 P.M. local time, a few hours later. Cruising into stronger head winds now in the equatorial region, the airship was moving at far less than top speed. Still, it had managed to cover three fourths of the distance from San Francisco to Tongareva.

Sailing majestically through the deepening darkness, the *Grand Eagle* held true to its adjusted course. Tracking and defense systems were still on ready status, even though there had been no further trouble from the Soviet carrier since the jet assault hours earlier.

In the airship's mess facility on Deck B, Paul Brandon and the government man, Haddock, sat at one of the long tables. Most of the off-duty personnel had eaten dinner at six, and now the room was almost empty.

Haddock glanced toward Brandon's tray and its half-eaten food. "What's the matter, Doctor—not hungry?"

"Not really."

Haddock nodded, but did not probe. He did not have to be a psychologist to know the man was worried, or to guess at the reasons. He tried to make conversation.

"Have you ever been in the South Pacific?"

"What? Oh, no ... I haven't." Brandon drained his coffee cup and set it down somewhat impatiently. "When do you think they'll have some idea who that murdered man was on Wake Island?"

Haddock sighed. "Hard to say. All the agencies are checking the photos and fingerprints against their files, but that could take quite a while. There are automated systems that simplify some of the procedures, but most of the files still have to be checked through individually." Haddock tried to sound reassuring, but he was concerned himself. "It takes time."

Brandon shook his head slowly. "I don't like it—Carla having to play this kind of waiting game with someone who's already killed three men outright and twenty-seven other people indirectly."

"I don't like it either, Doctor. But at the moment, there's not much we can do about it." Pausing briefly, Haddock asked, "What kind of chances do you think Lorenz has now?"

"I don't know. Assuming we get to him sometime early tomorrow, and his condition remains stable, his chances of surviving the operation are a little better than fifty-fifty. But I can't make you any promises. There are so many things that could go wrong, and Carla doesn't have even half the drugs or equipment she might need to handle a problem."

Haddock nodded, his own face mirroring Brandon's grim look. Rising, he said, "Well, let's get back upstairs. I don't like being away from things for too long."

"Right," Brandon replied, getting to his feet. He allowed the seat to swivel back beneath the table and picked up his tray, following Haddock to the waste receptical.

When they reached the command deck's control center, the two men headed toward the general. Smalley was conferring with Colonel Curtis, Major Tate, and Lieutenant Colonel Foster. As Brandon drew near, he could see that the four officers were looking over printout sheets listing the remaining missiles in the primary defensive system and computer projections of how long they might last in a renewed assault.

"Any word from Washington?" Haddock asked as Smalley looked up.

"Nothing worth mentioning. Just a few routine checks on our systems status." It had been a trying day and Smalley was beginning to look slightly fatigued. "Oh, and we sent some high-speed telemetry to Edwards Air Force Base for retransmission. All the recorded data from the computer's tracking and control logs, made during the Russian sortie this afternoon. The video tapes, too. Seems the boys in Washington want to look the stuff over to see what they can learn about Soviet air tactics." Smalley scratched his neck, smiling faintly. "Probably end up as some sort of training film."

"And nothing about the dead man on Wake?" Brandon asked.

Smalley shook his head. "Something may turn up yet, but there's always the possibility that there's just no data on him in any of the files."

Haddock began to pace slowly, staying within range of the others. "We've got to find out the man's identity. It may just tell us who the Soviet agent is, and I'd rather know that before we get there."

"So far," Smalley commented, "the photo doesn't match any of the data we've received on the survivors. Of course we still haven't pictures of them all, yet, so if it turns out that the dead man's photo matches that of someone *listed* as being alive on the island, then we'll know the man there is an impostor."

"If it matches," Haddock added.

Brandon frowned. "We'd better hope it does. Carla should be warned."

176

Haddock considered it. "I don't know. It might be better if she isn't."

"What do you mean?"

"Think about it," Haddock said. "As it is now, with the killer's identity intact, he probably feels he can just sit tight and hope the *Kiev* reaches the island first." He paused. "But suppose the man begins to fear that he's no longer safe with his little masquerade. Suppose Dr. Jennings reacts somehow to the truth about him, gives it away that she's on to him. Then what? Don't you see? It could put her in more danger."

Brandon was silent a long moment. He knew Haddock's words were true. The logic was reasonable. But it was becoming hard, if not impossible, for him to think objectively about Carla and the menace that was so near to her.

Further debate on the issue was cut off as Elizabeth Jordan approached from the communications console and extended a folder of facsimile printout sheets to the general.

Smalley took them and flipped open the cover. "What's this?"

"The photos and data on the Trans-Pacific jet crew you requested," Beth answered.

"We were supposed to get those hours ago. What happened?"

She shrugged her slender shoulders. "Near as we can tell, sir, there was some kind of foul-up at the airline's main office in Manila. These have just been transmitted from the relay station in Hawaii. Copies should be reaching Washington about the same time."

"All right, Beth," Smalley said, smiling to let her know he did not blame the delay on her. "Thank you."

Smalley glanced at the top two photos, showing the faces of the ill-fated jet's pilot and copilot. He looked at the neat uniform coats and the friendly and competent expression, then shook his head sadly. "I'm afraid these won't help us much. What we really need is information on the passengers."

Brandon reached out and took the folder from Smalley. "What will happen to the agent if we identify and catch him?" he asked Haddock.

Haddock pondered a moment. "If you're thinking of a trial, it doesn't work that way. He'll be kept in a special prison, of course, and we'll try to get as much information as we can out of him."

Brandon glanced up. "That's the worst that will happen to him? A mass murderer?"

Haddock shrugged. "It may not be justice, Doctor, but there are other considerations to be taken into account. The spy game has its own rules. Someday we may need to trade him for one of our own captured operatives."

Brandon shook his head and returned his gaze to the photos in the file. He flipped past the photos of the pilot and copilot and encountered pictures of the two stewardesses, Maggie Newcombe and Jill Laudon. As he studied their faces, it occurred to him that someone was missing here. He flipped back through the printout sheets and discovered that the second and third ones had stuck together. Separating them, he glanced at the face on the third sheet. He was about to close the file and return it to the chart table's top when he stopped and looked harder at the third sheet.

"Where's the last data you received from Washington?" he asked suddenly.

It was John Curtis who located the facsimile sheets and laid them on the table in front of Brandon. "Here—why?"

In answer, Brandon pulled a photo from the new file and placed it on the chart table, then shuffled through the other material until he located the photo transmitted from Wake Island. Looking up at the others, he said, "What do you think?"

The men looked at the two photos, side by side, comparing the faces. The angles were different, and in the one from Wake Island, death had contorted the features somewhat. But there was no mistaking the obvious.

"It's the same man!" Haddock admitted, and the others nodded in silent agreement. "Who is he?"

"That's what makes it strange," Brandon said oddly. "It's the jet's *navigator*, according to the label on the photo."

"The navigator." Smalley echoed the words. "The report from Tongareva was that the navigator had been killed in the crash, along with the pilot and copilot."

"No, wait," Haddock said quickly. "They presumed he was killed, but the body was never found."

Brandon frowned harder at the deepening mystery. "But how did the navigator end up on Wake Island? Surely the plane wouldn't have left without him. He was needed."

"Of course, ordinarily," Haddock replied, his eyes returning to the two photos once again. "But maybe it begins to make sense now, the whole thing about how the hijacker was able to take over the plane." He hesitated, looking through the materials. "The report from Wake Island said that the flight crew left the plane briefly while it was refueling and unloading some cargo. There was something about a personnel lounge. If the hijacker was able to pick a moment when the navigator lagged behind, or was separated for even a moment, he could have killed him and exchanged clothes, then gone on out to the plane."

Brandon protested, "But the other members of the flight crew would have known it wasn't the same man."

"Not necessarily. If they had already taken their places in the cockpit when the imposter arrived? They wouldn't have been looking for anything unusual, and it was dark then at that time of the morning. A KGB agent might have managed it."

Smalley agreed. "Yes, and he wouldn't have had to fool them for long. As soon as he was in the cockpit, he could have pulled a pistol and taken over."

Brandon asked, "So where does that leave us?"

"It's a mixed blessing," Haddock admitted. "Now we know another part of it, another piece of the puzzle. But as far as identifying the Soviet agent, I'm afraid we're back where we started. After the crash, the man must have assumed another identity—pretended to be a passenger, and played it by ear."

"But if that's what happened," Brandon said anxiously, "the killer could still be any one of at least four or five men, and we have no idea who."

"Unfortunately true," Haddock said reluctantly. "And that's not a pleasant thought. . . ."

On Tongareva a little after 9:00 P.M. Jill Laudon strolled through the stand of coconut palms surrounding the medical research facility. Overhead, a full moon was rising in the indigo sky, peering over dark clouds and touching their edges with silver. The sea breeze was balmy and pleasant, and the moonlight filtering through the palm fronds cast quavering shadows upon the sandy soil at the girl's feet.

It was better out here, Jill thought. The atmosphere inside had begun to feel too confining, too worrisome. Helping Carla with the meals and tending to some of the patients had kept her occupied, and she was grateful for the distraction. Still, there was no escaping the memory of the terrible crash, or the stranger and perhaps more terrifying threat that now hung over them.

Beyond, the sound of the surf was soothing. Waves that had traveled untold miles broke powerfully over the surrounding reef, sending diminished undulations of foamy water to lap upon Tongareva's shore. Here in the semidarkness, there was at least an illusion of peace.

Jill walked slowly, her arms folded, breathing in the exotic smells of the island and the sea. She felt tired, but knew she would find it difficult to sleep. She paused and leaned momentarily against the angled trunk of a palm. The view reminded her of another night in Hawaii when she, Maggie, and several of the other stewardesses, including the one who had died in the crash, had found some free time and got to see more than just the immediate area around the airport. They had all gone to a luau that night, and it had been fun. But the other girls had dates—even Maggie, surprisingly—and Jill had ended up feeling like a fifth wheel. In fact, she ended up doing exactly what she was doing now—admiring the romantic view alone.

The recollection brought a momentary twinge of sadness, and Jill pushed herself away from the rough tree trunk and continued her walk.

She'd taken only a few steps when a sudden movement to her right, a little ahead of her, made her halt again. From the dark and shadowy form of a tree another shadow separated and became the silhouette of a man. Jill froze in cold terror.

In the next moment, though, the man stepped into a flickering shaft of moonlight and his features became visible in the pale glow. He smiled at the girl's wide-eyed look. "Do you always spook that easily?" Alex Copley asked.

Instantly, Jill's fear gave way to irritation. "What are *you* doing out here?"

"Same as you, I guess," Copley replied, still amused at her reaction. "I just got fed up with that whole scene back there. Nobody's saying much, but the hostility that's floating around is too much."

"I think most of it's worry," Jill said, then her pretty face twisted into a frown. "And if there *is* hostility, you've sure been helping it along."

Copley brought a hand to his chest, feigning a wound to the area of his heart. "See what I mean? Even you."

Jill shook her head and turned away, starting back toward the building. She was in no mood for this kind of chit-chat.

"Hey!" Copley called after her, following. "You'd better not stay mad at me. Especially not after I've gone and done you a favor."

Jill halted, glancing over her shoulder. "Now what are you talking about?"

"Look here. I've brought something I thought you might want."

Jill watched as Copley held up two objects in the pale light filtering through the palm fronds above. Recognizing what he held, finally, she started toward him.

"My flight bag—Maggie's, too," she said with some agitation. "What are you doing with them?"

"Take it easy—I just got them out of the wreckage a little while ago. Thought you might appreciate the change of uniform."

Jill eyed him suspiciously. An act of kindness did not fit her notion of Alex Copley, and she wondered what he was up to now. Or even if he was telling the truth about why he had the bags.

Still, she was in need of her things. The clothes she was wearing were fairly bedraggled, and even her makeup kit was still in the flight bag. Maggie would no doubt appreciate getting hers back as well.

Reluctantly, Jill reached out and took the two bags, which Copley extended with unexpected courtesy. She looked them over briefly, then returned her gaze to Copley.

"You shouldn't have been out there, in the wreckage. Dr. Jennings said it was dangerous."

Copley shrugged. "I know what she said. I'm not sure I believe it. But either way, whatever cargo the plane was carrying is in the lagoon now, and the back of the plane seems safe enough."

"Maybe," Jill said, hesitating a moment before speaking again. "That still doesn't explain it."

"Explain what?"

"Why you bothered to get our bags. Why should you care about helping us out?"

"You see—there you go again! Why are you so touchy? What have I done to get you so down on me?"

"It's more a case of what you *haven't* done, to help out around here," Jill said, finally venting some of the antagonism she had felt since the day before. "Let's just say you didn't exactly impress me with your bravery after the plane crash."

Copley considered it a moment. "All right, so maybe I panicked a little. I don't go through an air crash every day, you know, and I never made any claims for bravery anyway. Let John Wayne do the heroics."

"You'll understand if I don't sympathize a great deal," Jill told him. "Carla and Maggie and I had to do most of the work getting people out of the back section. *We* had to risk the danger of an explosion. It wouldn't have hurt you any to help out."

Copley sighed. "So I guess I'm selfish, too, as well as a coward, huh?"

Jill studied him. "You're being awfully generous with the self-criticism, aren't you?"

"Might as well clear the air. I'm just trying to be friends."

"Why?"

"Why? Do I need a reason?"

"People usually have them," Jill said. "And I can't help wondering why you're being nice all of a sudden."

"What's wrong with being nice? I'm always nice with the right kind of people . . . people I like."

"And you like me?" Jill said warily.

"Sure. Why not? You act like you've got your head together, and we're about the same age." He grinned. "You're pretty, too."

Jill turned away from him again. "That's pretty transparent, don't you think?" she said.

Copley stepped closer. "You don't think I mean it?"

"No. And I don't care, anyway." She put the straps of both flight bags over her shoulder and started to head toward the building, some three hundred feet away. She had taken only four steps when he caught up with her.

"Wait a minute—" His hand touched her shoulder.

"Now what?"

As she turned to face him, Copley said, "If you don't believe I mean what I say, I guess I'll just have to show you."

In the next instant, his arms were around her, somewhat roughly, pinning her own arms by her sides. He had moved quickly, catching her by surprise. As she was about to yell, Copley forced his own lips against hers, kissing her hard.

Jill struggled within his grasp ineffectively. Copley was not a large man, but he was strong, and he seemed not about to let go. Jill tried to force herself to think clearly, to remember the best way to handle such a situation. Something in her mind told her to kick out at him, to use anything as a weapon against him. But her coordination had deserted her, and her muscles seemed incapable of responding.

She had stopped struggling, despite a dim realization that Copley was not holding her as tightly as he had. *Why?* She shoved away from him suddenly and stood there for a moment, breathing hard. Copley stood his ground but did not try anything else. Jill could not see his features in the shadows in which he stood, but she had the impression his face held a stupid grin.

Jill straightened the flight bags' straps again on her shoulder. With deliberate emphasis, she said, "Thank you *very* much, Mr. Copley . . . for reminding me just how much of a jerk you really are!"

Her rage threatening to dissolve into tears, Jill turned and fled, running the distance back to the building. She stopped a short way from the door, hesitating a moment in the darkness, trying to calm herself.

Trembling, Jill felt more anger than fear. She was angry with Alex Copley, of course, but more than that she was angry with herself. So what if he was moderately handsome? He was still a conceited louse who thought about nobody but himself. It was no great surprise that he had tried that, but Jill had expected more of herself. Even now, she felt confused about her reaction. Under the circumstances, even the fact that Copley had been attracted to her could not be much of a compliment.

Using the back of her hand to blot away the moisture welling up in her eyes, Jill glanced in the direction of the lagoon. Her vision briefly blurred by the tears, it took a moment more to focus on the surface of the water and to understand what she saw.

Her first thought was that she was seeing a reflection of the moon, somewhere out there near the center of the lagoon. But the position was all wrong. The moon was behind her—it couldn't be reflecting in the water from that angle.

Forcing herself to look harder, Jill's eyes cleared and she could see that the strange light was not upon the surface of the enormous lagoon of Tongareva, but came from well within its depths, ebbing up from some unknown source and flickering in the lagoon's center like cold fire. She felt an odd chill watching it, but finally tore herself away from the sight and returned to the building.

Still trembling slightly, Jill went up the steps and entered, heading for the main room. Before she could reach it, she saw Carla hurrying from the back room where the injured were being cared for.

As Carla approached Jill in the hallway, the stewardess gripped at her arm. "Carla—there's something funny going on out in the lagoon. I—"

"Can you tell me later?" Carla snapped, rushing on to the radio room.

Jill followed, caught up in a new feeling of anxiety, and watched nervously as Carla fumbled impatiently with the lock on the radio room door. When it was open, both women were inside in an instant, Carla moving quickly to the transceiver unit.

Carla switched it on, waiting for its circuits to warm up and wishing fervently that it were one of the new all-transistor models. As soon as she could, she triggered the transmit switch and spoke into the mike.

"ZK1DL calling USAF NA1 . . . Paul, this is Carla. Are you there?"

There was the usual momentary silence, then an unfamiliar voice crackled through the speaker. Another pause, and then Paul Brandon's voice was on.

"Yes, Carla—what's up?"

"It's Lorenz, Paul," she transmitted. "The diuretics are finally causing too much potassium depletion in his system, and the digitoxin isn't keeping him as stable. Over."

There was a pause again, then Brandon's voice came back. "Can you take him off the hydrochlorothiazide and use only the spironolactone? Do you think you can keep his heartbeat stable until morning?"

Carla's voice was strained as she replied, "I can try, but I don't think it's going to be enough. *Paul, I don't think he's going to last until morning . . . .*"

CHAPTER NINE

"**H**ave you got everything you need?"

Maj. Donald Shaffer, the *Grand Eagle*'s medical officer, kept pace alongside Paul Brandon as the five men walked quickly down the long corridor from the decks at the nose of the great airship back to the main elevator, roughly 180 feet forward of the craft's center. Brandon was busy making the final fastenings on a flight suit borrowed from ship's supplies, a close fit over the special uniform he had been wearing all day.

"I think I've got everything I can take—certainly not all I need," Brandon replied soberly. He checked his watch as they reached the elevator at the end of the corridor. The time was midnight. His watch had already been corrected once since leaving San Francisco and now it would have to be adjusted again, for as they drew nearer to Tongareva they were just entering the next time zone. "How long will it take us to reach the island?"

Lieutenant Colonel Foster, the fifth man of the group which included Brandon, Shaffer, Smalley, and Haddock, answered Brandon's question. "A Harrier can get you there in a little over an hour."

Brandon frowned. "That's not good for Lorenz. We've already lost two hours since Carla told us his condition was worsening."

"Couldn't be helped," General Smalley replied. "We had to get within range for a jet to make it there and back, and we're just now crossing the equator. There's still about nine hundred miles between us and Tongareva."

"Which is still cutting it close," Foster reminded. "The maximum range for a Harrier without midair refueling is only a little over seventeen hundred miles. If we get stronger head winds and the *Grand Eagle* doesn't make up the difference in the next two hours, our pilot will likely end up in the drink."

The men were silent as the elevator descended the short distance to the top deck of the Harrier bays. As the doors whisked open, they quickly strode out and headed for the spiral steps that led down to the planes. Shaffer handed Brandon his medical kit and equipment.

"I wish I could go along," Shaffer told him seriously, "but there's only one jet that can carry a passenger."

Brandon nodded. "I wish you could, too. But if I can get his condition stabilized, Lorenz may be able to hold out until you arrive in the morning."

This was Brandon's first time in this part of the airship, but he had neither the time nor the inclination to sight-see. As they reached the lower level of the forward Harrier bay, Brandon could see that Captain Lee, the officer who doubled as helicopter pilot and Harrier flight leader, was already suited up and standing on the catwalk beside his jet.

Brandon walked uneasily on the honeycomb catwalk flooring suspended above the bay doors below. As he reached Lee, the young air force officer extended a spare flight helmet to him. Brandon put down his kit and took the helmet, holding it awkwardly for a long moment. He slipped it on and secured the strap, then turned to the others.

Haddock pulled something from his coat pocket and offered it to the doctor. Brandon saw that it was a small automatic pistol, in a holster with two short straps on it.

He took it reluctantly. "You think I'll need this?"

"I hope not," Haddock told him. "But it would be foolish sending you into this kind of a situation without some kind of protection."

Brandon deduced from the strap arrangement that it was a leg holster and fastened it in place just above his ankle, pulling the trouser cuff back down to conceal the weapon's presence. He straightened.

"Are the Russians going to know I'm flying to the island?"

"Probably," Smalley answered. "But we have a few tricks we can pull in case they try anything. Good luck with Lorenz."

Brandon nodded, then turned and started up the steps that gave access to the plane's cockpit. He halted abruptly as a buzzing sound came from the tiny radio transceiver clipped to General Smalley's belt.

Smalley removed the unit and brought it near his lips. "Yes, John?"

With the helmet on, Brandon could just barely make out the crisp Texas intonation of Colonel Curtis, still at the control center of the command deck. He leaned closer, straining to make out the words.

"Sir, we've received a message from Washington," Curtis was saying. "I thought you'd want to know."

"What is it?" Smalley inquired.

"The investigators there have run across something a little strange," Curtis explained. "You'll remember that Dr. Jennings gave us a little background information on most of the crash survivors, including the minister, Father Daniels? Well, the investigative team has been checking and double-checking to substantiate the man's story about prior service in Vietnam. The fact is, not only can't they find any record of that, they can't find any evidence that a Brian Daniels was ever in the Air Force."

Smalley frowned at the news, considering the possibilities for a long moment. "What about his civilian documents?"

"All in order, sir. Everything else checks out all right."

"Thank you, John." Smalley clipped the radio back to his belt and exchanged glances with the other men. "What do you think?"

"We've been looking for a flaw in one of their stories," Haddock said. "Maybe this is it."

"Maybe," Smalley halfheartedly agreed.

"It must be," Brandon commented. "If the man *isn't* the KGB agent, then why would he lie about his military service?"

"I don't know," Smalley replied. "The question is, assuming the man *is* the agent, why would he lie about something that could be so easily checked?"

"Perhaps it was only something he felt he had to tell Carla, to explain his familiarity with aircraft. Perhaps he didn't think the remark would be relayed to us for checking."

Haddock was now beginning to look skeptical. "It doesn't seem like the kind of mistake a KGB man would make. Strange. It doesn't figure any way we look at it."

"Maybe not," Brandon conceded. "But with the safety of Carla and the others at stake, it makes no sense to take chances. I think this Father Daniels is going to have to be put at the top of the list of suspects."

"Maybe. You'll have to play it by ear." Smalley had a sudden thought and unclipped the tiny transceiver from his belt once more. He handed it to Brandon. "Here—put this in your pocket. I've got a spare unit up on the command deck."

Brandon took the device and held it in his hand. It was roughly the size of two matchboxes, laid end to end.

"We use them around the ship and back at the base," Smalley continued. "For longer range use, you'll have to extend the antenna and flip the switch on the back. It still won't transmit beyond thirty miles, but it might be a good idea if you let us know what the status is when we get within range of the island, just so we know what to expect. That operates on a special high frequency, and it should be more private than Dr. Jennings' shortwave set."

Brandon pocketed the device, but he looked skeptical. "Thirty-mile range? Out of something that small?"

"Don't doubt it," Smalley said with his characteristic broad smile returning briefly. "It's all integrated circuitry. Cost Uncle Sam three hundred dollars apiece, so treat it kindly."

Brandon nodded, reached out reflexively to shake the extended hands of Smalley and Haddock. Then he climbed up and into the open cockpit of the two-seater Harrier, into the back. Captain Lee showed him how to buckle the harness into place.

"Sorry there's not more room, Doc," Lee told him as he observed Brandon's indecision over where to place his equipment. "You'll have to stow that gear between your knees if you can—just so it doesn't fly loose. I don't want it bouncing off my head."

"I'll do my best," Brandon told him. He was able to get his medical kit between his legs, just barely, but had to leave the smaller equipment case in his lap. He resigned himself to holding it securely for the duration of the flight.

The two-seater Harrier was a modified version originally intended for training purposes, with a longer nose section and a correspondingly longer tail section for balance. The canopy stretched over a wider curve to enclose the longer cockpit.

As that canopy closed over his head, Brandon watched Smalley and the others go back along the catwalk to the bay wall, where the chief NCO stood by the controls. Brandon's seat behind Captain Lee was slightly higher, giving him a clear forward view. He tried to make himself comfortable, but the narrow cockpit and his own tension made it impossible.

There was a sudden, deep humming sound as the bay doors slowly began to open beneath them. The electric lighting of the bay offered at least a feeble sense of security compared to the dark void coming into view below.

As soon as the bay doors were locked into position, and before Brandon really felt he was ready, the plane started down at the end of its launching crane. The action was smooth, but it was a disconcerting feeling even so. Brandon watched the well-lit bay disappear from view as the plane emerged into the open night sky. It was the first time he had been outside of the craft since boarding it, and Brandon was again astonished by the scale of the mammoth airship.

Captain Lee turned his head back and said, "Doc—if you'll plug that cord from your helmet into the jack in front of you, you'll be able to hear me after I start the engine."

Brandon reached up and felt for the cord, tracing it down to the plug on the end. Feeling for the socket, he located it and patched into the communications circuits.

In the next instant, a deep tremulous whine started up, ebbing through the craft and gaining in pitch and power. Sound-proofing in the cockpit did not shut it all out, nor did the enclosing helmets. In another moment, there was a slight shift in the jet's position as the full power of the vectored-thrust turbofan engine was reached, expelled downward through the four exhaust nozzles. The jet's weight was balanced now.

Brandon could not help a slight feeling of anxiety as he saw the hook overhead disengage from the launching crane and retract within the fuselage. For a long moment, the Harrier hung beneath the great airship, then gradually it began to drop as power from the turbine was redirected to the rear.

Communication with the airship controller momentarily ceased, and as the jet began to accelerate away from the *Grand Eagle*, Brandon took the opportunity to ask of Lee, "Just how fast does this thing go, anyway?"

In his helmet earphone there was the brief sound of a laugh, then he heard Lee reply, "Our maximum speed's seven hundred thirty-seven miles per hour. You are in a hurry, aren't you, Doc?"

Brandon sighed inwardly. "Right. Let 'er rip." As his eyes began to adjust to the darkness, he could see the ocean's surface far below, coldly illumined by the light of the moon. Ahead on the horizon though, a mass of black cloud formations blotted out the stars. "Is it going to be hard finding Tongareva at night?" I know they don't have an airstrip radio beacon."

"I think we can manage without," Lee's voice replied. "Our navigational system is linked by radio to the *Grand Eagle*'s computer. They've got the island's relative position locked in, and can guide us most all the way. Just relax, Doc—we've got some flying ahead of us. . . ."

On the command deck of the airship, Colonel Curtis was awaiting the return of General Smalley. Taking a position near the radar console, he studied the screens covering the rear quadrant.

"Any activity on the *Kiev*?"

The technician did not take his eyes away to reply. "Not yet, sir. It might take them awhile before they pick up our jet and realize what's happening." The man fell silent again, until a tiny blip separated itself from the larger dot that was the *Kiev*. "Something's lifting off now, sir."

"A pursuit jet?" Curtis asked.

"Could be, Colonel."

Curtis moved quickly to the RPV console at the right of the main aisle. To the control officer he snapped a fast order.

"Get two mini-RPVs out there, between us and the *Kiev*. Use the ones with ECM gear. Lay down a screen across that Soviet jet's path."

"Will do, sir." The control officer activated the system and opened the RPV bay doors. Before a minute had elapsed, two of the small unmanned aircraft had been launched from the guide rail and were circling back in the direction of the Soviet aircraft carrier.

Both of the tiny craft were equiped with ECM—electronic countermeasures—systems that could effectively scramble the radar signals sent out by a jet. One of the systems operated by purely electronic means, while another worked by spewing out a spray of metallic particles. Infrared detection would be countered by special flares.

In the darkness, the only hope the Soviet pilot would have of intercepting the American jet would be by the use of his sensors. And in another minute or two there would only be a wide band of clutter, effectively blinding the Russian equipment.

The RPV control officer watched his display screens. "Do you think they might try to reach the island, sir?"

"No, not yet. They're still a bit out of range," Curtis replied. "And we can make sure they don't try it later, either."

Watching the screens for several more long minutes, both men were relieved to see that the Soviet jet did not go beyond the barrier. It had called off its pursuit and was returning to the deck of the *Kiev*. Curtis watched for another few minutes to be sure nothing else was attempted.

"Keep the RPVs in the air for a while yet, just to be on

the safe side," he told the controller. Straightening, he glanced forward to the great window, where the lights of the departing Harrier had already faded into the gloom. "The Russians really shouldn't mind Brandon reaching the island," Curtis said after a moment. "It's probably the only chance Lorenz has. . . ."

"Dr. Carla!" Mary Akaru came trotting heavily into the back room of the medical research facility, glancing hastily around at the patients who lined the sides of the room on their improvised cots, then catching sight of Dr. Jennings emerging from the curtained-off area occupied by Stefan Lorenz.

Carla's features, already grim, took on an added look of concern when she saw her assistant's barely concealed fright. "What is it, Mary?"

The older woman gripped her arm, pulling Carla in the direction of the main room. "Come—you must see!"

Carla had rarely seen the woman so disturbed and went with her quickly. It was darker now in the main room, with only one light at the far end illuminating the area. It was a few minutes before twelve on the island, and most of the crash survivors were sleeping, resting as best they could in the chairs and benches.

Mary brought Carla to a rear window, facing the inner stretch of Tongareva's narrow landmass and the emerald lagoon which covered 108 square miles. Outside, the moon was partially obscured by clouds now, throwing only a faint glimmer of light on the water's surface.

"What is it?"

Mary Akaru pointed, thrusting a stubby finger toward the center of the lagoon. The words she uttered softly were spoken with a mixture of awe and fear. "It is the ghost fire."

Carla looked harder in the direction Mary indicated, and finally saw the greenish-white light that flickered in the depths of the lagoon. She had heard Mary speak of the phenomenon many times, always with a certain reverence, but this was the first time she had actually seen it herself. For all its eerie quality, her mind still sought a rational explanation.

"You're sure it isn't connected with the wreckage?"

"No—too far," Mary insisted. "The wreckage is much closer. No, I tell you, I see the fire before, Dr. Carla."

Still staring at the sight, Carla asked, "What causes it?"

"Some say it is a *taniwha*—a spirit of the dead." Mary paused, watching the eerie fire in the water, her hand gripping the cross suspended on the chain around her neck as if to reaffirm her Christian teachings at a moment when the older island beliefs surged within her. Turning to Carla suddenly, she said in a low voice, "It is a bad omen. When the fire comes, someone *dies.*"

Carla was not one to be swayed by superstitions, but even so, the words sent a chill along her spine. "Maybe . . . maybe not."

"It has always been true," Mary insisted.

Carla sought a way to calm the woman's fears. "A lot of people did die, Mary . . . in the crash. Maybe that's why the fire is here."

"No. It always comes before. Never after."

There was a sound behind them, and Carla turned quickly. Jill Laudon was approaching the window, rubbing the sleep from her eyes in an almost childlike fashion.

"Something wrong?" she asked as she reached Carla's side. Before either woman could answer, Jill saw what they had been observing. Her eyes widened slightly in recollection. "That's what I saw before! That strange light in the water. I was beginning to think I was just seeing things."

Even as she spoke, the pale luminescense in the lagoon ceased its flickering, slowly fading from view. In another moment it was as if it had never been there at all.

"Back in the war," Mary said slowly, "some sailors they went after the light in their PT boat. They tore open their boat on a reef, but they still found nothing."

Carla knew what Mary must be thinking. The fear on her features must surely be for her husband, James, despite the fact that he was improving. No, it was not James Akaru who was near death at the moment. It was Lorenz. For a moment, Carla began to feel some of the same irrational fear that threatened to overwhelm her assistant. She resisted the feeling. There was no time now for anything but clearheaded thinking.

She checked her watch. It had been roughly an hour since she had last spoken by radio to Paul Brandon. He should be arriving soon.

"Jill," Carla said suddenly, "I can use your help. Come on with me."

The two women headed for the small kitchen and

storage area, where Carla looked briefly around. Settling on the six empty stew cans left from the evening meal, she handed three to Jill and carried the others herself.

"What are these for?" Jill asked.

"Paul said we have to put out some kind of signal lights," Carla explained as they walked quickly and quietly back down the hall, heading for the front door and the outside. "The pilot will have to see where to land."

Carla led the girl around the back of the building to a small storage shed near the generator. She moved past the empty gasoline cans to the one can that still held gas and began to pour gasoline into the stew cans until each one was about a third full. "Okay, I think there's enough left for your three cans," she told Jill.

Removing rags from a box on the shed's shelf, Carla pushed one into each of the small cans, then carefully picked up three of them by the edges of the open tops, her other hand supporting their weight from beneath. Jill followed suit, walking behind Carla as they headed around the building once more and started through the stand of palms. "There's a clear area about four hundred feet ahead," Carla told her. "The ground is pretty firm there."

They walked the rest of the distance in silence, following as straight a path as the irregularly spaced palms would allow. The darkness was unpleasantly close around them, and the footing a bit uneven.

Coming out into the clear stretch of land a short distance from the beach, Carla halted, pausing to select the best position. Then with Jill's help, she began to place the six cans in a wide pattern roughly forty feet across, with two cans on each of the three sides. The side facing the ocean was left open.

Carla pulled a box of matches from her pocket and waited, her eyes searching the dark sky for some sign of the approaching plane.

"This Dr. Brandon," Jill asked softly. "He's a friend of yours, isn't he? Maybe more than that?"

Carla glanced at the girl for a moment, then returned her gaze to the sky. "Yes. At least, he was."

She tried to see the time on her watch, but the luminous dial was too dim to read. The plane should be arriving. It *must*.

In the next instant, as if in answer to an unspoken

prayer, a tiny dot of light became visible on the horizon. It grew steadily larger as the plane sped toward them.

Carla quickly struck one of the matches and dropped it into the nearest can, standing back as flame flared out. She ran to the next, igniting that as well, until after a moment all six cans were blazing with tiny fires. The burning gasoline illuminated the section of open land, marking the safe area's border.

Carla and Jill backed away from the spot, almost to the line of trees. They stood close together as the wind caused the flames to writhe and dance in the darkness.

The approaching jet came in low, circling the area slowly as some of its thrust was directed down through its exhaust nozzles. Coming around the second time, the pilot shifted entirely into vertical landing and hovered in midair, jockeying his craft into position above the area marked with flaming beacons.

Main landing gear dropped down from the nose and center of the Harrier, while the balancer wheels folded down from the wing tips. The jet's downdraft extinguished two of the burning cans, but by then the plane was well positioned and descending.

It was the first VTOL craft Carla had seen firsthand, but it made little impression upon her. Her mind was on too many other things, not the least of which was Paul Brandon. Carla had thought of Paul perhaps a hundred times since leaving San Francisco a little over a year ago, and now he was here.

The jet touched down gently, tentatively, then settled more fully onto its landing gear. The sound of its turbofan began to diminish.

Carla approached as the canopy was opened, but Jill held back, staying near the edge of the stand of palms. A dark figure emerged partway from the cockpit, a silhouette that Carla did not recognize as Paul Brandon until after he had removed his flight helmet. She reached up to take the equipment he lowered to her.

From the cockpit Captain Lee said, "Wish I could stick around, Doc, but if there's any more trouble from the *Kiev*, the *Grand Eagle* is going to need all the aircraft she's got."

"I understand," Brandon told him, stretching stiffly as he eased out of the cramped seating arrangement. He checked his watch. It had taken exactly one hour and fifteen minutes to reach the island. The airship was a good deal slower.

"Just tell the others not to take too long in getting here."

"Will do. Watch your step getting down."

Brandon climbed out and over the side, careful with his footholds, then dropped the rest of the distance to the ground. Regaining his medical kit from Carla, he directed her away from the aircraft.

Captain Lee immediately closed the canopy and started up his engine. When it had reached full power, the jet lifted off and gained a little altitude, turning toward the ocean. Gradually channeling thrust back to the rear again, it accelerated and soon disappeared into the darkness. In seconds the high-pitched whine of its engine was replaced by the steady sounds of wind and wave. Brandon and Carla faced each other, silent for a moment.

Carla broke the silence. "Paul . . . I'm glad you're here."

Brandon studied her face, the face that he had not seen in so long, a face that had haunted more than a score of dreams. "Carla, I . . ." He hesitated, then abruptly said, "How is Lorenz?"

"He's alive. That's about all." Carla turned to look at the cans of gasoline with their improvised wicks. The ones that had not been extinguished by the jet's landing had finally burned themselves out. "We'd better get back there."

They reached the edge of the stand of palms and Jill joined them. There was only time for hasty introductions while the three of them hurried back toward the medical research building, with Carla leading the way.

Standing in the doorway as they approached were Alex Copley and Peter Benson, apparently awakened by the sound of the Harrier's landing and takeoff. Benson peered anxiously into the darkness.

"Was that a plane?" the businessman said. "Has help finally arrived?"

"A doctor's been flown in," Carla replied quickly. "The rest of the rescue party should be here by morning."

"A doctor?"

Benson sounded annoyed, but Carla was in no mood to discuss it further. She started up the steps with Brandon following, and at that moment an electronic signal beeped loudly within the building. Carla pushed past the others and ran inside as quickly as she could. Brandon knew the sound as well, and hurried close behind her through the unfamiliar hall.

Within the main room, Professor Arturo Maca was just rousing from sleep, and the mute man, Martin Sandersen, was still dozing. Father Daniels stood at the doorway to the room where the critically injured were housed.

Rushing past the minister, Carla entered the back room. Maggie Newcombe was already there, standing halfway into the curtained area where Stefan Lorenz was sheltered. Maggie looked panic-stricken as the sound coming from the monitoring circuit of the electrocardiograph continued.

"It just went off," she blurted. "I think he's dead!"

Carla squeezed past the woman, rushing to one side of the cot. She examined the bearded scientist's still form even as Brandon knelt opposite her on the other side. Carla switched on the EKG's monitor strip. The needles did not move, marking only a straight line.

"His heart's stopped," Carla said quickly. "He's fibrillating."

"Get the sheet down!" Brandon ordered.

Carla knew what he planned, but replied, "I don't have the equipment you need—"

"I brought a portable unit!" Brandon opened the equipment case he had brought from the Steinman-Keller Institute and removed a small device only four by nine inches in size: a six-pound portable defibrillator only recently developed by a British heart specialist in Northern Ireland.

Brandon had the cables uncoiled in a moment and began to smear electrode paste on the defibrillator paddles. The transparent gel was a sterile lubricant which prevented a serious burn to the patient's skin. As Carla exposed Lorenz' chest, Brandon asked, "Is your EKG unit protected against a burnout?"

"Yes, I think so."

Brandon left the EKG electrodes in place, where they could monitor Lorenz' heartbeat. Switching on the small defibrillator unit, he placed one of the two paddles against the man's right front side and the other under the left armpit.

"Stand clear."

Carla pulled her hands away and watched as Brandon activated the device. A nickle cadmium storage battery within powered the circuit, firing a four-thousand-volt charge through Lorenz' chest for 1/250 of a second.

Lorenz' torso jerked violently as the charge caused sudden muscular contractions. Then his form went limp once more.

Carla's eyes shot to the monitor strip emerging from the EKG unit. The ink tracings on the graph showed a brief surge of electrical energy, then resumed a straight line again.

"It didn't work!"

Brandon frowned. "Stay clear, I'll try again."

The defibrillator unit took a fraction of a second longer to recharge its circuits this time. When it was ready, Brandon triggered it once more.

The same four-thousand-volt charge. The same violent physical response from the unconscious man. If it failed this time, Brandon wondered whether there was any point to a third attempt.

But this time, after the initial high surge on the EKG, the ink tracings did not return to a straight line. They began to trace out a weak but rhythmical pattern across the paper graph.

"It's beating again," Carla said hopefully.

Brandon watched the graph for a long moment, then set the defibrillator unit aside. He opened his medical kit and brought out an injector and several drug vials.

"I think we can keep him stable for a while," he told Carla. "But I'm not going to feel safe about him until we get him into the airship's operating room."

Carla nodded silently. And though her immediate concern was still for the critical condition of Lorenz, she could not help glancing toward the doorway, where most of the others now stood, looking in on their activity. They all seemed concerned, of course, but Carla knew that one of them was viewing the scientist's treatment with more than normal concern.

"Paul," she said softly, almost under her breath, "his safety isn't all we have to worry about. . . ."

At that moment on the Soviet aircraft carrier *Kiev*, arc lights burned with their cold glow, illuminating the flight deck. Near the forward end of the deck, sailors wearing brightly colored life vests worked to position a large and bulky object which had been towed up from the hangar deck below. Once the thing had been maneuvered into position, its low wheels were secured and locking pins were extended to mounting plates on the deck. Straining against the wind sweeping across the vessel, the Soviet sailors worked to remove the tarpaulin that covered the device. Finally, all that remained was to pull two heavy cables out to the side and connect their multipinned plugs to recessed receptacles on the deck.

As the men returned to the hangar deck, Adm. Nikolay Bakhirev and Capt. Konstantin Dashkevich were overseeing the work of another group of technicians. These men were busy adjusting special equipment built into one of the Freehand VTOL jets. Bakhirev nodded approvingly at the progress of that work, but clearly was not happy with everything.

"We must maintain top speed from here on out," he was saying. "We have already lost valuable time."

Dashkevich nodded, somber-faced. "An unavoidable loss, Admiral. The currents in this part of the ocean do not favor us. Once we have crossed the equatorial currents our progress will improve. But we still cannot hope to match the speed of the airship."

"Normally, no," Bakhirev admitted. "But now their own progress has slowed, and we do not have to match their speed to keep them from gaining their objective."

Dashkevich still seemed to have doubts, but did not voice them. He was silent a long moment, absently stroking the scar along his jaw. "There have been no further transmissions from Petropavlovsk—no further orders from Moscow. I do not like it."

Bakhirev slapped him on the back, a resolute look on his own firm features. "You worry too much, Captain. The orders we have already received must still stand. And I assure you, we have what we need to carry them out. . . ."

CHAPTER TEN

Paul Brandon sat on the hard wooden chair squeezed in between Lorenz' cot and the wall, his body too tired to protest the discomfort of the unyielding seat yet still too tense to truly rest. He longed for daylight, hoping the coming of dawn would bring at least some semblance of reality to the bizarre situation in which he found himself. He had arrived on Tongareva in darkness, seeing little of the low coral island. He might just as well be on the moon, he thought. The luxuries and pleasures of San Francisco seemed farther away than mere miles could account for—they seemed removed in time as well. He was a stranger in an alien setting, with unknown dangers lurking both within and without. Only one thing kept it from being worse.

Brandon looked across the cot, past Lorenz whose shallow breathing rasped in the near-silence. In a chair on the other side, partially sheltered by the sheets used to curtain off Lorenz' corner of the back room, Carla Jennings slept. She was slumped in her seat, one folded arm across the EKG equipment, cradling her head. In the muted gray light that filtered through the curtains, she looked very much as she had the last time he had seen her, a year ago. But now she looked exhausted and worried, even in sleep.

Something about that look, about her vulnerability as she slept in the midst of the human wreckage of the crash, made him want to go to her, to hold her. And yet the memory of her leaving still hung as a barrier before him. That, and the realization that however different he might wish things were, he could not change the past. For that matter, the look of vulnerability was a kind of illusion as well. Carla was every bit as competent as he was, and as independent.

Time was passing slowly, far too slowly for comfort. Brandon checked his watch, for what was probably the hundredth time in the last four hours. He had already examined some of the other critically injured survivors while Carla was still awake, but there had been little additional help he could offer. Carla's examinations and preliminary treatment had been thorough. Nothing else could be done until the people could be transported to the better-equipped facility of the *Grand Eagle*.

Brandon tensed suddenly, hearing something out of the ordinary. It took a moment to realize that the sound was that of the electrical generator outside the building. What had been a steady, monotonous hum was now a coughing sputter.

The lights dimmed, now flickering, now fading, matching the erratic sound of the gasoline engine. The spasms continued for another moment, then abruptly all was silence. The research facility was plunged into darkness.

Carla Jennings stirred in her chair, then sat bolt upright. "Paul!"

"Your generator's gone out," Brandon said quickly, carefully working his way around the cot to reach her side. "Is there more gasoline?"

"No—I used the last of it for the flares." She paused for a moment, then asked, "What time is it?"

"About four-thirty. I take it the sun won't be up for a while yet?"

"No. There are some candles and a flashlight in the storeroom. We'll have to get them." She brushed against Brandon as she left her seat. Reaching out, she took hold of his arm with sudden concern. "Paul—with the electricity off, the EKG monitor won't work. There won't be any warning if Lorenz has another attack."

"I think he'll be all right for a moment. If necessary we can leave someone with him to alert us. Let's get those lights spread around."

"All right." Carla moved past him, conscious of their closeness in the darkened room. "I'll lead the way."

Taking her hand, Brandon followed her into the main room. It was only a little less dark here, with a faint amount of illumination entering from outside. Brandon remembered there had been a full moon earlier, and wondered if the clouds had now completely obscured it.

Carefully they threaded their way through the close clutter of equipment tables and sleeping survivors, reaching the corner of the hall. Turning, it was only a short distance to the kitchen and storage room. But in the windowless inner room the darkness was complete.

Carla traced her way across the room, hands extended and probing. When her fingers made contact with the table along the wall, she felt upon its surface for the flashlight.

With a click of the switch, a spot of light brightened the wall, illuminating the rest of the room with its glow. Carla handed the light to Brandon, turning again to search through the drawer of the table for candles. She quickly located the box with its six-inch cylinders, stocky and utilitarian. On the top shelf there were a half-dozen candle holders with glass chimneys. Brandon helped with them, and in a few minutes had the first four of them lit.

"We'll put a few in the back room," Carla said as she worked, "and the rest in the lab. We can use the flashlight if we need to go anywhere else, or to the radio room. . . ." Her voice trailed off as realization dawned. "Oh, Paul—the radio! We won't be able to contact anyone now."

"They should be here in another four or five hours at most," he reassured her. "After that it won't matter."

"Perhaps not." She started to pick up two of the lit candles in their holders. "Let's get these out there."

"Wait a minute," Brandon halted her. "Before the others wake, I think we should check something." He was still wearing the flight suit over his borrowed airship uniform, and now he reached into the large pocket sewn along the leg. Extracting a packet of facsimile sheets folded almost flat, he straightened the photos out and spread them across the tabletop where the combined light of the candles provided a fair glow.

"These are all we have so far of the passengers," Brandon explained. "We couldn't get them to you before."

Carla studied the faces looking out from the glossy paper, occasionally picking a photo up to get a better look. One appeared to be of Alex Copley, and she was not surprised to see that it was a police photo. The ones of Professor Maca and Peter Benson were of poor contrast and looked old.

"I'm afraid these don't help much," Carla told him. "One of them could be an impostor, I suppose, but I just can't tell." She paused a moment. "What about Father Daniels and Martin Sandersen?"

"They couldn't locate photos for either man," Brandon told her, then asked, "What about this Sandersen? You said he seems to be in shock—mute, almost catatonic."

"Yes. His condition seems real, but I don't know whether it's a result of the crash or something else."

"Could he be faking it?"

"I . . . I don't know." Carla hesitated. "He'd have to be awfully good at it."

"The man we're looking for would be." Brandon was silent for a moment, thinking about what he had learned before leaving the *Grand Eagle* and about the cautions both Haddock and Smalley had given him. "Carla," he said finally, "there's something . . . a report that came in about the time I left the airship. It may turn out to be nothing, but it's a puzzle. The information you told us about Father Daniels' air force background. . . ."

"Yes—he was a pilot."

"So he said. But there are no records of his having been in the service. None at all."

Carla's expression was brooding, disturbed. "Could it be a mistake of some kind?"

"I suppose. And it doesn't necessarily mean he's the agent anyway. But it's a piece that doesn't fit."

She made no direct reply, seeming almost reluctant to consider the possibility that the man she knew as helpful and compassionate could in reality be a cold-blooded murderer in disguise. Carla changed the subject.

"Paul, there may still be more reserve gasoline at the clinic, over on the west side of the island near Omoka village. And there's a portable fluoroscope unit that I never got around to bringing here. It might be a good idea to check some of the more seriously injured before they're moved again."

Brandon considered it. "All right. Maybe after the sun's up. But first I want to take a look at the passengers that were killed. Maybe . . . just maybe, there's something there that will tell us what we need to know. . . ."

Dawn was breaking as the *Grand Eagle* steadily narrowed the gap between itself and Tongareva. On the command deck, the early morning glow was just beginning to augment the night lighting illuminating the instrument consoles.

The rear doors swung open and General Smalley entered the control center. He was wearing a fresh uniform and looked alert and ready, despite the fact he had slept little during the night.

Haddock was waiting for him near the helm console, as was Colonel Curtis. Curtis spoke first as Smalley approached.

"Good morning, sir."

"Let's hope it is," the general said dryly. "How's everything going, John?"

"Well enough so far. There's been no further activity from the *Kiev*." Curtis paused a moment, glancing back toward the control consoles in the rear of the area. "I've sent a fast recon RPV back for a look."

"Good. Has there been any contact with the island?"

At this question Curtis frowned. "Commo can't raise them, sir. We don't know whether their radio's out, or what. Which is doubly bad, since we received this update from Air Force Intelligence a few minutes ago."

Smalley took the report sheet extended him. "About Daniels—the minister?" He frowned hard, studying the message. "Blast! We should let Brandon know at once. You're sure there's no way to reach them?"

"Not by radio, sir. And now that the sun's up, I don't think we can spare a jet for another run."

"I suppose not." Smalley folded the message methodically and gazed for a moment out the great window that was the forward wall of the command deck. "We should be there soon. But I don't like the way that weather's shaping up out there. The head winds are already slowing us down."

Curtis stepped over to the navigation console, where the navigation officer and a number of technicians were working with the computerized systems. Picking up a printout sheet, Curtis brought it to Smalley.

"We've got new photos from the Pacific weather satellite," Curtis told him. "This one's the latest." He pointed to a light gray swirling mass near the lower edge of the grid-covered picture. "It looks as if the tropical storm may miss the island."

"Maybe," Smalley said. "It's hard to second-guess one of those things. Whatever it does, it's still going to kick up a lot of wind for miles around. We'll have to get in and out of there as fast as we can. I don't want to put this ship through that kind of test just yet."

"Sir!" The voice came from behind, from one of the RPV control officers. Smalley and the others headed for the console.

"It's coming within range," the control officer told them, indicating the screen on the RPV console. The television image was electronically enhanced to compensate for the lower light level. The *Kiev* showed up as a small dark spot upon the surface on the ocean.

"Take it in easy," Smalley instructed the controller. "We just want a look."

The jet RPV covered the remaining distance quickly, and soon the telephoto image was nearly filling the screen. Even so, detail on the surface of the large Soviet aircraft carrier was difficult to make out in the poor light.

The controller said, "Looks like two planes on deck, sir."

Smalley did not answer immediately, waiting instead as the image grew a little larger, the RPV circling now to keep a position above the ship. Peering hard at the television screen, Smalley finally said, "No—*one* of them's a plane. The other is too boxy . . . no wings, either."

"Some kind of crated equipment?" Curtis suggested.

"Why would it be there?" Smalley replied. His eyes still riveted to the image, he observed, "There's some kind of movement now, at the center. Can you get a closer view?"

Before the control officer could answer, the television screen went crazy. The image dissolved into a jumbled pattern of light and dark, then faded abruptly to gray and did not change.

"What happened?" Smalley demanded. "Has the camera gone out on us?"

The controller checked his readings, quickly testing backup circuits. "Negative, sir. All the other signals have ended, too. The bird has been destroyed."

"Destroyed? Have you got it on tape?"

"Yes, sir. I'll run it." The man put the video tape equipment on rewind briefly and then started the tape up again on playback. It looked the same as before. He tried again, this time switching to the slow motion circuit.

"There!" Smalley said suddenly. "Just before the signals stopped altogether, there was a flash of light from the deck."

Curtis understood, but showed surprise. "A laser?"

"It must be. We knew the Russians were developing a system. I just wasn't aware they had a shipboard model ready." Smalley considered it a moment. "I wish I knew its range. It's probably limited, but still . . ."

"It may not matter," Curtis said oddly, glancing toward Haddock. "Since Washington has ruled out any direct contact with the *Kiev*. Unfortunately, the Russians seem to be under no such restrictions."

Smalley seemed not to hear the remark, or to notice Haddock's obvious discomfort. The general turned quickly and headed for the radar and allied sensors console. "Something's up," he said softly.

Haddock followed, reaching the area a step before Curtis. "What is it?"

"I don't know," Smalley replied. "But they didn't want us to see something, I'll wager."

The radar technician was busily adjusting his set. The entire lower quadrant of the screen appeared hazy. "I don't know what kind of gear they're using, but they've jammed the rear sector."

Smalley smiled faintly, knowing his hunch was right. "What about infrared?"

On the adjacent screen, a small red dot had appeared from the direction of the *Kiev* and was moving south. Its rate of progress appeared slow on the screen, but the readouts on velocity showed the craft was a jet.

Smalley turned to Lieutenant Colonel Foster, a short distance behind. "Scramble the Harriers. I want them ready!"

"*Yes, sir.*"

"It doesn't look like a direct approach," Curtis said, studying the screen. "Their jet's maintaining a course parallel to ours so far."

"That may be only a charade. He's still too close for comfort."

Within moments, six Harriers came into view from beneath the great airship and went into a holding pattern, circling wide. Smalley noted their positions on both the radar screen and the television screens that showed a complete view of the sky.

On the infrared sensor's display, the Soviet jet continued along its flight path, maintaining a course only a few miles to the starboard side of the airship. Long minutes passed. Outside, the sky brightened as the sun rose well above the horizon.

The Soviet jet was now even with the airship—now passing it—neither slowing nor wavering from its course. Smalley watched the screen for several more minutes, then quickly said, "The pilot's making a run for the island! *Foster*—turn him back—"

As orders were given to the Harrier pilots, the six VTOL jets pulled out of their holding pattern and roared away on a course that would intercept the Soviet jet.

Smalley watched the television monitors as the jets closed on the Soviet pilot. Even at the considerable distance involved, the potential conflict was happening much closer to the *Grand Eagle* then he would have preferred. But there was no helping it now.

The Harriers were almost upon the Soviet jet. The six pilots pressed their engines to the limit, gaining the speed necessary to overtake the craft ahead.

Almost at the last moment, the Russian pilot pulled up into a steep climb, then rolled right, eluding the pursuing craft which roared on beyond their target. Captain Lee swiftly duplicated the move, leading his pilots back toward the jet once more.

The Soviet pilot continued to take evasive action, apparently unwilling to yield to the threat posed by the six

American craft. As the bizarre aerobatics continued, the seven craft drifted closer to the area of the *Grand Eagle*.

Smalley's look of concern deepened. "What's he trying to accomplish? He must know he can't elude them forever—he can't reach the island." To Curtis he said, "Get on the Soviet aircraft frequency—warn him off."

As Curtis moved to comply, the Soviet jet suddenly banked to the left, swinging away from its southern goal and returning north. The Harriers followed, attempting to ensure its retreat to the *Kiev*.

"Wait!" Smalley said, holding up a hand to halt his second-in-command. The general watched as the jet continued. It seemed to be giving up in its effort, but its flight path was carrying it almost directly toward the great airship. Smalley's hands clenched. His face tightened in concern. "I don't like it. He's coming too close, and with our own jets right behind him we can't risk using our on-board weapons systems. Foster! Get those jets off his back . . . give us some clearance!"

Colonel Foster snapped quick orders into the microphone of his headset unit, but the timing was too close. Even before the Harriers could pull up out of range, the Soviet jet had made one last correction in its course and was now pointed directly at the nose of the *Grand Eagle*.

It did not hold that trajectory for long, but a few moments was all it required. This time, its assault was not with missiles. A different device built into the fuselage of the craft became its weapon.

"*Look out!*" Smalley yelled, instinctively turning and diving for the deck's flooring.

As the Soviet jet loomed large within the forward television monitor, nearly everyone on the command deck was reacting, swiveling away from the front of the ship. At the helm, Lt. Col. Stewart Gardner shoved his junior officers aside—for both men were frozen at the controls—and lunged for the controls of the turbo thrusters, jamming the buttons down hard in an effort to deflect the nose of the airship.

In the next instant, a dazzling flash of light erupted from the leading edge of the Soviet jet. The brilliant ray flooded the interior of the command deck, reaching across half of the section even as the nose of the airship rotated away with ponderous effort. For a split second, all details of the control center vanished in the intense light's glare.

Immediately, the Soviet jet pulled up and away, rocketing past the airship with its pursuers still in the process of pulling clear of the area.

General Smalley rolled over, fighting his way up from the deck. Others near him also struggled to regain their seats, looking dazed and bewildered. For a brief instant, Smalley himself seemed dazed. He stared blankly at the floor, eyes trying to make out the fragmented object that had fallen loose when he gained his feet. Finally he made it out. It was his meerschaum pipe, broken in his diving fall. He picked up the pieces absently, then coming alert suddenly, looked about the command deck for damage.

Oddly, there was none visible. He had half expected an explosion, and for an instant the intense flash of light seemed to bear out that fear. What he saw next brought sudden understanding.

At the helm, Stewart Gardner was still on his feet, though leaning for support against the console. Turning slowly, awkwardly, Gardner faced away from the front window, mouth agape, staring blankly into thin air. Right hand probing fitfully, he stepped forward. Gardner's foot caught on the leg of a technician who had not yet arisen from the deck and he stumbled, sprawling to the flooring. Smalley reached him only a split second after John Curtis.

As they helped Gardner to his feet, he stared past their faces, looking at nothingness. "I . . . I can't see. Sir!"

"It's all right," Smalley reassured him. "We've got you. Everything's all right." The general found himself repeating the phrase again, and wishing he could know for sure that everything *was* all right. To Curtis he said, "Get someone up here. We've got to get him down to medical."

John Curtis nodded, looking around. There were several others who had been unfortunate enough to be looking toward the forward window when the flash erupted. They also were blindly groping, confusion and near-panic on their features. Curtis headed for the communications console, leaving Smalley to steady Gardner.

"Cut those turbo thrusters!" Smalley bellowed at the two junior flight officers as they scrambled back to their seats before the helm. "Get us back on a stable course. *Tate*—get your weapons people back at their posts."

Haddock worked his way over to Smalley, aghast at the effects of the assault. "Good Lord, what happened?"

"I'm getting sloppy," Smalley said bitterly. "Should have expected something like this." With Haddock's questioning gaze still upon him, he explained. "The plane—it's one of their craft fitted with a laser designator. It's a device used for pinpointing targets so that missiles or bombs can home in on them. It's not a powerful laser—it can't damage the ship. But its effect on human eyes . . . I guess they figured they could stop us by blinding the crew. A second faster and they might have succeeded!"

Out beyond the airship, Captain Lee pulled his Harrier out of its climb, initiated to give the *Grand Eagle* a clear shot at the attacking jet. He had seen the flash of light that illuminated the nose of the airship, but he did not wait for confirmation of damage or injuries. He angled off in the direction the Soviet jet had taken and pushed the Harrier to its top speed. A quick check via radio assured him the other jets were with him in the chase. Lee did not know if the *Kiev* had other aircraft outfitted with laser designators or not, but he was determined that before many more minutes passed they would have one less.

The Soviet pilot was pressing his own craft to its limits as well, keeping ahead of the Harriers initially. But that distance was not great to begin with, and as the jets drew nearer the position of the *Kiev*, the gap narrowed. Slowly but surely, the slightly greater thrust of the Harriers' engines were allowing them to overtake the fleeing craft.

Captain Lee, well in the lead of the loose formation, was in range now. Maneuvering his jet so that the Russian craft stayed within his sights, he momentarily considered the missiles waiting with deadly power beneath his wings. Then, thinking better of it, his hand passed the missile controls and settled on the trigger of the two Aden 30-mm machine guns. Lining up his sight carefully, he fired a burst.

Chattering a throaty roar, his guns fired only a second. The first rounds were low, passing beneath the body of the Soviet craft. The rest of the burst hit home, chewing its way through the tail section of the fleeing jet.

With a sudden harsh squall of sound, the turbines within the Russian jet began to shred, sending a torrent of fragments spiraling back. Lee pulled up quickly to avoid the debris, watching as the craft started to lose altitude. He waited until he saw the Soviet pilot eject and the chute pop before circling back, making sure he did not come within range of the *Kiev*'s weapons systems.

The orange chute billowed open and caught, the pilot dangling beneath it. Below, the damaged jet arced toward the surface of the ocean, starting to tumble as minor explosions within its frame rocked it. An instant before slamming into the waiting waters, the remaining fuel ignited and the craft burst into a bright fireball, splashing into the ocean in flaming bits.

Continuing to circle for the moment, Captain Lee searched the horizon, peering in the direction of the *Kiev*. As his plane came around again, he thought he could make out a number of tiny specks of light. His own tracking instruments showed nothing in the area.

"Eagle, this is Flight Leader," Lee said into his microphone.

"Roger, Flight Leader," Foster's voice came back.

"Their bird's in the drink. Did you sustain much damage?"

"Negative," Foster replied. "No structural damage, although our main forward camera was affected. Four crew members were injured."

"Sorry to hear that," Lee transmitted. "Tell me, are you picking up any bogies to the north?"

There was a slight pause, presumably while Foster checked with radar and allied sensors. "Negative, Flight Leader. Everything in that area is pretty well scrambled by their gear. Why? Have you a visual?"

Lee turned trained eyes once again toward the horizon. This time he could be sure. There were indeed aircraft approaching from the *Kiev*. "Affirmative, sir. More jets from the carrier are on the way. I estimate six . . . maybe seven."

"Are they headed our way?"

"Hard to tell, sir. Look's like they may be going around."

"If they go for the island, intercept," Foster's reply came quickly. "But if they make a move for the airship, stay clear. Our defense systems are on. Your beacon signals have been locked in for identification so you won't be fired upon by our own missiles, but you'd be better off out of the area."

"Understood," Lee radioed. His fellow pilots were in a closer formation now, and they held back, waiting to see what move the approaching Soviet jets would make.

It did not take long to find out. The Russian planes maintained a heading toward Tongareva, giving the massive airship plenty of latitude. They were at a point almost even with the *Grand Eagle* when Lee directed his jets toward them in an effort to intercept the Soviet craft and turn them back.

Lee and his pilots reached the area in a matter of minutes. But the Soviet craft avoided contact, banking away in unison, with a precision that was almost uncanny. More minutes passed as the Soviet craft continued to evade the American Harriers. They were getting no closer to their goal—the island—but neither were they being turned away.

Just as the American craft were making another approach, all six Soviet jets executed a swift maneuver, pulling up into a steep climb. Surprised, Captain Lee watched the move, sharp eyes trained on the jets' silvery forms. Something he had wondered about since their first maneuver seemed suddenly confirmed.

On the command deck of the *Grand Eagle*, General Smalley watched the progress of the chase on the television monitor. Behind him, a technician at the radar console called out suddenly.

"Sir—there's something else out there."

Smalley moved quickly to the console and studied the screen. He could make out only the six American and six Soviet craft, and even these were partially obscured by the effects of the Russian equipment.

"Where?"

"To the east, sir." The technician indicated the portion of the radar screen. "Their ECM gear faded for a moment, and I could make out blips farther out than the other aircraft."

"How many?"

"At least six more."

Smalley frowned. "We should have picked them up on infrared by now."

"Not from that angle, sir. They've really swung wide, and with the sun just coming up, our infrared isn't much use in that quarter."

Even as Smalley was starting toward Colonel Foster to alert the Harrier pilots, Captain Lee's voice was coming over the console speaker. There was an odd edge to it as he spoke.

"I think we're chasing robots."

Foster arched an eyebrow and spoke into his mike. "Repeat, please—"

"Pilotless planes," Lee replied quickly. "Their maneuvers

are too tight for them to be manned. And I can't see anyone in the cockpits."

"Decoys!" Smalley said sharply. "Tell them to forget those Russian RPVs and go after the other jets to the east. They must turn them back!"

Foster relayed the orders, along with approximate coordinates from the brief radar sighting which had been made. He watched his own display as the Harriers banked away from the pilotless planes and headed east.

"We can't keep this up forever," Smalley said with concern. "They have more aircraft than we do—if they should get all their ships in the air at once, we wouldn't have a *chance* of stopping them from putting men on the island ahead of us."

From the radar console, the technician called out, "Sir—they've switched off their ECM gear. The screens are clear in that sector now."

"Are there any more planes lifting off the carrier?"

"Negative, sir."

Smalley was glad of that, at least. But the encouragement was short-lived.

"Trouble," Foster said suddenly. He pointed to the display on his console. "Now that the Harriers are in pursuit of the manned jets, the Russian RPVs are taking out after them."

"Our pilots will be caught in between—they can't fight those odds." Turning to Major Tate at the weapons console, Smalley asked, "Are those RPVs within laser range?"

"No, sir," Tate replied. "They're about a half mile beyond maximum range. We could use our missiles, but I hate to chance it with our own jets so close."

Smalley considered it. There was only a little time in which to act. There was no doubting that the Soviet RPVs were armed, and their maneuverability had already been aptly demonstrated.

"How many strike RPVs do we have?" Smalley asked of the main controller.

"Three, sir—four, if we convert one of the recon models."

Smalley frowned. "That would take too long. Launch the three you have at once. They're going to be outnumbered, so try to take at least three of the enemy ships out as soon as possible."

"Yes, sir." The control officer signaled at once to the other two console operators across the aisle on the command deck. One console could be used to control all three RPVs, but for the maneuvers required, independent control would be essential.

An officer and a noncom at each of the first three consoles activated the equipment. Already at the bottom of the great airship the RPV bay was opening. In another moment three BGM-34C remotely piloted vehicles extended into the open sky at the end of their launching arms. As controls at Consoles One, Two, and Three were activated, all three robot craft came alive, their turbojet engines whining up to full power.

Releasing from their arms, the RPVs dropped and began to pull away from the *Grand Eagle,* gaining in speed as they banked in the direction of their Soviet counterparts.

On the command deck, General Smalley had returned to the main radar console and was studying the screen intently. Far ahead, Captain Lee and his Harrier pilots were gaining ground on the Russian jets. Their chances for turning back the Soviet craft seemed good, as long as the robot craft now pursuing them did not catch up. Haddock came up behind Smalley, looking worried.

"They still haven't got any more ships in the air," Smalley said thoughtfully. "But we can't count on it staying that way for long."

Haddock also studied the screen, with its abstract symbols for men and machines. "What can we do?"

"We're going to have to make sure they don't launch any more, and that they can't use the ones they already have out."

Haddock looked up suddenly, concern on his features. "You know our orders—Washington wants no direct actions taken against the *Kiev.* We can defend the airship and block attempts to reach the island, but beyond that we can't—"

"Defending the *Grand Eagle* and reaching Tongareva first are exactly what I'm concerned about," Smalley cut him short. "It's the Russians' game now, and we can't play by our own rules and be expected to win!" Smalley went to the chart table and picked through the reconnaissance photos taken of the *Kiev,* selecting an overhead view of the flight deck. Then he turned and headed for the last inactive controller at RPV Console Four. Haddock followed, looking puzzled and concerned.

Smalley addressed the control officer at Console Four.

"Have the maintenance crew convert the special recon model at once," he said swiftly. "Leave the television cameras in place, but load all the explosives pods on it that it will hold—"

"Now wait a minute!" Haddock snapped. He took hold of the general's arm, then released his hold quickly as Smalley glared at him. "You can't take action against the *Kiev.* If their carrier is destroyed and Soviet lives are lost, there's just *no way* State can patch things up. There'll be the devil to pay. You simply cannot attack—"

"Give me some credit for intelligence," Smalley snapped, showing real irritation for the first time. "If I wanted to destroy that carrier, there are air-launched cruise missiles on board that could sink it in the bat of an eye. And kindly remember that on this airship I am still the commanding officer."

"All right." Haddock fought for control. "I'm sure you can understand my *concern.* But *please* tell me what you're planning to do."

Smalley's gaze became cool once more, and there was the slight trace of a smile returning to his normally cheerful features. "There's a tactic the Japanese used against some of our carriers, back in World War II. It's old, but highly effective. A slight variation will do the job, I think, and keep your people happy as well."

"I hope so."

Smalley returned his attention to the console. "We'd *all* better hope so. . . ."

In the air a mile and a quarter from the *Grand Eagle,* an odd conflict was taking shape. The three RPVs launched from the airship were about to intercept the Soviet robot planes. As they came within range, each of the American RPVs aligned itself with a target, approaching from the rear. At signals relayed from controllers on the airship's command deck, the RPVs' targeting systems locked onto the last three Soviet robot craft. Almost simultaneously, each RPV launched one of the four Sidewinder heat-seeking missiles it carried.

Too late, the Soviet machines seemed to sense their danger and started to pull up, trying to climb away from the threat behind them. But the Sidewinder missiles homed in on the Soviet jet exhaust and could not be shaken. In less than two seconds the missiles struck home and blasted the robot planes into shredded fragments.

Even before the fiery flash could fade, the first three Soviet RPVs of the formation banked away from their trajectory, redirected by controllers on the *Kiev* to give up their pursuit of the Harriers and instead turn to confront their new attackers. The remote-controlled planes executed a hard maneuver and banked again, seeking to bring the approaching American RPVs into line with their own weapons systems.

An eerie aerial battle began, with planes flown not by pilots but by technicians a goodly distance away, watching television monitors and the displays on their control consoles. Unimpeded by the stresses of gravity and inertia that limit the maneuvers of piloted craft, the RPVs were free to operate at the limit of their mechanical capabilities. The remotely piloted planes of both nations were climbing and banking with G forces no pilot could withstand, and with the swiftness of their computerized systems were responding far quicker than human reflexes could have managed. The battle was set now, the playing pieces committed.

A Soviet robot plane scored its first strike, as a missile from its pod flashed out and caught one of the airship's RPVs dead-center. Fragments began their drop to the sea below, minor explosions still flaring out in the machine's final death-throes.

But if there was celebration on the *Kiev*, it was doomed to be short-lived. For in the next instant the Soviet craft was itself struck by a missile from one of the two remaining American RPVs. And now it was down to two and two.

Banking and diving, the remaining craft began a spiraling, whirling dance as each sought to bring the opposing machines into position for attack. As computer-generated commands took over for human controllers, it became impossible to distinguish between evasive actions and direct assaults. What would in the past have been a war of nerves and reflexes was now a war of microcircuits and programming sequences. All maneuvers were coordinated by the real-time computers, until all movements began to appear almost choreographed, with destruction scheduled for the grand finale.

The second American RPV was hit an instant later, lingering a fraction of a second too long within range of its Soviet counterpart. Now there was only one jet left against the two remaining Soviet craft. Abruptly, on new commands fed into the circuits by its human controllers, the computer plotted a new maneuver for the RPV.

Diving, it followed the flaming debris of the second American craft as it plummeted toward the surface of the Pacific a mile below. Immediately, the two Soviet craft followed it, lining up their tracking systems on the dot of flame that marked the jet's position—a dot of infrared light that began to merge with the burning wreckage ahead of it. Ready to fire the killing shot now, the Soviet craft locked onto the target glow, arming their heat-seeking missiles.

At once, the American RPV cut power, its turbojet engine still free-spinning but drawing no fuel. Signals from the airship changed its control surfaces and brought it into a tight loop, pulling away from the path of the falling debris.

But the Soviet craft had already launched their missiles. The slender rockets were flashing out now, not to be recalled. But the target they were now locked onto was not the American RPV, but the burning wreckage slanting toward the waters below. Both the missiles and the robot planes had temporarily lost track of the RPV and were chasing an already doomed craft.

Completing its loop, the American RPV had reignited its engine and was coming over on top of the two Russian machines. Locked within its sensors now, the two robot planes were easy targets.

Twin missiles snaked out, each homing in on a target, and in another second both Soviet craft were destroyed in a blaze of incandescent heat. Its mission completed, the lone remaining RPV began to circle, awaiting further orders, and with one missile yet remaining.

On the *Grand Eagle*'s command deck, Lieutenant Colonel Foster watched the progress of the RPV battle as well as the Harrier interception on his console's display screen. Speaking into his microphone, he said, "Flight Leader, this is Eagle."

"Roger, Eagle," Captain Lee's voice came back.

"Do you need any help out there? We've got a strike RPV free and willing to assist."

"Negative," Lee replied, a slight edge on his voice. "We've just about got our comrades corralled out here, and I think we can manage to persuade them to turn back. Just keep your wind-up toys clear of the area and let us do our thing."

"Acknowledged, Flight Leader," Foster said, smiling slightly. "Let us know if you change your mind."

Beneath the *Grand Eagle*, a new RPV was emerging from the bay, newly outfitted with explosives pods latched beneath its wings. Similar to the other turbojet remotely piloted craft, this converted recon model was an experimental unit, with VTOL deflection thrusters added to the basic design and additional control circuitry to operate them. As the launch arm whined to a smooth halt, the craft's turbojet started up, building power. Most of the RPVs stored aboard the *Grand Eagle* did not have conventional landing gear because of their airborne recovery systems. This one, however, was equipped with standard gear.

General Smalley stood behind Control Console Four, looking at the television monitor showing the RPV. "Keep it low, out of the carrier's radar sweep if you can. Otherwise you won't have a chance of getting near it," Smalley was saying.

The control officer nodded. "Automatic approach, sir?"

"Yes, but switch to manual once you've got the *Kiev* in visual range. What I've got in mind is going to take a human hand at the control, and a steady one at that. Now this is what we're going to do. . . ."

Dropping away from the launch arm, the modified BGM-34C picked up momentum quickly, attaining its top speed of over seven hundred miles per hour in a matter of seconds. Banking in a wide arc which carried it away from the airship, the RPV continued its shallow dive until it appeared for a moment that it would plummet directly into the sea.

Pulling out gradually, the small robot craft assumed level flight and stabilized, only a few feet above the surface of the ocean. It sped on in the direction of the Soviet carrier, barely skimming the waves and looking like a torpedo which had leaped free of the water.

Long minutes later, on the bridge of the *Kiev*, Adm. Nikolay Bakhirev studied the ship's radar screens, listening at the same time to radio transmissions from the Soviet jets. On his firm features was a look of growing dissatisfaction.

"They are not going to make it," he said softly, but loud enough for the ship's captain, Konstantin Dashkevich, to hear. "I had hoped our little ploy might work, but I can see now that we should have sent a full squadron to begin with. They are turning back our planes."

"We can try again, sir," Dashkevich offered. "We can have more jets up from the hangar deck within ten minutes . . .

perhaps less. The airship is apparently operating at close to its limits now, and they have already lost many of their RPVs. I do not believe they have many more craft to deploy."

"I think you may be right." He nodded. "Certainly they cannot hope to match our total number of men and aircraft."

At one of the forward windows which spanned the entire breadth of the bridge, the ship's political officer, Ivan Grigorovich, stood with binoculars scanning the horizon. The conflict ahead was too far to have any hope of seeing it directly, but still Grigorovich gazed. At least, he thought, he would be able to see the returning Soviet jets, once they came within a reasonable range. In fact . . .

"The jets are returning," he said abruptly. "I can see one of them now."

Bakhirev looked up from the radar screens in surprise. "Impossible. They are still too far out. You can't be seeing them yet."

"But I do!"

Bakhirev looked at the screen again. "There is nothing registered out there that would be within visual range."

"It is very low—perhaps damaged," Grigorovich insisted. "Perhaps our radar is not picking it up."

The admiral hurried to the front of the bridge suddenly, a fearful suspicion dawning. "Are there others? If they are the jets, then there should be more than one!"

At the front window now, he could see the object as well. It was large enough to see without glasses, moving impossibly fast. Without a radar lock, there would be little chance of using either the automatic antiaircraft guns or missiles to strike it.

The American RPV roared on, continuing its screaming trajectory straight at the bow of the Soviet carrier.

"It is going to hit!" Bakhirev shouted, hands gripping the sill of the window with sudden force.

Hurtling on, the RPV seemed certain to impact with the carrier. But at the last moment the small craft pulled up, slowing, climbing higher above the waves and then above the level of the ship's deck. Thrust now was directed through the VTOL nozzles and braking force applied. The RPV rapidly lost its momentum as it neared the center of the ship, finally slowing to the point that it was virtually hovering above the ship's deck. With its television cameras relaying images of the carrier's flight deck, the RPV was quickly but carefully steered toward the forward elevator, which was still in the up position.

Oddly, the landing gear was still locked up in flight position. The small robot craft settled gently down, its fuselage coming to rest against the surface of the deck, tilting at a slight angle as power was shut down and the engine silenced.

Moving to the windows at the port side of the bridge which faced the flight deck, Bakhirev and Dashkevich stared down at the now still RPV. Both men's expressions wavered between puzzlement and consternation.

"Are they mad?" Bakhirev said under his breath. "What are they trying to do?"

Dashkevich started for the intercom, planning to alert the hangar crew. "It will have to be moved at once. It is blocking the elevator."

"*No*—wait." Bakhirev took the binoculars from Grigorovich and refocused them, gazing down at the sleek fuselage. "It may be a trick."

"*Sir!*" The voice was that of the technician at the ship's communications console. "We are receiving signals from the airship—a message of some sort."

The man fell silent again as he proceeded to write the transmission down. Finally, he tore the sheet free of its pad and delivered it to the two senior officers.

Bakhirev took it from Dashkevich's hands. "Is this all of it?"

"Yes, Admiral," the technician replied. "The message was repeated again after that. In fact, it still is being transmitted."

Dashkevich's look of concern grew deeper with each line of the message he read. "It is loaded with explosives—armed and ready to detonate!"

"I can read," Bakhirev said irritably. "According to this, any attempt to move the device or tamper with it will cause the firing mechanism to activate." Bakhirev looked away for a moment, mind racing. "If that explosion were to set off the weapons and fuel in the hangar area, it could blow the ship apart!"

The thought was not lost on Dashkevich. His command of the *Kiev* had only begun three months earlier. The possibility of the vessel's destruction was a nightmare, and a nightmare that now could easily become ugly reality.

"Do you see what they've done?" Bakhirev said grimly.

"So long as that would-be bomb is lying there, we can't use the forward lift. The rest of our jets are locked in the hangar. They're too big to be taken up on the rear lift."

Dashkevich fought to find a solution. There seemed to be none. "With no landing gear the craft will not be moved easily from the spot. We could drag it away with one of the tractors, but that would surely detonate the explosives."

"You have demolition experts on board," the admiral said suddenly. "Get them up here at once, and your aircraft mechanics as well. Maybe they can tell us something about the device."

"Yes, Admiral—at once."

Dashkevich alerted the necessary crew members by intercom. Within minutes, all had assembled on the deck of the *Kiev,* inspecting the deadly RPV from a respectful distance. The brief passage of time also brought something else into view.

"Look—the jets," Grigorovich said, and at his words both Bakhirev and Dashkevich looked up to observe that the six Soviet jets had indeed returned from their unsuccessful attempt.

"They must be warned," Bakhirev said swiftly. "Direct them to stay clear of the American craft. The disturbance of their landing might detonate it."

"There is room enough to avoid it," the captain replied. "But we cannot take the jets below for servicing now."

"Have them lashed to the deck. They will have to remain there until we have solved this problem—and solve it we *must,* as quickly as possible."

"I wonder," Grigorovich said speculatively. "I would not put it past the Americans to try a bluff. Perhaps the device would not really explode if moved."

Bakhirev turned his hard gaze on the young political officer. "You may well be right," he told him. "But who among us will be fool enough to find out. . . ?"

A few minutes before noon in Washington, D.C., four men met in Under Secretary Martin Pretori's private office at the State Department. Besides Pretori, Secretary of Defense Lewis Scoville, Gen. Eldridge Adamson, and Adm. Jonathan Hadley were present.

While the others took seats in chairs around the office, Scoville remained standing, pacing back and forth in front of

Pretori's desk. After the last few days of almost constant meetings, the absence of the CIA director was a jarring note.

"Where *is* Hoyt?" Scoville asked suddenly.

"Tied up for the moment," Pretori reminded him. "That status report for the congressional subcommittee."

"This is absurd." Scoville ran a hand over his bald head as if to smooth down nonexistent hair. "From the reports coming from the airship, there's a young war brewing out there. Yet suddenly the President is incommunicado." He turned to General Adamson. "Have you seen him this morning? Has *anybody*?"

The chairman of the Joint Chiefs of Staff shook his head. "I don't think anyone has since last night, outside of a few White House staffers, and I haven't been able to get anything out of them. All I know for certain is that he hasn't left Washington. *Air Force One* is still in its hangar."

"Unfortunately, that tells us very little." Scoville abruptly ceased his pacing and took a position near the end of the room, facing the others. "What are we going to do? We can't be expected to just sit on our hands while the whole situation in the Pacific blows up! The *Kiev* is continuing its direct assaults on our airship—and now it has blinded members of our crew, perhaps permanently. They can't be let off the hook merely to save what's left of 'détente.' "

Admiral Hadley nodded in agreement. "I still think we need a substantial naval force in the area . . . a show of strength that the Russians will understand."

"It's a little late for that," General Adamson commented.

"To be fair," Martin Pretori said from behind his desk, "we should consider the possibility that the President is unavailable right now because he's in contact with Soviet representatives here, especially after what he told us last night."

"Perhaps," Scoville said dryly. "But I still don't think we can afford to deal with those people. And some unwritten 'understanding' with the Russian leader is almost totally worthless."

The young Under Secretary of State rested his chin on folded hands. "I don't think he's trying to work any deals. All he wants is to avoid having this thing explode into World War III."

"He's going to need more than his political popularity to accomplish that."

Admiral Hadley shook his head hopelessly. "We're stymied. We can't take any action without the President's approval."

"I don't know," Scoville said slowly. "With the Vice-President out of Washington an emergency action might be possible."

"Only if you declared that Evans is incapacitated," Pretori cautioned. "And I don't think you can afford to risk that. He could hang us all out to dry. . . ."

At that moment in the Executive Wing of the White House, Herb Ettleman was about to unwrap a sandwich he had ordered sent into his office. A buzz on his intercom interrupted him before he could take the first bite.

Ettleman pressed the button on the device. "Yes, Edith?"

"There's a call on line two," his secretary's voice replied. "A television person—Archer Grant."

"Find out what he wants," Ettleman said, cringing somewhat at the mention of the name.

"There's another call, too, sir—the Secret Service chief on line one."

"All right. Thanks, Edith." Ettleman shifted his sandwich to his other hand and picked up the phone handset, using a finger to punch the button for line one. "Ettleman here."

The press secretary listened to the voice at the other end for a long moment, his face going suddenly pale. "When?" he said softly, his voice tense. "Is the Vice-President on his way. . . ?"

There was a long silence, then Ettleman replied, "I see. Yes, thank you. I'll get on it right away."

Ettleman hung up the phone gently, then looked down and noticed the sandwich still in his hand. He laid it back on the plate and wiped his fingers with the embroidered square of White House linen that had covered it.

Quickly, he left his desk and tossed note pads and a file folder from his desk into a slim attaché case. He grabbed his topcoat from the rack by the door and headed out of the office.

Ettleman had nearly reached the outer door, ignoring the presence of his secretary, when the woman called after him. Hand clasped over the phone, she kept her voice low as an added precaution.

"What shall I tell Mr. Grant?" she asked of Ettleman's back. "Will you call him later? He wanted to know something about a press conference of some kind. . . ."

Ettleman paused briefly at the door, facing her. "Tell him I can't speak with him now. Maybe later, although I'm not at all sure." Almost to himself, he added, "As far as the press conference goes, it's going to be a lot sooner than we thought. . . ."

CHAPTER ELEVEN

At 7:00 A.M. on Tongareva, Jill Laudon stood in the doorway of the medical research facility. She was wearing a clean stewardess uniform, and her freshly washed face bore the simple artistry of makeup once more, now that her flight bag had been salvaged from the wreckage.

Jill looked out upon a troubled morning, where the golden light of the rising sun clashed with dark and ominous clouds pressing in from the southwest, dividing the sky above into light and dark hemispheres. The wind from the southeast was nearly continuous now, bending the coconut palms toward the sea.

The others inside were all awake and had eaten what little there was left of the food stores, heated over Sterno. According to Carla and Paul Brandon, help was very close now. For Jill, that help could not arrive too soon.

The young stewardess ran a hand through her blonde hair, trying to imagine what it would be like to return to her usual routine. In the back of her mind was the realization that her flights for Trans-Pacific would never be the same again. She sighed uneasily, her nerves still on edge, and turned to go back into the building. She halted abruptly as she saw Alex Copley approaching, then tried to go quickly past him, her eyes focused on the floor.

Copley put his arm across the narrow hallway, blocking her path. "Hold it a minute, will you?"

"Get out of my way," Jill said curtly.

"Look, I just want to say something." Copley hesitated a moment, waiting until her eyes reluctantly met his. "I want to apologize for last night. I'm sorry about what happened."

222

"I doubt that," Jill replied quickly. "But let's just forget it, okay?" She tried again to get past him, but he still would not move. "I've got things to do."

Copley ignored her remark. "I should have known better—I shouldn't have tried something like that with a girl like you."

Jill's posture straighened, her look hardening. "I don't know what you're up to now, but I really haven't got the time to waste. Now do I have to do something silly like scream or punch you in the nose, or will you let me by?"

Copley fell silent, studying her for a long moment with a look she could not fathom. Then, saying nothing further, he stepped aside and let her pass.

A short distance away, Paul Brandon bent over a shrouded form which lay upon the timber floor of the raised storehouse. The stench within the closed building was sickening, but Brandon had forced himself to examine most of the bodies, concentrating on the male passengers in an effort to find some clue to the Soviet agent's identity. Whoever the impostor was, the man he had replaced had to be here.

Holding a handkerchief over his mouth and nose, Brandon raised the canvas and studied the last inert form. The man's face was discolored from contusion. Brandon tried to compare it with the photos of those listed as survivors, but it was an impossible task. It had been the same with most of the others, and Brandon began to wonder if he was wasting his time.

The crash victim wore a pale yellow shirt, now stained with dried blood, and the collar was open. Brandon caught sight of a neck chain and pulled it into the open, revealing a small St. Christopher's medal. It was an added bit of irony, Brandon thought, that the patron saint of travelers had been unable to help this one. There was a jacket, folded and relatively intact, lying between the man and the crash victim next to him, so that it was hard to know to whom it had belonged.

The jacket pockets were empty, except for a crumbled ticket for Trans-Pacific Flight 47. The dead man's trousers held a small amount of mixed change from the United States, Hong Kong, and the Philippines, along with a wallet whose identification cards labeled him as a British journalist from Hong Kong named Whitfield. Brandon replaced the wallet and was about to cover the body once more when he noticed the man's left hand. There was a pale band of skin on the third finger that suggested a ring had been worn there. Brandon wondered where the ring had gone. And when.

He pulled the canvas back over the body and straightened up, sighing. Then he left the building and bolted its door.

As Brandon headed back to the main building, he noticed the minister, Father Daniels, standing outside. Daniels, if that was truly his name, was looking in the opposite direction, toward the wreckage of the jet airliner.

He turned as Brandon approached, his expression vaguely troubled. He managed a friendly good morning, then added, with a nod toward the wreckage, "You know, every time I see it I still wonder how any of us managed to survive."

"Yes," Brandon said coolly. "Especially in your case, I imagine."

Daniels looked puzzled. "How so?"

"Carla told me you were up toward the front of the passenger section, where the plane broke up." Brandon watched for some sign of suspicion or uncertainty, but saw only what appeared to be understanding.

"Oh, yes. It was terrible. The jet was literally tearing apart around us. Only by God's good grace did I escape without serious injury." Daniels fell silent for a moment, then with lowered voice he said, "Tell me, have you made any progress with the other problem?"

"Other problem?"

"Yes, in finding out who the hijacker is," Daniels replied in a confidential tone.

Brandon felt taken aback, but said only, "No . . . not yet."

"It was quite a shock when Dr. Jennings told me what had happened," Daniels continued. "But of course it did explain the crash here, so far off course."

"We may not know for some time," Brandon said, and it was not truly a lie. He wondered if a KGB agent would be so brazen as to ask such a direct question. Perhaps, if he wanted to find out how close they were to the truth.

He was about to return to the main building and Carla when he noticed that Daniels wore a large ring on his left hand. It looked to be silver, with a black stone bearing on its face a Christian cross inlaid of some other material.

"That's an unusual ring," Brandon remarked, seeing that Daniels had noticed his interest.

"Yes—a memento of my last post in Asia," the minister explained. "A village craftsman made it for me after we had built a church in the area. He told me he made it from a silver spoon, which I suspect had been stolen from a French garrison decades ago. Perhaps I shouldn't have accepted it, but for me it was a symbol of the bond that had been forged between us."

Brandon nodded. The explanation seemed too complex to have simply been made up. Then again, perhaps that was the intent. "I'd better get back inside," he said. "There's still a lot of work to do."

He reentered the main building, but the work remaining was not what occupied his mind. He found Carla in the back room, where she and Maggie Newcombe were making their rounds among the injured, and motioned to her.

"Carla—could I talk to you?"

She saw from his expression that he wanted to speak in private. "Yes, of course." Turning to Maggie she asked, "Will you keep an eye on things for a moment? Especially Mr. Lorenz—"

"Certainly. I'll give a yell if there's any problem."

Carla followed Brandon out of the back room, then directed him into the storeroom. She closed the door behind them and turned to face him.

"Did you find anything?"

"I don't know. With the conditions of the bodies it's hard to be certain. I might have overlooked something, but I just don't know." He paused, frowning. "Carla, I want to know something—why did you tell Father Daniels about the hijacker?"

The question seemed to catch her by surprise. "*Tell* him? I didn't tell him, intentionally. He overheard Jill and me talking about the murdered crew members, and there just wasn't any way I could avoid explaining."

"You didn't mention that you knew about the connection with Lorenz?"

"Of course not. Give me *some* credit."

Brandon tried to avoid responding to the hurt look on her face. After a moment's pause he said, "You realize there's a strong possibility that Daniels is the man we're looking for?"

Carla nodded slowly, with a certain reluctance. "I know it's possible. But to tell you the truth, I really don't think it is him."

"Why not?"

"There's nothing I can put my finger on—no proof, really." She hesitated. "It's just a feeling. I think we can trust him."

Brandon let his skepticism show. "Under the circumstances, I don't think we can afford to trust any of them."

"You've only just met them. I've had a longer chance to observe them. I don't know who the killer is, but I don't think it's Father Daniels."

Brandon shook his head slowly, glancing away. "I wish you wouldn't rely on feelings so much. It's not that easy to tell about people. Not even about people you think you know."

Carla frowned, catching something in his tone. She stepped closer. "Paul . . . what's bothering you?"

"Nothing." He hesitated, then seemed to sigh inwardly, resolve setting his tired features. "I didn't want to bring it up before, but maybe I'd better get it over with once and for all."

Carla waited in silence, sensing what was coming. Her hand moved awkwardly to straighten a loose strand of hair.

"Why did you leave San Francisco without telling me?" Brandon's tone was calm, his words unhurried. "You could have called or left a message. But you didn't even send a letter. You just disappeared without leaving any forwarding address or anything. Why?"

Her eyes shifted uneasily away from him. "When I heard about this research project, I thought it would be a good opportunity, something worthwhile. I . . . I didn't tell any of my friends when I left."

"*Friends*? I thought we were more than that."

"I guess we were." She paused a moment. "Paul, I really wasn't trying to hurt you or anything. I just had to leave, and I couldn't bring myself to call you. I don't know . . . maybe I was afraid if I heard your voice I wouldn't be able to go."

"Would that have been so bad?"

She turned and took a few steps away from him. "Yes. It would have been. It would have only postponed the inevitable anyway. I *had* to leave San Francisco. I just couldn't cope with it anymore . . . with what was happening between us."

Brandon leaned against the table, the trace of a sad smile on his lips. "I thought we got along pretty well. A few disagreements, perhaps, but nothing serious. At least, not until that last time, when I told you about the position I'd landed with Steinman-Keller."

"That might have been the finish," Carla admitted, "but it wasn't the start of it. I let you know how I felt before, but I don't think you really understood."

"I'm not sure I understand now. I'd thought you would be pleased—it was a fantastic opportunity for me. Surely you can see that?"

"Yes, Paul, I can see it. The salary was certainly far better than anything you could make at the hospital."

"That wasn't the only reason," Brandon countered. "The chance to develop my project, with the total resources that the institute could supply—those opportunities don't come often."

"I know," she conceded. "Really, I do understand what you're saying. But when you came driving over that day, in that expensive new sports car, it was . . . well, just the last straw."

"Why? What's wrong with having one? I can afford it." He hesitated, frowning at the reaction on her face. "You know, becoming a doctor isn't like entering a religious order—there's no vow of poverty demanded of us."

Carla's gaze was firm and unwavering now. "Maybe there should be. I don't know, Paul, I'm not a fanatic about money. It's just that after medical school I met so many doctors that seemed to have gotten their priorities twisted around. Not all of them. Not even most, but too many. They don't seem to feel anything about the people they're treating—they're just logging hours and adding to their bank accounts. And I just don't think that human sickness and suffering should be turned into a profit-making enterprise."

"I'll admit there are some that fit that description," Brandon replied. "But even so, there have to be compensations. You know as well as I do, it's a difficult life. The hours . . . the contact with people that can't be helped, for all your skill, new medicines and techniques. If you let it get to you and start taking it too personally, it not only affects your work, it begins to tear you apart inside."

Carla nodded, thinking about the past few days especially. "But that never seemed to bother you. Not the way it does me."

Brandon studied her. "You think not?" He shook his head slowly, all the old feelings coming to the surface once more, unwanted and yet unavoidable. "Would you have liked it better if I had turned down the position at Steinman-Keller? If I had stayed on at the hospital, working on a one-to-one basis with patients?"

"That's not the point. *You* wouldn't have liked it. You wouldn't have been happy approaching medicine the way I do, and that was the main problem."

"But I don't see why! The institute isn't just some cushy, dead-end job with a fancy title. It's important work. The project I'm developing with Steinman-Keller may benefit not just a few people, or a hundred, but *thousands.*"

"Those that can afford it," Carla replied. "And the institute will reap the harvest."

"They have to make a profit, naturally. They're in business. But what does that matter, if the project works? How do you put a value on life?"

Carla turned away slightly, and Brandon thought he noticed moisture in her eyes. "We've had this argument before, Paul," she told him softly. "I didn't like it then. I like it even less now."

Brandon felt as if he had slipped into a nightmare, repeating the same mistakes he had made before. He went to her side, putting his hands on her shoulders.

"Carla, I'm sorry. Seeing you again like this . . . the last thing in the world that I want is to dredge up all of that. I don't want to upset you. It's just that . . . well, you don't know how I felt when you left that way."

She reached up a hand to touch his face, and at the same moment, a single tear escaped to run down the gentle curve of her cheek. "Let's not talk about it now. There are just too many things on my mind, and I don't think we can settle anything by going through it all again."

Brandon hesitated, reluctant to agree. Perhaps the matter *was* settled, he thought finally, and he was just too stubborn to accept it. "All right. Whatever you want."

"Paul, I think we should get that fluoroscope over here, and the gasoline, too." Carla wiped at her eyes, stepping toward the door.

He sighed, then followed her. "All right. You're sure the fuel is still there?"

"Yes," she replied. "The islanders wouldn't use it . . . not unless there was a real emergency. They know how important the clinic is." She paused in the hallway, glancing back toward the far end of the building. "If James were well enough, he could take you over and show you where it is. But he won't be up to moving around for a few more days."

"You can draw me a map," Brandon told her. "It would be better if you stayed here with the injured."

"But maybe I should be the one to go. I know where everything is, and if Lorenz should need anything—"

"He's stable for the moment, and I've shown you how to use the defibrillator." Brandon looked away from Carla, toward the main room where the crash survivors were gathered. "I want to take a couple of the men along to help out with the equipment and gasoline. And to see if I can catch one of them in a mistake. . . ."

On the deck of the *Kiev* there was a flurry of activity. The ship's demolitions experts had cordoned off the area of the forward elevator, where the American RPV still rested. Tarpaulins from the lower decks and mattresses from the crew quarters had been piled around the small craft, and a few slipped carefully beneath the wing tips to prevent its shifting.

Admiral Nikolay Bakhirev was also on the deck, overseeing all that was taking place. Besides the precautions with the RPV, the hangar maintenance crew was busily transferring ten Hormone A helicopters to the rear half of the flight deck, using the slightly smaller rear elevator. The first few to have been brought up were tied down in place, and their rotors automatically brought around into full flying position.

One of the demolitions officers approached Bakhirev, with much the same fearful respect he held for the RPV itself. "Sir—we have placed the barriers as well as we could. Should the device explode, at least some of the force will be absorbed."

"But not enough directly beneath it," Bakhirev countered. "And that is where the greatest danger lies. I have ordered the aircraft, as many as possible, away from that part of the hangar, but the fuel supplies are still vulnerable. Have you made any progress with the device itself? Can it be deactivated?"

The demolitions man swallowed hard. "We *think* we know how it operates, Admiral. But the problem is that there are no external controls that might be switched off. And I fear that if we attempt to open the control section or remove the explosives pods, it might detonate."

Bakhirev was clearly displeased. "What about the radio

controls for our own robot craft—can't they be used to make the device take off?"

"Not without knowing the pattern of radio frequencies it uses, or the coding signals. It is possible that our own transmissions might even cause it to explode."

"Do what you can, then. I want everyone who might be of use working on this." Bakhirev dismissed the man and returned his attention to the rear of the flight deck. The naval infantry troops were emerging from the hatch at the rear of the main superstructure and were gathering near the helicopters, checking their weapons and forming up into groups even as the flight crews worked at readying their craft. As Bakhirev continued to watch, the leader of the group, a lieutenant, left the others and walked briskly to the spot where the admiral waited.

The man's dark uniform looked more representative of the army than the more traditional sailors' garb of the ship's crew. A black, beretlike cap tilted at a slight angle to his forehead bore a gold badge with a red star at its peak. Heavy black boots reached up almost to his knees, and his jacket was held neatly in place by a wide belt with diagonal shoulder strap. The holstered pistol at his side and the AK-47 rifle slung from his shoulder left no doubt about his combat role, and his gaunt Slavic features were assured and self-confident. He halted before the admiral.

"Are your men ready, Zagorski?" Bakhirev asked.

"Yes, Admiral. We only await your orders."

"Good. As soon as we are within range of the island, you will board the helicopters. The flight will take a few hours. Now, do you understand your instructions concerning the agent you are to contact, and what you are to recover?"

"Yes, Admiral."

"Return to your men, then," Bakhirev ordered. "I will alert you when the time is right. . . ."

The *Grand Eagle* cruised on, its turbines operating at full power. Within its central bays, the six Harrier jet aircraft were again locked into place, being refueled and having their weapons systems reloaded.

On Deck B, Elizabeth Jordan left the elevator and ran down the wide corridor, then turned the corner and headed toward the medical section. She only slowed her pace when she came within a few feet of the door.

Beth stopped almost within the doorframe, catching her breath and casting her worried gaze around the section's well-lit interior. Summoning up her courage, she stepped inside.

Within the surgery to her left, beyond the Plexiglas windows, Maj. Donald Shaffer and his assistants were preparing the room for the operation that would have to take place within a matter of hours. Shaffer looked up from his checklist and noticed Beth standing there. Her anxiety was apparent even at a distance of twenty feet.

Shaffer glanced about to see that everything was under control, then he left the surgery and walked toward Beth. "Can I help with anything?"

Beth seemed to be making an effort to bring her thoughts under control. "I just heard what happened. To Colonel Gardner . . . and the others."

Shaffer nodded grimly. "Nasty business. It could have been a lot worse though. Most of the injured ones I've treated and confined to quarters." His eyes shifted to the three-bed compartment at the far end of the section. "I've kept Gardner here. He got the worst of it, I'm afraid."

Beth followed the direction of his glance, then looked back at Shaffer, her features tightening. "How . . . how bad is it? Will he be all right?"

Shaffer studied her for a moment, the depth of her concern suddenly dawning on him. "Oh, yes—I believe so. I'm sorry if I've alarmed you. I've examined his eyes, and as far as I can tell, there is no *permanent* damage. But it will take a little time for him to recover. He's going to need help in getting around for a while."

"May I talk to him?"

Shaffer considered it. "All right. I don't think it could do any harm. Might even help a little. He's been mildly sedated, though, so he may be a little drowsy."

"Thank you, Major."

Beth turned and started toward the far corner, her steps hesitant and quiet. Gardner's reclining form came into view as she drew nearer the compartment at the end. His appearance was enough to be alarming. Thick gauze pads with opaque ovals covered his eyes, and more gauze ran across these and around his head. The exposed portions of his face were coated with an oily substance, beneath which the skin was slightly pink.

Beth approached slowly, at first uncertain whether

Gardner was asleep or awake. "Stewart?" she said softly. "It's me, Beth. . . ."

Gardner's head rolled toward her. "Beth? What are you doing here?"

She sat on the edge of the molded plastic bunk that extended from the side wall of the compartment. Her lips formed a smile as she tried to sound casual and reassuring. "What am I doing here? What do you think! When one of the crew told me what happened, I came down to see how you were."

Gardner remained silent. His breathing was steady but he seemed uncomfortable.

"The doctor says you're going to be all right. You'll be able to see again, after you've had a chance to rest."

"Yes, that's what he tells me." After a moment's pause he asked, "Who's in charge of the helm?"

"One of your junior officers from red shift, I think."

Gardner thought a moment. "Probably Kelly. Under the circumstances, he'd be the best choice. But he doesn't know this ship like I do."

"Just take it easy and don't worry about it. Colonel Curtis is backing him up, and I'm sure they can manage. You've done your job, and you got injured in the line of duty. You're entitled to a rest." Beth's worried frown returned and her lip quivered slightly. On impulse, she reached out and ran her fingers through his hair, smoothing it back.

Gardner stiffened under her gentle touch. His hand came up, located her wrist, and moved her hand away. "Beth, please don't do that."

"I . . . I'm sorry, Colonel, I shouldn't have—"

"I'm not pulling rank on you, Beth. That's not it at all." He relaxed his grip on her wrist, letting her hand come to rest in his. His tone became apologetic. "I'm the one that should be sorry. You've done nothing wrong."

"Why . . . why does something like that disturb you so?" She watched as his head turned away from her. "Yesterday, when I touched your arm, you looked at me so strangely. Why?"

"It's not because of you," Gardner replied, his voice low. "It's just that, it reminds me of something. . . of someone."

Beth hesitated, then said, "Your wife?" His silence was enough of an answer. "It's been three years," she said.

"Three years, Stewart. But you still belong to her, don't you?"

"I can't just forget I've ever had a wife and child, Beth. You don't shut off feelings that were that strong."

She looked away from him, fighting to control her emotions. "You know, at first I thought the project was going to be good for you. It gave you something to take your mind off things . . . it gave you a kind of purpose. But I've watched you day by day, becoming more and more submerged in your work, until there's just nothing else left. That's not good."

"You needn't worry."

"I can't help but worry!" Beth hesitated a moment. "They told me what you did up there. How you tried to divert the ship. You weren't thinking of your own safety, you were only thinking of the ship. As if your own life didn't matter."

"That's just conditioned reflex . . . good air force training."

"Is it?" Beth did not pursue the terrible possibility that hung in the air.

"Can we just drop it?" Gardner asked.

"If you want."

There was a long moment of awkward silence between them, and Beth began to wonder if she had finally pressed the matter too far. She had hoped that with time, he would begin to understand how she felt, enough so that she could draw him away from the past that was dead and buried. Now it seemed he did not want to be drawn away.

Finally, Gardner spoke. "How long before we reach the island?"

Beth sighed. "I don't know exactly. Soon, I think."

"I should be up there. The maneuvers are going to be tricky. Kelly hasn't handled the ship under these wind conditions."

"How could you help?" she asked plaintively. "With your eyes bandaged, you won't be able to see what's happening."

"I won't have to see to offer advice. They can report the readings to me as they go."

Beth glanced back toward the surgery. "I don't think Major Shaffer will let you."

"He might. He knows how important this mission is." Gardner paused. "Besides, it's only my eyes that need the rest."

Beth considered it for long, agonizing seconds. Then finally, her voice barely above a whisper, she said, "If the doctor says it's all right, I'll help you back to the command deck."

"You'll help?" There was surprise in Gardner's voice.

"Yes." Beth had her eyes closed tightly, shutting out the sight of Gardner's bandaged features. "If that's what you want, I'll help."

"I didn't think you approved of my obsession with duty."

"I don't. But I can't tell you what to do. And I'd rather be there to help out if I can, if that's all you'll let me be." Her voice was still low, but her words were coming faster now. "I'm not trying to diminish what you had. I didn't know your wife very well, but I know you loved her, and you'll always treasure her memory. I don't expect you to forget about her. I really don't. But we can't change the way things are, Stewart. I care about you, and I just wish you wouldn't shut me out."

"Beth, I—"

"You don't have to tell me again. I'll keep my distance if that's what you want." Her voice was tremulous, catching at her words. "If my being here on board is only going to bother you, I can ask to be reassigned . . ."

She bit off the last word and opened her eyes, afraid to say more lest she break down. But she could not avoid the tears that welled up in her eyes and rolled down her face, carrying their bitter taste to the corners of her mouth.

As the drops continued to flow, one of them fell upon the back of Gardner's hand. He touched the moisture with the fingers of his other hand, then brought both hands up to search the contours of Beth Jordan's face. Curious and probing, his fingers gently traced the paths of her tears.

Gardner started to speak, then seemed uncertain. Then gradually his expression changed, as the dismay over what he had caused became another emotion. Cradling her face in his hands, unable to see her troubled features, he drew Beth closer until at last their lips met, in a long and tender kiss that answered the questions in Beth's worried mind more certainly than words. . . .

On Tongareva, Paul Brandon stood by the inner shore of the island, facing the lagoon. Its enclosed emerald waters were unsettled, stirred into motion by the continuing wind. James

Akaru's small boat was at the water's edge, its bow partly on the sand.

Brandon bent to unscrew the cap from the tiny outboard motor at the craft's stern. It was a single-cylinder model, ancient-looking and weathered but obviously well maintained. Its fuel tank was half full, and Brandon had considered the possibility of using the fuel in the generator for a few moments of electricity—enough to contact the *Grand Eagle*. But the fuel would be needed for the trip to Omoka village, and besides, he was not certain what the mixture of marine fuel and oil from the outboard would do to the more sophisticated engine of the generator.

Brandon put the cap back in place and turned as he heard the others approach. Carla was in the lead, bringing the map she had sketched, showing the location of the clinic and its interior layout. Most of the others had followed—Father Daniels, Jill Laudon, Peter Benson, and even Alex Copley. Mary Akaru and Maggie Newcombe had remained within the building, as had Professor Maca and the mute man, Sandersen.

"I hope you can find the fluoroscope from this sketch," Carla told him as she reached his side. "I've drawn the clinic as well as I can remember it."

"I'll manage," Brandon replied. He glanced over to where Father Daniels stood. "I could use some help. Care to come along?"

Daniels considered it, then nodded. "Yes, of course."

Carla knew what Brandon thought about Daniels, and what he was planning. If he was right, she did not want him to be alone with the man. She looked to the others. Alex Copley was not the most reliable of people, but at least he was young and strong.

"Mr. Copley—Paul might need someone else, too."

The young man had taken up a position near Jill Laudon. He frowned at the suggestion. "I, uh . . . I'd like to help, but I think maybe I'd better stay here. I'm not much good in boats anyway."

The businessman, Peter Benson, had a disgusted look. There was no one left but him now. Passing Carla, he muttered, "You should know by now that you're not going to get any help out of him! I'll go. It will give me something to do."

Carla tried to conceal her worry as first Daniels and then Benson climbed into the tiny boat. She watched as Brandon pushed it out into the water, getting his trouser legs wet before stepping into the small craft himself.

Brandon started up the engine and waited as it sputtered into life, then he turned the boat toward the southwest and headed out into the lagoon. His course away from the shore would take him very near the spot where the cargo section of the wrecked airliner had submerged, but at the moment, even the deadly substance within the lagoon seemed less dangerous than the presence of the unknown killer.

Carla returned Paul's wave as he pulled away, feeling a pang of remorse at having let him go. She watched for a long while. Omoka village was roughly six miles away by boat, across the northwestern tip of the atoll. It should not take them too long to reach the clinic, load the equipment and reserve gasoline, and return. So long as nothing went wrong.

Finally, Carla turned and started back toward the building. The talk she had with Brandon was still very much on her mind, but she knew she had to force herself to think about her patients and the danger that was still so close.

The others were beginning to disperse now, but Jill joined her as she headed back. "I'll be glad when the rescue team gets here," the young stewardess said, her face showing the effects of worry and fatigue. Smiling faintly, she added, "Not that you've been inhospitable. . . ."

Carla did not reply, her eyes still focused ahead.

Jill frowned slightly. "Carla—is there something wrong?"

She seemed to hear Jill for the first time. "What?"

"I said, is there something wrong? You seem preoccupied."

"I'm sorry. I guess I was just thinking about everything we have to do." She stopped momentarily, turning to glance back at the lagoon. Some thought, below the level of consciousness, was nagging at her. She stood staring off across the lagoon's emerald water, the wind blowing her auburn hair as she tried to recall the vague recollection that had flashed so briefly through her mind. She turned away again and started for the building once more.

Jill was watching her now, more intently than before. "Are you worried about Dr. Brandon?" she asked.

"Yes," Carla replied automatically. "I mean, yes, I'm concerned about him, but I'm sure he can manage all right."

"I suppose so. He seemed to know how to handle a boat."

"He should. He used to go sailing with some friends of ours, back in San Francisco. In fact, he—" Carla fell silent suddenly, a chill feeling seizing her. The mention of the boat brought to mind something she had just seen, so that the disturbing recollection that had eluded her finally solidified.

Carla whirled, looking out across the lagoon. Brandon and the boat were almost out of sight in the distance now, beyond recall.

Jill caught some of the terror in her eyes. "What is it?"

"Oh, Jill—the navigator. I mean, the agent who replaced him," Carla cried. "*I think I know who he is. . . !*"

As the boat neared the shore at Omoka village, Paul Brandon glanced back at the lagoon, wondering if he had made the right decision in leaving Carla to handle the patients, and especially Lorenz. Worse, he wondered if he was right about Daniels. There was the frightening possibility that the Soviet agent was still back there with Carla, in a group that was now diminished by three men. Brandon looked again at the two men in the front of the boat. Both were silent, peering ahead at the approaching shore.

Omoka village was at the westernmost point of the island, near Taruia Passage, largest of the three channels that connected the sea with the central lagoon. The largest village and administrative center of Tongareva, Omoka was the port of call for ships serving the islands of the Cook chain. Those ships came for the island's copra, and to bring new supplies of canned meat and other goods. The visits were long months apart, and it was easy to understand why Tongareva was known as one of the loneliest spots in the South Pacific.

Brandon eased the boat in toward the wharf, and Daniels reached out with the bow rope to tie it up. In another moment, the three men were standing on the sun-bleached wooden planking, appraising the village and the silent crowd of islanders gathered a short distance from the wharf. There were many children and old people among them, but few young men and women. In years past, the island's population had been diminished by both nature and man—storms, diseases introduced by the Europeans, and in the 1800s, slave raids by Peruvian ships. Now there was a new, more subtle force at work. Young islanders dissatisfied with Tongareva's spartan existence were steadily leaving, seeking their future on the larger islands and in New Zealand, where jobs and better schools beckoned. Many of the older people feared the islands ways were being lost forever.

As Brandon and the others approached, the islanders backed off, keeping their distance. Brandon wondered if they were always so suspicious of strangers, but then he remembered the warning that had been given them about the danger of contamination from the wreckage. Had he known the legend of the ghostly fire, which had burned again in the lagoon last night, he might have better understood their reaction.

"Come on," he said to Daniels and Benson. "We'd better get to the clinic."

The three men walked through the village, to be met with more curious stares from islanders who were normally open and friendly. The clinic was not difficult to find, following Carla's instructions.

Inside the small building, Brandon located the fluoroscope equipment and began to pack it into its trunklike case for carrying. "Mr. Benson, there should be a can of gasoline out back—will you see about it?"

Benson nodded, heading for the rear door of the building and leaving Brandon alone with Daniels.

"It will probably take the two of us to carry this," Brandon said as he worked. He could feel the weight of the small automatic pistol Haddock had given him in the pocket of his borrowed airship uniform, where he had transferred it from the leg holster. He wondered if he would have to use it. In his other pocket was the tiny radio transceiver. The *Grand Eagle* was probably within range now. Brandon hoped that when he used the device, he would be able to report that everything was under control.

Brandon tried to think of a question that might trip up Daniels—that would expose him. The problem was, he did not know enough about his background to adequately set the trap.

If the agent kept up his charade until the *Grand Eagle* arrived, there was the chance he might feel compelled to make a grandstand play which could endanger Carla and the others. Brandon wanted to settle it here and now if he could, but he was rapidly running out of time. He glanced at his watch. It was a quarter after nine. If the agent knew how close the airship was, he might never have come along in the boat. Assuming he *had*.

There was another possibility, though. A possibility that held enormous risk.

Brandon waited until Daniels had lifted his end of the fluoroscope case with both hands. Ready to release his own end if need be and go for the pistol, he said, "You wanted to know if I had any ideas about the hijacker?"

Daniels' look was curious. "Yes, of course."

"At the moment," Brandon said, quietly, "my prime suspect is you."

He watched Daniels' features for the man's reaction. A trained Soviet agent would not give himself away easily, but there would be an instant of surprise during which a man's composure might be shaken. An instant only, but Brandon hoped it might be enough to reveal the truth.

Daniels looked stunned. Far from being wary, the man's expression was merely incredulous. "Why on earth do you say that?"

"Your air force records turned out to be nonexistent."

"That's impossible."

"I'd have no reason to say it if it weren't true," Brandon said firmly. "We've been checking into everyone's background."

Daniels was silent a moment, then his shock became a firm insistence. "Well, there's got to be some kind of foul-up. I *was* in the Air Force. And I can most certainly assure you that I had nothing whatsoever to do with the hijacking. Why would I? What possible reason could I have?"

"I think you know," Brandon replied. He was playing a dangerous game, and knew it. But there seemed no other way.

Daniels was still holding on to the fluoroscope case, his pose relaxed. The initial shock passed from his features and he regarded Brandon speculatively. "What are you trying to do, Doctor?" he asked finally. "Bluff me into some kind of confession?" When Brandon did not reply, he added, "I guess after what happened you have to suspect everyone, but if you think I'm responsible, you've got the wrong man. And I'm sure an investigation will prove it."

Brandon studied him for another long moment. It was either the truth or a splendid acting performance. Daniels had said nothing to indicate that he knew more was involved than a mere hijacking. An agent would be clever enough to avoid that, of course, but he had an odd feeling that Daniels was exactly what he seemed.

"All right," Brandon said, with a wry smile he hoped would be convincing. "It was one way of finding out."

Daniels regarded him oddly. "If you're really worried about this hijacker, then we'd do well to get back to the others as quickly as possible."

Brandon nodded silently, still not completely convinced of Daniels' innocence. At that moment, the rear door opened and Benson entered with a five-gallon can of gasoline, leaning away from it to balance its weight.

"There's only the one can," he said.

"We'd better head back to the boat," Brandon replied. He started for the door, carrying his end of the fluoroscope case as he led the way out of the cottagelike clinic building.

As they walked, the thought occurred to him that he should sound out Benson as well, just to be on the safe side. If it should turn out that the agent was neither of these two men, then it meant he was still at the research facility with Carla. That possibility was perhaps the most frightening of all.

Unlike Daniels, there were some things about Benson that had not come from the man's own statements to Carla. He tried to visualize the investigative report that had been sent along with the businessman's old passport photo.

Trying to sound conversational, Brandon said, "I imagine your wife will be glad to see you back safe and sound, Mr. Benson."

Benson looked at him oddly. "At the moment, I don't have a wife."

Brandon feigned ignorance. "No? But I was sure the survivor's report for notifying relatives listed you as being married."

Benson shook his head with annoyance. "I *was* married, but I was divorced last month." He held up his left hand briefly, then shifted the gasoline to it from his right. "Or didn't you notice the lack of a wedding ring?"

Brandon still maintained a puzzled look, and it seemed to get on Benson's nerves. "Look, what do I have to do," he said sarcastically, "show you my checkbook stub with the first alimony payment!"

"Sorry," Brandon apologized. "Someone must have made a mistake."

"Obviously," Benson said. He continued to walk alongside Brandon and Daniels, whose pace was slowed somewhat by the heavy fluoroscope case.

Brandon knew all about Benson's divorced status from the report that had been transmitted to the *Grand Eagle*. He wondered if an impostor would have known. He might, if he had looked through the man's personal papers and checkbook.

He remembered the crash victim's body in the storehouse—the one whose hand seemed to be missing a ring. There was no certainty, even, that it was the body of the man replaced by the impostor. And if it were, did the missing ring mean anything? Brandon remembered the unusual ring Daniels wore, which had a seemingly reasonable explanation. Or was it instead a wedding ring that was missing—not stolen by the agent, but merely absent because there was no further need to wear it?

Brandon glanced quickly down at Benson's left hand. It was evenly tanned, with no mark of a ring. But in a month's time, the man's finger could have become tanned as much as the rest of his hand. So there was still no certain answer. Nothing to point to either of the two men.

And if it were another—? Brandon remembered that Alex Copley had refused to come along. Had he a reason more sinister than Brandon had thought?

The three men reached the wharf and headed for their boat. Brandon studied the face of Father Daniels as they set the case down upon the wooden planking in preparation for loading it aboard the boat. Daniels was still regarding him curiously, but still seemed to be playing out his role as a man of God.

Brandon was running out of ideas. And time as well. Just as he was wondering if he had set himself an impossible task, a commotion started among the islanders of Omoka who had gathered to watch them.

The shout had come from one near the edge of the group, then several more spoke out in excited voices . . . voices tinged with wonder. In a moment, there was a confused cacophony of agitated yelling as the entire group pointed to the north.

Benson set down his gasoline can and looked to see what had aroused such reactions. Standing beside him now, Daniels also looked.

Brandon saw it as well. The mammoth, torpedolike cylinder of the *Grand Eagle* could be seen approaching the northern shore of Tongareva, less than a mile out, its huge propellers driving it steadily on.

Both Daniels and Benson stared out toward the horizon,

seemingly spellbound by the sight. Brandon forced himself to look away from the airship and moved to a position a short distance behind both men. Soundlessly slipping the small automatic pistol from his pocket, he held it unobstrusively at waist level, covering both Daniels and Benson. It might be an unnecessary move, but it was far better to be prepared.

He had to know. He had to know *now*, before they returned to the other side of the lagoon. If he could trust them, fine. If not—

Brandon tried to recall the name on the identity cards in the wallet of the dead man, back in the storehouse. If he was wrong about it being the replaced man, then what he was planning would tell him nothing. The prognosis was bad, he thought, but there was simply nothing else left to try, short of attempting to keep both men under guard while crossing the lagoon.

Brandon braced himself. "Whitfield!" he called out, using the name of the foreign journalist who supposedly was dead.

Daniels turned, almost at once. He looked into Brandon's eyes with renewed curiosity . . . curiosity that turned quickly to concern at sight of the pistol. "What!"

Benson did not turn. His eyes remained fixed upon the distant form of the *Grand Eagle*. But as Brandon continued to watch both men, he became aware of the fact that the muscles of Benson's neck were tensing, his ears moving slightly as the skin at his temples tightened.

He finally turned, his expression fixed as he saw Brandon and the automatic. "Are you insane!" The words came smoothly from his lips, with the same irritable impatience as before. But now there was something else as well—a sound of total self-control and a wary alertness.

Brandon turned the gun away from Daniels, toward Benson. "I think you're off the hook, Father—"

In the next instant, Benson whirled in a movement that was almost explosive in its unexpected quickness. Darting behind Daniels, he shoved the minister violently at Brandon and dove for the boat.

Brandon fell back heavily as Daniels collided with him, spilling them both to the wooden planking. He lost his grip on the pistol, and to his horror, saw it spin toward the edge of the wharf. Making a futile grab for the weapon, still impeded by the weight of Daniels' fallen body, Brandon clawed the planking in an effort to pull himself nearer the gun.

Teetering on the edge, the pistol seemed to waver for a moment, and a moment only. Then it slipped over the side, splashing heavily in the water below.

As Daniels moved to recover his balance, Brandon crawled to the edge, still grabbing for the sinking weapon. As the ripples spread out from its impact, its shadowy form could be seen drifting down through the clear water, settling on the bottom in a mass of sharp coral, captured there and inaccessible.

"Look out!"

The voice belonged to Daniels, and before Brandon could respond, the man had grabbed him, pulling him headfirst over the edge and into the water. At virtually the same moment, a bullet whizzed past them with an audible rush followed by a muffled, popping noise. Benson had produced an automatic with a silencer, and he kept on firing almost wildly, pinning them down.

Above the startled screams and cries of the islanders as they started to flee, the roar of the outboard motor grew loud, and Brandon caught a glimpse of the boat pulling away from the wharf. Scrambling back up to the wooden planking, both men stayed low.

"He's heading back to the other side!" Brandon snapped.

"We may be able to catch him with another boat," Daniels replied. "But he's armed and we aren't."

A moaning outcry caught their attention suddenly, and both men turned to the land's edge near the wharf. Most of the islanders had taken cover now, but three remained, one of whom was sprawled upon the ground. An elderly man, with a crimson wound at the temple.

Brandon moved to his side quickly, examining the man. But there was nothing to be done. "Dead . . ." he told Daniels soberly. "Instantaneous. One of the wild shots—"

The youngster at his side wailed louder, and the other islander looked on with grim understanding. The islander spoke. "The ghost fire came last night, telling us someone would die. It always speaks the truth."

Brandon looked at him oddly, but there was no time for questions. He looked wildly back to the lagoon and the boat which was gaining more and more distance. "We've got to stop him."

Daniels, for all his quick-thinking actions, still seemed stunned by Benson's transformation. "What's wrong with him? What kind of criminal is he?"

"He's a Russian KGB agent," Brandon replied. "He's after Lorenz and something in the wreckage. Worse yet, there's a Russian carrier on the way."

"What can we do?"

"I don't know. Even with a gun I couldn't stop him at this distance." Brandon fell silent, his mind racing. Then suddenly he recalled the tiny radio transceiver in his pocket.

Pulling the device free, he turned it on and depressed its transmit button. "*Grand Eagle*—this is Brandon—"

It was General Smalley's own voice that answered. "Thank the Lord you're all right—we were getting worried. Listen—we had an update on Daniels. He's all right—"

"I know," Brandon replied, glancing toward the minister. "We've got an emergency here! The KGB man is Peter Benson. At least, that's the man whose identity he's assumed. He's gotten away from us here at Omoka village and is heading back by boat to the research facility where Carla is. Is there any way you can stop him?"

There was an interval of silence, then Smalley's voice returned. "We could use the helicopter. It will take us ten or fifteen minutes to slow down and get it in the air."

"That might be too long," Brandon transmitted. "Besides, he's armed. If your crew gets too close, he'll fire on them."

"We'll see what we can do," Smalley's voice replied. "We haven't got a radar fix on the boat yet. Probably not enough of it to register. Are there any other boats out?"

"There will be. We're going after him."

"All right. But take care."

The transmission ended, and Brandon looked toward the islanders who were approaching once more, now that the danger was past. "Is there another boat we can use?"

At first his question was only met with stony silence. Then the man who had seen Brandon attempt to help the wounded islander came forward. "That launch there." He pointed to a boat tied up at the wharf. "It is mine. You may use it."

"Thank you." Brandon hurried over and put the gasoline can in the boat, then started to work the fluoroscope case toward the edge of the wharf.

Daniels joined him, helping to get the case over the side and secure within the launch. Climbing in, he took the seat opposite the pilot's while Brandon released the lines and pushed the boat out from the wharf.

Scrambling in, Brandon took the pilot's seat and started the engine. Turning the rudder hard to one side, he brought the bow around and headed out across the lagoon, opening the throttle to full. Spray kicked up behind them as the boat sped over the surface of the lagoon.

Ahead, still almost a half-mile out, the *Grand Eagle* cruised on, steadily fighting the winds stirred up by the perimeter of the great storm that was many miles to the southwest. Angled into the wind, the mammoth craft drew nearer with each passing moment.

The motor launch was faster than the boat Benson had taken, but with the lead he had from the start, there was still an outside chance he might reach the other side. What he might do if he did reach Carla and Lorenz first, Brandon did not know.

Abruptly, there came a buzzing signal from the tiny radio transceiver. Holding the wheel with one hand, Brandon brought the device closer to his ear.

"Brandon—are you monitoring?"

"Yes," he transmitted. "We're pursuing Benson."

"We know. We have you on both visual and infrared systems now. Benson, too. You're about two miles behind him."

Brandon noticed the *Grand Eagle* swinging around slightly, repositioning. "What are you going to do?"

"Just keep your distance . . . and your fingers crossed."

Smalley's voice faded and Brandon pocketed the radio unit. Still steering a straight course for the fleeing boat, he kept an eye on the massive airship that was growing larger in the sky.

Abruptly, a flash of brilliant light erupted from the starboard side of the airship. It stabbed out at the boat in the lead, focusing on its target with pinpoint accuracy.

Benson's boat jumped as if it had struck a submerged rock. A small geyser of water vapor and wood splinters sprayed upward as the airship's laser beam scorched its way through the bow of the boat, nearly cutting it in two. Stalled by the sudden inrush of water, the damaged vessel pitched forward, flipping Benson into the lagoon.

Brandon knew full well what it was, but Daniels stared

ahead in amazement. Their borrowed launch raced on, aiming for the spot in the lagoon's northern end where the wrecked boat was beginning to sink.

In another few minutes, they reached it. Brandon cut the throttle and steered the launch into the area carefully, avoiding some of the larger fragments of charred wood. Benson was clinging to a piece of floating debris, dazed, still clutching his automatic.

Alert to any sudden movement, Brandon reached over the side and wrenched the gun free. Then he and Daniels pulled Benson into their own boat.

The man was stunned, but seemed to have no real injuries. He settled back weakly as Brandon secured his wrists with part of the bowline.

"Let's get him to shore," Brandon said to Daniels. "We're going to have to get Lorenz up to the airship's surgery as quickly as possible. . . ."

Minutes later, the *Grand Eagle*'s helicopter was lifting off its platform as Brandon eased the launch into shore. Benson was capable of walking now, and Brandon directed him toward the research facility, holding his own gun leveled at the dripping man.

No one was visible outside the building as they approached, and Brandon began to worry that Lorenz might have suffered another attack. But then as they neared the door, Carla Jennings appeared in the doorway.

Brandon smiled at her, expecting to see her relief at the capture of the murderous agent. But there was no relief in her eyes. There was only quiet terror.

Brandon halted abruptly. Behind Carla he could see the older stewardess, Maggie Newcombe. There was a different kind of fear on her features, and in her hand was a small pistol— Carla's own—held very close to the back of Carla's head. Brandon's indrawn breath caught and held within his lungs.

"You gentlemen just move on inside," Maggie said nervously, the Australian edge to her voice more pronounced than usual. "I'm not used to this sort of thing, so please don't make me hurt anyone."

Brandon and Daniels exchanged glances, then started slowly for the door. Brandon still guided Benson at close range, the pistol on him at all times.

"*Hold it right there*," Maggie said suddenly. She

motioned toward Benson. "Untie him—*now!*" She pressed the gun closer to Carla's head for emphasis.

Brandon looked into the worried eyes of the young woman who meant so much to him—more than he had ever realized. He did not know if Maggie would carry through with her threat. He did not want to find out.

Reluctantly, he released the rope that bound Benson's hands. Rubbing his wrists, the Soviet agent turned slowly, studying Brandon.

"A wise move, Doctor. Now I trust you shall continue to be wise." He reached for the pistol, slowly, carefully, never taking his gaze from Brandon's own eyes.

There was nothing else to do but hand it over. Brandon slowly extended the gun to him, wishing with all his heart that he had considered the possibility of a *second* Soviet agent.

Overhead, the helicopter was circling, Captain Lee at its controls, looking for a place to land. Benson observed it a moment, his soaked clothes still dripping. With his free hand he brushed aside the hair that was damply stuck to his forehead, and blotted at the slight trickle of blood beneath his nose.

Turning to Brandon, he said, "I presume you have a means of talking to the crew?"

Brandon nodded slowly.

"Good. Then you will tell them that I am in command here, and that if they want all of your people to stay alive, they will keep that helicopter from interfering."

"It's coming to pick up Lorenz," Brandon said quickly. "He needs an operation—"

"*Tell them!*"

Brandon did as he was told, using the tiny radio unit. Then he entered the building under the watchful eye of Benson and Maggie Newcombe, who maintained her hold on Carla.

"Paul, I'm sorry," Carla said softly. "I didn't realize until it was too late. I remembered seeing him brushing wet sand from his pants legs, and I knew he had to be the one who was in the cockpit when the plane crashed." She remembered too how she herself had crossed through the shallow water to reach the shattered cockpit section, even as the Russian agent must have done to join the other survivors, moments after the crash. She knew now that he must have changed coats with the real Peter Benson in the confusion and taken his attaché case. Telling Maggie Newcombe of her revelation was her second mistake.

In the main room the others waited in one corner, where Maggie had kept an eye on them from the hallway—Jill Laudon, Professor Maca, Alex Copley, Martin Sandersen, and Mary Akaru. Of them all, Jill seemed the most astonished by the senior stewardess' actions.

The young girl looked at her co-worker with a mixture of anger and hurt. "Maggie—how could you?"

"Just save your moral indignation for someone else," Maggie snapped, her harried gaze never leaving Brandon and Daniels. "I didn't have any choice. I've been carrying things for them to Hawaii for three years. If I'd refused to go along, they would have made sure the authorities found out. This isn't how it was planned, but it's too late to worry about that now."

Jill blinked. "*Planned*?"

"You didn't really think we got switched to Flight 47 by accident, did you?" Maggie said sarcastically, a nervous whine to her voice. "Oh, yes, of course you did. You would."

Jill recalled the two stewardesses they had replaced, almost at the last minute. The reason that had been given was food poisoning. And now the need of it became clear. As senior stewardess, Maggie was responsible for checking the passenger list at all stops. When the Soviet agent left the rear compartment at Wake Island to take over the plane, someone had to cover for his absence. That job had been Maggie's.

"Enough!" Benson snapped brusquely. "None of that is important now. I know that the carrier is on its way, and will be here shortly. We have to wait."

Brandon looked around the room. The others were in no position to help, and with one gun at Carla's head and another in the hands of a trained KGB killer, there seemed nothing he could do.

"Lorenz *can't* wait," Brandon said earnestly. "The *Kiev* won't be here for many hours yet. Lorenz' condition has already declined, and he simply won't last much longer."

"You're lying," Benson said flatly.

"It's the truth. If you've been briefed on him, then you know his history of heart disease. That's why I'm here—I'm a specialist. The surgery I'm planning is a long shot, but it's the *only chance he has*!"

Benson studied him for a long moment without a trace of emotion on his features. "Are you saying that you could operate on him here?"

"Here?" Brandon glanced about the primitive facility. "No, of course not. But on the airship there's a complete surgical facility, with another doctor and trained nurses. We could—"

"Impossible. Lorenz is not leaving this building until the carrier arrives."

Brandon stared at him with firm resolve. "Then he will die, before the ship ever gets here. Can you afford to let that happen?"

Benson remained silent for a long moment, considering possibilities. He began to chew at his lip. To Maggie, he said, "Is it true, about Lorenz?"

Maggie hesitated. "I'm afraid so. I've been keeping an eye on him while you've been gone. He looks bad."

"Your leaders must want him pretty bad," Brandon prodded further. "*Can you afford to let him die*?"

A heavy silence fell upon the room. Outside, the wind howled, rattling the windows of the research facility, an ominous reminder of the storm that was passing barely out of range of the island. Tense minutes passed.

Finally, Benson glared harder at Brandon. "No. I cannot allow that to happen. We are going to have a little arrangement, Doctor. I will allow you to operate on Lorenz. But Dr. Jennings and the others shall remain here as hostages."

Brandon looked quickly to Carla, who was standing rigidly still with Maggie close behind her. His worried glance was mirrored in Carla's own eyes, but she said only, "It will be all right, Paul. Just make sure Mr. Lorenz is all right."

"Oh, I have no doubt he will," Benson said. "It's his only hope of seeing you all alive once this is over. Do you understand that, Doctor?"

"Yes."

"You answer too easily," Benson replied suspiciously. "That could be a mistake. There must be no doubt in your mind that I am serious about what I say . . . *deadly* serious. You might feel tempted to renege on our agreement." He glanced about the room, still keeping Brandon in view. "No, I think you need to be convinced . . . graphically."

He brought his pistol around quickly, leveling it directly at Jill Laudon. He squeezed the trigger.

"*No!*"

The anguished shout came from Alex Copley. Even as the silenced automatic fired with its muffled popping sound,

Copley had lunged forward in front of the frightened girl. The bullet hit him in the side, spinning him partway around. He crumpled to the floor.

Benson quickly brought his gun around to cover the others before anyone could try anything. "Steady! Don't make me use up any more of my hostages."

Jill Laudon stared in horror at Alex Copley, who was virtually at her feet. She seemed shocked . . . numb . . . disbelieving. Then finally she knelt, putting tentative hands on Copley's shoulders.

Copley's features were contorted in pain. "I must be crazy!" he gasped, breathing in heaving spasms which brought new anguish to his features. "Why'd I do a dumb thing like that?"

Jill looked up, a newfound anxiety in her voice. "He needs help!"

"There will be time for that," Benson said curtly. "I must commend Mr. Copley for his surprising display of bravery. But I *warn* you all that any similar displays will prove fatal." He turned to Brandon. "Now do you understand how important it is that you return Lorenz?"

Brandon nodded, his features taut and grim.

"Good. Now you may contact your airship again. The helicopter may return, with one pilot only. And I want the side doors left open, so that I may see it is empty. You—" he gestured toward Daniels—"you will help him carry Lorenz outside, *carefully*, but then you will remain behind with the rest. . . ."

Minutes later, the helicopter had left the airship to return to the island, landing in a clear area a short distance from the medical research facility. Brandon waited outside, standing next to the cot on which Stefan Lorenz lay. His medical kit and defibrillator equipment sat alongside.

Shutting the engine down, Captain Lee stepped slowly out of the helicopter and made his way to where Brandon and Lorenz were. Stopping before the doctor, Lee glanced cautiously toward the building.

"Are we ready to go, sir?"

Brandon looked back and saw Carla, barely visible in the doorway. Maggie Newcombe was apparently guarding the others now, for Benson himself was keeping Carla under the barrel of his gun.

"Yes," Brandon said faintly. He bent to pick up his end

of the cot, setting his medical kit between Lorenz' feet, and swinging his equipment case around his shoulder by its strap.

Together with Captain Lee, he carried Lorenz' cot like a stretcher. The helicopter had already been prepared, the bench seat in the middle folded back to make room for the cot. Taking a position on his knees alongside the cot, Brandon steadied it while Captain Lee started the helicopter's turbines and increased their power to takeoff speed.

Brandon had only time for a last swift glance back at the research facility and Carla before the craft started up, maintaining level flight as it turned for the mammoth airship floating above the northern end of the island. The thought that Carla's life depended on what he did in the next few hours would only make the operation that much harder.

Major Shaffer, General Smalley, and Haddock were waiting in the helicopter hangar at the top of the airship. As the Bell UH-1N lowered to the deck on its lift, the three men rushed to meet Brandon. Close behind them, Griffith and nurse Lynch pushed a lightweight wheeled stretcher.

Haddock spoke first. "What happened? I thought you had Benson secured."

"I did," Brandon said quickly, supervising as Lorenz was carried from the elevator and shifted to the stretcher. "The senior stewardess is working for the Russians, too. She had a gun on Carla and the others."

Haddock frowned, more at himself than Brandon. "I should have considered that possibility. Airline personnel are sometimes used as couriers. Their constant traveling makes them valuable."

"The *Kiev* is still a fair distance back," General Smalley told him next. "But they'll be within helicopter range soon enough."

They walked quickly along, returning through the missile section and reaching the elevator. The descent to the lower level of the ship and the long walk through the corridor that stretched to the nose of the great craft seemed to take an eternity. Time that neither Lorenz nor the others could well afford.

At last they reached the medical section of Deck B, and Lorenz was wheeled into the surgery to be prepared for the operation. Brandon and Shaffer scrubbed, slipping into OR green surgical garb.

"What are you going to do?" Haddock demanded.

"Perform the operation as best I can," Brandon replied tersely. "And then return with Lorenz to the island."

"We can't just hand him over to the Russians!"

"We don't have a great deal of choices," Brandon snapped, anger rising in his voice. "Benson's left no doubt of what he'll do to Carla and the others if we try anything. I won't let you endanger them."

Haddock fumed. "There's got to be a way."

Brandon turned for the surgery. "If I think of one, I'll let you know. . . ."

Putting his face mask in place, he headed for the cabinet at the side of the operating table. On a tray on top, hermetically sealed in a thick plastic covering, was the artificial heart. The device he had worked so long and hard to develop at the institute. And it would be used to save not *one* life, but many. If it worked . . .

Shaffer took up his position at the table, checking to make certain Lorenz was stable. At the end, Griffith tended to the anesthetic while the nurses positioned the trays of surgical instruments and the heart-lung machine.

The power supply for the artificial heart had not been completed yet. An external battery pack would have to suffice temporarily.

Shaffer looked up at Brandon. "I think we're about ready, Doctor."

Brandon approached the table and Lorenz. He tried to concentrate solely on the difficult operation that lay ahead, remembering each critical step of the procedure. But still haunting him, burned deeply into his memory, was Carla's face and the frightened look it held as he left. . . .

CHAPTER TWELVE

Carla Jennings shifted uncomfortably on the wooden bench positioned near the window of the medical research facility. She looked fearfully toward the man who had called himself Peter Benson, hoping that her movement would not be misconstrued. Benson sat beside her on the bench, away from the window where he could not be a target for marksmen. His own eyes still darted quickly back and forth among the other people in the room. Maggie Newcombe was positioned at the other side of the laboratory area, where she could cover them all from the opposite angle.

Glancing down at her watch for the hundredth time, Carla saw it was 2:00 P.M. Paul Brandon had been gone with Stefan Lorenz for a little over four hours now. She wondered how the operation was going and what Benson's reaction would be if it did not go well.

With great hesitancy, she finally asked. "Would ... would it be all right if I got up and walked around a bit?"

"No," Benson said quickly and firmly. "Stay where you are. You have already moved around enough."

Carla glanced around the room, her eyes taking in the faces of the others. All of them seemed as anxious and fearful as she herself felt. All of them except Martin Sandersen, who still seemed almost catatonic, and Alex Copley, who was slumped in a chair at the other side of the room, a wide swath of gauze and adhesive tape dressing across the side of his bare chest. Carla had given him pain-killers, and he was now only semiconscious. She was glad Benson had at least allowed her to treat the gun-shot wound. The bullet had missed Copley's vital organs, but muscle tissue had been torn and one rib cracked from the bullet's passage. The boy had been in great pain.

Even now, Jill Laudon sat next to Copley, and the worry on her features seemed as much for his health as for her own safety. How much of it was guilt over the fact that Copley had taken a bullet meant for her, Carla could not guess.

Time had been passing with agonizing slowness. It was bad enough waiting on the outcome of Lorenz' surgery, without the overhanging threat of Benson's ugly automatic, so near and menacing. And somewhere out there, she knew, a Russian aircraft carrier was drawing steadily closer to the island.

"This Dr. Brandon," Benson said suddenly. "Is he good?"

Carla looked at him soberly. "One of the best."

"I hope you are right."

Carla studied him a moment, before his penetrating gaze forced her to look away again. His last remark seemed not so much a shadowy threat as concern on his own part. She imagined he must be fearful of failing in his mission. Then Carla remembered that his mission had so far required him to murder three people, and many more as a direct result of the crash. A chill ran through her as she thought about the total insanity of it all, of people who dispensed death as readily as she dispensed medicines to treat the injured.

A sound started up in the distance, muffled at first, then gradually growing louder and more distinct. Benson seemed to notice it about the same time as Carla, and in another few seconds everyone else heard it as well. Their faces angled toward the window with varying degrees of anxiety.

The helicopter was returning from the *Grand Eagle.*

"Get up," Benson told Carla, prodding her with the automatic. He motioned her toward the door, staying close as they walked slowly along, then halted her a short distance from the open doorway. He kept the pistol close to her head.

The helicopter drifted down, gently settling on the same spot where it had landed before. Captain Lee cut the engine and emerged from the front of the ship, walking around to help Brandon with the stretcher. Brandon emerged at the rear of the stretcher, still clothed in green operating garments. Even the rubber surgical gloves still covered his hands.

The two men brought the stretcher and its burden forward, setting it down on its legs a short distance from the medical research building. Brandon looked up toward the doorway at Carla and Benson, his surgical mask hanging loosely about his neck.

"Tell your pilot to return to the airship," Benson shouted.

Captain Lee responded immediately, the young officer going back to his helicopter and starting the turbines. Once in the air, he headed for the *Grand Eagle* once more.

Benson started to emerge with Carla, then, remembering the relative accuracy of the airship's laser systems, he hesitated. Turning toward the back he commanded, "The rest of you—outside!"

One by one they emerged into the open, all except for Copley, who was barely conscious now. Maggie Newcombe kept a nervous guard from the rear as the group assembled in front of the building.

Moving closer to the stretcher, Benson stared at it with sudden alarm. For the sheet that covered Lorenz' still form had been drawn over his head. One arm partially protruded from beneath the sheet, limply hanging, and of a deathly blue-white pallor.

Brandon approached Benson slowly, his worried eyes shifting from Carla to the Soviet agent. A look of utter failure and anxiety set his features.

"*No,*" Benson said under his breath.

Stopping halfway between the stretcher and Benson, Brandon said, "I'm sorry."

Steering Carla ahead of him, Benson stepped closer to the covered form, stopping almost even with Brandon. On his face apprehension mingled with open skepticism. Briefly glancing back at Maggie Newcombe, he snapped, "Check him!"

Walking quickly, but keeping an eye on the others, Maggie headed for the stretcher. Reaching it, she bent toward the covered form with reluctance. Her pistol still alertly poised, the fingers of her free hand reached out and touched the exposed wrist tentatively.

The arm was flaccid in her grip. There was no pulse, and the skin felt cold to the touch.

She looked back at Benson fearfully. "He's dead!"

"Are you *certain*?"

"Yes!"

Brandon looked uneasily at Benson, less than a few feet away. The man's gun was still pressed very close against Carla's temple.

"Uncover the face," Benson ordered, a nervous sweat beginning to appear on his forehead.

Maggie Newcombe started to obey. Her gun covering the others, her hand reached for the corner of the sheet and began to lift it. Behind her at a short distance, Benson shifted his position slightly, his view blocked by Maggie's shoulder.

Brandon saw the gun in Benson's hand move several inches away from Carla's head, briefly pointing away from her as Benson sought to see past Maggie.

There was no waiting any longer. With one explosive motion of Brandon's tennis-trained body, he leaped toward Benson, grabbing the hand that held the gun and forcing it upward, away from Carla. Brandon's other gloved hand shot to the exposed skin at the back of Benson's neck, clamping down firmly.

A shot fired into the air as Benson's finger involuntarily squeezed the trigger. His entire body jerked violently, twisting awkwardly in a grotesque posture.

Maggie had started to turn toward them when suddenly

the sheet-covered form on the stretcher came to life. The sheet fell back as Col. John Curtis lunged from the stretcher, his long arm knocking the pistol away from her hand.

Benson was slumping to his knees, eyes glazing, but was still clutching the automatic. Though weakened and faltering, he resisted Brandon's attempts to wrest the gun from his grip.

Curtis scooped up Maggie's pistol and ran toward Brandon and the struggling Benson. Grabbing the silenced gun in Benson's hand, he threw his weight against it, burying its muzzle in the sandy soil.

Brandon freed one hand from his struggle and swung hard at Benson's jaw, surprising himself more than anyone else as the Soviet agent collapsed limply to the ground. Brandon looked up quickly at Maggie Newcombe, but the senior stewardess, now disarmed, was standing weakly still, staring at the unconscious agent in mute horror.

Carla rushed to Brandon's side as he straightened. Her eyes darted to the fallen Soviet agent, puzzled and questioning. "Paul—how—?"

In the next instant the question seemed unimportant. Impulsively, she embraced him, thankful for his safety.

Brandon returned the intensity of her embrace, but said, "Careful—"

Carla had already noticed the hard, boxy object concealed beneath the jacket of his surgical garb. Stepping back, her look of curiosity returned.

"I think the battery's dead by now," Brandon said, reaching beneath his jacket to switch off the device. He held out his left hand, carefully peeling off the adhesive tape that had secured the small defibrillator electrode to the palm of his rubber glove. He repeated the procedure with his right hand, then withdrew the electrodes and their cables through the long sleeves of his jacket. All that remained was to remove the small defibrillator unit from where it was strapped around his upper torso. "There wasn't much of a charge left on it, but it held out long enough to work."

Colonel Curtis straightened up, still keeping an eye on the unconscious agent. Reaching up to his left arm, he undid the small tourniquet Brandon had applied in the helicopter, just before touching down. He rubbed his arm carefully, glad to feel the pulse returning at his wrist. Now that circulation was returning, and the effect of the chilling spray Brandon had applied to the skin was beginning to wear off, Curtis' arm was regaining its usual warmth and color.

Fresh concern showed suddenly on Carla's features. "Paul—what about Lorenz? Is he all right?"

"Yes. So far, at least." Brandon peeled the surgical gloves from his hands. "The operation went well, and Major Shaffer finished up." He glanced skyward. The helicopter had not gone all the way back to the airship. It was hovering high overhead, with Captain Lee keeping an eye on what was happening.

Colonel Curtis waved a signal to Lee, then turned back to Brandon and Carla Jennings. "There isn't much time. We're going to have to get those crash survivors aboard the airship."

"We need to check some of them before we move them," Carla told him, "Paul brought a fluoroscope unit over from the clinic."

Curtis gave it thought. "All right. We'll transport the least injured first, and while the helicopter is making its trip, you can be checking the others." He motioned toward Benson and Maggie Newcombe. "Let's get them inside where we can secure them. . . ."

Overhead, the massive airship was now at an altitude of less than a thousand feet, and still descending. Its length literally spanned the narrow strip of land that separated ocean from lagoon. Slowly, ponderously, the ship repositioned, stopping above the area of the lagoon in which the fragmented cargo section had gone down. Heading into the wind, the craft's propellers were adjusted to hold it in position. Automatic checking systems working the control surfaces and turbo thrusters came into play, bringing the *Grand Eagle* into a stable hold.

Near the center of the ship, directly behind the two Harrier bays, the heavy equipment bay was the scene of hurried and purposeful activity. During much of the flight, airship maintenance crew members had worked to cover most of the bay's flooring and walls with wide sheets of plastic film, sealing the edges with plastic tape. Four of those same crewmen were now donning wet suits and scuba gear. Since the airship's planned operations were to take place almost entirely over water, a small number of the crew had been trained in underwater recovery techniques with the thought that unsuccessfully netted RPVs could still be returned if their flotation devices kept them near enough the surface. Now that training was about to be put to a different test.

"Zip those suits up tight," the master sergeant in charge of the group cautioned them. He passed around tubes of a special waterproof cream. "Use this on your faces—cover all the exposed area. The less contact with that chemical in the lagoon, the better."

The four men finished their final adjustments as the large bay doors began to open. Above, at the top of the thirty-five-foot-high equipment bay, powerful winches were ready to unwind their lengths of cable.

One of the divers stepped close to the edge of the open bay, peering down at the lagoon's surface some two hundred feet below. "We could do without that wind," he commented soberly, then joined the others in climbing into a round, open framework enclosure that had been nicknamed "the birdcage." Connected by cable to a smaller winch, the cage was hoisted a few feet in the air while a fifth crew member handed in the coiled cables the others would need. Then the cage was swung beyond the edge of the bay and the winch reversed.

Wind began to buffet the cage and its human cargo almost as soon as it started its descent. The closer it came to the water's surface, the farther it arced out and away from a true vertical. The cable played out slowly, controlled from above.

Reaching the surface, the cage settled a few feet into the water, then stopped. The water lapped around their legs, bearing a grayish scum—apparently some of the leaked missile fuel powder had floated to the surface. The men slung heavy cables over their shoulders, checked their air-hose mouthpieces to be sure their regulators were operating properly, then one by one they left the cage and descended into the water.

There seemed an abrupt change as the sound of the wind no longer reached their ears. All they could hear now was their own breathing, and the disturbance their bubbles made in the water.

The wrecked airliner's cargo section lay roughly thirty feet ahead, almost flat upon the sandy bottom of the lagoon. It looked relatively intact, which would greatly simplify recovery operations. Its raw ends beckoning, the cylinder of metal was tilted slightly off of true level, pointing toward the shore.

There were no fish now in the immediate area, though at a distance both the brightly colored tropical varieties and gray sharks could be seen. It was almost as if they knew and understood the danger.

Approaching the wreckage, the four divers looked first for cracks and tears in the fuselage—places that might cause it to weaken and break apart if moved. They found several minor splits in the outer skin of the plane, but the main structure seemed relatively sound.

The men split up into two teams, moving to each end of the cargo section. Uncoiling their cables, they prepared to pass them under the fuselage.

The task would be easier at the rear of the wreckage—the underside of it was raised slightly off the sandy bottom by coral growths. The first diver took his end of the cable and started under the edge. There was perhaps a foot of space between the fuselage and the bottom in one spot near the end. But passage through that space was hampered by both the coral protrusions on each side of the gap, and by the added bulk of the diver's air tanks. Struggling to bring his end of the cable through the gap, the man's chest scraped against the bottom, his tanks wedging against the underbelly of the wreckage.

From the other side, the second diver reached to meet him halfway, to take the cable the rest of the distance. Coral growths on the far side were closer, restricting the second diver's passage. Carefully squeezing in between the coral, the diver was keenly aware of the fact that too much pressure against the sharp edges of the growth could result in a cut, not only of his wet suit, but of his arms or shoulders as well. He did not know how much of the powdered missile fuel was still in suspension in the water here, but he had heard the report of the fuel's effects on the man who had only absorbed some of the chemical through the pores of his skin. What the highly toxic substance would do if taken directly into a raw wound was anybody's guess.

Try as he might, the second diver could not reach across the remaining distance to where the first man held the end of the cable. It was still more than a foot beyond his grasp.

On the opposite side, the first diver made a loop of the cable's end. Holding the connector clamp in one hand, he fed out a length of cable, letting its own natural springiness expand the loop forward. When it had reached out an extra foot and a half, the second diver grabbed hold and securely gripped the loop. Carefully working his way back out of the tight channel between coral growths, the second diver brought the end of the cable free and started up and over, to be met by the other diver. Working on the clamps, they started connecting the two cable ends together.

At the forward end of the wreckage, there was virtually no space at all between the bottom and the fuselage. Both divers at this end worked for more than five minutes trying to locate even the slightest gap through which the cable could be fed.

In another moment, the first two divers joined them, but were also stumped by the impossibility of the problem. There seemed to be no way the cable could be placed.

One of the men suddenly swam up to the side of the wreckage and pointed to the cabin windows. He motioned with the end of the cable, showing how it could be passed through the windows on both sides of the fuselage and directly through the cabin.

Using his diving knife, he hacked at the double-paned glass for half a minute before finally realizing that it simply could not be broken in that way. The window was too tough, and the water impeded his movements.

Sheathing his knife, the man looked down at the shark stun rod tethered to his weight belt. Unhooking it, he held it in his hands tentatively, then leveled it at the second window from the end and jabbed forward, directly at the glass. On the first strike, the shotgunlike shell at the end exploded with a sharp jolt. The concussive force shattered the double-paned window, forcing the fragments inward in a slow-motion tumble.

Passing his end of the cable through the jagged opening, he motioned for one of the other divers to follow suit on the other side of the fuselage. In a moment, the second window had been breached, and a diver entered the wreckage to guide the cable the rest of the distance.

The men were securing the connectors on top of the wreckage when they noticed the presence of the sharks for the first time. While the dreaded killers of the deep had been maintaining their distance before, they now were circling ever closer to the wreckage and the men.

Momentarily disregarding their danger, the first diver pulled a dye marker from his belt and popped the flotation tube. As the marker spiraled to the surface, it began to release a bright yellow dye that would be visible from the equipment bay of the airship.

A minute passed. More seconds ticked by, while the sharks grew bolder in their passes. Then finally, there was a splash above as two large cables, their ends connected to a string of weights, descended into the lagoon.

They were still not directly above the wreckage, but from their angle, it was apparent that the airship had been shifted a few degrees to bring it more in line. Two of the divers swam out to intercept the cables, unfastening the weights that bound them together.

One cable had to be hooked to each of the "slings" that went around the fuselage. The divers had begun making the connections when the sharks closed in still more.

Swimming through the contaminated water, passing the toxic substance through their gills, they would be dead in hours or less. But for now, their danger was real and imminent.

Two of the divers continued to work on the cable connections while the others moved out to keep the sharks at bay. Among the four, there were only two of the stun rods still usable. And the number of sharks in the area was already up to a dozen, increasing with each passing minute.

Making a pass too close for comfort, one shark was repelled by the first diver as he struck at the beast's blunt nose with the side of his stun rod. But when one left, two more took its place. They were approaching from all sides now, slowly circling, testing their prey's reactions.

On the top of the fuselage, the diver at the rear of the wreckage completed his connection, quickly swimming to the other end to assist the other diver there. As the two men worked at the last connection, a large black shark—the species dreaded most by the islanders—approached dangerously close. Both men's stun rods had been expended. They were useless now, except as clubs. First one diver and then the other struck out with their rods, fending off the *papera*'s deadly advances.

Seeing their danger, the other men returned to assist. As the large shark made another close pass, the diver nearest him jabbed out with a charged stun rod. The end of the rod connected a short distance behind the eye, firing its shell.

Its side ruptured by the concussive force, the shark wriggled through the water, tail down and moving fitfully. From the raw gash seeped a steady discharge of blood, spreading slowly through the water.

Quickly now, all four divers worked at the connector,

finally securing the last cable. Their leader motioned for the surface, and all began the slow ascent. Below them the eerily beautiful world of clear water, coral, and white sand erupted into a nightmare scene.

Aroused into a frenzy by the blood of the mortally wounded black shark, the others swarmed about its sinking body. The entire area became gray with sharks, obscuring even the presence of the wrecked fuselage section.

Swimming steadily but evenly toward the surface, all four divers sought to reach the cage and its relative safety before the attention of the sharks focused next on them. In the frenzied state they were now in, they would likely attack anything within reach.

Clambering into the cage, the divers began to signal wildly, arms raised to the massive airship which so dominated the sky above them. Long seconds passed while the turmoil beneath the water's surface continued, then at last the cage started up with a sudden lurch.

Following the instructions they'd been given, the four men did not remove their mouthpieces. They continued to breathe the air from their tanks as the cage was drawn steadily back up to the airship.

Below, the large cables drew taut as the winches began to exert pressure on them. Peering down from their cage, the divers could see the cargo section of the wrecked airliner shift position slightly as it lifted from the bottom.

Abruptly, their cage seemed to halt in its ascent. For as the heavy cargo section was being lifted, its weight was causing the airship to lose altitude. The cage seemed almost ready to start back to the water's seething surface when controls on the command deck activated release valves leading from the *Grand Eagle*'s ballast tanks.

Tons of water cascaded down from vents near the ends of the airship, shutting off at the precise moment to equalize the weight of the cargo section. The *Grand Eagle* returned to its original height, and the cage continued up.

Below them, the surface of the water broke as the fragment of the downed jet emerged. As the winches in the equipment hold maintained their steady pull, the cargo section rose steadily higher, water spilling from the open ends. Because of the differing placement of the cables, the section was not level. The forward end of the section was lower, and the winch controlling its rise had to have its speed increased briefly to bring the end up.

Within six more minutes, the entire fuselage section had been brought up into the spacious equipment bay. The remaining maintenance crew members, now cloaked in impermeable garments head to foot, manned spray tanks filled with chemicals to neutralize the effects of the leaked fuel powder. They coated every inch of the cargo section, directing the spray inside as well.

The four divers were next, and they waited for the hosing down, still with masks in place and breathing from their tanks. But before that took place, the master sergeant in charge of the bay operations donned gloves and approached the first diver. Observing the gray scum that coated the man's wet suit, he extended a sterile glass slide and scraped some of the material onto its surface.

The master sergeant then dropped the slide into a plastic bottle and capped it. He placed that in a plastic bag and sealed the top. Handing it to one of the crew, he said, "Get this up to Major Shaffer right away. . . ."

On the command deck, General Smalley watched the activity in the equipment bay on one of the television monitors, his expression troubled. Turning to the radar and allied systems console, he asked, "What's the position of the *Kiev* now?"

The technician glanced up from his equipment. "They're about sixty-five miles out, sir, and they're maintaining top speed. But their helicopters are going to get here a lot sooner than the carrier."

Smalley frowned. "That doesn't leave us much time."

Near him, the government man, Haddock, looked concerned. "Can we get the last of the people up before the copters reach us?"

"Maybe," Smalley replied softly. "Maybe not. But even if we *do,* it's going to be cutting it awfully close. And if the Russians know we've got both Lorenz and the prototype, they're not going to just quit and go home."

Hearing their conversation, Lieutenant Colonel Foster approached, respectfully, but with an anxious look. "Sir—with Lee and the other pilot tied up with the helicopter, we can't launch more than four of our Harriers. And Lee is the flight leader."

"I know that," Smalley said with some irritation. "But

we can't stop the shuttle while there are still injured down there, waiting to be brought up."

He hesitated for a long moment, and Haddock spoke up. "I think we should avoid any further conflict with the *Kiev*. So far there's been no loss of life on either side as a result of actions between the two vessels."

"I intend to keep it that way," Smalley replied, pulling the fragmented pieces of his pipe from his pocket and absently fingering them. Glancing up at the helm, his eyes settled on the officers there, and behind them, Stewart Gardner, who had reluctantly been allowed to assist while final maneuvers had been made in approaching the island. Smalley started to look away, then suddenly something about Gardner's bandaged head brought his attention back. His eyes narrowed in thought. Turning suddenly to the radar console once more, he asked, "Are those Soviet helicopters within visual range of us yet—can they see what we're doing?"

"Negative, sir," the technician replied. "But they will be within fifteen or twenty minutes at the most."

Moving quickly to the communications console, Smalley pressed the intercom switch for the equipment bay. When the master sergeant in charge responded, he ordered, "Forget about securing the cargo section! I want you to get that crate with the prototype out of there as fast as you can—you know the markings to look for." Switching to the helicopter hangar circuit, he said, "Have Captain Lee wait—he's got a passenger for the return trip."

Motioning for Haddock to follow, he explained, "I'll walk you to the elevator, and tell you what I have in mind. . . ."

In the island's medical research building, Paul Brandon and Carla Jennings readied the last of the injured for transportation. Father Daniels had remained behind to assist, and he and Colonel Curtis were presently carrying one of the stretchers into the main room, to be ready when the helicopter returned.

"Sorry about the misunderstanding, Father," Curtis was saying. "You'll have to admit, it did look bad."

"Just how did they manage to lose my records?" Daniels inquired, setting down the stretcher and starting back with Curtis to the rear room.

"They weren't really lost. It turned out that Air Force Intelligence had pulled your complete file and all duplicate records. They had them in their security section."

Daniels looked puzzled. "Why?"

"For safety's sake, I guess," Curtis replied. "They didn't elaborate, but they left the impression that you were doing some work for them."

Daniels stopped in his tracks. He looked strangely at Curtis, eyebrows raised. "Hardly. I'm not even in the Air Force anymore. When I first went back to Southeast Asia as a missionary, I *did* agree to keep my ears open for any information about POWs that haven't been returned, but nothing more. I made it clear to the officer who spoke to me that I had no intention of passing along tactical information."

Curtis shrugged. "Perhaps they were merely being overly cautious."

Brandon and Carla passed them on the way, carrying another stretcher into the main room. As they set it down, a sound from the outside attracted their attention.

Brandon looked out the window. "The helicopter's back. After this trip, we'll have to start on the bodies of the dead."

Carla nodded grimly, glad that she would not have to assist in that part of the transfer. Looking out at the helicopter, she frowned at the sight of a man she had not seen before, emerging from the craft.

"You know him?"

"Oh yes," Brandon replied. "Only too well."

Haddock looked around briefly, then quickly headed for the building. As he entered, he walked directly to Brandon and then stopped to survey the room. His gaze rested a moment on Benson, slumped in one of the chairs, his hands bound and his eyes closed. Near him, Maggie Newcombe was also seated, and also tied securely.

Haddock studied the man. "How long will he be unconscious?"

"Quite a while," Carla answered. "Maybe twenty-four hours. I've given him a fairly strong sedative."

He nodded, then his eyes shifted to Maggie Newcombe, his face hard and unyielding. "So this is his accomplice? The killer's helper?"

Maggie seemed unnerved by the tone of his voice. "Now just a bloody minute—I didn't kill anyone! When this thing started, there was no mention of anyone being killed. It was just to be a mock hijacking."

"Either way, the results are the same," Haddock replied. "You're in this thing up to your neck. Maybe if you hadn't taken charge and released Benson after he had been captured, it would have been another matter, but—"

"I had to do that!" Maggie whined. "If that Russian ship got here first, and I hadn't helped him, my life wouldn't have been worth a cent."

"Maybe. But we're in charge now, and if you want any kind of special considerations at all, you'd better be prepared to cooperate with *us*. . . ."

At that moment activity in the airship's equipment bay was continuing at the same frantic pace. An extendable catwalk had been brought alongside the cargo section wreckage, and a crewman with face shield and gloves was using an electric saw to cut through the aluminum skin of the fuselage. He followed a rough line marked on the outside after the position of the desired crate had been determined.

Near him, a weapons handler was busily wiring a small explosive charge which could be activated by remote control. Several large magnesium and phosphorus flares were wrapped up in the hastily assembled bundle, ordered up by General Smalley. Small additional charges had already been placed on the cable connectors, at the point where they touched the fuselage. They would be triggered by the concussion of the main charge.

On the command deck, Smalley continued to watch the crew's progress on the television monitor. His expression grew more concerned with each passing minute.

"Eight minutes to visual range, sir," the radar technician reported on the nearness of the Soviet helicopters.

Smalley frowned but said nothing in reply. He continued to watch the monitor as the crewman made the last cut in the cargo section's side.

The men carefully peeled back the aluminum skin of the fuselage and exposed the interior of the section. The crate they wanted was visible, secured by several straps.

Working quickly now to cut through those straps, the crewmen freed the crate from its pallet and tipped it back, bringing the end through the raw opening. It weighed at least two hundred pounds, and as they moved it, the suspended cargo section shifted slightly.

Tying a lifting harness around the crate's sides, one of

the men reached for the cable from the small winch that had been used to lower the divers earlier. As he strove to keep his balance, he was keenly aware that one slip could send him plummeting through the open bay doors two hundred feet to the water below. The wind howled ominously through the bay, as if confirming the danger and adding its own dire warning.

On the monitor, Smalley watched as the crate was hoisted free of the cargo section. In another moment, the main explosive charge had been placed, and the crewmen were quickly pushing the fuselage siding back to its original position.

"*Five* minutes to visual range, sir," the radar technician called out.

Smalley spoke into the intercom. "Seal it and start the winches—get that thing out of the bay and start it down!"

Working feverishly, the crewmen covered the cut edge of the panel with aluminized repair tape intended for minor patches on the airship itself. Their job finally done, the men moved clear as the winches overhead started unwinding cable, steadily lowering the cargo section back toward the surface of the lagoon.

It had taken a little over six minutes before to haul it up. Now they had less than five to lower it. They could only get it down within fifty feet of the water in that amount of time. But perhaps that would be enough. . . .

On the island, Paul Brandon peered anxiously out of the window facing the ocean. His features tensing suddenly, he told the others, "I can see them—they'll be landing any minute!"

Maintaining an open formation, the ten Soviet helicopters rushed toward the beach. The first ones were setting down even as the last were crossing the span of water between the edge of the reef and the land itself.

The bulbous-nosed Hormone A helicopters settled carefully on the sand, their double rotors slowing to idle speed. The pilots of the craft kept their engines going, ready to lift off at the first sign of an attack from the hovering airship.

Lieutenant Zagorski and eleven of his naval infantry troops piled out of the first helicopter while more soldiers emerged from each of the other nine craft. In a moment, 120 trained fighting men with weapons ready had gathered at the island's edge. There was no longer any pretense that the *Kiev* was involved in a rescue mission.

Zagorski shouted for four squads of his men to take up positions near the building and the American helicopter, which was waiting with its own engines idling. As he directed them, one of his sergeants pointed to the airship and its dangling cargo with an urgent look.

"Sir—they are hoisting the wreckage!"

Zagorski looked and saw that the cargo section was moving slowly up toward the open bay. "They cannot be allowed to take the prototype!" he yelled. He motioned to one of his men, armed with a small rocket launcher. "Aim as I direct you," he told him, watching as the soldier brought the narrow tube to his shoulder and looked through the sights. "Better that it be destroyed than given up to the Americans."

The trigger was depressed. A sudden whoosh of propellant fired the projectile from its tube, straight for the side of the cargo section, still hanging less than 60 feet above the water, and only 140 feet below the *Grand Eagle*.

Impacting in the cargo section a split second before the remote signal could be used to detonate the explosive charge, as Smalley had planned, the rocket accomplished the same purpose. A brilliant flash erupted within the suspended fuselage as both the charge and the rocket's own explosive detonated.

Firing almost simultaneously, the special charges placed at the top of the section ignited and burned through the cables supporting the wreckage. Lurching free, the cargo section plummeted the remaining distance to the lagoon, its interior a white ball of burning phosphorus. Even as it sank beneath the surface, inextinguishable flames still raged within it, followed by several minor explosions as air trapped within the other crates became superheated.

Zagorski watched the smoldering wreckage briefly through the clear water of the lagoon. The fuel canisters no doubt accounted for the brilliant flames, he thought. Surely there was nothing left that could be salvaged by anyone.

His primary concern now was Lorenz, and he hurried toward the building where his men had already taken up positions. He glanced toward the helicopter, where Captain Lee waited uneasily.

His attention snapped back to the building as Carla Jennings and Paul Brandon emerged, carrying one of the stretchers, apparently starting for the helicopter. Behind them, Colonel Curtis and Father Daniels brought another injured survivor. Already waiting in the open air were two other stretchers with their human burdens. Haddock emerged cautiously, pulling Maggie Newcombe along, her wrists still bound.

"You will halt there!" Zagorski commanded in surprisingly good English, the wide semicircle of armed troops backing up his words with chilling effectiveness. "Where is Lorenz?"

"He's dead," Brandon said unconvincingly.

Zagorski studied him hard, leveling his rifle with almost casual disregard, the sling still running over his shoulder. "I think you are lying."

Carla said nothing, watching worriedly as the Soviet officer looked with probing eyes at the people on the stretchers. Of the four, three of the injured were men.

Zagorski studied the people standing before him. He did not fail to notice that Maggie Newcombe's hands were tied.

His voice flat, he said, "A red star is rising in the heavens. . . ."

Maggie responded quickly. "Our destiny is the world." Leaning away from Haddock with an urgent look, she said, "He's lying! The one they carried out is Lorenz."

Zagorski's eyes narrowed slightly. "You know the countersign," he replied. "But you are not the agent. Where is he?"

"Whitfield is dead," Maggie told him. "I was part of the operation. He told me the countersign, in case something happened."

"What happened to Whitfield?"

"They were chasing him across the lagoon in a boat. The airship fired on the boat and he went into the water. The sharks . . ."

Zagorski turned toward the lagoon, where almost a dozen fins were visible, circling about a central point not far from where the burned-out wreckage had sunk. He looked back to Brandon and Carla Jennings, and the man on the stretcher they had carried. Silently, he strode closer, peering intently at the unconscious man's face.

The man was covered with a sheet reaching up to his neck. The top of his head was bandaged so that the hair was not visible. His face and neck were slightly pink, suggesting he had just been shaved. Zagorski lifted the sheet. A bandage covered the man's bare chest.

Brandon said stridently, "This is *not* Lorenz. I'm telling the truth."

There was the trace of a smirk on Zagorski's gaunt features. "Do you really expect me to believe you?" He noticed a bulge at the end of the stretcher. Reaching down, he gripped the end of the sheet and yanked it free.

There between the man's feet was an attaché case. Zagorski picked it up, examining the Czechoslovakian initials at the top edge.

"S.L.," he read aloud. "Do you mean to tell me that does not stand for *Stefan Lorenz*!" Turning quickly to two of his men, he commanded, "Take him back to the helicopter."

"*No*," Haddock protested. He backed off as rifles were swung in his direction.

As the stretcher was being carried off to the helicopter, Zagorski cast a worried glance at the hovering airship. Without the suspended cargo section, the *Grand Eagle* was now rising higher.

Addressing his next statement to Colonel Curtis, he said, "I suggest that you do not attempt to prevent our return to the *Kiev*. Not unless you want to be responsible for the death of Lorenz. I think you would have a hard time explaining that to the people of the world."

Haddock managed a defeated look. "I speak for the State Department. We will take no action that will endanger Lorenz."

Zagorski motioned his men back to the helicopters. He was about to leave when Maggie Newcombe spoke out.

"What about *me*?"

Zagorski turned, looking at her dispassionately. "Our orders say nothing about you. Consider yourself lucky that they do not." With that he hurried back to the first helicopter and climbed aboard.

One by one, the ten Soviet craft lifted off the beach and swung around toward the north. The thunder of their rotors lingered for a long moment, gradually fading with their departure.

Haddock watched them go, the worried look still on his features. "We don't have much time, gentlemen—we'd better get finished up here and *get out*. . . ."

On the command deck of the *Grand Eagle*, General Smalley stood near the helm. To the flight officers there he said, "We may have to bleed a little helium. With the cargo section and

270

some of our ballast gone, it's going to be too hard to hold her down."

Using the helm's intercom circuit, Smalley pressed the button for the equipment bay. As the master sergeant in charge responded, he asked, "What's your report on damage down there? Did that explosion do us any harm?"

"Nothing serious, sir," the voice came back. "One of the bay doors took a little flak, but I think we can patch it."

"Good. Get it done."

At the rear of the control center, Major Shaffer pushed through the double doors and hurried toward Smalley. In his hand was the small bottle with its glass slide.

Smalley turned as the doctor approached. "Is that the sample?"

"Yes," Shaffer replied. "I've been examining it under the microscope."

"What about the lagoon? Are the chemicals we've brought going to be enough to neutralize the leaked fuel?"

"I think so, but we may not need them. This scum that was floating on the surface and contaminated the divers' wet suits—it's plankton."

"What?"

"Plankton—small marine organisms, the beginning of the ocean's entire food chain. Apparently they've been ingesting the powdered fuel. It kills them, of course, but it stays within their system when they float to the surface." Shaffer paused a moment, examining the sample with a certain curious respect. "We know from the initial report given us on the fuel that when it's absorbed into a living organism, it's eventually broken down into separate elements which are not in themselves toxic. So it's possible the lagoon will be free of any contamination within a few more days."

"That ought to ease a lot of minds in Washington." Peering out through the forward windows, he said, "Now we've got to complete the transfer operation. With both that storm out there and the *Kiev* getting closer, we can't afford to hang around much longer." He sighed. "We've done all we could do here."

Major Tate, the weapons control officer, called forward, "Sir—what about the RPV we've got parked on the *Kiev*? Shall we bring it in?"

Smalley considered it only a moment. "No, not just

yet. Let's leave her there a little while longer, just in case. . . ."

Forty-five minutes later, Paul Brandon and Carla Jennings were standing outside the medical research facility. The helicopter had already taken the last of the dead to the airship, where they would be taken to Deck C's storage holds for the trip to Hawaii. Rising now above the airship once more, the helicopter would be returning to the island in a matter of minutes.

Brandon knew it was returning for him. He surveyed the rather bleak island, thinking of the primitive conditions in which Carla had been working for the past year.

"How do you manage here?" he asked suddenly. "How do you stand it?"

Carla looked around the island with different eyes, seeing the trees, the ocean, and the shore, remembering the islanders she had come to know and understand. "It's beautiful here. It really is, Paul. Don't judge it by what's happened in the past few days." She hesitated, brushing back a strand of wind-blown hair from her face. She seemed calmer now that the greatest danger had passed. Or perhaps it was only fatigue, catching up with her. "Tongareva has been good for me," she began again. "After you've been here awhile you get used to the island, to the quiet, slow rhythm of life. Sometimes you wonder if you could ever go back to that turmoil we call civilization."

Brandon was silent for several minutes, listening to the sounds of wind and wave, trying to understand. Then another sound intruded as the helicopter settled down some distance away, engine slowing as Captain Lee waited.

"Do you think you could go back?" Brandon asked her. "Now, I mean?"

Carla studied him a moment. "Now?"

Brandon turned toward her, putting his hands on her shoulders. "Come back with me. After the crash survivors are taken to Hawaii, the airship will be returning to California. We—"

"Paul, I—"

"We could try again," he continued. "I know there are things we don't agree on, but still—"

"Paul, please don't say any more," Carla pleaded, her expression uncertain and pained. "I'm not sure if I know my own feelings anymore, and anyway, no matter what I want now, I *have* to stay here."

Brandon's hopes fell. "You have to . . . or want to?"

"There's no other doctor here, Paul—I can't just go off and leave the islanders without medical help." She glanced back toward the building, where Mary Akaru was still tending to her husband. "James is recovering, but there are some things that Mary can't handle in the way of medical emergencies. If any of the islanders got sick . . . if one of them should *die* because I'd left—"

Brandon nodded reluctantly. "You don't have to explain. You're right, of course. I understand the responsibility you have here."

"It's more than responsibility. I *care* for these people. I want to be able to help them when they need it." She hesitated, her eyes looking deeply into his. "You do understand, don't you?"

"I'm beginning to." Brandon looked toward the waiting helicopter. Captain Lee was not pressing—he gazed out to sea, giving them their privacy. "I've got to go back with Lorenz. If anything should go wrong with the artificial heart, I'll have to be there. I guess we both have our duties to perform." He looked at Carla somewhat wistfully. "I don't really want to say good-bye. . . ."

He pulled her closer, kissing her gently. It was a long and bittersweet moment, and he wondered if it would be the last time he held her in his arms. All about them, the wind of the passing storm became stronger.

Reluctantly, he pulled away. "I have to go. They can't wait any longer."

Without glancing back, he hurried toward the helicopter and stepped up into the cabin. In another moment, the craft was in the air, heading for the airship's top hangar.

Minutes later, on the command deck of the *Grand Eagle*, General Smalley was conferring with Haddock and Colonel Curtis. Standing with them, her hands still bound, was Maggie Newcombe.

"Assign her quarters," Smalley was saying, "and post a guard. I don't want her wandering around."

Maggie looked anxiously toward Haddock. "You said if I cooperated—"

"I'll do what I can. But you're not through yet," Haddock said flatly. "I want a list of the agents in Hawaii for whom you've been acting as courier, although I'm sure they'll all be gone by the time we get there."

Colonel Curtis said, "I still wonder if we should have let the Russians have Lorenz' attaché case."

"There was nothing important in it," Maggie said morosely. "Believe me. I searched through every inch of it as soon as I had the chance."

Haddock's features bore a grim smile as he held up the luggage tag he had removed from the case while still on the island. "Then I'm glad you didn't know about the microfilm he was bringing us. . . ."

As Haddock and Curtis were taking Maggie Newcombe toward the rear doors, Paul Brandon arrived on the command deck. He brushed past the others, hardly noticing them.

Taking up a position near the wide front windows, Brandon looked down at the island and the distant form of Carla Jennings. The feeling of emptiness that had been a part of his life for the past year began to settle upon him once more.

Haddock and Smalley exchanged glances, then the general took up his usual position near the helm.

Smalley said, "Gentlemen—get us out of here before anything else happens."

At the helm, the flight officers punched in new commands and returned the ship's control from automatic to fully operational. One of them announced, "Leaving stable hold, sir."

Turbo thrusters at the nose and tail of the massive airship started up, swinging the Grand Eagle slowly around. The view through the command deck's large front windows began to change, the island slowly being lost from sight.

In another moment, the Grand Eagle had its new course set in and locked. The massive rotors at its tail spun faster as the turbines reached full power, and the airship pulled away from the coral atoll known as Tongareva. . . .

Miles out, on the deck of the Kiev, the ten Soviet helicopters were returning. Adm. Nikolay Bakhirev watched their landing approach with a look of relief.

"They are back without incident . . . good."

"Yes," Captain Dashkevich agreed. "It is unfortunate that they had to destroy the prototype."

"Another can be built," Bakhirev said confidently. "At least we have Lorenz."

The ship's political officer, Grigorovich, pointed down

at the forward end of the flight deck. "We also have a problem," he observed. "The American RPV."

"The men are still working on it," Dashkevich said.

Out on the flight deck, as the helicopters began unloading their troops and the man on the stretcher, the demolitions personnel were still attempting to find a way to bypass the tamper-proof controls on the RPV. One of them was moving a small electronic instrument along the fuselage, a few inches above the metal surface, while the man next to him was searching for a way to disarm the explosives pods themselves. The first man looked questioningly toward the other, but the second only shook his head grimly in reply.

On the bridge, Bakhirev turned to Dashkevich. "If we can disarm the device, I am sure our technicians will find its design of interest. But for now, Captain—set in a course for Tahiti. We have a schedule to meet, and a guest to entrust to our waiting comrades. . . ."

Belowdecks, the stretcher was being carried through passageways and compartments by two of the naval infantry soldiers. Finally reaching the sick bay after several minutes, they carefully transferred their burden to an examining table. The *Kiev*'s medical officer directed their activity, then dismissed them.

Turning to the unconscious man, the medical officer proceeded to attach electrodes from an EKG unit. He switched the device on and watched the chart feed out. Puzzled as he scanned the fluctuations, he switched the unit off and reached for the stethoscope about his neck.

Placing the bell of the instrument against the patient's chest, he listened to the heartbeat. It sounded strong and regular in its rhythm. A frown set the man's features.

Moments later, on the bridge of the Soviet carrier, the medical officer appeared at the top of the companionway and headed toward Bakhirev. The admiral seemed surprised to see him.

"Yes—what is it?"

"I have examined Lorenz," the officer told him. "At least, an initial check."

"What is his condition?" Bakhirev asked. "Will you be able to treat him?"

"I can find nothing wrong with him," the officer said with some exasperation. "His heart is that of a normal man—the characteristic sounds of a valve disorder are simply not present. One would almost think it was an entirely different person. . . ."

Those words lingered in the air between them for a long moment, as both men's expressions showed dawning realization. In the next instant, Bakhirev was hurrying for the companionway that led to the lower decks, the medical officer close behind him. When they reached the sick bay, Bakhirev went directly to the unconscious man and studied him intently. He snatched up the EKG strip and looked at it for a moment before crushing it in his fist.

"Those bandages," he said abruptly, pointing to the man's chest and head, "remove them!"

The medical officer complied, carefully at first, then more quickly, seeing no wounds beneath the bandages. In a moment, the man's dark hair was revealed.

"Lorenz is an older man, with gray hair!" Bakhirev snapped.

Jostled by the movements, the patient roused slightly from his unconscious state. His eyes did not open, but he muttered something faintly, almost in delirium. The words were clearly in Russian.

Bakhirev cursed under his breath and ran for the ship's intercom, leaving the stunned medical officer still staring down at the semiconscious Benson. He jabbed the button for the bridge.

"What is the position of the airship—*quickly*!"

"Still out of range of our weapons systems, Admiral," Dashkevich replied. "It is moving at top speed now . . . the winds are assisting it."

Bakhirev felt a chill cut through him as he remembered the flight deck above. The American RPV was still blocking the forward elevator, so no jets could be launched. The helicopters, even if they could match the speed of the airship, could in no way hope to stop it.

"They have him," Bakhirev said weakly, bitterly, knowing full well the report that Grigorovich would send back on his performance. "They have Lorenz . . . and there is not a thing we can do about it. . . ."

Twelve hours later in Washington, D.C., it was 9:20 A.M. A large crowd of newspaper reporters and television staffers were gathered in the auditorium of Walter Reed Hospital, their low, agitated voices creating a confusing murmur of sound. Both film and television cameras had been set up for the last few hours, and the lighting had been ready for an equal amount of time.

Caroline Simmons, a member of a network news team, stood clutching a newspaper. "Insanity," she was saying to Archer Grant. "This town is nothing but one big crock of insanity. Ettleman promises us a press conference one day, and then the next he tells us to come out here for a special address by Evans. And look at this—"

The blonde young woman flourished the newspaper. "There's a big story here based on a government press release saying that the crash survivors from Trans-Pacific Flight 47 were rescued and are due to arrive in Hawaii early this afternoon. But the whole issue of the radioactive materials shipment is played down almost to nonexistence, and the aircraft that Ettleman described as being top-secret is suddenly lauded by the government as a marvelous new tool for emergency operations and natural disasters!"

Grant nodded smugly. "You're still new in Washington. Wait till you've been here awhile." He sighed. "And don't worry about the airship—our affiliate station in Honolulu already has a camera crew standing by to cover the arrival."

"A lot of good that does us here," she replied. "And what about Evans? Does he really think he can just ignore the whole matter of the potential nuclear contamination?"

"I suppose he can try," Grant said, frowning curiously as several White House staffers appeared at the side of the auditorium's stage. "The funny thing is, I have a feeling that the biggest news flash is yet to come. . . ."

Seconds later, White House Press Secretary Herb Ettleman appeared, closely followed by Vice-President Drew Russell. Secret Service men could be seen in the wings, along with several medical personnel.

Russell, normally noted for his smooth manner and flashy grin, was uncommonly severe in his appearance. He looked faintly ill at ease.

The camera lights were on now. Film and video-tape were rolling, and live coverage was being sent back to the studio for transmission to network systems in New York. At the cluster of microphones on stage, Herb Ettleman announced, "Ladies and gentlemen . . . the President of the United States. . . ."

There was a slight swell of voices from the left side of the audience as newsmen there got a glimpse of the wheelchair being halted in the wings. Helped to his feet by Secret Service men, William Evans rose slowly and unsteadily, then made his way to the rostrum, the two agents close behind him but not supporting him. Dressed in the gray pin-striped suit he usually wore to press conferences, Evans looked pale and drawn.

Standing before the microphones, he took a moment to survey the crowd and the faces he had come to know among the news media. For whatever else seemed wrong with him, his eyes were still bright and alert.

"Members of the press," Evans began, his voice calm and steady, "fellow Americans, those of you who are watching and listening at home now, or at your offices—I speak to you all this morning with some difficulty. What I have to say is unpleasant for me, but it must be said. I have delayed too long as it is."

There was no reaction this time. Not even a disquieting cough. Evans had their attention fully now, and his weakened form had almost hypnotic power.

"For some time now," Evans continued, "I have been suffering from diabetes." He paused to let the words sink in. "Perhaps I was wrong to keep that fact a secret from you, but that was the decision I made. My personal physician has been treating me for quite some months, and the problem seemed to be under control. However, my condition has gradually been worsening, despite all treatment." He hesitated. "I was urged by my physician several weeks ago to enter the hospital for more extensive tests and treatment, but due to a number of critical international developments and another recent cause for concern, I . . . perhaps unwisely . . . delayed hospitalization. That decision exacted its price yesterday morning. I was brought here at that time in great secrecy, in a diabetic coma.

"From the preliminary tests, I am still a long way from death's door. However, the doctors assure me that my system will stand the best chance of continuing in some degree of health if I am removed from the stress of the presidency. More importantly, *you*, the people of this grand nation, deserve a national leader who is fit . . . one who is free of the shadow of an incapacitating illness. My term of office is not up for several years yet, and there is always the danger that some grave mistake in judgment could be made by those who surround me, in a moment of fallen leadership. I have taken pains so far to prevent that from happening, but I, like any mortal man, cannot guarantee the future."

Evans paused briefly, glancing toward the others with him on the stage. "For that reason, I do hereby announce today my resignation from office, effective at twelve noon. Vice-President Drew Russell will be sworn in immediately thereafter. If he has the kind of support and assistance I have been so fortunate to receive, I am certain he will make as fine a president as has ever honored the Oval Office."

He hesitated, seeming to falter momentarily. Then, looking once more over the assembled group, he said weakly, "I think . . . that will be about all for now. . . ."

As the two Secret Service men helped Evans back across to the side of the stage and the waiting wheelchair, there was complete and utter silence in the room. Everyone seemed stunned by the unexpected announcement. Then, almost simultaneously, groups of people arose to honor the man whose nobility had moved them. Their applause merged into an ovation that swept the room. It continued, growing steadily in volume and fervor, long after Evans had disappeared from sight. . . .

EPILOGUE

New Year's Eve in San Francisco—normally a festive time for people in the city that was his home, Paul Brandon thought. Yet for him, the past two weeks since his return had been completely devoid of holiday spirit. As he sat at a table at No. 9 Fisherman's Grotto, looking out at the fishing fleet now docked for the evening along the wharf, it was hard for him to feel that a new year was beginning.

Brandon was in no mood to enjoy the rustic beauty of the popular seafood restaurant. He recalled only too well that it was the same place where he and Carla had dined with the Nortons for the last time, but he said nothing about it when Philip Norton and his wife had suggested it this evening.

"Are you still with us, Paul?"

Brandon looked up, realizing that Norton was speaking. "What? Sorry, Phil. I guess my mind was elsewhere."

"So we've noticed," Margery Norton replied. Phil's wife was a decided contrast to her conservative educator husband, a vivacious redhead who liked nothing better than to arrange parties for her husband's associates and friends. "Phil was just saying that he thought the spaghetti and crab meat sounded good, and *I* said I thought I preferred the Creole sauté. How about you?"

Brandon glanced halfheartedly at the menu. "I don't know. Either sounds good."

"You still haven't told us what you've been up to." Phil Norton said. "When I tried to call you that night after you gave the lecture for my group, I couldn't locate anyone who knew where you were, except for someone finally at Steinman-Keller who thought you had left town to attend some sort of conference on new surgical techniques."

Brandon managed a good-natured smile. "That's about it."

Margery Norton looked at him cajolingly. "Are you sure you won't come to our little get-together later and help us ring in the new year? Remember—you still owe us an appearance after last time. . . ."

"No. Thanks for the invitation, but I don't think I can."

"Now I won't accept a refusal," Margery said with smiling firmness.

"We'll see."

While Phil Norton checked his watch, his wife looked across the room with sudden recognition. "Oh—there's a couple I wanted to invite to the party and couldn't reach. I've *got* to go talk to them." Tugging at her husband's arm, she added, "Come along, Phil—where are your manners tonight?"

Norton shook his head slightly and grinned, reacting to Brandon's wry look. He left the table and followed his wife to the other side of the room.

Brandon returned his gaze to the wharf below, watching the water lap silently about the boats moored there. He was still debating with himself about whether or not to accept the Nortons' after-dinner invitation. Margery's "little get-togethers" had been known to include thirty or forty people. The idea of all that frivolity seemed somehow hollow and unappealing. But perhaps the company would help, he thought. Perhaps that was exactly what he needed most.

He almost did not hear when someone near him asked, "Pardon me—may I join your table?"

Brandon turned, about to explain that Norton and his wife would be returning shortly. The words froze in his mouth as he looked at the young woman standing so near.

Carla Jennings frowned slightly at his surprised expression. "I can't say that's much of a welcome, Paul." Her frown softened into a gentle smile.

"*Carla—*" Brandon was stunned for an instant, then he quickly got to his feet and pulled out the fourth chair for her to sit down. He glanced briefly to the other end of the room, where the Nortons waved back. "I should have known something was up. When did you get back?"

"About two hours ago," Carla explained. "I tried calling your place, but you weren't home, so I called Phil and Margery. They said you were all going out tonight. I just did have time to change and freshen up."

Brandon said nothing for a long moment, content with just looking at her. The worry that had shadowed her on the island seemed to be gone now. Her features were vibrant and full of color, and her auburn hair was combed in a simple style that gleamed. She wore a wool dress suit of emerald-green hue, and a strand of pearls around her delicate neck.

"What happened?" Brandon said at last, almost reluctant to bring the subject up. "I thought there was a problem with your leaving."

"There was," she admitted. "But about four days after you left, the supply ship we'd been expecting finally arrived. It had been anchored at Manihiki island during the storm. The new resident doctor the Cook Islands Government had been promising to send for months was on the boat."

"Didn't you know he was coming?"

"No, but I should have, he told me. Seems he sent a letter telling me about it," she replied, rolling her eyes. "The letter was in the mailbag the supply ship brought!"

"So you left on the supply ship?"

"Yes. They were docked for a while, loading copra. I had to contact the World Health Organization's representatives by radio and explain, and then get my things ready. The trip back to the main island, Rarotonga, took a week." She grimaced at the thought. "It was a horrid voyage—I was seasick most of Christmas. Then I caught a jet back this morning, and here I am. What about you?"

"You mean, after I left the island? Well, in Hawaii, we

transferred down with all the injured, and Lorenz too, of course. I've never seen so many government agents in my life as I did that day."

"How is he now?"

Brandon crossed his fingers in a hopeful gesture. "The device is working, Carla. Even if we have to remove it eventually, the rest his own heart is getting may be enough to allow corrective surgery on his valve problem." He shook his head wistfully. "I'm sitting on one of the biggest medical news items in recent history, and I can't let a word of it out. At least, not yet."

Carla's expression became more serious. "The work you've done, Paul—the research for the institute—it *is* important. I realize that now, even if I couldn't see it before. I know it will all be put to good use."

"I'm going to make sure that it does," Brandon told her. "I've already spoken to the people at Steinman-Keller. I don't want to make a cent off the artificial heart units, once they start production. And I've persuaded them to set aside a certain percentage of the units for patients who couldn't afford them, otherwise. For them, it's as much a tax write-off as it is a humanitarian gesture, but the effect is still the same."

"I'm glad to hear that. I really am."

Thinking back about Tongareva, he said, "I'm sorry about the islander Benson killed. I can't help feeling it was my fault. If I hadn't pressed Benson to reveal himself the way I did—"

"You couldn't help it, Paul. All things considered, it's a miracle no one else was hurt."

"Maybe so. But I guess I'll always wonder." He paused a moment, as another thought crossed his mind. "The other islanders were talking about some kind of ghost fire being responsible for the old man's death. You know them pretty well. What were they talking about?"

Carla sighed. "I wish I had a good answer for you. There's a weird glow sometimes in the lagoon—maybe it's some kind of natural phosphorescence, but no one has ever found out. The islanders have a legend about it foretelling death among them. To tell you the truth, I don't really think it's just a silly superstition anymore."

"Well, at least it's all behind us now."

"Yes."

Brandon reached across the table and took her hand. "What *about* us?" he said tenderly. "We're two doctors . . . do you think we might be able to patch up our differences enough to make a go of it?"

"I don't know, Paul," she said honestly. "But I hope we can. And I guess if I didn't think it was worth a try, I wouldn't be here now."

Brandon considered it a moment. "Do you want to go to that party at the Nortons?"

"Not really. Do you?"

Brandon shook his head. "You know," he said finally, "there's a rather scruffy-looking Christmas tree standing in a bucket of water in my utility room. Do you think it's too late to decorate it?"

Carla returned his cautious smile. "It's never too late . . . for anything you really want. . . ."

THE END

REFERENCES

The following research bibliography may be of interest to those who wish to delve deeper into matters presented in this book.

AIRSHIPS

1. Allen, Hugh. *The Story of the Airship*. Akron, Ohio: Goodyear Tire and Rubber Co., 1932.
2. Ege, Lennart. *Balloons and Airships*. New York: Macmillan Publishing Co., Inc., 1974.
3. Hunt, Jack R., et al. "The Many Uses of the Dirigible." *Astronautics & Aeronautics,* October 1973, p. 58.
4. Kirschner, Edwin J. *The Zeppelin in the Atomic Age.* Urbana, Ill.: University of Illinois Press, 1957.
5. Lehman, Ernst A. *Zeppelin—The Story of Lighter-Than-Air Craft.* New York: Longmans, Green and Co., 1937.
6. Litchfield, Paul W., and Allen, Hugh. *Why Has America No Rigid Airships?* Cleveland: Corday & Gross Co., 1945.
7. Morse, Francis. "Cargo Airships: A Renaissance?" *Handling & Shipping,* June 1972, p. 47.
8. Morse, Francis. "The Nuclear Airship." *New Scientist,* April 7, 1966, p. 12.
9. Morse, Francis, et al. "Dirigibles: Aerospace Opportunities for the 70's and 80's." *Astronautics & Aeronautics,* November 1972, p. 32.
10. "Nasa, Navy Study Feasibility of New Uses for Airships." *National Observer,* November 22, 1975, p. 1.
11. Nørgaard, Erik. *The Book of Balloons.* New York: Crown Publishers, Inc., 1971.
12. "Nuclear Power for Airships? . . . Old Idea Has New Possibilities." *Nucleonics,* December 1965.
13. Pearson, John F. "Don't Sell the Airship Short." *Popular Mechanics,* September 1974, p. 112.
14. Vaeth, J. Gordon. *Graf Zeppelin.* New York: Harper & Brothers, 1958.
15. Whitehouse, Arch. *The Zeppelin Fighters.* New York: Ace Books, 1966.

THE SOVIET NAVY

1. Baldwin, Hanson, et al. *Soviet Sea Power.* Washington, D.C.: Center for Strategic and International Studies, Georgetown University, 1969.
2. Farquharson, W. John. "Soviet Naval AA Cannon Persists in Missile Age." *U.S. Naval Institute Proceedings,* October 1974, p. 109.
3. Herrick, Robert W. *Soviet Naval Strategy: Fifty Years of Theory and Practice.* Annapolis, Md.: United States Naval Institute, 1968.
4. "How Russia Is Tipping the Strategic Balance." *Air Force Magazine,* January 1975, p. 48.
5. Polmar, Norman. *Soviet Naval Power: Challenge for the 1970's.* New York: National Strategy Information Center, Inc., 1972.
6. Saunders, Malcolm G., ed. *The Soviet Navy.* New York: Frederick A. Praeger, Publishers, 1958.
7. "Soviet Ship Tried to Jam Carrier's Defense System." *Miami Herald,* November 25, 1975, p. 7-A.

NEW TECHNOLOGY

1. Ballenberger, Walter. "On the Way to Tactical Aircraft Robotics." *Astronautics & Aeronautics,* June 1975, p. 28.
2. Chant, Christopher. *Aircraft.* London: Octopus Books, 1975.
3. "The Electronic Arsenal." *Time,* March 3, 1975, p. 58.
4. Hudock, Robert P. "The Electronic Battlefield: A Tactical Revolution." *Astronautics & Aeronautics,* June 1975, p. 6.
5. "Industry Observer" (item concerning navy plans for a remotely piloted powered airship). *Aviation Week & Space Technology,* September 1, 1975, p. 9.
6. Kantrowitz, Arthur. "High Power Lasers." *Astronautics & Aeronautics,* March 1975, p. 52.
7. Klass, Philip J. "Advanced Weaponry Research Intensifies." *Aviation Week & Space Technology,* August 18, 1975, p. 34.
8. Klass, Philip J. "Current Systems Still More Cost Effective." *Aviation Week & Space Technology,* September 8, 1975, p. 53.
9. Klass, Philip J. "Mini-RPV Program Spawns Wide Range of

Vehicles." *Aviation Week & Space Technology*, July 14, 1975, p. 49.

10. Klass, Philip J. "Pentagon Seeks to Channel Research." *Aviation Week & Space Technology*, September 1, 1975, p. 50.

11. Miller, Barry. "Bombing System Emphasizes Simplicity." *Aviation Week & Space Technology*, September 15, 1975, p. 59.

12. "Navy Plans Studies of V/STOL RPVs." *Aviation Week & Space Technology*, September 8, 1975, p. 17.

13. "Navy Testing Sea Recovery of Mini-RPVs." *Aviation Week & Space Technology*, September 15, 1975, p. 64.

14. Powell, Craig. "The Saga of Fat Albert." *National Aeronautics*, April-June 1974, p. 10.

15. Reilly, James P. "Part 1: High-Power Electric Discharge Lasers (EDL's)." *Astronautics & Aeronautics*, March 1975, p. 52.

16. Russell, David A. "Part III: Gasdynamic Lasers." *Astronautics & Aeronautics*, June 1975, p. 50.

17. Stanford, Phil. "The Automated Battlefield." *New York Times Magazine*, February 23, 1975, p. 12.

18. Taylor, John W. R., ed. *Jane's All the World's Aircraft 1973-74*. London: Jane's Yearbooks, 1973.

19. Tsipis, Kosta. "The Accuracy of Strategic Missiles." *Scientific American*, July 1975, p. 14.

20. *United States Air Force Fact Sheet: Remotely Piloted Vehicles.* Andrews AFB, Md.: Office of Information, Air Force Systems Command, September 1974.

21. "U.S.-Soviet Nuclear Arms Race." New York *Times*, May 29, 1974, p. 4-C.

THE SOUTH PACIFIC

1. Barth, Ilene. "Cook Islands." *Travel*, November 1974, p. 55.

2. Crocombe, R. G. *Land Tenure in the Cook Islands*. London: Oxford University Press, 1964.

3. Freeman, Otis W., ed. *Geography of the Pacific*. New York: John Wiley & Sons, Inc., 1951.

4. Grattan, C. Hartley. *The Southwest Pacific Since 1900*. Ann Arbor, Mich.: University of Michigan Press, 1963.

5. Laborde, Edward D., ed. *Australia, New Zealand, and the*

Pacific Islands. London: William Heinemann, Ltd., 1952.
6. "New Zealand." *Encyclopedia Americana,* 1974 ed., Vol. 20, p. 245.
7. *New Zealand Official Yearbook—1969.* Wellington, N.Z.: Dept. of Statistics, 1969.
8. Paxton, John, ed. *The Stateman's Yearbook 1974/1975.* New York: St. Martin's Press, 1974.
9. Price, Willard. *Adventures in Paradise, Tahiti and Beyond.* New York: The John Day Company, 1955.
10. Reed, Alexander. *An Illustrated Encyclopedia of Maori Life.* Sydney, Australia: A. H. & A. W. Reed, 1963.
11. Shadbolt, Maurice. "Paradise in Search of a Future." *National Geographic,* August 1967, p. 203.
12. Shadbolt, Maurice, and Ruhen, Olaf. *Isles of the South Pacific.* Washington, D.C.: National Geographic Society, 1968.
13. Tudor, Judy. *Pacific Islands Year Book,* Sydney, Australia: Pacific Publications, 1972.

MEDICINE

1. D'Alonzo, C. Anthony. *Heart Disease, Blood Pressure and Strokes.* Houston: Gulf Publishing Company, 1960.
2. "He's First Crime Victim of Volt Gun." Miami *Herald,* September 22, 1975, p. 1-B.
3. Longmore, Donald. *The Heart.* New York: World University Library, McGraw-Hill, 1971.
4. Marvin, H. M. *Your Heart: A Handbook For Laymen.* Garden City, N.Y.: Doubleday & Company, Inc., 1960.
5. "Mini Heart Machine Is Developed—Costs $880." Miami *Herald,* August 12, 1975, p. 22-A.
6. "Outlook Good for Artificial Heart, Pioneer Researcher Tells Surgeons." Miami *Herald,* October 11, 1975, p. 28-A.

WASHINGTON

1. Daniel, Jean Houston, and Daniel, Price. *Executive Mansions and Capitols of America.* Waukesha, Wis.: Country Beautiful Foundation, 1969.
2. Kennedy, Robert F. *Thirteen Days.* New York: W. W. Norton & Company, Inc., 1969.

3. "Nixon Look Given to Cabinet Room." Miami *Herald,* March 19, 1970, p. 20-D.
4. Truett, Randall Bond, ed. *A Guide to the Nation's Capitols.* New York: Hastings House, 1968.
5. *The White House.* Washington, D.C.: White House Historical Association, 1962.
6. Wolff, Perry. *A Tour of the White House with Mrs. John F. Kennedy.* Garden City, N.Y.: Doubleday & Company, Inc., 1962.